Alone

Also by David Small

ALMOST FAMOUS
THE RIVER IN WINTER

Alone

A Novel

David Small

W·W·Norton & Company

New York   London

Excerpt from "The Sense of the Sleight-of-Hand Man," copyright
1942 by Wallace Stevens and renewed 1970 by Holly Stevens.
Reprinted from *The Collected Poems of Wallace Stevens,* by
permission of Alfred A. Knopf, Inc.

Excerpt from "Ashes of Life" by Edna St. Vincent Millay. From
Collected Poems, Harper & Row. Copyright 1917, 1945 by Edna
St. Vincent Millay. Reprinted by permission of Elizabeth Barnett,
literary executor.

Lyrics from "I Don't Know Why (I Just Do)," lyric by Roy Turk,
music by Fred E. Ahlert. Copyright © 1931 and renewed 1959
by Fred Ahlert Music Corporation/Pencil Mark
Music/TRO-Cromwell Music, Inc./Redwood Music.

Lyrics from "I'm Looking Over a Four Leaf Clover," lyric by
Mort Dixon, music by Harry Woods. Copyright © 1927 and
renewed 1955. All rights for the extended term administered by
Fred Ahlert Music Corporation on behalf of Olde Clover Leaf
Music/Callicoon Music.

Lyrics from "Don Gato," Copyright © 1964, 1971, 1988 by
Silver Burdett & Ginn. All rights reserved. Used with permission.

The text of this book is composed in 12/14.5 Bodoni Book,
with the display set in Poster Bodoni and Bodoni.
Composition and manufacturing by the Haddon Craftsmen, Inc.
Book design by Margaret M. Wagner.

First Edition.

Library of Congress Cataloging-in-Publication Data
Small, David
Alone: a novel / by David Small.
p. cm.
I. Title.
PS3569.M284N49 1991
813'.54—dc20   90-49354

ISBN 0-393-02991-3
W.W. Norton & Company, Inc.
500 Fifth Avenue, New York, N.Y. 10110
W.W. Norton & Company, Ltd.
10 Coptic Street, London WC1A 1PU
1 2 3 4 5 6 7 8 9 0

For Jemry

Acknowledgments

I WISH to thank the John Guggenheim Jr. Foundation for its support during the early critical days of my work on what eventually, by many forms of indirection, led to the book in hand. In purely material terms, the help could not have come at a more auspicious time in my career as a novelist. In terms of what it did for my morale, the value is incalculable.

My thanks also to my friend and editor, Mary Cunnane, the other indispensable woman in my life, who kept telling me I was a writer long before I was ready to believe it myself. I owe a great debt to Donald S. Lamm, who has encouraged me at every turning in the road; and to Eric Swenson, whose few words at the right moment may very well have decided for all time whether or not I turned out to be a published writer of fiction.

And again, as always, I owe a great debt to Robert Russell, my teacher, mentor, and friend for lo these thirty years. Not least of all, I thank Bruce Allen, my old chum from Boston days, who read my work and took me seriously as a writer long before anybody else did.

It may be that the ignorant man, alone,
Has any chance to mate his life with life
That is the sensual, pearly spouse, the life
That is fluent even in the wintriest bronze.

—*from "The Sense of the Sleight-of-Hand Man"*
by Wallace Stevens

Part One

Self-Delusions

O n e

I *WAS* living alone again—had been for nearly a year—when I learned that my kid had set himself on fire.

Mostly you forget about people. They shuttle in and out of your life. You have your work to do, your bills to pay, your own particular set of worries—all of which conspire to make you blind to everything except yourself.

Nobody stays around anyway. You get tired of them or they get tired of you. Somebody dies or the family splits up. Friends move away. Usually you never hear from them again. Or you make a mistake, say or do something you shouldn't. One way or another, they all pass you by pretty fast.

That was why I hadn't seen or heard from either of them for years. Till she—my ex-wife, that is—called me that night from the burn center, very hysterical and overwrought, and told me what he'd done.

I WENT out there on a plane, but it wasn't any good. Apparently he'd been brooding about the circumstances of his life and somehow, at eighteen, it had all seemed so hopeless.

He'd gone down by the river, not far from where they lived, lugging his stepfather's can of gasoline for the lawn mower along with him, and there he poured most of the contents down over his head and set fire to himself with his cigarette lighter.

Then apparently he had a change of heart and jumped into the river to put out the fire. But it was too late to do much good. He was badly burned over most of his body.

He lingered for several days, but there wasn't much they could do. They did what they could, of course. One of them told me it wouldn't be the burns directly that decided the outcome, but whether or not his skin still had the capacity to retain enough lymph fluid to keep him alive long enough for the healing to restore the natural barrier again. When you're badly burned, the stuff just leaks out of you. There's nothing, no barrier, to keep it in your body. That's what kills you.

He wouldn't talk to us. Linda and I both went in to see him. We tried to comfort him, reassure him that he would get through this all right. Linda's husband, Michael, did the same thing. But he wouldn't talk to any of us.

I guess he thought we had let him down too many times and had decided he wasn't going to make the mistake of trusting us again.

It was awfully hard on Linda. She hadn't been the best of mothers, I suppose, but certainly no worse than most. He talked to the doctors and nurses but he wouldn't talk to us.

He lingered in what I suppose was terrible pain. But all I had for a certainty when I was granted entry into that darkened room to try my hand at comforting him was his unforgiving silence.

He died on the sixth day following his accident. We all called it "his accident" when comforting each other in the

waiting room. What was it other than an accident? Surely no
one would put himself through such agony on purpose if he
had the slightest idea of what it entailed beforehand. Surely
he didn't know what he was doing when he flicked on that
lighter and turned himself into a human torch. So it was an
accident, whether it was a deliberate act or not.

"We failed him, Earl," Linda kept saying over and over
again. She couldn't stop crying or blaming us both through
the whole ordeal. Michael came in for a lot of blame too, as
well as Keith's teachers. Particularly a man named Ordway
who had given him a bad time in fifth grade. It seemed that
none of us had taken the time to understand him.

"What was in his mind, to do such a horrible thing to
himself? How he must hate us, not to say a word to any of
us."

She cried all the time and blamed us each in turn when
she had breath left over from her sobs. She didn't mean to
be acid or nasty. Blame was the only way she had at the
moment for dealing with the awful pain and bewilderment
and guilt she felt.

After the funeral I got on a plane and came home. I don't
think it hit me till I walked in the front door of my house.

I set my bag down in the hall and groped for a chair in the
living room like a blind man. There, sitting on the edge of
my chair, with my head on my knees and my hands touching
my toes, like a baby curled in the womb, I let it come out.
There was a lot of it.

Afterwards, exhausted, I lowered myself to the floor and
slept. When I woke that evening I was all right—or as all
right as I thought I ever would be again.

T w o

I *WAS* reluctant to call Nola and tell her about Keefer's accident. We all called him Keefer, which was the name he had made for himself out of Keith when he was little.

She was in Myrtle Beach at the condo she had rented for the month of April in hopes the warmer weather might do her some good. Renting the condo had been Dwight Fister's idea. He was down there with her, looking after her. In February, I'd hired him in a last-ditch effort to avoid putting her in the hospital again.

It turned out to be a brilliant idea.

At first I had my doubts. It wasn't that he didn't have the qualifications. He was a registered practical nurse; he came with good letters of recommendation. But he was much younger—only in his early thirties—than the type I was looking for. I thought she would be better off with someone closer to her own age, preferably a woman.

I was also prejudiced against his appearance and mannerisms at first. Dwight was shaped like a pear. He spoke softly and had trouble pronouncing his *r*'s and *l*'s. The day I interviewed him, he was wearing a royal-blue turtle-

neck under a velour burgundy pullover shirt, which did
nothing to hide his none-too-incipient breasts. Throughout
our conversation, he sat with his hands capping the knees
of his wide-wale navy-blue corduroy slacks and looked at the
floor. He had a maidenly nervousness about him that I found
unsettling. I noticed that he had tassels on his loafers. I was
ready to hold that against him too.

The downy blond hair on his head and the backs of his
hands was almost white. Whenever he answered one of my
questions his pale eyelashes fluttered as he tried to look at
me directly. I saw a flash of eyes as startlingly blue as an
infant's before his gaze reverted to the floor.

I didn't think he would work out and tried to discourage
him.

"My mother's quite old now—seventy-seven."

"Oh, that's okay. I wike older people."

"She suffers from depression—very severe clinical depression. Do you know anything about depression, Mr.
Fister?"

"Oh yes."

"Have you ever been around anybody suffering from severe depression?"

"No, but I've wed about it extensivwee . . ."

I found it discouraging to listen to that speech impediment, which had the effect of trivializing everything he said.
But I'd had very few answers to my ad. Everybody except
Dwight wanted more money than I could pay. On paper at
least he had good qualifications. I asked him a few more
questions and hardly listened to the answers; then shrugged
my shoulders and gave him the job. What the hell, I thought.
I could always run the ad again in the spring and see if I
couldn't find someone more suitable. In the meantime he
would have to do.

As it turned out, he was better for her than all the doctors and psychiatrists she'd ever been to. Even in that first month I could see some improvement. That was why I especially hated to call her with the bad news. I decided to talk to Dwight about it first. I called after eleven, when I knew she would be asleep, and he would still be up watching television.

"Oh Arrow, that's tewwibble," he said when I told him the news.

When I asked his advice about telling Nola, he said: "You must tell her wight away, Arrow. It's not the kind of thing you can keep from anybody. Besides, she's a stwong lady. Very stwong."

I had never thought of her as strong, but I knew Dwight was right about one thing. There never is a good time to tell anybody bad news. I would just have to get it over with as soon as possible for both our sakes.

The next morning I called again and told her. When I was through she said, "What else can happen to us now?"

It was the kind of thing I had learned to expect from her, so I don't know why it upset me so much.

Not "poor Keefer," or "poor Linda," but "poor us"— really meaning "poor me." I flushed hotly and went blind with temper for a moment. I was about to say something that I would regret later. But I managed to hold it back. What good would it do to say something hurtful to her? I thought. Why make it worse for anyone? She was old, she would never change now. She hardly had known Keefer anyway.

So I let it go and told her I would see her when she got back, and I got off the line as fast as I could.

I wasn't sleeping well at nights. I've always had insomnia, a disease of the Nichol family, which I inherited from my maternal grandfather. But this new version, which came on me after Keefer's death, was much worse than the old kind I was used to.

I would take a couple of drinks before bedtime, to knock myself out, and it worked pretty well. But after an hour or so, I would begin to dream. Night after night it was always the same one.

In my dream, I see Keefer down by the river with his can of gasoline. He is having trouble making the lighter work. The flint is worn-out. He stands there, his narrow clothes soaked in gasoline. His long bony thumb repeatedly flicks the lighter's little wheel, trying to get it to work. Framed by his shoulder-length chestnut hair, his dark brows frown in concentration. His face, with its mixture of heavy stubble and acne, looks so grimly stubborn.

I am trying to wake up—trying to shout, Don't do it, Keefer! but I can't make a sound.

Finally the lighter works and he touches it to his clothes. A ball of fire rolls up and down the length of his body. I see him lurch uncertainly for the river. A smudgy cloud of oily smoke vaporizes on the air just above his head as he staggers about blindly, searching for the river right beside him.

Here I finally wake and find myself blubbering and crawling around in the bed on all fours in the darkness.

I had no breath in me—no sense of relief knowing what I'd seen was just a dream. It wasn't anything I could really wake up from. I knew for certain it had happened just in that way—just as I had seen it in the dream—and I knew that I was meant to see it night after night, for as long as it would take me to make peace with my memories of him.

When I had lain there a little while, the cold sweat beginning to dry clammily on my forehead and chest, and I had begun to recover myself, the sound of crickets in the back-

yard flooded into my consciousness like a sudden tide
through the black squares of the windows and filled every
cranny in the shadowy room with its dry steady din, till I felt
completely numb—as inhuman as the crickets themselves.

Then it was time to get up and go downstairs and fix
myself another drink and sit on the couch in the study to see
if I could read. If that didn't work, I got up and wandered
around the house and looked into each of the rooms, as if I'd
never seen them before. I had made a mess of my life. I
looked around the house like a detective, searching for evidence at the scene of a crime.

I bought the house two years ago when Marilyn first
brought up the idea of getting married. I thought a halfway
measure like that might settle her down, but it didn't.

It is not as nice a house as Linda and I had in the old days,
and certainly the neighbors are not as nice, but it is okay. On
one side lives a pleasant Pakistani with his Australian wife
and three small boys, whose pinched dark faces remind me
of the barefoot waifs pictured on the relief-fund posters I see
on the counter by the cashier in the little restaurant where I
go for breakfast in the mornings. They scream like starlings
from morning till night, accompanied by the yapping of their
excitable little dog. The woman, whose name is Fiona May
(he is known as Joe, since his real name is apparently un-
pronounceable), has told me that the dog is a Jack Russell
terrier. By whatever name, it is one of those little toylike
barky things that I have always despised. Fiona May is
blessed with superabundant energy. She is always knocking,
hammering, and tumbling things about over there. Joe is a
laid-back type, with a Cheshire-cat grin perpetually on his
face, whom she puts to work around the house on the weekends.

On the other side of me lives a fellow named Monty

Pickle, a thin, rather nervous man of middling age, who makes his home with his old father and a fat dog. In the summer, the elder Mr. Pickle walks around the yard with his pant legs rolled up and a dented broad-brimmed straw hat on his head. Mr. Pickle is hard of hearing. I hear him complaining in a loud unhappy voice to his son sometimes, usually about food. He hardly ever leaves the premises. His main passion seems to be feeding the birds and squirrels. I don't mind the birds, but I object to the squirrels. With all the extra rations, some of them get to be as big as prairie dogs. They are an awful nuisance. They come over the fence and dig up the flower beds and bury the peanuts that Mr. Pickle gives them all over my backyard. The old man is very emaciated, with a tight little cap of white hair on the back of his head that looks as if it were made of spun glass. Over the years, I've said hello a few times, but he has never answered me. He is either too deaf to hear me or too busy laying out seed for the birds.

Monty sometimes walks his fat dog past my house. It is an old orange chow with a bushy tail, wrapped as tightly as a noisemaker, on its back. If I am out front raking the lawn, he sometimes says hello; but after an exchange of greetings he falls silent and keeps on walking. It isn't that he doesn't want to talk. It is just that the circumstances of his life have left him speechless. He has a job somewhere—I believe he is an art teacher. But other than that, and his walks around the neighborhood with his dog, he never leaves the property either. In all the time I've lived next door, I have never heard the dog bark.

Ours is a carefully kept neighborhood—typical of the kind you find here in central Pennsylvania. In three seasons out of four, the Chemlawn truck regularly perambulates through our streets and stops before most of the houses. On

hot humid summer afternoons, the smell of chemical fertiliz-
ers sometimes hangs heavily on the air, but the lawns are as
green as billiard tables. The hedges are neatly barbered; the
trees are trimmed back into shapes like giant lollipops; the
flower beds are edged with scalloped concrete.

It is a place where you can keep to yourself. The neighbors don't seem to care what you do, so long as you don't do
it on their lawn. I like that. It suits me fine.

When Marilyn was here, she decided we were going to
transform the backyard into a lush private garden—our own
little private paradise. She said when the hedges grew tall
enough, we would slip out there on starry summer evenings
and make love in the grass.

"Won't that be fun?"

I didn't think so, what with the damned bugs, and my bad
knees, and a perfectly comfortable bed upstairs.

"Yes, but it would really be romantic, wouldn't it?"

See? I said to myself. This is what you get for getting
mixed up with a woman half your age. Next time you'll know
better.

I was feeling a little discouraged anyway. My dentist had
recently warned me that I ought to stop fooling around and
undertake the periodontal surgery that he had recommended nearly seven years ago.

"What if I don't?"

"Well . . . in a few years you might have trouble whistling
'Dixie.' Let's put it this way. You can get a little long in the
tooth, or have teeth no longer. Your choice."

I had also just paid my annual visit to my internist, Albert
Probst, another funny fellow, who chose the moment, as he
was stripping off a finger cot, after having plumped up my
prostate, to say: "Well, my boy, you've arrived at the age
where you probably ought to let me give you a sigmoido-
scopic examination."

"No thanks," I said. "I never sigmoid on a first date."

He thought it was funny, but I didn't. It was another one of those little reminders of how old and stringy a chicken I was becoming. I'd had altogether too many such reminders lately. I was in no mood to let him stick one of his trumpets up my rectum—or to lie out with Marilyn in the wet grass, either.

When we first met, I was forty-five and she was twenty-four. I was fast arriving at the age when hair stops growing on your head and starts growing out of your nose. She was lovely, but she was just a kid.

I met her at a reading I gave at Clouser State College, shortly after my book was reissued. I took her for one of the students, but she told me she was a teacher. She said her name was Marilyn Swenson. She taught fifth-grade English and science in Appletown, which is east of Harrisburg, and not very far from where I was living at the time. She was relatively new to the area, having been born and raised in northern Michigan (known by some as Yooperland, a word derived from the initials UP, signifying the cold and remote country of trees and bears and frozen tundra also known as the Upper Peninsula), and she had completed her education at the University of Michigan only two years ago.

"How do you like it?"

"Teaching? I love it." She flushed with pleasure as she said this.

Later I would find out how much the kids loved *her.* Two or three times a year, she would take an ex-student—usually a quiet self-possessed little girl, with a name like Melanie or Deirdre—to Pizza Hut on a luncheon date, and listen to yarns about the sixth grade. On Saturday mornings, adenoidal-sounding little boys would call her on the telephone and talk to her about their hamsters. It was plain they all thought she was wonderful.

I liked her right away. I liked her voice. I liked her mass of auburn hair and her ready smile full of big white teeth. I asked her if she would like to have dinner sometime, and she said yes without a moment's hesitation, as if going out on a date with a man old enough to be her father was not at all a repugnant idea, to her way of thinking. I was gratified to be accepted as a human being by someone so young. It was flattering; it was good for the ego. I had no idea it would lead anywhere, but it certainly did.

HER skin was soft and delicate as butter. Her long silky-soft hair, I learned, changed colors with the season. In the summertime, she was a tawny strawberry blonde. In the dead of winter, her hair darkened to the auburn shade I'd first seen when we met.

In the good weather, she loved to sun herself. From time to time I would leave my desk and go to the bedroom window, where I could look down on the piece of lawn where she liked to lie out in the sun in a little blue-and-red flowery bikini on an old faded beach towel. She had the very fair and delicate honey-white skin of her Swedish ancestry, and she didn't tan well at all. I liked to get up from my desk from time to time, when I knew she was out there, and go to the window and look down at her, lying all white like a domestic rabbit against the green grass. Spread in a luxuriant fan upon the grass above her head, her hair looked almost pink in the strong sunlight.

"Sometime, when you get rich from one of your books, can we go to Florida in the wintertime? And just lie out on the beach? You can stay in the room and read, if you want to. I won't mind. And can we make love in the late afternoons and then take a nap and go out to dinner and maybe

sometimes go dancing afterwards? Can we do that sometime?"

"We surely can. As soon as I get rich, we'll do that."

Well—I never got rich, and we never did that. It would
have been fun. We could have done it. I don't know why we
didn't.

The first time she stayed with me all night, I took her out
to breakfast at the International House of Pancakes the next
morning. She had pancakes with blueberry syrup on them.
She said she liked to try a different syrup each time. Sometimes she tried a different syrup on each pancake. Later in
the car, when I kissed her, I could taste the sweet berry
flavor on her lips.

She had the sweetest disposition of any woman I've ever
known. She wore jeans and her hair in a ponytail and liked
to hold hands when we went shopping at the malls. She
looked about fifteen, and I looked about a hundred.

When we drifted around the malls, or sometimes when I
took her out for dinner, or to the movies, women my age
darted me sardonic looks as if to say: *We know what you're
after, mister.* And they were right. They *did* know what I was
after.

It was wonderful to sleep with a young woman. I marveled
at the warm suppleness of her body. I loved the way she
walked around the house, twittering like a bird, in her spi-
dery little undergarments. When we made love, she smelled
like fresh-cut grass. Her wetness often soaked me to the
waist, as if I'd been wading up to my hips in her, and dried
tight like school paste on my stomach. When she did her
nails with that polish I liked, something which she called
Marshmallow and that looked like mother-of-pearl when it
dried, the room was full of a delicious smell like the essence
of bananas. Of course they knew what I was after. I was after

some fun for a change—something I was unlikely to get from any of them, since likely they were as beaten down and as discouraged by life as I was.

We quarreled—if you can call our sorrowful disagreements by that name—about two things: my drinking, and getting married. I didn't think I had a drinking problem, and I certainly didn't think we ought to get married.

Her father had been an alcoholic. His addiction, and eventual death, had caused her and her mother and her brothers and sisters a good deal of misery and heartbreak. She always looked at me worriedly when I went to the bottle for my evening cocktail. The atmosphere of silent anxiety she created about it every night spoiled a good deal of the significance and pleasure I took in this daily ritual, and I resented it—as well as her timid remarks about "the number of empties" (usually one) in the trash each week. I saw no harm in having a drink or three. I'd had my real brush with the booze right after Linda and I broke up a decade ago. If ever I was going to become a drunk, I told her, that would have been the time.

"I know," she said meekly.

But she didn't know, she still worried all the pleasure out of it for me, and it irritated me a lot.

As for marriage, I was touched that such a lovely young woman thought she wanted to marry me, but the idea was ridiculous. I'd spent most of my adult life being ridiculous. I had no intention of being a ridiculous old man to boot.

"Why not?" she asked in a pouty voice. She was like a child who intended to keep the subject going till she had her way.

"Because."

"Because why?"

"Because it's not a good idea. We're getting along just fine the way we are. Why . . ."

"Why what?"

"Why gamble with the arrangement? This way if you ever want to leave—"

"If you ever want to kick me out, you mean."

"No, I don't mean that. I mean what I say. If you ever want to leave, you can. No mess, no fuss. This way you're not tied to me."

"But I'd never leave you. I love you. You mean everything to me."

"You mean everything to me too. But in a few years I'm going to be an old man. I don't want you to be my nurse."

"You're not old, you're young. I'll take care of you. I'll keep you young."

"Maybe in a few more years when I start to look like Claude Pepper you won't be so sure of yourself."

She was a good girl. She still thought love covered all the contingencies. I hated to be the one to give her the bad news. But she was as sure of her position as only the young can be. She would give me a year to get used to the idea, she said. If I couldn't accept it by then—well, then she was afraid we both probably ought to get on with our lives.

"The trouble with you is, you come from an unhappy family."

"What's that got to do with it?"

"You think it's normal to be miserable."

"No I don't. I was happy before you brought this up again."

"You're not trying to protect me. You're just afraid, because of what happened the last time."

"Maybe you're right."

"Well . . . we won't talk about it anymore for now."

And we didn't. We talked about it very infrequently. And very quickly, my year-long grace period ran out.

Always a woman of her word, she came home from work

on the last day of school with some boxes she'd stopped at
the grocery to pick up, so she could pack up her stereo and
her Roy Orbison and Elton John records. She got her suitcase out from under the bed. She got her garment bag out of
the back of the closet. When she was finished, I helped her
carry everything downstairs and pile it all in her yellow
Volkswagen.

She was wearing sneakers and her Michigan sweatshirt
with her favorite pair of jeans, which, after repeated wash-
ings, were almost as white and soft as a pair of suede kid
gloves. Except for the kind of kiss she gave me, I could have
been sending my daughter off to college.

"Will we always be friends forever?"

"Always."

"Will you call me if you ever change your mind?"

"Yes I will."

"I love you, Earl. I always will."

I was touched by these declarations, even though I knew
they were absurd—which only made them all the more
touching. I never doubted her sincerity for a moment. She
was a good sweet girl with good looks and brains and she
was going back to Michigan to take a job teaching. Doubtless
within a month or two some nice young man would find her
and within a year they would be married. If they were the
marrying sort, the good ones didn't stay single for long. I
knew all this, as surely as I had gum disease.

I stood back and took a long last look at her. It seemed to
me that her pretty baby-face still wore the rosy flush of
infancy. Her orange lashes were full of tears, and her smile
trembled as she gave me a big hug goodbye. I had no doubt
that I was doing the right thing.

The little car sounded like a lawn mower when she started
it up. She ground the gears and it threshed jerkily into re-

verse and retreated swiftly down the drive into the road. Again she ground the gears, and the car sprang forward like a mechanical toy, and then surged down the street. She was still waving as she turned the corner.

I remember looking at the sky and thinking she'd chosen a good day for travel. Then I went back inside and closed the door and sighed a sigh that could only be described as one of relief.

I poured myself a liberal hooker of vodka and went out in the backyard to see how the Purple Gem I'd transplanted was coming along.

I spent an altogether calm and restful day, luxuriating in the sudden stillness of the house, which I hadn't realized I had missed so much.

But that night, I woke in the darkness in one of my cold sweats, and felt as if I was going to die before I saw the light of day again.

I told myself I would get over it, that this was the worst part of it—this being alone again at night, when I woke up. In a little while, I'd be used to it again. Surely, I thought, surely this time I've done the right thing.

Three

IF you are not your father's boy, then who are you?

Maybe you are self-invented. Made from bits and pieces of scrap collected from other men you've known here and there. Maybe they gave you some of the pieces. Maybe some of the pieces you stole. In any case, they don't all fit together. Or work the way they would, if they came from one place. I often think that's been my problem.

I must have had a lot of cocker spaniel in me at one time. I used to wag my tail whenever someone said a kind word to me. When somebody wanted me to do something, I would get right up and do it, I wanted to please everybody that much. As I say, I must have had a lot of spaniel in me. But I don't feel that way anymore. What with one thing and another, I guess I used it all up. Now, mainly, I want to please myself.

Still, you can't escape certain parts of your makeup, because certain parts of it don't belong to you. Those parts belong to other people. As I say, either you stole them or otherwise acquired them in some way. Or they may have been installed early without your knowledge or permission. These installations—such as the spaniel part in me, for example—tend to belong to the installers, usually your mother or father. Sometimes the equipment is very good and useful. Other times, it damned nearly guarantees you'll end up in a ditch sooner or later. Either way, you play the devil trying to get rid of any of it.

I remember my father so well.

Richie and I always called him Jack, just as we always called our mother Nola. Not to their faces, of course. But always when we were talking about them between ourselves. Jack and Nola seemed to suit them better. I still think of them by their given names, even today.

That last Thanksgiving we all spent together, nearly thirty years ago now, Jack made especially memorable by pulling the stove out of the wall.

He was preparing dinner—not an unusual thing for him to be doing when Nola was going through one of her episodes of depression. Gradually, with the help of a little whiskey, it occurred to him that he was tired of cooking these holiday meals she was always too fatigued, or too sad, or too sick, or too something, to do for herself.

We'd been sitting at the kitchen table, drinking beer and telling stories on each other, to see who could be made to look the most ridiculous.

That morning, we'd coaxed Nola out of bed for a light breakfast, in front of the parade on TV, with the rest of the family. Richie tried to keep her awake by kidding her about all the naps she made him take when he was a little kid.

"Geez, Ma, you used to feed me breakfast and throw me right back in. You'd get me up for lunch and then put me back down for the afternoon. Then, after supper, you'd pack me off for the night."

"I did not. You're a big fibber."

"Yes you did, Ma. I was the best-rested four-year old in the state of Maine. You did the same to Earl when he came along."

"That's why the back of my head's so flat," I said. "From all those naps you gave me."

"The back of your head is *not* flat."

"Yes it is, Ma."

"I can still sleep eighteen hours a day," said Richie. "I was born and bred to be a damned zombie."

"You boys think you're funny."

She was sitting in a bleary-eyed stupor on the old brown velour couch in the living room, dressed in a pair of ancient silk pajamas that Jack's mother had given him one Christmas eons ago—the navy-blue ones with the red piping raveling out in places; and over the top of these she'd pulled on his threadbare old yellowy-white terry-cloth bathrobe with the cigarette burns all over it. She hadn't combed her hair. Even back then, it was already more gray than blond, but you hardly noticed, her hair was so baby-soft and pale anyway, unless of course you got right up next to her. Like a lot of blonds, she wasn't aging particularly well. She sat there, her feet tucked under her, looking fat and slack in Jack's old bedclothes. She was so numbed over with sleeping pills and tranquilizers she could hardly hold her head up.

"Where you going, Ma? Back to Coo-Coo Cloudland?"

Her nebulous blue eyes fluttered open again. She smiled at Richie. He could say anything to her. She really adored him. She fumbled around with her coffee cup till she found the top of the end table.

"Land sakes, I can't seem to keep my eyes open today."

"Come on, Ma. Have another cup of coffee. You can take a nap later."

Jack made the mistake of putting in his two cents.

"Give it a try, Nole. Hell, the boys are home and it's Thanksgiving."

She flickered her eyes at him and spit a little hot fat in his direction.

"I *know* what day it is, thank you."

Apparently this remark used up the last of her strength. Her eyelids fluttered a few more times; her head rolled back and then forward; and then slowly she subsided to the cushions. We watched the details of this performance with the critical attention of experts. In two minutes, she was out cold.

When she started to snore, conversation became impossible. That's when we picked up the coffee cups and newspapers and moved to the kitchen.

"So much for breakfast," said Jack.

I was home from college but planned to make it short. I didn't enjoy these holidays with my family very much. Linda and I had already started going together, and she wanted me to go up there—up to Long Island, that is, where they lived—and visit with her and her parents for a few days.

She had lent me her nifty little Karmann-Ghia for this purpose, and Daddy, as she called him, had dispatched a hideously skinny geezer with a bony head like an old horse, whom Linda referred to as Cousin Vito, to fetch her back to Bergen Cove for the holidays and to wait for me. That was my excuse for getting away as soon as I could.

Richie was working for an air freight company in Tampa and had flown in on Allegheny for a few days' visit.

The day we arrived home, we found the household in its customary state of malaise. The draperies were drawn. The dishes were piled in the sink. The dust was an inch thick on everything. Richie always called it "Miss Havisham's house." This particular episode of her illness had gone on for nearly two months, and showed no signs of letting up.

It was unusual for her to get sick so early. Usually she waited till after Christmas. We used to joke about how she would open her presents and then go to bed till it was time to get up and go to Maine again. But this time, it looked like she might really stay in bed that long.

The first night we were home, Richie took me aside and shook his head dolorously.

"If it goes on much longer, Jack'll go right out of his tree."

I agreed with him. Privately I started thinking of ways I could avoid coming home for Christmas. Maybe Linda's folks would want me to come up there again. Maybe my friend Arthur Frankenwood would want me to spend the holidays with him.

Meanwhile we all had to get through this together. As we sat there at the kitchen table, drinking beer and kidding each other, I had the momentary illusion that we were making a pretty good job of it.

We were giving Jack the business about how he said "electwis-ity" instead of "electricity," and he was denying that he ever said it that way.

"Yes, you do," said Richie. "You talk just like Elmer Fudd sometimes."

"Where did that pesky wabbit go?"

"Dwat that wabbit."

We rocked from side to side, like Ray Charles at the keyboard, and laughed till the tears ran down our faces. Jack sat there smiling thinly as if to say: Wait a little while till it's my turn.

Just about then, we ran out of beer. Richie went to get another one and discovered it was all gone. Before I knew

what he was up to, he set a bottle of whiskey on the table.
Jack had stepped out for a minute.

"Are you crazy?"

He waved me off.

"It's okay. One or two won't hurt him."

Jack came back into the room.

"We're out of beer," Richie said.

Jack nodded and smiled. He poured himself a shot in his
beer glass and tossed it off; then poured himself another and
sat down. When I looked over a few seconds later, he was
pressing the neck of the bottle down over the top of his glass
again.

It always took him a few minutes to undergo a personality
change.

In the interval, Richie talked about tequila.

"Yeh, that's what we ought to be drinking. With salt and
lemon wedges. You got any tequila, Dad? I'll show you guys
how we drink it down in Mexico."

Jack looked up. In a glance, I could see we were in the
presence of Mr. Hyde again.

"I hate a holiday like this, with your mother in there lying
like a rag doll on the couch."

"Let's go wake her up. We'll feed her a couple of pep
pills. She's got some great uppers in the medicine cabinet.
There's every pill known to man in there."

"You stay away from those pills, wiseguy."

When Richie had lived at home he had stolen them all the
time, but he shrugged innocently.

"What would I want with her pills?"

"You just stay the hell away from them."

"Okay, okay, don't get excited."

"I'm not excited. I'm just telling you how it is. You keep
the hell away from them."

"Okay, okay."

"Goddam bunch of pillheads."

He poured himself another shot. Then he lapsed into one of his dangerous silences. We waited. Nobody was allowed to talk when he got like that.

He looked up and said:

"Hell, it's worse when she's awake. I don't think I can stand it today. I don't know whether I can sit across a table from her or not. I'm sick of holidays like this."

"Well at least we're having a good time," said Richie. "Have another shot, Elmer. Forget your troubles."

"I tell you what," said Jack. "Let's eat out. What do you say? To hell with eating a rubbery bird and looking at her. We'll go down to Lambert's."

"We can't do that to Ma."

This remark of mine exasperated Richie. For some reason he seemed to be egging Jack on that day.

"Don't be such a dink. We'll be back before she ever wakes up. We'll bring her a turkey sandwich, if that'll make you happy. Hell, she's out of it. She couldn't care less what we do."

"To hell with her," said Jack. "She hasn't known the difference between sleeping and waking for twenty years. I'm going to get rid of that damned bird right now."

For a minute I thought he was talking about Nola. He got up and slipped on the potholder mittens and took the roasting pan out of the oven. He pushed open the swinging door with his backside and disappeared into the living room. Richie and I looked at each other as if to say: What's he up to now?

We got up and followed him.

"Where you going, Dad?"

"I told you, I'm going to set this bird free."

He set the pan down on the rug and unlatched the glass

door to the sun deck. We stayed out of his way. It was always better to give Jack a little room when he'd had a few drinks. He got it open, picked up the pan, crossed the deck to the railing, and heaved everything—the pan, the potholders, and the half-cooked bird—in a great arc out over the lawn.

We watched the bird fly in front of the picture window and suddenly plummet out of sight, as if it had been shot out of the sky. Nola was still snoring on the couch.

"I guess it'll be dinner out today."

"Right," said Richie. "Lambert's. He's flying now. If he crashes, you and I'll go down and eat anyway."

"Good. I'm getting hungry. I can't sit around and drink like this all day without having something to eat."

Jack came in from the sun deck wiping his hands on the back of his pants.

"Now." He held up a finger. "Just one other thing."

We followed him back into the kitchen and watched him pull the stove out of the wall.

It was directly wired to the outlet. A spritz of white sparks spluttered out of the wall when he broke the connection. He was a big man, although not tall, with tiny feet and hands and big shoulders and big arms and a big belly as hard as a medicine ball. He was very strong. But he couldn't pick up the stove by himself, which he was attempting to do.

"What are you doing, Dad?"

He straightened up and hooked his thumbs in his pockets and cocked his head at us in that way he had when he thought we were being particularly stupid or lazy.

"Are you jerks just going to stand there? Or are you going to help me?"

"What are we supposed to do?"

"Grab an end and help me carry this thing out onto the deck."

"Geez," I said. "I don't know—"

"What the hell," said Richie. "Look at him. You know how he is. He'll ruin his back if we don't help. He'll be walking around here for months like a duck on a crutch."

"Okay, okay," I said. "Let's get it over with."

"Atta boy," said Richie.

We lugged the stove in through the living room and out the door onto the deck and helped him lift it to the top railing.

Then we stood back so he could have the satisfaction of pushing it over the side all to himself. It smashed into the half-frozen ground one story below with a very loud and gratifying crash. Instinctively we looked in the window at Nola. She lay there flat and motionless as a decal. She never even twitched a muscle.

Jack couldn't have cared less. He rested his elbows on the railing of the deck and calmly gazed over the side, like a tourist taking a Sunday-afternoon ride on a ferryboat in New York Harbor.

Richie commenced the noise he made through his nose when something particularly tickled him.

"What's so funny?"

"Everything. This family—that's what's so funny."

"You jackass. You're as bad as he is."

He threw back his head and laughed. He looped an arm over my shoulders. "That's right, Early. We're all a little crazy in this family."

We went down to Lambert's at sixty-seventy miles an hour in Jack's El Dorado. I held on to the dashboard while he took it down the hill into town. It was like going down a chute on a toboggan. Richie was rolling around in the back, cackling like a fool.

At the restaurant, Jack ordered us a big spread. Then, looking distracted, he excused himself, mumbling something about wanting to see if his pal Lambert was in the kitchen.

We watched him weave across the floor, lightly touching the tables and chairs of other diners, attracting their somber stares as he unsteadily made his way to the swinging door at the back of the room.

"What's that all about?"

"I think he likes the waitress. He probably went out there to cop a feel."

We couldn't help it; we began to laugh. Richie rolled his head back on his shoulders, the way he did sometimes when life got so damned funny he could hardly stand it.

"Ah ha-ha," he said to the ceiling.

"Why can't they act normal?" I said. "Like other people?"

"Forget it, Early boy. What fun would that be?"

Because I knew it would make him laugh, I told him how I'd gone in and asked Jack for a raise the summer before when I was working in the shoe factory as one of his tracers.

"I bet that went over big."

"He didn't even look up when I walked in. He was signing some papers. 'Well? What do you want?' he said. 'I've been working for you in the summers now for six years,' I said. 'I think I'm entitled to a raise.' That got his attention. You know how he squints at you when he thinks you're out of your mind? He gives me that look and he says, 'What am I paying you now?' and I said, 'You're paying me the minimum wage,' and he said, 'You're worth every cent of it. Now get back to work.' "

Richie laid his head back and laughed at the ceiling again.

"That's our Jack all right."

A moment later, Lambert came out of the kitchen in his shirt sleeves and apron with a big silly grin on his face which made him look like Victor Borge and told us that Jack had suddenly remembered an urgent appointment of sorts and had to leave by the back door.

We looked out the window. The El Dorado was gone. He was still pretty slick when it came to pulling the old disappearing act.

"Meal's all paid for, boys. So eat up. I'll give you a lift home afterwards."

"That'll be grand, Lambert. Thanks a lot."

"My pleasure. That father of yours—he's the riot act, ain't he?"

"He sure is, Lambert. We just laugh ourselves silly over it every day."

After Lambert went back to his kitchen, I put my elbows on the table and stared at the little reservoir of gravy on the summit of my mashed potatoes.

"I don't get it."

"Quit trying. They're both crazy as coots. Let it go at that."

On the way home Lambert insisted we stop and have a few shots of applejack with him. When we finally got back to the house, Richie went downstairs and wrapped his arms around the toilet bowl, where, from the sounds of it, he intended to spend the rest of the night. I left the light on in the upstairs hall and found the keys to the Karmann-Ghia and drove downtown again to see what had become of Jack. It wasn't good to leave him out on his own for too long. Eventually I found him in a little bar just around the corner from the shoe factory.

He was arm-wrestling all comers at a table in the back. He was drunk as a bird full of berries. Of course he was beating everybody. No doubt the fact that they all worked for him helped a little bit. I stood off and watched him for a

while. He was putting them down one right after another—
young guys who laughed and shook their heads in admiration and clapped him on the back when their forearms hit
the table.

His broad handsome face was red and sweaty, but he
seemed younger and happier than I'd seen him look in
years. He was a factory man, born and bred. He had started
in the factories when he was twelve, sorting lasts into bins.
He worked part-time in the factory in Ligget, Maine, all
through high school. Then he was out of them for a few
years, while he was married to his first wife, and took work
as a reporter for her father, who owned the local newspaper.

Afterwards, when he went back into the factories, he
quickly worked himself up to foreman and eventually
managed a succession of plants from Maine to West Virginia. Nola said that in twenty-three years of marriage she
had lived in twenty-eight different houses. I'd gone to eight
grammar schools, plus one private school, and four different
high schools. The only time we settled down for a little while
was when Nola made him stay put for three years while
Richie played sports in high school.

One time when I brought Arthur Frankenwood home
from college for the weekend Jack took us down to the factory and made a pair of shoes to show us how it was done. He
started right at the top of the factory in the cutting room and
went through every step all the way down to the shipping
room. At the end he gave the pair he'd made to Arthur. The
workers treated him like a little tin god. He was one of their
own kind who'd risen in the world and they loved and re-
spected him and understood his weaknesses.

I waited till just he and Dick Sowers were at the table and
then went over to them. Sowers was foreman of the finishing
room and one of Jack's favorite drinking buddies.

"If I didn't think I could whip every mother's son in that factory," Jack was saying, "I wouldn't manage it."

Sowers patted him on the arm.

"Aw come on naw, Dimesy. Don't go getting mean on me."

"I'm not getting mean, Dick. I'm just telling you how I feel."

"Why looky here, Jack! Here come one of your boys. Hello, Earl. You come down to have a beer with your dad, didja? How's school going?"

Nola couldn't stand Sowers. He invited them to dinner once and she made the mistake of agreeing to go along. He lived way out in the country, somewhere in the hills beyond old Route 22. When they finally found the place, he was taking a nap on the sofa. He seemed to have forgotten about his invitation, but insisted they stay for dinner anyway.

He sent his wife, who Nola said looked like a Russian peasant woman, outside to dispatch one of the chickens scratching in the dirt yard. Nola said she heard the chicken squawk when Sower's wife caught it and wrung its neck. Later she smelled the odor coming from the kitchen as the woman scalded it and prepared to pluck its feathers. It was a hot day. The windows were open but without screens. The air was full of the smell of chicken manure. Jack and Dick sat at the dining-room table drinking beer and sweating like a pair of hackney ponies at the county races. During the meal they shooed the flies off their food. Nola said it had been a horrible experience, one that she would never repeat.

"Good," Jack told her. "That's another place I get to go by myself."

Sowers insisted on buying me a beer. I sat down and sipped it and waited patiently for what I considered to be the right moment.

He was trying to persuade Jack to give his boy, Tony, another chance. Tony was a side laster who had the habit of not showing up on Monday mornings, and Jack had fired him some time ago.

"He's changed, Dimesy. You learned his lesson for him real good."

Jack said he'd think about it.

I figured the moment had come.

"What do you say, Dad? Let's call it a night."

He shook me off and sucked greedily on his beer bottle. He slammed the empty down on the table and looked me. His eyes had turned into those little mean glimmering slots, the way they did when he got crazy.

"You go home, if that's where you want to go. Tell your mother I'll be back in time to pay the bills before the end of the month. Tell her not to worry. There're plenty of groceries in the house."

"I'm not telling her that. Come on, now. You come home with me. You've had your fun."

Amazingly, without a further word, he picked up his change and cigarettes and walked out of the bar with me. It was an unusually mild night for the end of November. He wanted to put the top down for the drive home. He said the fresh air would do him good. I tried to talk him out of it but gave up when he pointed down the street and said, "You go and get in your goddam car and leave me alone."

I shut my mouth and started down the sidewalk. Before I reached the Ghia, the El Dorado roared into life and squealed away from the curb, shrinking with amazing rapidity down the dark alley. He took it right through the stop sign and fishtailed out onto Railroad Street. Another tire squeal, and the car disappeared from view. I jumped in Linda's little car and followed after him as fast as I could.

I tried to keep up with him, but his taillights kept growing smaller. He must have been doing seventy when he hit the railroad tracks. The car bucked him straight up in the air. His head and shoulders rose well above the top of the windshield but he kept his gaze fixed straight ahead and somehow held on to the steering wheel.

When he came down, his tailbone landed on top of the seat. Instantly, slick as a craphouse rat, he slid back down behind the wheel and sped up the hill. A few weeks later he would remember this long dangerous moment of levitation above the railroad tracks as a pleasant flying sensation, ruined only by the fact that he'd been peppered on the forehead by something that felt as hard as walnuts. Big bugs of some kind—probably moth millers or beetles, if beetles flew at night. Hurt like hell, he said, and rubbed his forehead, grown tender again at the mere recollection.

I didn't even try to keep up with him after that. My heart was beating too fast and I felt weak all over at the sight of what I'd seen.

If he wants to kill himself, I thought, let him. I don't have to watch.

I slowed at the cemetery to see if he'd taken the corner all right. Jesus was still on his pedestal, surrounded by the usual congregation of tombstones. The fence was still up. No sign of Jack. He'd made it around the corner all right. I began to breathe easier. We didn't have far to go now. We were as good as home.

When I pulled into the driveway, he was already in the house and all the lights were out. I figured he had gone to bed with his clothes on, as he often did at the end of a rampage.

The El Dorado was in the driveway with the top still down but no keys. I thought about going in the house and waking him up so I could get his keys and put the top up for him. But I didn't think he would like it very much if I woke him up.

Instead, I lighted a cigarette and leaned against the side of the car and looked down the lawn toward the horse barn, which tilted to one side like a lame ghost standing in the moonlight.

To hell with it, I thought. No sense in asking for trouble.

It was a nice night. The moon was out, very hard and bright. I got Nola's fat old lazy collie dogs off the rug in the laundry room and onto their stumpy unreliable legs and took them for a walk around the edge of our property: a nice long walk calculated to make me tired enough so I could sleep. All the booze and craziness had left me feeling wakeful.

The walk did the trick. The fat lazy dogs and I slept together in my bed as sweet and peaceful as a set of triplets till nearly one o'clock the following afternoon.

F o u r

WHEN Jack was feeling gloomy he used to say that
if you lived long enough, sooner or later life
would back up on you like a toilet.

"You can count on it," he said.

I think he was talking about old age, or bad
marriages, or disappointed ambitions, or some
combination thereof. I was never sure just what
"life" encompassed in this context and had no
desire to ask. I had no reason to doubt his word,
either. But I didn't think it would apply to me
any time soon. Especially if I got out of there
fast and made a life for myself somewhere else,
like Richie.

The Saturday following Thanksgiving, I
drove Richie to the airport and saw him onto
the flight that would take him back to his job in
Florida, where he said he had important work
to do; and then I set out for Long Island in
Linda's sporty little Karmann-Ghia to meet her
big brother, Mario, and her parents, Nicola and
Phil Stephano.

I was pleased that I had engineered such a
quick and relatively painless getaway from my
family, and I was full of schemes for pulling off
a similar escape at Christmas. I was twenty-

three and a junior in college. I had spent two years back-
packing and bicycling around the country after high school
before entering Bentham. I had earned my way by means of
a series of short-lived menial jobs. I had found it was possible to go anywhere so long as you didn't mind washing
dishes, cleaning public toilets, or sweeping out a joint after
hours.

Once, during those weeks when I was pedaling my bicycle
randomly from place to place and drinking in the country
(largely by pausing at most of the taverns along the way), I
asked a man in a watchcap and overcoat, who was sitting
next to me in a bar in a little town called Callicoon, if he was
a native. No, he said. He was just passing through. I asked
him how long he'd been in town. "Six years," he said. I
offered to take his picture with my Polaroid so he could have
it as a memento of our conversation. "No," he said. "I don't
want no picture, thank you. It's bad enough just getting up
in the mornings and looking at myself in the mirror without
having a picture around too."

Like that man in Callicoon, I was just passing through my
parents' lives, on my way to a happier destination. I planned
to be a poet; in fact I was counting on it. I knew I couldn't
support myself, much less someone like Linda, by writing
poems, so I had decided to knock off a couple of money-
grubbing novels first, following a plan similar in excellence
to the one set down by the inestimable Thomas Hardy, one
of the great writers whom I especially admired. If he could
do it, so could I. I knew a great deal of poetry by heart and
often quoted it as if it were proof:

Love has gone and left me and I don't know what to do;
This or that or what you will is all the same to me;

But all the things that I begin I leave before I'm through—
There's little use in anything as far as I can see.

or:

Thou hast bound bones and veins in me, fastened me flesh,
And after it almost unmade, what with dread,
Thy doing: and dost Thou touch me afresh?
Once again I feel Thy finger and find Thee.

In those days, I mistook my very ordinary talent for rote memory as evidence of incipient poetic genius. Soon enough I would learn the difference.

That afternoon, as I sped under the East River and emerged into the sunlight again and pointed the nose of the little car in the direction of Bergen Cove on the South Shore of Long Island where the Stephanos lived, I felt everything was right: I was only twenty-three—not so bad, really, for all the time I'd wasted.

I sped along with the window cranked down partway. The intoxicating currents of coppery autumn air ruffled my hair and patted me on the face as if telling me repeatedly that I was a good boy. I felt as exuberant and privileged as one of the Kennedy clan. Young Jack was on his way to the White House, where everybody under forty fancied he belonged; and I was on my way to see Linda, where I fancied I belonged. Surely the parallels must be significant. Ah, how wonderful to be young and full of promise, and not all used up and full of self-deluding lies like Nola and Jack and Richard Nixon.

I was especially eager to meet Linda's father, Phil.

Rumor at school had it that he was a gangster. Among other things, he was supposed to control the sales of all the

barbershop supplies on Long Island. One of the more fasci-
nating stories circulating around campus involved an anonymous salesman who didn't seem to understand that when it
came to talcum powder and after-shave lotion, Long Island
was the exclusive precinct of Mr. Stephano and his many
sample-case-toting minions. Despite repeated warnings, so
the story went, this earnest man, who insisted that it was a
free country, persisted in sticking styptic pencils and leather
strops in places where they shouldn't have been. It was said
that this man ended up in the trunk of a car at Jamaica
Raceway with a bullet in the back of his head and a bottle of
hair tonic shoved up his rectum. I didn't dare ask Linda if
such a lurid story was true; but I did ask her if her father
really was a member of the Mafia, as some people around
school claimed he was.

"Of course not, silly," she said and told me the story of
how her father had arrived in this country from his native
Sicily with just three dollars in his pocket.

"Momma worked as a seamstress; Daddy worked in a
barbershop at two bits a shave and fifty cents for a haircut.
They pinched and saved so he could open his own shop.
Then they pinched and scrimped some more, till they
scraped together enough to open a little restaurant no bigger
than a shoe box. After that, they were on their way."

In addition to the restaurant, greatly expanded since the
old days, Phil owned a string of barbershops, wholesale
businesses dealing in personal-care products and hotel and
restaurant supplies, some rental property along Sunrise
Highway in Nassau County, several thousand acres of farm-
land in Suffolk, stocks and bonds, and other forms of plun-
der beyond my ability to take in or calculate.

All of this had been accomplished by a man who could
barely write his name and who never read anything more

complicated than the *Daily News.* His was the quintessential American success story. Understandably Linda was very proud of him.

Of course, this tale of dogged hard work and eventual success secretly disappointed me. I was still persuaded that she was protecting him and that he would actually turn out to be a Mafia don—someone with the cruel swagger of an Al Capone; or someone riddled with cold-blooded eccentricities like Red Levine, the executioner, who always wore a yarmulke on the back of his head when he did a job; or someone who wrapped himself in the sinister silences of a Lucky Luciano and whose brooding figure was spiraled with blue cigarette smoke as he sat behind an elegant desk and meted out life and death.

What I got instead, when I drove through the gates onto the paving stones of the broad curve of driveway in front of their long rambling pale yellow house, was a little bandy-legged man clad in a Yankee warm-up jacket and a pair of baggy pants with a scant horseshoe of gray hair running from one jug ear to the other; a man with a pitted face who showed me all his teeth at once like a crocodile as he approached the car on sore feet and fumbled with the door handle. He was older than the parents of most of my friends, already in his sixties by this time, and already bothered by the arthritis and emphysema that plagued him so much in his later years.

I thought he was rather wonderful-looking in a mildly ferocious way, with his somber high cheekbones and hooded eyes—he reminded me of a picture I'd seen of Geronimo, the Apache Indian chief—but when he smiled at me like that, it gave his face an expression of voracious appetite or of sudden excruciating pain, rather than one of warmth or pleasure. I thought maybe I'd run over his foot. As he clawed at

my door and showed me all those teeth, I must have started
back in alarm, because I heard him growl, "Open the door,
for Chrissake! Come on, get outta dere!"

Later I learned that he did not often let himself go like
that. It was the excitement of my arrival that did it. Usually
he settled for a thin inscrutable smile and a short irresistibly
complicitous cackle when he wanted to register mirth or
approval—actions which I came to think were more in keeping with the savage dignity of his face.

I opened the door. He thrust an arthritic claw at me.

"Hallo," he said. "I'm Linda's fahdah. You must be Ur."

Just then Linda flew out of the house and down the flagstones with a squeal and threw herself into my arms. She
was followed by a big burly guy about Richie's age, with a
massive head and the dark expressive eyes of an operatic
tenor. When he was sure she was through squealing over
me, he stepped in and gave me his big paw.

"I'm Mario, Linda's brother. Hey nice to meetcha."

I liked him right away. He had even white teeth and an
perspiry awkwardness around strangers that put me at ease,
since I usually reacted the same way. When I had pulled in,
Cousin Vito, dressed in crow black like a chauffeur or an
undertaker, was polishing the limousine which was parked
under a cluster of convoluted trees that overhung the cobble-
stones of the driveway. Slowly during the greetings and introductions he had inched forward till he hovered just over
the knob of Phil's bony shoulder. A ghastly smile full of
pointy gray teeth suddenly raised the withered curtains of
his cheeks. I nodded my head in acknowledgment; he nodded in return.

From under the backseat I extracted the pea-green gym
bag that held my toothbrush and a change of ragged underwear (it looked like I'd taken a direct hit in the seat from a

load of buckshot) while the three men leaned together like a trio of barbershop harmonizers and squinted at us and showed us their exceptional dental work. They were as grotesque a set of human beings as I'd ever seen—with the possible exception of my own family. I swung my bag out of the car and put my arm around Linda and we started for the house. As we ascended the steps together, everyone started talking at once like a bunch of magpies and immediately I felt at home.

At dinner that night, I met Linda's mother. A small doe-eyed woman with gray hair and a timid smile, she said very little, although I thought I detected an ally in the encouraging looks she gave me. She excused herself early and retired to her room to lie down again—I had seen nothing of her before dinner. She had not been feeling well for some time, Linda said. The doctors could tell them nothing, and the family was very worried about her.

Mario and Cousin Vito had prepared the main dish—a duck-and-sausage-and-pasta concoction which was delicious. Both had worked in the restaurant kitchen in their time and they were the regular cooks of the household, although Anna, the housekeeper, officially claimed the title. They did let her serve the meal. She was a fat hairy shifty-eyed woman, with a low husky laugh, and when she set the steaming platters and tureens on the table, her big arms trembled, as if with passion.

During dinner, Mario told me that he was "vice president of Pop's company," but it was clear to me even then, that like Cousin Vito, he did whatever Phil told him to do.

He fiddled shyly with his wineglass, his balding forehead damp with perspiration, his flushed baby cheeks peppered with the permanent five-o'clock shadow of his race. His sports shirt was open at the throat. Amid the sinuous glint of the woven gold chains around his neck, I could see thick burls of hair attached to his chest like upholstery buttons. As if to reassure me that I was making a good impression on everybody, he smiled frequently and pleasantly at me throughout the meal, with teeth as dazzling white as coconut meat.

Phil had experienced a hot flash as he approached the table and had immediately divested himself of his string tie and heavy blue corduroy shirt. Throughout the meal he leaned on his elbows at the head of the table in his ribbed undershirt, sipped a little of the simple strong table wine, and puffed rapidly on an endless string of smelly crooked black cigars. He told me that twice a year he sent Cousin Vito into the city to buy them by the case at the only place that imported them from Italy.

"Nuthin' tastes good to me no more," he rumbled as he waved away various offerings of food. The others around the table received this information in silence and bent over their plates of duck and pasta, the platters of cut bread, the three carafes of Chianti gleaming like giant black pearls against the long white tablecloth. I learned that this was a formula he pronounced at every meal, much like a surly benediction. Other than that, he had little else to say. He seemed to be a man of few words and long rhetorical silences. But I noticed his yellow eyes suddenly sharpened to cunning pinpoints of light whenever Linda said anything. Plainly she was his favorite child.

Over the fruit and cheese, he said he had noticed the blemishes on my face and told me to cut out the milk and cheese if I wanted to get rid of them.

"Daddy! You're embarrassing him!"

"Whaddya mean? I'm only trying to help. What—are you embarrassed, Ur?"

"It's *Earl,* Daddy."

"I know what it is. Whaddayou embarrassed, Ur? I don't mean to embarrass you."

"No sir."

"Good. See? He's not embarrassed."

After dinner, he put his arm around me and said he wanted to show me his study. It was very nice: paneled in dark wood and furnished with rich-looking overstuffed chairs and ottomans in burgundy leather and outlined with brass upholstery tacks. He insisted that I sit down and have a little glass of brandy with him.

"Linda tells me you gonna be a pot."

"A poet, yes. Well . . . I hope so, at least."

Again I heard that good-natured but irrepressibly complicitous cackle escape from his lips, even as he raised a claw as if to repress it.

"They starve to death, eh? How you gonna eat?"

"I was thinking of teaching school."

"Oh. *Un' professore.* Well, I wish you much luck with your life. You're a nice boy."

The idea of teaching was new to me, but now that I'd said it, it sounded good. I thought I saw a new gleam of respect light up the corners of his yellow eyes.

"Linda: she likes you a lot, I can see."

"Thank you, sir. I like her a lot too."

He puffed on his cigar rapidly and narrowed his eyes as he studied me.

"Next week we goin' to Florida for a month. Me, Cousin Vito, Mario: everybody. I got a house down there in Pompano Beach. Right on da canal. Speedboat. Swimming pool. Everything. Why don't you kids come down for Christmas, eh?"

When I hesitated he said, "Don't worry about the money.

I know it's tough for you college kids. I'll send you the tickets, okay? I got lots of it; at my age I don't mind spending it."

"Gee, I don't know what to say, except thank you, sir."

With his stiff crooked fingers he patted my knee.

"Forget it. You come down. It'll make Linda happy. I like to see my lil girl happy. Just like you, eh?"

He showed me his teeth again in that cutthroat smile of his and made another growling noise deep in his chest which I took for laughter, and then he stood up abruptly and relieved me of the empty brandy snifter in my hand. I gathered the interview was over.

When we came out, Linda took me aside and whispered, "I think he likes you."

"Did you say anything to him about Christmas?"

"Maybe I put a little bug in his ear. Why? What did he say?"

"He said he'd send me tickets so I could come down and spend the holidays with you."

"Oh, that's wonderful. We'll have such a good time."

"Boy, you get whatever you want, don't you?"

"Yep." She batted her eyes at me. "I'm my daddy's little girl. He buys me whatever I want. Didn't you know?"

That night we went out to see a movie, mentioned in Linda's General Lit class, that she'd been wanting to see for months. She was a business major, with a minor in accounting, but thought she ought to take an interest in things like foreign films for my sake. It just happened to be playing in the little run-down theater in town. It was a French film, with subtitles, called *He Who Must Die*, and it was touchingly beautiful. We were practically the only ones in the place. As soon as the theater darkened, Phil, Mario, and Cousin Vito all fell asleep instantly, as if under posthypnotic suggestion.

"Look at those guys," Linda said affectionately. "They don't care about the movie. They'd rather be at the track. They only came because they knew I wanted to see it. I really love those jerks. They'd do anything for me."

While they slept, Linda and I held hands, munched popcorn and watched the movie, and otherwise thoroughly enjoyed ourselves.

"How can you stand that boring stuff?" asked Mario, awake again in the black-and-white world of a late fall evening and apparently made irritable by the sudden sharp wind on the sidewalk outside. We were waiting for Cousin Vito to bring the car around. Linda smirked at this remark.

"Who do you like—Bugs Bunny?"

"At least he's funny."

Phil gave a bone-cracking yawn and scratched at his whiskers. He had apologized earlier for not shaving that day; he said it irritated his skin. He also hated to dress up, he said, unless he was "outta town on business." Consequently he looked a little incongruous, in his stubbly beard and baggy pants with the collar of his vicuña overcoat turned up against the raw weather, as he opened the door of his limousine and handed Linda into the backseat.

"S'okay," he growled behind his collar. "At least she's got some brains. Not like you, stoo-pid."

"What are *you* talking about?" said Mario affably. "You fell asleep too."

The next morning after breakfast (at which Phil limited himself to a cup of coffee and a fragment of anisette toast, coupled again with the announcement "Nuthin' tastes good to me no more"), Linda and I followed the path around the swimming pool and cabana and down past the converted toolshed where Cousin Vito had lived in Spartan simplicity for thirty years, unlocked the gate at the bottom of the bar-

ren garden, and walked along the beach on the private cove
which formed the rear boundary of Phil's property and that
of his nearest neighbors. We held hands and threw stones at
the sandpipers and gulls.

Linda was a lithe, slender girl in those days with curly
black hair and a little round baby face and gravely serious
brown eyes above a red pouty mouth. She moved on long
legs with the sullen grace of a moody ballerina. She twitched
and tossed her glossy ponytail much in the proud and temperamental way that Jack's horses tossed their manes and
switched their tails when we let them out to pasture. When
she bestowed one of her dazzling smiles on me, it seemed a
rare and priceless treasure.

I thought I was in love, because most of the time when I
was with her I felt miserable. I carried my lust around with
me like grief. It weighed me down and made me ache for
release. I dragged it with me everywhere as if in the grip of a
low-grade fever that never got any worse and never got any
better either. I tried the obvious solution one night by slipping my hand up her leg, but she punched my nose so hard
that for a week afterwards I blew bloody gouts into my handkerchief.

I tried to carry my burden with dignity. But it preoccupied
me so much and made me so unhappy that often when I was
with her I couldn't think of anything to say, and so passed
much of the time in moody silences. That's the way it was
that morning as we walked on the beach and tossed pebbles
at the birds. She seemed to accept these silences of mine as
behavior one would expect from a poet.

On the drive back to Bentham that afternoon I tried to
ease my burden by resting my head in her lap and smiling up
at her tragically; but as she shifted the little car through its
puny but ferocious-sounding gears, the gearshift knob kept

hitting me in the head, till I finally gave it over and sat up again.

When I got back to my rooms, Arthur wanted to hear all about it.

"Did they frisk you before they let you in? Did they check all your orifices to make sure you weren't packing an ice pick? Did they want to cut off your dick in case it was loaded? Weren't they afraid you'd use it to shoot Linda?"

I told him he was very funny, which was what he wanted to hear. If he was smart, I said, he would let it drop right there.

DESPITE the irresistible offer of free tickets, I did not spend the holidays in Florida with the Stephanos that year after all.

Because on December 23, 1960, my brother Richie took a DC-3, cargoed with some contraband parakeets and a few bales of marijuana, into the side of a remote mountain in Mexico and effectively canceled Christmas for all time.

F i v e

"**Y**OUR brother was a wonderful young man."

"He was in the dope trade, Ma."

"How can you say that! That's not so! Nobody ever said that!"

"Yes they did, Ma. They told us that when Dad and I went down to claim the body. You know that, Ma. The plane was full of the stuff. Illegal parakeets too."

"Well, I'm sure he didn't know what he was carrying. He just flew the plane wherever they told him to. He was like that."

"Yeh, sure, maybe I'm the King of Siam."

"Don't you have any feelings for your poor dead brother? You're such a strange boy! Whatever happened to your heart?"

"I have plenty of feelings for him, Ma. But I'm not going to kid myself just because he's dead. He wouldn't want me to. If he thought I set out to do that, he'd come back and kick my ass."

" 'Just because he's dead.' Listen to you talk! I should think 'just because he's dead,' as you put it, would be the time to cherish your best memories of him. But you—you're a different kettle of fish altogether, aren't you? You never remember the good about people. Only the bad."

I admit I have always had the gift for seeing people in the worst possible light. But still I thought it a strange complaint for her to make. If I tended to look at life through the wrong end of the telescope, doubtless I had perfected the trick at her knee.

One of my sins, according to her, was that I reminded her too much of my father. I'm sure I did on the occasion of this lamentable conversation, which took place a little less than a year after Richie's death. To be told that I was like my father was a demoralizing accusation, since I didn't admire him very much. He thought he was a truth-teller too; but he was only a mangler—someone who tried to hurt you with the facts if he thought you deserved it. I didn't want that kind of meanness in me.

Sometimes now, when I look in the mirror to shave, it gives me a little shiver: the glittery-eyed spade-shaped face staring back at me with such catlike intensity some mornings is not mine but Jack's, come back to haunt me or to take over my body for a few extra days of hell-raising or people-mangling. But back then, I didn't think I looked or acted like him at all.

RICHIE was five years old when I showed up. His opinions about life and the nature of the universe were already formed, and they didn't include me. He was used to being an only child; he wanted to keep it that way. It infuriated him that Jack and Nola had sneaked off and bought another baby without even consulting him.

"Sometimes when Nola'd put you down for a nap I'd wait till she fell asleep on the couch and then I'd creep in your room and bat you over the head with your teddy bear."

He casually told me this one evening as he punctured the

lid on another can of beer during one of our talks at the
kitchen table. It was during that last Thanksgiving we spent
together, before he flew off for his rendezvous with his
mountaintop in Mexico.

"Hell," he said, grinning. "Had someone handed me a
two-by-four, I would have gladly laid it right between your
eyes."

"You must have really hated my guts."

"Yep. You really ruined everything when you showed up,
Early boy."

"I don't see how. You were always Nola's favorite. Jack
thought you were great because you could throw a football
fifty yards when you were only twelve. What more could you
ask for?"

He shot me a quick look.

"I don't know."

He seemed puzzled.

"You just ruined it, that's all."

He grinned at me again.

"You took up valuable space, ol' son. You used up pre-
cious oxygen. Somehow you just screwed things up."

I knew it was true. I couldn't find fault with an answer
that honest.

Richie was Nola's child by her first marriage to an affable
drunk named Hal. Jack had been married before too; he had
two children by that marriage, but they lived with their
mother and we never saw them.

I was the only issue by their marriage to each other—the
first of one; the second of two; the last of three; and the
fourth of four, as I used to like to say, in order to mystify
myself and others.

As brothers, Richie and I shared half the usual gene pool
and, if truth be told, probably not much else.

It wasn't easy being the sibling of someone who still

thought of himself as an only child. He used to beat me up regularly in order to relieve the terrible strain I put on his nerves.

Some days he brought his friend Dickie Buckwalter home from school. Dickie stood by and watched with interest while Richie knocked me around the room. I was always slow to defend myself and played right into his hands. Everybody knows a bully hates a good fight. What he wants is a weak-kneed sissy like I was, to hammer around at leisure. Finally even I would go berserk and try to stab him with a pen or a letter opener or a bread knife or anything I could get my hands on. Then Dickie would jump in and hold me down while Richie escaped out the back door.

Other days he did without Dickie's services and worked me over on his own. These fights usually started upstairs and ranged all through the house. We pounded each other from room to room—although mostly it was me who tumbled through doorways and sprawled on the floors. I scrabbled around on my hands and knees a lot and screeched obscenities at the top of my voice.

During one of our fights the ex-marine, who lived beyond the hedge behind our house, came to the back door with his .45 strapped on his hip and told Richie that he'd call the cops if we didn't cut it out. Richie answered the door. I was busy resting under the dining-room table at the time.

"I got a wife and a little girl, you know. They can hear you guys over here plain as day."

What he planned to do with that gun, I have no idea. This is America, where anything is possible. Likely I sounded as if I was having my throat cut; probably he brought it along just in case he ran into someone wielding a butcher's knife.

Richie came back and told me who it was and what he'd said.

"From now on when we fight," he said, "you gotta learn to keep your voice down."

Apparently I learned the lesson well. Marilyn often said that one of the things she especially liked about me was that I was so quiet. "You're so soothing to be around, Booby." Booby was one of her nicknames for me, although I always suspected it was not so much a nickname as it was a description. Of course she giggled and denied it when I told her that. Booby, she said, was just her way of calling me her baby boy. So was Hot Buns. I tried to get her to stop calling me those names, but she wouldn't. If you are foolish enough to get mixed up with a woman half your age, you can't expect to salvage much of your dignity. I really never had any illusions about that. Nor did I ever tell her the reason I was so soothingly quiet was that my brother probably had beaten all the noise out of me when we were kids.

When Richie wanted to watch TV, he wouldn't let me in the same room. It was a new invention in those days; we had the first one in the neighborhood: a big old ugly Dumont with a screen no bigger than my hand. Richie said whoever got to the set first had control of it till he gave it up. Naturally he always got there first.

If I strayed into the room, hoping for a glimpse of *Kukla, Fran, and Ollie,* he would glare over his shoulder and stick out his bottom teeth at me like Lon Chaney, Jr., playing the part of the Wolf Man.

"Outta here, pusbrain. Before I tear your dick off."

He was besotted with the thing, like a bear loose in the town garbage dump. He pulled his chair up close and planted one foot on either side of the tiny screen and rocked back and forth on the back legs of his chair. He turned the sound down so only he could hear it. Usually he had a dish of ice cream sprinkled with walnuts and chocolate sauce under his chin, which he shoveled into his face as fast as he could. All the while his eyes would be fixed on the screen, utterly fascinated by whatever was flickering there at that moment.

It made no difference to him. He couldn't get enough of it. Every thirty seconds or so he would lean forward and go through the dial rapid-fire, pausing here and there to gaze in absorption at some other intriguing image: a test pattern; a cartoon worm popping out of an apple; William Boyd, kicking up a cloud of dust on his white horse. Then he would give it a few clicks and watch another channel for fifteen or twenty seconds and then click it again till in about five minutes or so he had covered the whole 360 degrees and then he would start over again. There were only half a dozen channels in those days but he was always looking for another one. He figured it for a growth industry.

Finally he wore the teeth right off the dial. First it got loose and wobbly like a lid that wasn't screwed on tight and then one night it fell off while Jack was tuning in *The Texaco Star Theater.* Jack had to go out and buy a new set. I don't think he ever understood why the old one fell apart like that.

Nola was always patient with Richie. He was temperamental, like a racehorse, she said. You had to deal with him differently than you did with other people. You didn't put a racehorse in the same pasture with the other animals, did you? No, of course not. You treated them according to their temperament.

She told me I was lucky. I was blessed with an "even" disposition. "How I envy you," she said with a lethargic drawl, an affectionate tilt of the head, and a slow smile. She would never have to worry about me, she said. I would make out just fine.

Richie's racehorse temperament usually came into play when Jack wasn't around. Jack had no understanding when it came to people with bad nerves.

One night she was helping him get ready to go out—I suppose he was about sixteen when this happened. He had plans with friends that night. He was always rushing off to sports banquets or to the movies or to parties on the weekends. The whole house was set on end by his need to get off in time: to have his dinner carried to the bathroom so he could eat it between his shower and shave without any loss of momentum; to get the shirt he wanted out of the wash and ironed in time; for somebody—either Nola or me or sometimes even Jack, if he was home—to tie his tie for him. He never did learn to tie his own tie, although he held strong opinions on just how the knot should look.

Nola gave him five dollars in bills and change to go out on that night. It was a handsome sum in those days; but for some reason that evening it wasn't enough. In a sudden flare of temper he began to curse and threw the money back at her. One of the coins hit her so hard that it made a faint little intaglio of Ben Franklin on her arm, where it remained for a few minutes before turning into a bruise as purple as the petals on the irises Jack had planted under the clump birch in the front yard.

"That's it, young man! You're not leaving the house tonight!"

Nola's reaction caused him astonishment and pain. He swore and bellowed at her but she remained firm. When the usual bullying didn't work he switched tactics and began to whine.

"But it was an accident, Ma! I didn't mean to hit you! Honest!"

"I don't care whether it was an accident or not. If you

can't control yourself any better than that, then you'll just have to stay home."

He cried and gnashed his teeth and plucked at his hair and tore through the house, his face contorted in agony.

"Please, please, Ma! I'll never do it again! You don't have to give me any money or anything! Just let me go out! You can punish me all you want next weekend!"

At last, as his time grew short for getting ready, she relented. I suppose she thought he had learned his lesson and there wasn't any point in carrying things too far. She went to her purse and held out a ten-dollar bill this time. She shook the money in his face.

"Don't you ever do anything like that again!"

"I won't! I won't! I promise! Honest to God!"

His face literally quivered with sincerity. He was a good actor, I'll give him that. And he had the sense to look her in the eye, instead of ogling the money she was waving under his nose.

Satisfied that he was properly chastened, she turned over the money. He snatched at it eagerly.

"Thanks, Ma!" he cried and thundered up the stairs.

Nola smiled and shook her head.

"That boy," she said. "Doesn't he just beat all?"

From behind my bowl of chicken-noodle soup, in my place of safety at the dining-room table, I wasn't obliged to answer this, and so I didn't. But I had my ideas about it. I knew if I had thrown money at her, I wouldn't have gotten out of the house that night—except maybe by way of the downspout outside the window of my room.

Once, in a fit of pique, I made the mistake of asking her why she treated me differently.

"Why do you like Richie better'n me?" was the way I put it.

"Because he hasn't got a real father like you have."

Maybe she didn't hear the question. I hate to think that she admitted her preference for Richie straight out like that. I expected her to deny it and tell me that I had an equal place in her affections. Her answer put my famous disposition to the test. I was supposed to believe that he acted the way he did, not because he was an innately miserable son of a bitch, or a brat who'd been spoiled rotten, but because he was an orphan, sort of. My duty was to feel sorry for him and to accept my role as a backup son, a benchwarmer in her affections, against the day I was ever needed. I didn't think this was fair, and for a long time it troubled me.

Whenever I recall this dismal passage in my childhood, I always find myself back in Rockville Centre, Long Island, in Nola's shadowy bedroom in the big white stucco house on Rockaway Avenue.

In that room the rosebuds in the wallpaper are always swimming in a huge slow circle on the dark walls. The shades are drawn. It is always twilight in there, no matter what the hour elsewhere in the house.

I am ten years old, and I'm trying to get her to wake up but I can't.

I wave my report card at her.

"Look, Ma! Straight A's!"

She lies there with her mouth open, her nose pointed at the ceiling.

I waggle a drawing in front of her face.

"Look what I did in Art, Ma!"

But she doesn't stir.

I try entertainment. I croon the lyrics of her favorite songs. I know she likes them sad and melancholy. I sing them softly. I open my arms wide, just the way the regular crooners do.

"You made me love you,
I didn't want to do it,
I didn't want to do it—
You made me love you
And all the time you knew it. "

I get down on one knee and try her all-time favorite:

"I don't know why I love you like I do
I don't know why, I just do
You never seem to want my romancing
The only time you hold me is when we're dancing
I don't know why I love you like I do
I don't know why, I just do"

I try something peppier. I leap up and begin to strut around the room like some dandy in a Mummer's Day parade.

"I'm looking over a four leaf clover
That I overlooked before"

When entertainment doesn't work, I appeal to her intellect. I sit down on the floor and open up some of the books which Jack and I have stacked on the rug beside her bed. They come from book clubs and have been accumulating unopened for months, and they make a little wall almost as high as the mattress. I open the mailing cartons and put aside the bills for Jack. I sniff the new paper, the glue, the print. I riffle the pages and study the illustration on the book jacket. I love opening these packages. It's like having Christmas. I can't believe that she just lets them pile up. I always open anything I get in the mail the second it arrives.

"Look at this one, Ma! *Thirteen Clocks!* By James Thurber!"

When none of this works, I give up and leave. I can't help thinking that she's not really asleep; that she's only waiting for me to go away, so she can switch on the light and read, or do whatever she does in there all day long by herself. I have this idea in my head that she is just waiting for me to grow up and go away. Then Jack will come home from the office some evening and she'll rise up on one elbow and whisper, "Is he gone yet?" and Jack'll say, "Yes, he's finally gone. I packed his bags and threw him on a train heading west this morning"; and she'll toss aside the covers and dance around the room, and she'll be only thirty years old again.

Sometimes, when I'm feeling especially suspicious, I go outside and clamber up a tree onto the roof over the kitchen wing. From there it's an easy job to shinny up the downspout to the main roof, where I go hand over hand along the rain gutters, till I come to her windows. I hold on to the shutter and lower myself to the windowsill and brace my feet on the brick molding below. Once in position, I peer between the shade and the windowsill into the semidarkness of the room. It's too dark to see much, but I can just make out her silhouette on the bed, her nose still aimed at the ceiling like a catatonic spaniel on point. She hasn't moved an inch. I sigh. She's too smart for me, I think. I lift myself back up by the shutter and grab the rain gutter again.

Sometimes, if I'm feeling especially curious, I'll go around to Richie's window to see if he's still searching for boogers in his nose between shots with his Ping-Pong ball at the tiny homemade backboard that he's set up on his dresser. I watch him quietly for a few minutes: how he whispers to himself, digs in his nose, and gets set for his next shot. It makes me feel powerful to crouch by his window and watch him undetected.

After I've had enough of him, sometimes I haul myself up onto the blue slate shingles of the main roof. Carefully I make my way over the steep slippery surface to the chimney at the top of the house. I hold on to the rough bricks and gaze out over the treetops and roofs of the neighborhood. Up there, where there's always a steady breeze no matter how hot it is below, I feel like an eagle in the wind. I feel just like Jesus on the mountaintop, surveying all the kingdoms of the earth. Someday I'll catch her, I think. She can't fool me forever.

IF, like cigarettes, I was bad for her health, then Richie was definitely good for it. In high school, he played football in the fall, basketball in the winter, and baseball in the spring—all with skill and grace. She went to all the games in the enthusiastic clubby company of the mothers of the other players. Those four years were the happiest of her life.

She kept a scrapbook of his accomplishments. He was often in the papers. In his senior year, he was voted the best basketball player in the conference, although he was only five feet nine. He played four years of varsity football and baseball and was selected all-county in each sport several times. It took five bulging scrapbooks to hold the accounts of his achievements.

At best, he was an indifferent scholar. She was sure that if she hadn't gone to the principal and complained about his teacher, he wouldn't have passed senior English. The teacher was a difficult old maid who'd been around longer than the building. She had it in for him because he was a sports hero.

"You know how jealous people like that can be."

I said I certainly did.

No doubt better grades would have brought more scholarship offers than he got. People like that old maid tried to hold him back. They might fail in their attempts, but they created a certain atmosphere which was an impediment in and of itself.

Then there was his size. College coaches held a grudge against little people. As it was, he was still able to choose among some respectable offers from several small schools. He took what looked like the best and picked a relatively obscure college in the Florida panhandle. She didn't understand why he had to choose one that was so ungodly far away.

"It's the boy's life," said Jack. "Let him go where he wants."

"You!" she shot back venomously. "What do you care where he goes!"

Unfortunately, things didn't work out in the panhandle. Maybe her instincts were right after all.

At first, the problem was that he couldn't see to throw the football over his own linemen. They were much bigger than the ones he'd operated behind in high school. But he learned to drop back fast and spot his receivers almost by instinct. The real difficulty was the coach; he was unhappy no matter what Richie did. He simply wanted a bigger fellow for the job. He had his eye on a big strapping farm boy who was planning to transfer from a small school in Georgia if the details could be worked out.

Richie had never figured as second-string in any coach's plans before. It didn't fire him up, as it might have some athletes. Instead it affected his self-confidence. He wasn't the type to rise to that kind of challenge. Secretly he had always suspected that his athletic ability was a kind of magical trick that he might lose the knack of conjuring at any minute. That was what seemed to be happening to him now. He told me this one night over the telephone.

"Well . . . cheer up and do your best," I said.

"What the hell would you know about it?" he said bitterly.

He was right. I didn't know anything about the problems of athletes.

He suffered a shoulder separation in the third game of his freshman season—just as Nola and Jack were preparing to fly down and see him play on the following weekend. The injury finished him for the year. Early the following season, playing in the last quarter of a runaway game as backup for the new boy from Georgia, he injured a knee, and that finished it. Soon afterwards he dropped out of school.

Jack gladly would have paid to have him finish his education. He made that plain during the series of long desperate telephone calls that Richie made home in the aftermath of his injury. Nola and I listened in on the extensions. We offered up driblets of commiseration and encouragement. But only Jack gave him any useful advice.

"What the hell. Things like this happen. Stay in school and I'll pay for it. So you won't be able to play football—big deal. You'll live. Who knows? You may even thrive."

But Richie said it was too embarrassing to stay on, now that he'd lost the scholarship.

"I thought the idea was to get an education."

Richie agreed that that was probably the point.

"I'll send you to another school. Under an assumed name, for Chrissakes, if it'll make you feel any better."

Richie thanked him and said he'd think about it. The next thing we knew, he'd dropped out of school.

Too mortified to return home and explain his failure to hometown fans and friends who had expected such big things of him, he decided to stay down South. He qualified for a commercial pilot's license and got a job flying freight for a small company located near Tampa.

It broke Nola's heart when he decided to stay in Florida. As someone whose feelings were easily hurt, she naturally felt aggrieved. She thought it was selfish of him to stay so far from home when he no longer had a good reason to. She could only conclude that he no longer cared about her feelings. She related her grievances in a long candid letter. After several weeks, he responded with a postcard, addressed to us all, which had a picture of a pelican on it.

"I'll bet he's got some girl down there," she said as if it were a scandalous development.

Then she lost him—suddenly and altogether and forever. Not to some girl, as she had feared, but to a remote mountain in Mexico.

Jack and I arranged to have the body flown by air freight from Tampa to Portland, Maine, where it was met by Parker Foss, the undertaker, and transported to Dunnocks Head for interment in the Nichol plot at Burr's Cemetery.

He would rest, Nola decided, with her parents—between Dillard, who had taught him to play baseball, and Fatima, who had made his childhood glorious by feeding him home-made tollhouse cookies and angel food cake. She wanted him back in Dunnocks Head where she said he belonged. She wanted him next to her parents, who had loved and nurtured him when he was a little boy.

That left only one space in the plot. Presumably that one was reserved for Nola, since she had already caused to have erected a headstone, as white as a sugar cube, inscribed with the year of her birth in the bottom left-hand corner and the

first two numerals of the current century on the right-hand
side, with space to accommodate the final strokes of the
stonemason's chisel. Where Jack eventually came to rest was
obviously his own affair.

The day we buried Richie she said to me in a sick whisper,
"Your brother was the only person who ever understood me.
I don't know what I'll do without him."

I said: "You still have me and Dad."

The words must have struck her heart like bullets of ice.

We were walking toward the car. She was leaning on me
heavily. Jack was still by the gravesite, talking with the
meager assembly of other mourners who'd turned up—
mostly distant cousins with Adam's apples bigger than their
chins, and old great-aunts and -uncles, solemn and wrinkled
as sea turtles.

Nola patted the back of my hand and looked up at me.

"You," she smiled wanly. "You have your own life to
live."

S i x

WHEN I was a kid, I needed explanations. I climbed around the outside of the house and looked in windows for the answers. I learned things in a variety of ways.

I see Jack sitting on the bed with one shoe off. It looks as if he's talking to someone on the other side of the room, but nobody's there. "I don't understand it," I hear him say through the open window. He grabs a handful of hair and lets his chin drop to his chest.

Quietly I clamber along the rain gutters to the other side of the house to see what Richie's doing. He's whispering to himself—something about the clock running out. He flips the Ping-Pong ball in a hook shot over his head. It ricochets off the miniature backboard and flies across the room. Cat-quick, he catches it before it hits the floor, dribbles once, sets and shoots. This time he scores. "Rawrrgh," he whispers hugely. "Rawrrgh," the crowd at the Garden goes crazy as he hits for two at the buzzer.

I leave him cheering to himself, and climb to the rooftop. I hold on to the chimney. I gaze at the diamond dust of the stars overhead. What a beautiful night! Down below I hear Richie tuning up to play his drums: the clashing beat of the cymbals on the high hat; the tonk-tonk on the cowbell; the hollow staccato of the sticks on the edge of the raspy snare drum; the powerful thud-thud of the tom-tom.

I learn lots of things.

I know that my mother started life as Nola Nichol. Eventually she married my father and became Mrs. Jack Dimes. Jack likes to say that when she married him, she doubled her net worth overnight.

"Nichols and Dimes," he said when he swaggered over to her that fateful night they met at the dance hall in Arrowsic. "Sounds like we're just meant to be together."

"It's Nichol, not Nichols," she told him. "Besides, no matter how you look at it, we'd be just a bunch of small change."

Sometimes she tells me new things when she wakes up from one of her naps. Often she likes a little snack at such times.

"Early boy, will you be nice and fix Momma some buttered popcorn? Oh thank you!"

Or:

"Momma's really hungry. Will you make her some nice peanut-butter crackers and bring them here to me on a tray with a glass of milk? That's a good boy."

I am happy to oblige, since these bowls of popcorn and plates of peanut-butter crackers often lead to knowledge.

Jack finds little flattened khaki-colored dots of peanut butter on his pillowcase. The cracker crumbs and popcorn kernels in his bed keep him awake and thrashing at night.

"Damn fool can't even get out of bed to eat. Now don't you go making her any more of those peanut-butter goddam crackers and popcorn she likes to lie around and gump down all day. You hear me, Earl? You let her get out of bed and make her own damn snacks—eat 'em at a table like a normal human being, for a change. You hear me?"

I hear him all right. But he doesn't understand what's going on or how important it is to my education. With a fine sense of my own moral superiority, I keep on making her the buttered popcorn and peanut-butter crackers, albeit with a little more secretive cautiousness than before.

If she feels like talking, I settle on the furry white rug next to the piles of unopened books from the book clubs. I clasp my knees and get ready to listen. She nibbles her popcorn thoughtfully. The drapes are still drawn. It is twilight in the room as usual. She frowns, clears her throat, and stares into the popcorn bowl.

She begins to talk in a slow wondering voice full of surprise and sadness. She's not talking to me. She's talking to something else in the darkened room with us. I'm just there, overhearing what she says.

I learn how shy she was as a child. How the other children tormented her on the playground, singing awful songs they made up about her—songs she could never get out of her head afterwards. She sings in a sad little voice:

> *"Nola, Nola*
> *Did a lil dance*
> *Nola, Nola*
> *Lost her rubber pants!"*

They change their tune when she blossoms into a beautiful girl in high school. Then she torments her old tormentors by doing no more than remaining as shy and fey as ever, only now lovely and achingly inaccessible.

When she is a senior, she starts seeing a boy from Bath. He is a few years older, already out of school, and works as a meat cutter in a grocery store owned by a man named Thurston Smith. The boy plays basketball for the Bath town team. His employer is one of the team sponsors. Nola goes to all the games she can. When he races down the court, his hard white body sails up under the basket as if rising on the roar of the crowd. It makes her feel all damp under her clothes. Her boyfriend is the best player on the team. His name is Hal McGann. He will turn out to be Richie's father and an alcoholic, but not much else.

By this time, she's met Jack at the dance hall in Arrowsic, and they've had their famous conversation about nickels and dimes. Hal doesn't dance. He works late at the store most nights anyway, so Nola goes to the dances accompanied by her mother, who sometimes plays piano for one of the local groups, or with her girlfriend, Dolores, whom her parents don't approve of because she has what they call "a reputation."

I learn all about Dolores, too. How she goes out in the gravel parking lot at the dances and sits in Bobby Whitfield's Model A and tipples bathtub gin with him in the darkness. Then, flushed with alcohol and excitement, they come back in the warm crowded softly lighted rooms to dance and perspire together.

After high school, Dolores goes up to Boston and gets a job with the telephone company. She meets a rich man and becomes his mistress. Years later, she meets up with Bobby Whitfield again. They marry. Everybody thinks it's so romantic. Because here they were so much in love in high school, and then they meet again years afterwards and discover they're still in love, and finally get married.

One night they get into a fight, and Bobby shoots Dolores. The bullet doesn't kill her, but it leaves her paralyzed from the waist down. She tells the police it was an accident and

Bobby doesn't go to jail. After that, Bobby is a devoted husband. I even know what they look like, because Nola stays in touch with Dolores, and once they come to visit. I watch Bobby unload the wheelchair from the back of the car and set it up in the driveway and lift Dolores out of the car onto the chair. She's fat and laughs a lot and her henna-colored hair is thin. Nola tells me she was beautiful once, but I don't believe it. Bobby has a big fleshy nose and kinky hair. Neither of them looks capable of passion to me.

Sometimes Jack is at the dances. Whenever he sees Nola, he comes right over. He cuts through the crowd as if nobody else exists. It makes her heart beat fast.

More than once he looks around in pretended earnestness and says with a feigned note of concern: "Where's the boyfriend tonight?"

She's always terribly embarrassed by this question; she doesn't know why she is, but she is.

"He had to work late at the store."

"Aw, too bad. Guess you'll have to dance with me."

He doesn't wait for a reply. He leads her out into the swaying crowd of humid dancers. It's like she's been drugged. She lets him drag her around the dance floor. It reminds her of the comedian's act she sees one night when Dillard takes her to see vaudeville at the Keith Theater in Portland. The comic uses a human-sized rag doll for a prop. He's got it dressed in a red evening gown with a rag mop on its head for hair. He puts the lady rag doll in a chair, offers it a drink from his pocket flask, but it keeps falling over. *Had enough already, hey?* The rag mop falls off its head. He picks it up and puts it on the doll's lap. *Here you go. Hold on to your hair, dear.* The audience loves it. The orchestra strikes up a tango. The comedian steps into the stirrups on the doll's feet, which the audience hasn't noticed before, and very dramatically dances with it all around the stage. The crowd thinks it's a scream.

Nola feels just like that doll. If Jack ever lets go, she'll slide right down the front of him and stretch out on the floor. She lies stricken and wilted in his arms. She can't get her legs to work right. They have gone limp as noodles. She can feel everything he owns, from his breastbone on down to his kneecaps. If he doesn't take her back to her seat pretty soon, she's afraid she'll wet her pants.

Sometimes he draws back and shoots her a look from under his heavy eyelids and says: "Why don't you tell the basketball player to go dribble his ball in some other part of town? So you 'n' I can get together."

"I couldn't do that!" She can hardly breathe.

"Why not?" He loves to get her flustered. It makes her mad that he can do it so easily.

"Because we're—we're almost engaged. As soon as he gets the money for the ring."

He tightens his arm around her waist and brushes his lips against the hair on her temple.

"Baby. So far as I'm concerned, *nobody* is engaged. Not till the day they're married. And maybe not even then."

Oh, that makes her heart beat fast, all right!

So do the bad stories. Somebody is always whispering in her ear when the basketball player is not around. *Did you hear what he did at the dance in Ligget the other night? He punched a hole right through the men's-room wall! When they asked him to leave he got into a terrible fight, and the police came and dragged him off to jail!*

When they try to eject him, he spins around the cop on duty at the dance hall and knocks him down a flight of stairs. The cop sits up woozily on the sidewalk outside and blows his whistle. By the time Jack figures he'd better leave, there are six more cops waiting for him outside. They play bull-in-the-middle with him. When he charges one side, the ones behind him beat him on the back with their nightsticks. When he turns on them, the others move in and do the same. He keeps turning and charging, trying to break out of the ring. "Why don't you bastards fight like men!" he cries, and their heads drop a little to see him standing there with the blood running out of his hair, still challenging them contemptuously. "Come on! Come on, you priceless pride of pinheads! Drop those sticks 'n' I'll take you all on! One at a time or all at once, however you like it, ladies! Come on! Come on, you goddam fairies!" They beat him senseless, since he seems to require it, and drag him off to jail.

When she hears the story, it makes her feel hot all over. She knows the reason he did it: why he got so angry and punched a hole in the wall, and then fought with all those policemen. It was because she wasn't there. That's why he did it. Because he was so frustrated and disappointed that she wasn't there. She is as sure of it as if he'd told her that himself.

Then one day, out of the blue, she learns that he's gone and married Sylvia Wiggens, whose father owns the newspaper in Ligget. By this time she has her ring from the basketball player. But the news about Jack still makes her feel bad. She knows it's silly, but she can't help it. Gradually the story comes out that Sylvia is pregnant, so Jack had to do what he did. Still, she feels let down about it.

She marries the basketball player and moves to Bath. But it doesn't work out right. Thurston Smith takes him for a few drinks after work every payday and then invites him back to the store to play a little game of twenty-one. Every week he wins back most of Hal's paycheck. He feels so good about it he gives Hal a raise.

But the business goes sour. Thurston offers Hal a cut if he'll help him burn down the store for the insurance money. Hal gets liquored up and lets himself into the store one night at three in the morning. He sets fire to a stack of newspapers and cardboard boxes that he piles up around the furnace. Nola is outside in the car waiting for him. She has no idea what he's up to. He comes running out of the store looking wild-eyed and jumps in the car.

"Drive!" he says. "Drive like hell! 'nless you want to spend the rest of your life in jail!"

Thurston collects his insurance money and moves to Florida. Hal never sees a penny of it.

Sometimes she sits alone with a cup of coffee and looks out her kitchen window which overlooks the street and lets herself think about Jack. She wonders how different her life would have been if she'd married him instead of Hal. She knows Jack is not happy either. She knows this, because whenever she's up Ligget way, she always stops by the newspaper office just to say hello. He looks so happy when she drops in on him like this.

"Mother and I were on our way to Waterville, so I thought I'd stop by and say hello. She's waiting for me in the car."

"God, I'm so glad you did. How are you? You look wonderful."

She likes the way the typewriters stop clacking when she enters the newsroom, how the other reporters pause to look at her with admiration and yearning before they resume typing again. It tells her that she's still pretty. She loves the way he sits at his desk and just smiles at her as she approaches. The expression on his face seems to say: *Well I'll be: truly here is balm for my damaged soul.* He rises at the last second and holds out his hand: "Nola. Goddam. How good to see you again."

He calls her whenever he is down her way too. If she can, she joins him for a cup of coffee and a piece of pie at the diner in Wiscasset, where they are less likely to run into any busybodies from Bath who might get the wrong idea.

A few times they meet down at Popham and walk along a wild and lonely strip of beach together. They talk about how their marriages aren't working out, haltingly at first, and then more freely later on. They listen to each other's pitiful stories and shake their heads dolefully. How sad things don't work out better, even when you try so hard. Once, he tries to kiss her, but she says no, she couldn't do that, it wouldn't be right.

"I know, I know," he says in a chastened voice. He looks out to sea. "It's just that I—well, never mind about that."

She wishes he'd finish his sentence. She hates it when people do that. She's pretty sure he was going to say that he loves her. If so, he was right to stop. Still, she wishes he wouldn't start up and then leave her dangling like that. That's not fair, either.

She can tell he is suffering. She lets him put his arm around her sometimes, if it seems appropriate in connection with the conversation they're having.

In the fifth year of her marriage, just as it begins its final collapse, Nola gives birth to Richie. It's a stupid mistake, but that's the way it happens. Hal is drinking more than ever. Some nights when he comes home he is so fall-down drunk that she locks him in the bedroom. He's perfectly affable when he's drunk. It's just that he falls down a lot and won't shut up. Sometimes when she locks him in the room, he climbs out the window and down the fire escape and is found weaving about in the street out in front of the apartment house, dressed in nothing but his union suit. It is a miracle he isn't run over by a passing car, but everybody in

town has learned to slow down and be on the alert out in
front of his house. When he gets too much for her to handle,
she calls Dr. Moody, who comes over and gives him a shot
that puts him out of his misery for the night.

On one such occasion, the doctor turns to her and says:
"Well, my dear, I'm afraid you might's well give it up. I
don't think this fellow is ever going to get any better. Do
you?"

For some reason this remark, made by a fatigued physi-
cian in the middle of the night, impresses her in a way the
obvious circumstances of her life have not. While Hal lies
snoring heavily on the bed, she calls Dillard and asks if he
will come and get her and the baby. He doesn't ask questions; he just says he will. Hal is still passed out in the
bedroom when they load up the car and drive off.

When Jack reads the divorce announcement in the *Portland Press-Herald,* he borrows a car and drives right down to
Dunnocks Head and asks her to marry him.

"But you're already married."

"I know, but if I get a divorce. Jesus, Nola, I've always
been crazy about you. This is our chance to be happy. What
do you say?"

Her heart flutters fearfully. Here is rescue after all, just
when she was beginning to feel most hopeless about living at
home, a divorced woman with a small child. She glances
timidly at his body, lean as a rake handle, buttoned into his
three-piece beige suit with the light-blue chalk stripe. It is a
cheap suit and looks it, but it makes her feel tender towards
him. She can teach him how to dress better. She's always
had an eye for fashion. She sees swiftly the lovely sculpture
of his throat above his starched collar, one button open at
the neck; his loosened silky blue tie stamped with tiny red
diamonds bunched inside the top of his vest; the glint of the

tiger's-eye ring on the pinky of the hand that lies loose and half coiled and dangerous-looking in his lap.

Her frightened eyes rise to his smiling lips and the milk-white blade of his eager face. A little dark-blond leaf of wavy hair clings like a piece of fancy plasterwork to his smooth untroubled forehead. He is too handsome. Too handsome for her. It troubles her to look at him. She can't look into the mesmerizing sapphire-like fire of his eyes. Yet as she looks away, she knows she wants him more than she's wanted anything in her life. If she doesn't marry him, if they don't take this chance to right their lives this time, she'll probably regret it the rest of her life. She studies her hands for a minute, as if she were thinking it over, but really only to collect herself. When she thinks she can speak again, she raises her head and smiles.

"Yes I will," she says in a faint breathless voice.

He gives her a passionate kiss which flattens her lips against her teeth and hurts her mouth.

"Thank God," he says. "I think you just saved my life."

He speeds back to Ligget and tells Sylvia he wants a divorce. She screams and throws things, tells him she'll never give him one. His two little kids stand in the middle of the floor and cry. They don't know which way to turn. Their faces distorted, they hold their arms away from their bodies a little, with their hands curled, ready to hang on, if only they knew which parent to grab on to. Hastily he packs a valise and flees to his mother and father's house, two streets over.

The next morning when he shows up for work, his father-in-law fires him. He applies at the shoe factory, but things are slow. That winter, he and his father go into the woods and cut cordwood and make a little money that way. It is bitter cold that winter. The trees are hard as iron. By lunchtime, his sandwich is frozen stiff. He has to cut it into pieces with his pocket knife in order to be able to eat it.

The next spring they hire him on at the factory and things get better, at least in that way.

Four years go by. It's hard on both of them. Dillard can't abide having a married man paying court to his daughter. Even though Jack is separated from his wife, it's still scandalous. So far as he's concerned, the son of a bitch is no good.

I know the rest of the story too.

How he gets her pregnant in a ditch one day out in the country when he loses control of himself. And how they go down on the train to Boston to take care of it and how he faints and how it doesn't take and she has to go back a second time and this time when she gets home it does and she has it on the toilet and Fatima has to send for the doctor in the next town so it won't get around Dunnocks Head.

And it happens again and this time it's me and they talk about going down to Boston again; only he thinks the divorce might come through, and it does, and they get married, and I don't end up down the toilet like the other one.

How, long ago in the little house in Ligget, she lets the furnace go out. And when he comes home drunk that night he grabs her head and holds a straight razor in front of her eyes and tells her he'll cut her up so bad that even her parents won't recognize her if she ever lets it happen again, and how he acts like he doesn't remember a thing about it the next morning.

I know how scared and lonely she was in that little rented house in Ligget. It was crooked; all the doors and floors were crooked. It leaned out over a gully full of trash as if exhausted and about ready to fall in and join the rest of the debris at the bottom of the gulch—which it did eventually, only we weren't there anymore.

Fatima and Dillard drove up from Dunnocks Head once a week and brought them groceries. If not for those, she doesn't know what they would have done. She doesn't tell them anything—how he hits her sometimes, how he threatened her with the razor. She is too ashamed and frightened. Her father never liked him. He warned her not to marry him; he said he was no damned good, but she went ahead anyway.

She walks to the front gate, where she can see the Kennebec showing like little blue bits of picture-puzzle pieces through the leafy trees at the bottom of the hill.

The sight of the river makes her feel better. On its way to the sea, it runs right through Dunnocks Head, in full view of her parents' house. That common thread of water links her with her mother and father.

She has no friends. Ligget is Jack's hometown. His ex-wife and kids still live there. They have the town's sympathy; people think she's just a whore who broke up a nice family. Nola thinks Ligget is a hole: she hates the town, she hates the people. There's nothing there but ugliness and the shoe factory.

She wants to go home. She wants somebody to take care of her again and be nice and not mean. She longs to sleep in her narrow bed upstairs at the back of the house, under the archipelago of rusty water stains on the ceiling, where it is cool and dark and quiet. She wants to hear the distant sound of the sad train whistle which haunted the nights of her childhood and made her feel so sweetly and safely melancholy.

She misses the vegetable-rank smell of Fatima's parlor. She holds herself together with memories of plants in terracotta pots arranged on steplike shelves, luxuriant vegetation dreaming in the watery sunlight filtering under the dark-green shades in the niche made by the bay window: African violets, their furry jade leaves cut in little heart shapes as from suede cloth, and tiny pink starlike flowers shyly peeping out; elephant-eared caladiums with blood-red veins and purplish jagged stains on their tender flesh, like horrible bruises.

She longs to drink in the sight of her mother's fat overstuffed beet-red chairs, covered in mohair with a nap as prickly as an unshaven man's chin, scattered about on the shiny linoleum of the parlor floor like bumper cars abandoned on a rink at a park closed for the season.

She wants to lie back in one of the prickly chairs and watch Fatima's back sway back and forth on the piano stool, as she pounds the yellow keyboard of the upright into submission with one of her illiterate renditions of "The Washington Post March" or "Roll Out the Barrel." She wants to register the effect the vibrations have on the framed print of watermelons and oranges over the piano and watch it slowly go crooked on the wall. And as her sweet loving but largely unconscious mother continues to play havoc with the notes of popular tunes, and the picture crawls on the faded wallpaper to an even more crooked angle, she wants to smooth one of the homemade crocheted doilies against the prickly arm of the chair and study between her fingers the beautiful details of its strawberry pentagrams and blissfully forget all about being grown up.

Take me home! she wants to cry when they come once a week with the groceries. I want a homemade doughnut! I want to hear you play the piano again! I want to sit in one of your prickly chairs and watch the picture go crooked on the wall. I'm so tired, Mother and Daddy. I just want to sleep sleep *sleep* by myself in my own room again.

But she says none of these things. Instead, when they get ready to leave in the car, she hugs herself and murmurs with

downcast eyes, "Careful on the drive home," and waves as
they pull away from the curb.

> *Where you goin', Nola, Nola*
> *Whutchu doin', Nola, Nola*
> *Nuthin', nuthin'*
> *Kick her in the oven, oven*
> *No place, no place*
> *Hang her by a shoelace, shoelace*
> *Nola, Nola*
> *Stuff her in a stroll-ah!*

She's in her seventh month. She can't sleep at nights. The
nights are awful. Lying there in the dark next to him, her
wakeful thoughts are worse than nightmares. Sometimes she
gets up in the middle of the night and makes bread, kneels
by the bathtub, does some laundry on the scrub board. If
these things don't calm her, she dresses, creeps out of the
house, and walks up and down the dark hills of the sleeping
town.

"Where the hell have you been?" he asks one morning
when she comes in. He's sleepy and irritable, sitting at the
kitchen table in his soiled paisley bathrobe, breakfasting on
the toast and coffee he's had to make for himself.

Instead of answering she sits down and lights a cigarette.
The sudden crushing burden of her depression leaves her
speechless. He waits, his big shoulders hunched in anger.
Her eyes are full of tears. She hasn't got any words, she
hasn't got any answers. All she can do is blow smoke at the
ceiling. He waits for what he considers a reasonable length
of time, then reaches out and pastes her a good one with the
back of his hand. She hits the wall and falls to the floor.
Stunned, she sits there under the table. He finishes his cof-

fee, pushes back his chair, and goes into the bathroom to shave.

She waits till he shuts the door. Then she scrabbles off the floor, plucks Richie from his bed, and runs with him in her arms across the snowy yard to Mrs. Kendall's house. They lock the doors. She calls her father.

"What's wrong, daughter? He didn't hit you, did he? I'm just waitin' for him to do something like that—I know he will, sooner or later—so I can get my shotgun and come up there and blow that son of bitch right out his back door and off the porch and down into that gully, with the rest of the trash where he belongs."

No, no, she says. Nothing like that. I'm just a little homesick, that's all.

"Can Richie and I come and stay with you and Mother for a little while? I just miss you both so much, that's all."

"Where are you now?"

"I—I'm at Mrs. Kendall's."

"Is Richie with you?"

"Yes."

"Stay there. Don't you go back to that house. I'll be there as soon as I can get there."

You see? she tells me. *My daddy knew all along what I was going through. I didn't fool him—not for a single minute.*

JACK doesn't show up at the house till New Year's Eve, although she's been expecting him, half hopeful and half afraid, ever since she walked out on him three days before Christmas. When the inevitable knock comes at the door on that snowy night, her heart flutters sleepily like a broody hen suddenly elevated to a higher roost. She knows it's him. She can feel him outside; she's felt him drawing closer all day. It's like atmospheric pressure building up, like pressure on the windows, getting ready to blow the glass to smithereens if it doesn't let up soon.

Dillard won't let her answer it. He goes to the door instead. Just as he suspected, it is the son-in-law he despises—standing there under the harsh needlelike blaze of the porch light with a handful of snow swirling around his head, dressed in a hulking disreputable secondhand raccoon-skin coat which fits him like an oversize ape suit, and a flat porkpie hat jammed on his brow. In one raveling gloved hand he holds a bottle of champagne; in the other, two hollow-stemmed glasses. Standing there in his busted gloves and porkpie hat and the horrible moth-eaten coat and the black muffler up around his nose, which he lowers like a mask with a free finger to show his pearly teeth, like an audacious turnpike thief revealing his identity to the victim he is just about to rob, he looks a perfect fool.

"I'd like to speak to my wife, please."

"I doubt if she'd like to speak to you. Wait here. I'll see what she says."

He is dead set against it.

"You'n' the kids can live here," he says. "You know that. You don't have to have anything to do with that son of a bitch ever again."

He always refers to him as "that son of a bitch," never by name—as if "son of a bitch" is the only acceptable euphemism or substitute for the actual obscenity of the man's name itself.

When he sees she's going to talk to him anyway, he makes her promise not to let him in the house. "Don't let that son of a bitch in my house," he says. He makes her promise to keep the storm door between them. So, against her father's wishes, she goes out to talk to Jack to see what he wants; and when she sees the blade of his handsome face smile so beautifully at the sight of her, it's like a stab in the heart. He pops the cork on the champagne. He passes her a glass through the crack in the door. She lowers her face to the wide shallow bowl of the glass. She drinks. The tawny wine sprays her cheeks and upper lip. She loves champagne, loves to watch the bubbles rise in the hollow stem, loves the tiny tickle as they break on her face. It makes her close her eyes and smile.

"Come back to me," he says. "You can walk around town all night for all I care. I'll never go out with the boys again if that's what it takes. I love you, Nola. I need you. I want to take care of you and Richie. I want to make a good home for you and him and the baby when it comes. I want to get someplace in the world. Be somebody. So I can give you and the kids the kind of things you deserve.

"Someday we're going to have a beautiful house. We're not going to live in that shitbox in the gully forever. You're going to wear beautiful clothes and have plenty of money. Our kids are going to go to the best schools. They're going to college; they'll never have to struggle like me. They'll always have good jobs. They'll have kids, Nola. They'll bring their babies to our house. We're going to have a wonderful life."

When she comes back into the parlor that night, Dillard knows at a glance that she's going back to the son of a bitch. But when she tells him, all he says is, "Remember: we're here, if you ever need us."

"Your grandfather was a wonderful man," she says to the corner of the room. "I wish he and Mother had lived longer. I wish they were alive now so I'd have somewhere to go. Someone to talk to other than you, little boy. Oh—I thought I was doing the right thing. I was big as a house with you.

The thought of washing up permanently on Mother and Daddy's doorstep with two kids in tow was more than I could bear. So I went back. Going back was the only choice I had."

Jack is as good as his word. He rises in the world. He's restless, hardworking, smart. In time he works in New York City managing a business that manufactures expensive handbags. Later he manages a series of shoe factories in Pennsylvania. These jobs pay good money. When she gets real bad he's able to send her to famous doctors and prestigious institutions.

We move from Maine to Pennsylvania to Maine to New York to Maine to Pennsylvania again. We live in lots of different houses—sometimes two or three in a year. For a while, in one little shoe town in Pennsylvania, we live in a hotel. The address I give at school is: Room 409, c/o the Jimmie Wilson. Every night we eat in the dining room. I can have whatever I want. Usually I have the baked ham with raisin sauce. Mr. Honey always waits on us. I love Mr. Honey. I pretend he's an old family retainer.

Richie and I attend eight different grammar schools and one horribly run-down private school located in an old Quaker hotel in the Catskill Mountains. How Jack found out about the place and what possessed him to send us there remains a mystery. But it is where he sends us one time when she goes back to that sanitarium in western Massachusetts that she is so fond of, where they give her nice hot baths and wrap her up in bay leaves and gauze like a mummy so she can't move and leave her with her head pointing east in a room with a positive energy field for hours at a time.

He buys her a Cadillac. Every summer she takes us to Maine and rents a tall gaunt cottage built on a ledge that looks out over a dark-purple ocean. The cottage is only a few miles from Dunnocks Head, not far from her parents and her childhood home. They still keep her bedroom just the way it was when she was a child. We spend a lot of time there so she can sleep in her old room. When they pass away, first Fatima and then Dillard within six months of each other, we still keep going to Maine in the summers, and the first thing we do, even before we go down to the cottage, is drive by the old house on Nichol Avenue to see what fresh outrages the new owners have perpetrated in our absence. "Oh my God," she says. "They've torn off the porch and painted the place brown! Oh my God, my God! I never should have sold it!"

Sometimes Jack comes up, with the idea of staying a few weeks, and parks his Cadillac next to hers on the rise of tall blond grass in front of the cottage. But he's restless; he's always restless on vacations. He can't sit still for a minute. We make him irritable.

"Jesus Christ!" He leaps out of the wicker rocker as if something just bit him on the ass. "Don't you kids *ever* shut up?"

His legs twitch at night. He can't sleep. He thrashes around, he wraps himself in the sheets till he can hardly move. It's worse than popcorn and cracker crumbs. He goes out on the couch in the living room and reads paperback books all night, whatever's there in the cottage: *Dr. Hudson's Secret Journal; Goren's Rules of Bridge.* He has never learned to relax, he says.

"Work is the only form of relaxation I'm good at."

We're all expert at indolence, and accord this remark the contempt it deserves. Inevitably he cuts short his stay and speeds back to his life in the city, much to everybody's relief.

"He's got a woman in the city," she says. "I know he has. He doesn't think I know, but I do."

"A woman in the city?"

It sounds exciting.

"Be quiet," she tells me. "Finish your breakfast. Go down to the cove and take a swim with your brother."

"I ain't doing that. Not after yesterday. The son of a bitch tried to drown me again."

"Don't talk that way!" she flares. "Don't you try and talk like your father to me."

I learn things in other ways. Sometimes I learn by accident.

I'm eight years old, maybe younger, when I push open their door one night. He's standing in his underwear, swaying over her. He's got her by the hair. She's down on her knees at his feet, crying softly. He's got the pistol in his hand, the one he keeps wrapped in an oily cloth in a shoe box at the top of his closet that I get down sometimes and pretend to play Russian roulette with in front of the mirror. He's got a baffled but determined look on his face. I can tell he's drunk and out of his mind again.

"No no no," she whispers. "Please please."

"Why not?" he says. "Give me one good reason."

Unsteadily he bumps the muzzle against her temple as if looking for a place to plug it in.

He looks up. I see the murderous glint in his red-rimmed eyes. His eyes widen as he sees me frozen in his doorway with my arms held out stiffly from my sides, as if trying to maintain my balance in weightless space. He flies into a rage. In some unremembered ignominious fashion I am thrown out of the room and warned in a terrible voice not to come in again.

Outside the door, whimpering and fretting to myself, I don't know what to do. I'm scared of him, scared of what he'll do to me, if I go back in there again. I'm scared of what

he'll do to her too. I'm too cowardly to open the door again.
All I can do is whimper and bite my fingers and try to hold
the noise back so he doesn't hear me. I crouch at the key-
hole, but I can't see a thing. He stuffed it with toilet paper
long ago. All I've got are the voices through the painted
wood. I bite back the animal noises in me and press my ear
to the door. *Don't don't,* says one. *Why not?* says the other.

I strain to hear everything the voices say, but they fall
away to urgent whispers and are lost to me for minutes at a
time. I bite my fingers. I fix my eyes on the full moon as it
slowly rolls like a marble up the black sky outside the row of
windows on the wall opposite. With my eyes fixed on the
hard round moon, I crouch there and listen as hard as I can.
My hair feels as if it is standing on end, straining to hear too.
Silence: oh there's so much dreadful silence on the other
side of that door!

I fall asleep. I must have fallen asleep. Or into a catatonic
state, brought on by sheer terror. Else, how can I explain the
gap in my memory? Because the next thing I remember is,
she's holding me.

"It's all right, all right," she whispers.

She hugs me, holds me. In her bathrobe now, her long
hair in her face, some of it in my mouth, her eyes bagged and
haggard with weariness.

"Hush," she says. "Hush, hush. It's all right. Daddy's
asleep now."

She holds me. She's got the pistol in one hand, the heavy
blunt bullets in the other. She's not dead, and neither am I.
But I can't look her in the eye. All I can do is blubber. She
knows what a coward I've been.

Through her gold hair, I see his white hairless shins and
alabaster feet hanging off the edge of the bed. In the circle of
light thrown against the roses in the wallpaper, by the lamp

overturned on the rug among the scattered unopened books from the book clubs, he sprawls in a swirling debris of mattress, pillows, and bedclothes like a tree ripped up by the roots.

THERE are other times, other ways that I learn.

Sometimes I learn by example, as on the day he beats me up by mistake.

I walk in on him and Daryl Wilhide as they're having a few martinis together in the living room while the women are out shopping. Before I can back out of the room again, he spots me.

"So you're on the wrestling team," he says. "Well, now. Why don't you show me what you know?"

A scrawny little fellow with a head like a baby bird, Wilhide stands on the coffee table in his stocking feet and giggles into his martini as Jack stalks me, gets me in a half nelson, whips me around the room. Jack weighs 220; I weigh 103. I bounce off the couch. I fall into the fireplace. I hit the floor. Jack pins me fourteen or fifteen times. Wilhide stands on the coffee table and cackles like a fool through it all. When I grow up, I decide, I'll kill the scrawny little son of a bitch for this.

At last he lets me crawl off. When the women get home, I'm in the little bedroom off the kitchen. My lips are puffy. One of my eyes is swollen shut. I've got brush burns from the rug all over my body, and I can't lift my left arm.

"My God." Nola puts a hand on my forehead. "What in the world has he done to you?"

I say: "He showed me how to wrestle."

She gets a steak out of the refrigerator and tells me to press it against my eye, it'll take the swelling down.

After dinner, Jack comes back to see me. He looks a little embarrassed and ashamed of himself. He sits on the bed and pushes my hair back off my forehead.

"How you doing, kid?"

"Okay," I say.

"I guess I was a little rough on you."

He rubs his chin thoughtfully, smiles at me. He's got beautiful teeth, his eyes are pebbly-blue. He's a handsome man, broad-shouldered in his white shirt and loosened tie, with a dark-blond wave of hair always on his forehead like a little piece of pargeting. I think to myself: I hope I look just like him when I grow up.

"Sometimes you probably wonder why I'm tougher on you than on your brother."

I never noticed, but I nod my head solemnly. It looks like we're having a man-to-man talk. I don't want to louse it up by saying something stupid.

"Yes, I bet you have."

He smiles and tousles my hair again.

"Well, I'll tell you why—only keep it to yourself. It's because I expect great things of you. Your brother, he's an athlete. Maybe he'll be a professional, who knows? But you're the smart one. You got something special in you, I can see it. But you're too soft and sensitive, son. You're too much like your mother in that respect. So if I'm tough on you sometimes—like today, in the living room there, maybe I was a little rougher on you than I should have been—it's because I want you to grow up so you can take things. Take what life has to dish out and still come back for more. I want you to learn to stand tall like a man. You understand what I'm trying to say?"

I shake my head yes. I'm so happy he's talking confidentially to me like this that I don't trust myself to speak.

"That's my boy," he says. "How's that eye coming along?"

She never figures out a way to leave him permanently. Sometimes she takes us out of school and we get on a train and ride for two days. We go across flatlands, through mountain gorges, we travel across deserts. We sleep in train compartments. The porter makes up our beds at night. We eat whatever we want in the dining car. I like the sound of the ice tinkling like little cowbells in my ice water. I love to see the world sliding by outside the dining-car windows.

We end up in motels or hotels in towns we've never been to before, with open suitcases scattered all over the floor. She's bent over on the edge of the bed, sobbing hard.

"I can't," she chokes out. It's awful how the words hurt her coming out, like someone trying to hold back vomit.

"I can't. I can't. We have no money. There's no place we can go."

She calls him then.

"I think I'm getting sick," she says.

She tells him where to find us. After a day or two, we hear a soft knock at the door.

Richie and I scramble for it and throw it open.

"Dad!"

Nola lifts her head off the pillow, slides to a sitting position on the edge of the bed. She's got on the little black dress he likes, but her hair is uncombed and she is in her stocking feet. Somehow his arrivals always catch her by surprise.

We dance around, we tangle ourselves in his arms and legs at as many points as we can. He drags us across the room till he reaches Nola. She stands up and falls into his arms. We hear her sigh his name in relief. We step away and watch them hold each other, holding on silently, as if for dear life. Holding each other for so long that Richie and I test each other with a look and can't help breaking into smiles. Rescued again, our faces seem to say.

No: she never finds a way to leave him.

> *Nola, Nola*
> *Whutchu gonna do?*
> *Nola, Nola*
> *Eat a little rue.*
> *Nola, Nola*
> *Eat a little dirt.*
> *Nola, Nola*
> *Have some more dessert!*

S e v e n

WHEN I visited Bergen Cove at Thanksgiving, Phil had told me that he and Mario owned "da leg of a nag," as he put it, that was scheduled to run at Pimlico at the end of the season.

It had been agreed that he and the boys would stop at Bentham and take Linda and me along to Baltimore on the appointed weekend—the second one in January, right after the start of the spring semester. Mrs. Stephano was not up to traveling and had no interest in racetracks anyway. She was to remain home under the watchful eye of Anna, the housekeeper.

I had no more interest in seeing Pimlico than presumably Mrs. Stephano did, particularly at that time of the year, even though Phil assured me it was one of the most beautiful institutions in the world. But I *did* like the idea of staying at the first-class hotel he said he'd have Mario book us into, and of having dinner at Tío Clemente's, a restaurant, he growled in a low suggestive gravelly voice, "that maybe you kids'll like, eh?"

He lazily blinked his yellow eyes at me and punctuated each of these relatively innocuous words by slightly tapping the smoky air above his bald head with the glowing tip of his cigar as he said them, as if they contained much hidden meaning. At the same time he smiled at me, shooting me another glimpse of that astonishingly painful-looking grimace full of peg teeth, before his heavy cheeks, flushed and shiny with wine, collapsed again into his customary deadpan expression. That grim piratical smile signaled complete confidence in my understanding, but I had no idea what he meant.

Later Mario took me aside to whisper that Tío Clemente's was an experience I shouldn't miss, if I could help it. That he was fat, and obviously given to the enjoyment of good food, added special authority to his opinions about restaurants, so far as I was concerned.

I left Bergen Cove basking in a sense of bewildered pleasure, feeling like one of Dickens's orphans who suddenly and inexplicably is taken into the warm benevolent keeping of an unknown benefactor. Why I considered Phil's interest in me to be such a mystery I mark down to my peculiar condition of arrested development at the time. I was twenty-three, to be sure; but I was still an inexperienced hand in many ways. My interest in books and my absorption in the suffocating problems of my family had ill-equipped me to deal with the obvious. Hadn't Linda told me, with a perky little waggle of her head, that her daddy was ready to buy her anything she wanted? I was naive enough to think that her remark was a comic exaggeration. Even if I had taken it literally, it wouldn't have occurred to me that it might include boyfriends as well as material goods.

Richie's death had a sudden calamitous effect on my ideas of what constituted good fortune. I was no longer interested in fine food, or free lodging, or in going anywhere with anybody. I tried to buckle down to my studies, but I couldn't keep my mind on my work. I kept fretting about how they were managing at home without me.

I told Linda what was troubling me, and said I wanted to go home and see how they were doing, instead of traipsing off to Baltimore for the weekend. I apologized for ruining everybody's plans. I said I thought I could talk Arthur into giving me a lift home. She was disappointed; she contended that a trip away at this time would probably do me some good.

"Can't you go home next weekend?"

"I've got a test I have to study for."

"Well—if you don't want to go with us, I understand."

I didn't think she understood at all. With a growing sense of irritation concerning why any explanation was needed, I tried to keep my patience and explain it to her the way you would to a spoiled little three-year old.

"It's just that I'm worried about them. I don't think I could go off and have a good time, with that on my mind."

A flutter of panic crossed her face.

"You don't mind if I still go with Daddy, do you?"

I assured her that I didn't. I told her to go and have a good time for the both of us, and to be sure to thank her father again for inviting me.

"He'll really be sorry that you're not coming with us."

"I'm sure you can explain why."

"Well—I'll try," she said.

It was at this point, when my exasperation with her was reaching its limits, that she surprised me with one of her gestures of sudden generosity. It was part of a pattern of behavior that would become so familiar to me later on.

"Here." She rummaged in her purse briefly and tossed me the keys to the Ghia.

"Take my car. Then you won't have to beg Arthur for anything. He'll want you to help him with his Chaucer or something. This way you'll be free as a bird. Hey, wait a minute."

She dug further into the jumble of lipstick tubes and chewing gum. "I can give you some gas money too—"

Full of gratitude, I gave her a chaste brotherly kiss on the cheek and told her that she was a wonderful girl, which made her beam with pleasure like a little child. Then, well in advance of Phil's expected arrival, I stole out of the parking lot in Linda's little car and drove the forty-five miles or so to the sooty little town of Aldridge, where the gypsy practice of Jack's trade had beached him for the last three years—one of the longest sojourns in any one place in his entire career.

We lived in a long low house with a big mortgage, built into a hillside on a ridge east of town, surrounded by three acres of lawn and baby trees and shrubs that we'd planted. Downslope, to the northeast of the house, was a small grove of fairly well-established pines, where we buried Nola's fat old dogs as they keeled over one by one, sublime victims of old age and the high-cholesterol diet of table scraps that she fed them.

Below the grove was a shallow muddy pond banked on three sides by thick brambles of musk roses. Below that, and running along the edge of the lawn as far south as the small eggshell-colored barn, were about ten acres of sloping fields that we'd fenced in for pasturing Jack's motley collection of horses—two dirt-colored mares with hammerlike heads, and a palomino gelding that was full of worms when he bought it, and still was nothing but a bag of bones. Why he kept them on the premises I couldn't imagine. He never did anything with them that I could see, other than feed and water and fetch the vet for them, except to lean the hams of his big forearms against the top rail of the white board fence from time to time and watch them graze in the pasture.

When I swung down into the circular driveway on that lowering gray afternoon and pointed Linda's car at the garage doors, I was not prepared to see the stove still on the lawn—still balanced on one corner like a cubist piece of garden sculpture, looking very white and hard-edged against the dark-green background of the yew hedge.

Of course it had been there at Christmas too, when I came home to make the long trip north with them for Richie's funeral. But we were all numb with grief and in a hurry, and if I even glanced at it, it hadn't meant anything to me, other than just another one of Jack's messes that would have to be cleaned up and hauled away sometime when time allowed.

The day after he pushed it over the side, he went out and replaced it with the best stove Nola had ever had in her life. Although what she wanted it for was another matter. She rarely used it for anything, except to boil hot water for instant coffee. A hot plate would have served her just as well and saved him a lot of money. But he'd done it. He'd made amends for his folly in the usual way—by spending lots of money on something that nobody particularly wanted.

It was delivered on the afternoon of the day he bought it. That was part of the bargain. Either get it there today, or no deal. But it arrived too late to be of much good, so far as lunch was concerned. So, when we all finally piled out of bed that day, Jack went out and got us several piping-hot containers of take-out from the little Chinese restaurant that had just opened up in the square downtown next to the bank. It was all part of his self-imposed penance for being a bad boy the night before. Usually it was a pleasure being around the place for a few days after one of Jack's escapades, when he felt he had some failing to make up for. We sat around the kitchen table and slurped wonton soup and licked our chops over the barbecued spare ribs, the pork fried rice, and the Lobster Cantonese, and poked fun at Nola for sleeping through all the excitement the night before.

"I don't think it's one bit funny," she said while sucking on a barbecued rib, and we all laughed hilariously—albeit Jack a little sheepishly.

"I think you ought to leave it there on the lawn," I said, meaning the old stove. "As a monument to Family Life."

That got a laugh too.

But when I came home that afternoon in Linda's car and saw it still balanced there on a little breadcrust of snow in the fast-failing light, I sat behind the wheel and stared at it till my stinging eyes made it wobble and dance like ectoplasm.

I waited a few minutes till I got hold of myself and then went into the house. They were sitting in the kitchen over coffee. She was in her robe and pajamas, and her hair was standing up on the back of her head where she'd apparently slept on it all afternoon. Jack was in his shirt sleeves and slippers having a cigarette. It looked as if I had walked in on them at a particularly dreary moment. They were surprised and happy—even relieved, I think—to see me.

"Why Early," said Nola, sounding pleased. "What are you doing home?"

"Hi, Ma."

"Good God," Jack said, grinning, "look what the cat dragged in. I thought you were going to the races."

I noticed the difference in him right away. He looked thin and sick.

"I was, but I decided to come home instead. What's for dinner?"

"I thought I'd fix some chop suey."

"I could always come back later."

He laughed.

"Well, wiseguy, you can always have a grapefruit with me, if you like. Your mother's got me on this diet she found in the newspaper. I've lost twelve pounds already."

"No wonder you look awful."

"Are you kidding? I've got forty pounds to go."

"Well, go easy. You don't want to overdo it."

"Your mother's worried too."

He grinned at Nola, who, in old pajamas and bathrobe, was languidly watching us from her seat at the table in the breakfast nook, nursing a cup of coffee that looked as if it had gone as sour as a sinkful of old dishwater.

"She's afraid I'm liable to get so good-looking again that I'll have to fight off all the women down at the factory with a stick."

"You leave those women alone," she said. "They have enough problems without you bothering them."

"You'd better cut it out," I said. "A quick drop in weight like that isn't good for you."

He pointed his thumb at me and cocked his head at Nola.

"Listen to him. He's been on my back to lose weight for years, and then when I do, he wants me to stop." He looked at me again. "God, you're a lot like your mother—you're both like one of those damned old Studebakers: nobody can tell whether you're coming or going."

They put on a brave front for my benefit that weekend. Even Nola tried her best to stay awake, although she didn't get dressed or ever get around to combing her hair, so far as I could tell. But she was conscious mostly, and smiled weakly in my direction whenever I entered a room.

On Saturday night we even played a few listless hands of crazy eights before we crept off to our beds, relieved to be alone in the dark again, and free of the pretenses which we'd kept up for each other's sake.

When I was ready to leave for school on Sunday afternoon, Jack walked me out to the car.

"Don't you think you ought to get rid of that sometime?"

I nodded in the direction of the ruined stove, still balanced white-on-white against the threadbare snow in the backyard.

He shot me a look.

"I've got a man coming tomorrow to haul it away."

Looking haggard and troubled and a little ludicrous in his baggy slacks, he gave me a determined smile and waved goodbye as I started up the driveway. In the rearview mirror, as I turned into the road, I saw him still waving. His pant cuffs flapped against his ankles as smartly as yacht-club pennants snapping in the breeze against their flagpoles.

This image of him, standing in the wind on the edge of the drive, looking thin and haggard, with his pants flapping around his legs, stayed with me down at school. It disturbed me. Sometimes it materialized on the page of Ruskin or Carlyle before me, as I tried to study. It woke me up at nights. Three weeks later, I hitched a ride with Arthur and went home again.

He had lost another eight pounds and admitted this time that he wasn't feeling right. He had given up the grapefruit diet, which he said was the root cause of his problems.

"It was the damned diet. It left me weak as a kitten. You couldn't keep a fruit fly alive on that diet. Your mother comes up with the damnedest ideas. I don't know why I let her talk me into these things."

He had gone back to his usual fare: thick slabs of rare roast beef slathered with mushroom sauce, with mashed potatoes and gravy on the side; steaks and fries; beans and hot dogs with the special cabbage salad he had invented, made with lots of sliced-up green olives, carrot shavings, and mayonnaise; the coffee ice cream with walnut topping that he ate in the evenings while sitting on the sofa in front of the

TV with Nola. But that wasn't working either. He was feeling nauseous all the time and leaving most of his food on his plate. And he was still losing weight.

"That goddam diet has caused me to lose my appetite. It'll probably take me months to get feeling right again."

He told me he was having trouble sleeping at nights. That was not like him at all. Ordinarily he fell asleep the second his head hit the pillow. Now, when he finally did drift off, he often woke a few minutes later bathed in sweat. He found himself going into the bathroom in the middle of the night to check his temperature with the old thermometer of dubious accuracy that lay in the medicine cabinet among the litter of Nola's extensive pharmacopoeia of nostrums and knockout drops. He seemed to be running a mild fever on and off, although it was hardly noticeable, only two or three degrees above normal. He always woke in a sweat at daybreak, he said. Usually he felt pretty good after that, if a little weak. His temperature was always normal in the mornings.

"I've got some kind of a virus I can't kick, that's all. My system's all fouled up. If I could get a good night's sleep—"

"Go see Dr. McSherry," Nola said. "Get him to give you a vitamin B-12 shot. That'll fix you up."

He turned on her.

"You go get one in your ear, if you want to. I'm not going to that quack."

He finished up with his usual spiel about doctors.

"If you got anything more wrong with you than a cold, they don't know what to do. They have to make it up as they go along. Thanks but no thanks. I don't want to be one their guinea pigs."

"Well then, take one of my sleeping pills, so at least you can sleep at nights."

"No thanks. Last time I took one of your so-called sleeping potions I was up on the roof every night for a week, baying at the moon. Don't you remember?"

"Oh, land sakes." Nola pushed away her cold coffee cup. "You talk some sense into him, Early. He won't listen to me."

McSherry was the dapper little pill pusher who wrote Nola's pep-pill prescriptions whenever she called him on the telephone and said she was running low. I liked him, and so did Jack. Sometimes he came up to the house and talked horses with Jack down by the fence. He was also known to leave a waiting room full of patients from time to time and go out in the backyard behind his office and work on his putting for a few minutes. Although Jack liked him personally, he had no use for doctors as a matter of principle. One had vaccinated him with a dirty needle when he was a kid, and he had damned nearly lost his arm because of it. It was his policy to avoid them at all costs. Under the circumstances, I thought McSherry was just the man for the job.

"Why don't you go see him, Dad? He knows what you're like. He won't try anything silly on you. He might be able to help."

"God," he sighed. "Don't I just love it when the two of you go into collusion against me. All right, all right. I'll go see the son of a bitch."

I told him to call me with the results, and two weeks later, he did. He sounded good on the telephone.

"He put me in the hospital for some tests. I told him I'd give him twenty-four hours. Then I was clearing out of there. He said that was okay, that was all the time he needed. So I went in there, and they poked and prodded me and stuck things in various apertures and took a picture of my chest, and then I went home. Hell, they didn't find a thing. He called me back into his office a week later, and said my white blood cell count was a little elevated, but other than that, they couldn't find a thing wrong with me. He thought maybe it was stress or depression, so he gave me some Librium and sleeping pills to try. And, by God, I have to say I think it worked. I feel pretty good again."

"Good," I said. "Well . . . stay in touch."

"I will. Say, when are you coming home again? I think your mother likes having you around the place. Particularly—you know . . . right now."

Midterms were coming up and Linda was feeling a little put-out and neglected by all my scurrying back and forth between home and school, so I hadn't planned on going home anytime soon. But one night, around three o'clock in the morning, I was called to the telephone, and it changed my mind in a hurry.

It was Nola. I could hear the edge of hysteria in her voice, although she was doing her best to keep it under control.

"You'd better come home. Your father's sick. I can't—I can't cope with this alone."

She had got up in the middle of the night, very careful not to disturb Jack, who was making horrible noises in his sleep in the other bed. She couldn't stand it; she had to get out of there. She was worried sick about him anyway, she said. He was still losing weight and he hadn't been acting right. With Nola, as with all of us, sometimes worrying about somebody made her aggravated by everything he did. In this case, it was Jack's snoring. She put on her robe in the dark and felt her way out of the room with her hand in front of her, so she wouldn't run into the edge of the door, as she had one night. She'd gotten a big knob right in the middle of her forehead that night. She reminded me that Richie and I had had a marvelous time over that one the next morning at breakfast.

"But why were you walking around in the dark, Ma?" we

kept asking her, till finally out of exasperation she'd said, "Because I *like* to, sometimes," and as she sat there, looking mad at us, with that big knob right in the center of her forehead and two black eyes like a raccoon, we'd snickered ourselves silly. Well, she wasn't going to repeat an experience like that again, if she could help it, but she still didn't want to turn on the light either and disturb Jack, so she felt her way out to the light switch in the hall.

She might as well have saved herself the trouble. She was in the kitchen. She thought it might be nice to have a real cup of coffee for a change, such as Jack made for her sometimes. As she was standing there, trying to figure out the intricacies of the coffee maker, Jack crept up behind her and gave her the fright of her life. She supposed she had startled him too, when she had jumped and cried out like that, because he started to swear at her, and said she was "a goddam nervous Nelly," and always had been, and if she'd sit the hell down and get out his way he'd make the damned coffee for her. He had an old moth-eaten army blanket slung over his shoulders.

"Why are you dragging that horrible thing around with you?"

"Because I got the chills," he said. "Is that all right with you? Now sit down and get out of my way, so I can do this little job."

As he poured the coffee, she wondered aloud in a meek voice from her place next to the salt and pepper shakers in the breakfast nook if there were any more cookies in the house. He said he would investigate. He found some tollhouse cookies that weren't too stale and put some on the tray with the coffee and brought it over to the table.

"He looked so horrible, lugging that tray over to the table, with his shoulders bent and that old blanket hanging off him."

"Get to the point, Ma."

"Shut up and let me talk. It's my nickel."

She was so worried, she said. He looked so awful. She thought she'd better not look at him anymore. But that didn't help. When she bit down on her cookie, she was so nervous that the crunch sounded just like a cat biting down on the skull of a mouse.

She tried to make pleasant conversation. She told him what good cookies he had found for them.

"I told him they were almost as good as Mother's. You know what he said? He said, 'Your mother's been dead for fifteen years'! That's all he could find to say by way of an answer to my attempted pleasantry.

"Well, I knew he was feeling just miserable. He always talks that way when he's feeling really bad. He gets like a bear with a sore backside. Then I noticed he was just sitting there. Just sitting there. Looking at his coffee cup. He hadn't even taken one sip. I said, 'What's wrong, Dimesy?'

"Oh, Early! He looked up at me, so sweet, with a little smile on his lips, and he said, 'I don't think I can even lift it up.'

"It nearly broke my heart when he said that. When I think what a strong man your father has always been! I went over to his end of the banquette and told him to scootch over and I held the cup to his lips and he took a sip. 'There,' I said, 'isn't that nice? Have a little bite of cookie.' His eyes were closed. The tears were just running down his cheeks. I don't think I ever saw your father cry before. Only he wasn't exactly crying; he was just so exhausted, apparently, by the effort of sitting there upright in the booth with me.

" 'God,' he said to me in a whisper. 'I could just lay my head down on your lap and go to sleep forever.'

" 'Don't talk like that!' I said. 'What are you trying to do—scare me witless?' I waited for him to make some smart remark about my wits, but he didn't say anything. I said, 'Would you like to go back to bed now?' and he nodded, and I helped him back to the room and got him untangled from that smelly old blanket, and lifted his feet up under the covers for him. He's so weak, he had to hold on to the wall in the hallway. Oh Early, I'm so afraid. I think he's really sick! Really sick!"

She paused, as if for refutation, but I was so full of forebodings I didn't know what to say. Then I heard her whisper, "Oh my God! I don't know what I'll do!"

"Try to get some sleep. Call McSherry in the morning. Get him in to see him as soon as possible."

"I don't think I can," she whispered. "I'm just so worn out by all this. Can't you come home and help me with your father?"

"I'll get a ride," I said. "I'll be there sometime tomorrow. Now try to get some sleep."

So I went home again and saw for myself that he was a very sick man, although he kept on denying it and still blamed it on the grapefruit diet.

This time McSherry sent him to Crackenberry, an internist of some reputation at the Pressman Clinic in Harrisburg. He was the one who found the tumor on Jack's kidney.

When the biopsy report came back and McSherry told him it was cancerous, Jack started downhill fast. He had lost a cousin and an uncle to the disease and had always dreaded it, certain it would catch up to him someday and torture him unmercifully. His "cancer attacks"—shooting pains in the rectum, usually brought on by a long trip behind the wheel of a car—were another thing Richie and I used to kid him about when we were kids. "Dad's having another cancer attack," we'd say, and fall together on the backseat, laughing hysterically like a pair of hyenas. It made me wince to remember it now.

He got so bad during the slow painful weeks that he had to endure, while he waited for the test results, and then for Crackenberry to get him in to see Payne, reputedly the best surgeon around, and then for Payne to schedule him for surgery, that I thought he was going to die. But following the operation and some chemotherapy, he began to improve rapidly.

When he came home from the hospital, he stripped off his shirt and showed me his incision. It was healing beautifully. The doctors told him that he healed with the speed of a young boy—not at all like a fifty-three-year-old man. He was proud of that. Over the course of several weeks, he showed me the scar many times again and repeated what the doctors had told him about his amazing recuperative powers.

Through all of this he'd steadily lost more weight, till now he was about as skinny as that old wormy palomino of his down in the pasture. His face was sunken and drawn, and all his clothes hung on him as if he were made from a few sticks, like a scarecrow. But he seemed happier and more relaxed— more at peace with himself—than I'd ever seen him before.

One afternoon, when we were sitting out on the deck, enjoying some mild fragrant early-spring breezes together, he cocked his head and, leaning over the arm of his Adirondack chair, fixed me with one of his patented squinty blue-eyed glowers. "I'll tell you something," he confided. "You wouldn't believe the experiences I had when I was lying in there sick. The things I saw—unbelieveable. I can tell you this, though: there really is life after death."

I must have looked skeptical, because he narrowed his eyes and drew back his lips and stuck out his jaw at me pugnaciously, as if getting ready to throw a punch if I gave him any back talk.

"You can bank on it, pal," he said. "I've been there. I know what I'm talking about. I've seen it for myself."

When I didn't try to refute this with arguments about how you're liable to imagine anything when you're delirious, it seemed to pacify him and restore his faith in me, because he sank back into his chair and decided to confide in me some more.

He smiled and said softly: "I saw your brother. He told me to say hello."

He was smiling at me sweetly as a saint. I wanted to laugh and cry at the same time. It made all the little hairs on the back of my neck stand up. Suddenly I couldn't see because of the tears that had dimmed my eyes. I reached out blindly and gave his poor bony hand a squeeze, and we sat there, saying nothing to each other, holding hands like a couple of girls, and looked out over his pasture and his scraggly horses, to the blue ridge of mountains in the distance.

E i g h t

NEAR the end, they catheterized him and drugged him up and left him pretty much to himself. He had a nice peaceful room on the second floor of the clinic, down at the far end of the hall, out of everybody's way.

He didn't know who I was, or who Dick Sowers was, or who anybody else was, and it all seemed to be a matter of supreme indifference to him anyway. When you spoke, he'd look at you for a moment, then look away again, as if he'd made up his mind not to bother with you.

His bed was cranked up a little at the top. He stared at the wall opposite the footboard as if he saw the answer to everything between his toes—scrawled there on the wall, in a language we couldn't see.

Some of the men from the factory came to see him. They sat with their caps on their laps and tried to talk to him, just as though he was the same man they'd always known. But when he looked at them and then looked away and didn't answer, their feelings were hurt and they were confused.

I told them not to take it personally.

I said, "It's the disease. It's gone to his

brain. He can't talk anymore. He doesn't know anybody. I don't think he even knows where he is. Although I expect he still likes to have the company."

Some of them broke down when I told them that. A lot said they weren't coming back anymore. They couldn't stand to see him that way. I said maybe it was best: just stay away and remember him the way he used to be.

I would have liked to have done that myself.

Nola was too sick to go see him. It was probably a good thing. It would have broken her heart—and, God knows, he had already done that often enough.

I dropped out of school and took a part-time job in the produce department at the Weis Market. Every night after work I took a sandwich, which the nice Pennsylvania Dutch lady at the deli counter fixed for me, and went over to the hospital and sat with him while I watched the news and ate my dinner.

I didn't try holding any one-sided conversations with him. When I was finished with my sandwich and the news, I kissed his forehead, said goodnight, and cleared out of there as fast as I could.

I was getting good at leaving the scene as quickly as possible. I remember passing the door of his bedroom one day just before he went into the hospital for the final time. He was sitting on the edge of the bed in his underwear with his hands dangling between his scrawny thighs. He was so exhausted that he was crying. He raised his head and looked at the ceiling. I heard him say in an anguished whisper, "Why is this happening to me?" I covered my ears and fled the hallway before I overheard any more unanswerable questions.

Some philosophers say a man who is a slave to his lower emotions is led into thickets by the world's distractions.

They believe a man ought to be rational and without desire. A sensual man is never free, they say. He never gains what they call true control over his spirit. All his life he struggles with the wrong things. He lives unwittingly of himself. As soon as he ceases to suffer, he ceases to be.

It certainly seemed to be true of Jack. At least the part about the suffering. Jack was one of the more distracted human beings who ever lived. He was always gnashing his teeth and smashing things and getting into fights to relieve the terrible tensions he felt, particularly as a young man. He never had a moment's peace that I know of, till the end, when he was too doped up to know he was having one. Finally he was beyond the reach of all forms of suffering, including some of his favorites like sex and alcohol. And the minute he stopped suffering, he ceased to be. Long before he ever stopped breathing.

That was the way it went, till they called me one morning at the market, to say that he'd passed away during the night.

We took him back to Ligget and buried him next to his mother and father on a hillside overlooking the Kennebec. Ligget is all hills anyway. So whether you are alive or dead, you're bound to be whatever it is you are on a hillside.

We got an auctioneer in and sold the house, the horses, the automobiles, and the extra furniture she wouldn't need in the new little house that she'd bought for herself and the dogs. By this time, she was down to just two old tricolor collies.

Nola needed the cash. Jack had made good money, but he had the knack of spending it faster than he could make it. He died with no life insurance of any kind. He left behind lots of bills, including the mortgage, installment loans on the cars, some financing for part of my college tuition, feed bills for the horses, and lots of hospital and medical expenses his medical insurance didn't cover. Fortunately the value of the house had appreciated considerably. After she paid off everything, Nola had enough left over to buy her new little house outright, and she put the balance on interest at the bank in order to provide herself with a small income. It wasn't much, but it would keep her and the dogs in biscuits for a while. Someone at the bank told her she would be eligible to collect reduced social security benefits at age sixty-two. "So far as I'm concerned, sixty-two can't come too soon," she told me.

During all of this, Linda was going through her own bad time. Her mother's inscrutable illness was getting worse, and she wondered whether she ought to drop out of school too and go home and try to be of some help. Phil didn't think it was necessary and ordered her in his harsh peremptory fashion—which I know hurt her feelings—to quit calling home all the time and attend to her studies.

I made it down to Bentham some weekends, but now that I'd dropped out, I felt out of place and uncomfortable. I was feeling particularly morose anyway and I suspected, perhaps unfairly, that Arthur and my other so-called friends, made up of a small supercilious circle of English literature majors and the self-styled theater group who regularly performed in the Green Room theatricals on campus—and even Linda herself to some extent, who despised all these people except Arthur, who she said at least had retained the remnants of some common sense—I suspected that they all regarded me as the victim of some horrible disease, possibly contagious, and that they really wanted nothing more to do with me.

It may have been that they were merely busy. Bentham is a demanding school. They had already expressed their sympathies, both because my father was sick and because it had forced me to leave school. Certainly that should have been sufficient. But I kept on obtruding my sorrowful face into the

middle of their busy schedules when for all intents and pur-
poses everything to do with me should have been finished
business. It was probably only paranoia on my part. Nothing
makes you feel so isolated among the young and hectic as
having serious illness in your family—except for being seriously ill or permanently incapacitated in some way yourself.
They'll forgive you if you die—maybe even start a fund in
your memory. But I suspect it irritates almost everybody if
you insist on being chronically ill or permanently screwed
over, and yet gamely try to keep up with your more fortunate
brethren.

As Jack's illness dragged on, I went down to school less
and less. Linda and I kept in touch by telephone in a sort of
half-hearted, desultory fashion. Our conversations were dull
and listless. We didn't seem to have much in common anymore except our family miseries, and these were driving us
apart rather than together. Over the telephone wire, neither
of us seemed quite real or relevant to the other. We were
both too damned numb to care. This was the moment when
we could have gone our separate ways, mercifully, with no
hard feelings on either side. Except for Phil's intervention, it
might well have turned out that way.

I always had to initiate the calls to Linda—she never
called me. In fact, I half suspected that she'd taken up with
someone else in my absence and was just waiting for the
right moment to break the news to me. (I was right about
this—and surprised too, despite my suspicions—although I
wouldn't learn a thing about it for years to come.)

If only I'd had the sense to stop calling her, our relationship—or whatever it ought to have been called, since I see
now that on my side at least it was based almost entirely on
sexual frustration—would have died the natural death that it
deserved.

Phil, on the other hand, often telephoned *me* during this

time. Sometimes Nola would be out of bed, flapping around the house in her bathrobe and pajamas, and she would answer the ring. Immediately I would know it was him on the line again because she would always make a face and cover the mouthpiece and whisper, "It's that horrid old *Italian* man again."

Besides, if I was within twenty-five feet, I could hear him shouting through the earpiece in the raspy irascible voice that he reserved especially for dealing with the exasperations brought on by all forms of modern technology except the automobile, which he would merely sit in while others drove and did what he told them to do. Had Phil had his way, we would still be communicating by drum and signal smoke.

My daily rounds consisted in doing the minimum amount of housework around Nola's house and seeing that she got something to eat and took her medication. I also saw to it that the poor old dogs, poofed out in their dull matted snarly coats, were led down the back steps on their spindly legs to effectuate a more or less daily poop in the backyard. That, and sleepwalking through my work among the fruits and vegetables in the produce department at the Weis, and visiting my nearly insensate and stupefied father in his stuffy room at the Pressman Clinic. Phil's calls were always a welcome break in this horrible routine, and always cleared my head immediately, like a dose of smelling salts.

"Hallo hallo!" he shouted down the line. "Hallo, hallo, who's dis? I wanna talk to—goddam, what's wrong with dis ting? Hallo hallo!"

I held the phone away from my ear as he began knocking it against something at his end—most likely against the edge of the Moorish stand in the hallway, a little filigreed treelike thing carved in dark wood and inlaid with pieces of enamel, where I'd seen a telephone sitting, on my visit to the house in Bergen Cove. He hammered the receiver about like a pipe smoker clearing his briar against a fence post, apparently with some idea in his head of getting it to work right.

Usually it took me a minute or two to get him calmed down long enough to realize that he actually had me on the line.

"Ur! Ur, is that you, eh? Heh, heh."

This was followed by some gratified gurgly growling sounds deep in his throat.

"Hallo, hallooo. How are you, eh? It's nice to hear you again. I been trying to reach you all week but they keep giving me the wrong numbah."

"Hello, Phil!"

"Hallo, hallo? What the—Ur, you still there?"

"Yes, Phil!"

I always had to shout in return, so he could hear me over his own voice, or as if I didn't trust the telephone company either. Satisfied the technology was holding up under the strain of this connection, we would make the appropriate inquiries about the sick, and he would usually end by saying that he hoped I would be able to travel home with Linda to visit with them all again sometime soon; and then he would slam down the receiver, usually while I was still in the middle of thanking him for his call.

This string of telephone calls puzzled me as much as they pleased me. I was glad he cared about me and my problems at a time when no one else seemed to. But I didn't understand why.

One night, when he'd had me summoned to the telephone, he told me that if I needed any money for tuition, or anything else when I started back to school, I should come to him.

"Don't go da banks," he said. "Those thieves. They want blood outta cabbages."

I thanked him. I was flattered. I told him that I thought I would be able to manage all right without his help. This was pure New England bluff, because I had no money for school, didn't know where to get any, and certainly wasn't going to ask Nola. Phil got so mad when I made, what seemed to me, this modest refusal, that for a moment I thought I had Donald Duck on the other end of the line.

"Don't insult me when I offer you help! Whaddayou, think it's a disgrace when somebody offers help with your life?"

"I'm sorry. I didn't mean any—"

"Listen to me! Don't insult me like this! You hear me?"

"Yessir, I hear you, Mr. Stephano."

"Okay. Okay." He sounded somewhat mollified. "I tole ya, call me Phil. Nobody calls me Mr. Stephano except maybe for a few waiters lookin' for a big tip. Listen: you need it, you take it. Hear me? It's no disgrace. You pay me back whenever you can. Okay?"

"Yessir. Thank you very much."

"Good, good. You're a nice boy. How's you fahdah? Any beddah? Aw, too bad. I'm deeply sorry for your troubles."

Shortly afterwards, at the conclusion of these ritual inquiries, he hung up. And I had a sense that in a way all his earlier telephone calls had been preliminary to the point that he'd just made so emphatically: that from now on, if I ever needed any help, he would see to it—and he would take it amiss if I didn't come to him.

I didn't realize it then—I was really too stupid to know what was going on—but Phil had apparently adopted me and made me his son-in-law long before Linda and I had any idea of getting married.

I suppose this talent for—what? Acting on assumptions before anyone else knew what they were? Inventing reality by embodying his schemes with money, equipment, and employees? Whatever you called this ability for knowing what was going to happen before anyone else did, even if he had to invent it himself—by whatever name you called it, it was likely the gift that had made him a rich man.

That spring, it seemed there was no end to death and disaster. Shortly after I got back from Maine, Phil called again to offer condolences (he'd sent a stupendous wreath to the funeral home in Ligget, by far the largest, which Nola considered inappropriate and which had put her in a snit: *Why would he do such a thing? He didn't even know Dimesy),* and he asked me if I would mind doing him a favor.

"Missus Stephano is going in the hospital—they gonna try a lil surgery. See what they can find. My lil baby Linda should be here, eh? So she can smile on her mother when she comes outta the ether or whatever. I wonder—d'you mind driving her home for me?"

"Certainly, sir. I'd be happy to."

Of course Linda was perfectly capable of driving home herself—and *she* had the car. All I had was the use of the secondhand Rambler convertible that Nola had already bought to replace the El Dorado that she couldn't afford anymore, which I borrowed sometimes to go back and forth to the Weis Market, or to the bank, or the drugstore, to get her prescriptions filled, and which I had to park in the distant reaches of the parking lots because the transmission was so touchy that sometimes I couldn't get it to go into reverse gear. (Years later, when she got Tito, her cocker spaniel, I would sometimes see the two of them flying down the road in the selfsame old rattletrap, only now the blue was faded to a dull gunmetal finish and one of the taillights was

usually broken from where Nola had run into various ob-
structions that had impeded her progress in getting from
here to there. Usually the dog would have his head out the
window as the car careened past me, his ears flapping in the
breeze like the unbuttoned chin straps of an old-time aviator's helmet. Tito would be straining forward, doing his
noble-dog bit, peering straight ahead at the road with the
solemn *sang froid* of a fighter pilot in a power dive.)

But I was more than pleased to take on the role of Linda's
gallant. It was obvious that Phil considered me part of his
circle now, and he wanted me on hand as his own crisis came
on the boil.

He growled appreciatively, told me Linda would be expecting my call, and nearly broke my eardrum when he
slammed down the receiver. Linda picked me up at the
house. From there we drove on to Bergen Cove.

After months of feeling bad without evident cause, Mrs.
Stephano had agreed to undergo exploratory surgery. She
was a shrewd woman. When she came out from under the
anesthesia, she wanted to know what time it was. It was
twelve-fifteen. She had gone on the table at nine forty-five.

"Well—that didn't take long, did it?" she said quietly
and closed her eyes.

Everybody in the room knew she figured that whatever
was wrong with her, it should have taken longer than that to
fix it.

Unfortunately, the poor woman's instincts were right. The
doctors had found an inoperable tumor the size of a boccie
ball on the aorta, just above her stomach. They took one
look and closed her like a book. The whole thing had taken
under forty-five minutes.

When the family came back into the room that night, after
their conference with the doctors—the room now crowded

with flowers and relatives from Queens, Northport, some from as far away as New Paltz—Mario couldn't help himself and broke into big operatic sobs at the sight of his mother smiling wanly at him from the pillows.

"Mario—stop, stop," she admonished him weakly.

But Mario lost his grip completely. He prostrated his clumsy body by the side of her bed and twisted her hands within his own and howled ferociously at the ceiling like a madman.

His balding head glistened in the light of the bedside lamp as he hid his face from the sympathetic gaze of the crowd of relatives surrounding the bed like figures in a creche. Crying so passionately made him sweat freely. His big nose ran like a river. His sallow face grew shapeless as a reflection in a puddle of water. He had no handkerchief. He wetted the front of himself till I could see his dark nipples and some of the buttons of his chest hair showing through the material of his white shirt.

Linda went in the bathroom and got him some toilet paper to cry into. Cousins, aunts, and uncles consolingly crowded near while Mrs. Stephano, the color of cigar ash, lay quiet and sweetly serene under the white sheets and feebly stroked his head.

At last Phil grew exasperated and started swearing at him.

"No, no, Phil," I heard Mrs. Stephano say in a piteous voice. But her hand fell away limply to her chest, as if surrendering Mario to judgment.

Phil said something else to him in Italian and actually started to raise his crooked hand as if readying to cuff his cowering head. But he was restrained from going further when a matriarchal figure dressed in black stepped forward, an elderly lady from upstate, whom the others addressed as Aunt Tessie, and apparently someone of great standing in the family hierarchy, who told him solemnly that it was a wicked thing for a father to mistreat a sorrowing child.

The doctors gave Mrs. Stephano six months, but she got it over with in under six weeks.

During that time, I practically lived at the house in Bergen Cove, leaving only to drive Linda back to Bentham for her final exams and to return one weekend on my own, to see how Nola and the dogs were getting along. Nola thought I had deserted her, and she was right. I had.

I felt bad about it, especially during that gloomy weekend I spent with her. Although I doubt she intended for me take it literally, she did say that I had a life of my own to live. I was determined to try to do just that. The distractions of my old passion for Linda sharpened painfully again under the pressure of living in the same house that awful summer. Everything was falling apart. With everybody suddenly dying like flies around us, we glommed onto each other desperately. I also needed a few surrogates to fill in the other vacancies in my life. Phil and Mario would probably do nicely in this regard, I thought. My mother couldn't help me. Incompetent even in the smallest matters, she had never been able to help me in any practical sense. As a teller of sad but elucidating stories she was excellent. But I had heard all of the good ones by the time I was twelve. And it seemed to me that I could only go on helping *her* by putting myself at risk: by living at home; by doing her shopping for her and seeing that she got her prescriptions filled; by doing the heavy lifting around the place. In this scenario, the bench-warmer son finally comes into his own. But I wanted no part of the role. The time for that was long gone. She would have to learn to take responsibility for herself. She would have to find her own way of dealing with desolation, just as Linda and I were trying to do. Nobody was going to take care of her anymore. Certainly not me. I thought all of these thoughts, and they left me aching with a bad conscience.

On the night of the day of Mrs. Stephano's funeral, Phil and Mario and Cousin Vito drove over to Roosevelt Raceway, where Phil bet two hundred dollars on the Perfecta and won over thirteen thousand dollars in return. They had invited me to go along, but I chose to stay at home with Linda and Anna. Linda had told me she was not upset that her father and the others had gone to the track as usual on the day of her mother's funeral.

"You could have gone if you wanted to." She took my hand and smiled. "But I'm glad you didn't."

She explained that Phil was a proud man. Too proud to make much of a public show of grief over something he couldn't change. He would do his mourning in private in his own way. The thing was, the planet would go on wobbling through the darkness, no matter who died.

She knew that he had loved her mother deeply—deep, deep down, on some pure harsh indivisible level that didn't show, an old love with no flesh on it, just a bag of bones now, but proud, and needing no words or any gratuitous gestures. He would take refuge in the comfort of his regular habits. She accepted this. He would go to the track. He would place his bets as usual. He would win a few and lose a few. He would light another one of his stinking cigars and study his program, and go on with his life in the best way he knew how.

Mrs. Stephano was interred in consecrated ground following a baroque funeral mass conducted by Father Palumbo of St. Anne's, the church where she and Phil had been parish members for thirty-five years.

Shortly afterwards, in Father Palumbo's oak-paneled study, I began to take instruction in the Catholic faith, while professing great admiration for the writings of Cardinal Newman—especially the essays entitled *The Idea of a University,* some of which I had actually read in one of my courses at Bentham. It seemed politic to mention this, since my intention was to stay on good terms with him. As a matter of record, I had been baptized a Methodist, but had rarely darkened a churchyard door since.

In one of our six meetings, I promised to bring up my children in the one true faith. In some ways, I felt I was being adopted by all the parties concerned: Father Palumbo, the Catholic Church, Linda, and—of course—Phil. But it was really the secular parties to the adoption whose approval I was seeking.

And at the end of that summer, before the same altar where Mrs. Stephano's casket had rested so recently within a bower of hothouse flowers, Linda and I were joined together in what Father Palumbo and others were pleased to call "Holy Matrimony."

N i n e

EIGHT hundred people attended our wedding and reception. I knew only a handful. If I'd had my way, we would have crept off and gotten married by the town clerk. But that wasn't what Linda wanted, or Phil either—or even what I'd agreed to, when I signed on with Father Palumbo.

Except for poor Mrs. Stephano, who was truly devout, the rest of the family were fairly nominal Catholics, so far as I could see. They took a practical view of the church. It was an important local institution, just as were the schools, the banks, and the local branch of the Sons of Italy. They followed form in matters of baptism, marriage, and burial, and made it a point to attend Mass during the major celebrations. Phil, of course, gave generously to the church. He had a pagan's inherent respect for any supernatural powers that possibly might be operating in the local vicinity and therefore have a hand on the levers of his prosperity. It was only prudent to propitiate these forces regularly with little offerings of tallow and fat. It was no different from dealing with the local pols on zoning matters. I also dimly perceived that the wedding was to be a moment of high drama in the lives of the Stephano clan; in their minds the only proper setting for a performance of this magnitude was St. Anne's. Anywhere else was unthinkable.

Arthur Frankenwood was there as my best man. Leslie Crowthers, leader of the theater rats at school, drove out from the city that morning to be there, which impressed me, since I had never thought he was much of a friend of mine. He'd already started work at Bergman & Childress as one of their book salesmen. Six years later, as it turned out, he played a big part in getting B&C to publish my novel, and became my editor in the process. Considering the pain he's put me through, I don't know whether to bless him or to curse him.

Nola was there too, looking shrunken and out of place, dressed in a strand of imitation pearls that had turned yellow with the years, and a green sateen dress which looked awful on her. An old red-fox stole that had once been her mother's was slung around her neck—the kind where the black hinge in the fox's jaw bites the other fox's tail in order to keep the whole contraption in place on the shoulders. She kept it on during dinner because she said the air conditioning was giving her a chill. She had on a hat too, a little shiny-green pillbox affair of straw, with a fishnet half-veil. It had been knocked askew on her head by Phil when he introduced her to Cousin Gino, an important member of the General Assembly in Albany, with an expansive flourish of his arms.

I watched her finicking with her plate of filet and lobster tail from our places of honor at the table on the dais. She was seated right in front of us. I couldn't catch her eye. She kept them lowered as she pushed a baked tomato around on her plate. She was trying to ignore the attentions of a deeply tanned gray-haired man in a red Palm Beach jacket and yellow slacks on her right, who seemed ready to bite her on the neck if she didn't talk to him. Her mouth was tightly pursed against the intrusion of this friendly importunate man. She had on far too much rouge, and her face looked powdery and drawn. She hated crowds. She hated strangers, especially noisy friendly strangers—and all of these people were noisy and friendly. She looked miserable, and I wanted to thank her with a smile for being on hand, but I couldn't. She never looked up.

At one point during dinner Linda leaned over to me, apropos of nothing, and said, "Your mother's quite a character, isn't she?"

I think those were the kindest words she ever found to say about her.

At first she said she couldn't come to the wedding because of the dogs. Even if she could find a kennel for them for the weekend—which she didn't want to do, because they were so old and rickety and so dependent on her that they were like a couple of babies—she was afraid of driving the Rambler as far as Long Island because the transmission had begun to act up again on her way home from the cottage that summer. She wasn't feeling particularly well either, she said. That's why she'd decided to come back from Maine before Labor Day. To come home and rest—not to run around the countryside. I understood this perfectly, and told her it was all right if she couldn't make it. But Phil finally talked her into leaving her animals behind "with a trusted friend," as he put it—Dr. Perlmutter, the vet, as it turned out in this instance—and dispatched Cousin Vito with the limousine to fetch her back to Bergen Cove for the weekend, where he and everybody else treated her like visiting royalty.

I met so many people that weekend it was impossible to keep them straight.

I remember at the reception Linda introduced me to a

series of Uncle Tonys. "Say hello to my other Uncle Tony from upstate," she would instruct me, and I would turn on my heel and shake the hand of yet another one of her duplicate uncles.

Some of them still had on their hats and coats, and were in a hurry to get back to Utica or Kingston or wherever it was they'd come from. Usually a dark expressive hand, sparkling with a diamond ring, would withdraw a big cigar with a flourish from the middle of a dark saturnine face. With a glitter of pearly teeth, this new Uncle Tony would pump my arm with enthusiasm. Another pair of hot dark eyes with whites the color of cooked onions would examine me appreciatively from head to foot.

"Hallo, kid. Welcome to the family."

A fifteen-piece orchestra dressed in baggy dinner jackets did its best to imitate the sounds of Guy Lombardo and the Royal Canadians. There were two open bars on each side of the room and three bottles of Piper Heidsieck on each table when we sat down to our meal. A mob of priests suddenly materialized at the reception like a multitude of blackbirds. One of Linda's cousins, as it turned out, and his friends from the nearby seminary. They stood around wolfing down food and drink and cake as if they hadn't been fed in a week.

The men paid to dance with the bride—Mario's idea. The one or two priests who tried it got to dance with her for free. I thought it was crude and demeaning, but Linda said it was the custom. I sat at Nola's table and watched Linda twirl across the dance floor with a succession of men while Mario worked the crowd for more business. The gray-haired man had finally given up and she was sitting by herself.

"You don't look well. You look like you're running a fever or something. Are you all right?"

I assured her I was fine.

"Tell me when you two get ready to leave, will you?"

I nodded.

"We're going to sneak out the side door in a little while. We don't want to attract any attention."

"Well, tell me before you go. I don't want to sit here thinking you're still here, and you're not. Will you do that for me?"

"Okay, Ma."

Just as the party was reaching its crescendo, I slipped over and told her we were leaving.

"Take care of yourself, Early."

"Don't look so tragic, Ma. We're only going to the Poconos. I'll see you in a couple of days."

"All right, son."

Mario and Linda were waiting for me by the side door out in the lobby. He'd brought the car around and parked it right outside. We were all ready to go. Through the ballroom door I'd closed behind me, I could hear the bogus band begin to play "Seems Like Old Times," and for a moment the sentimental fruitiness of the saxophones quavering out the melancholy old tune filled me with inexpressible sadness. A sudden sense of utter desolation and loneliness swept through me like a cold wind. In my mind's eye I saw Nola, in her moth-eaten stole and her hat knocked askew, still sitting alone at the desecrated table in the ballroom, the melted butter for her half-eaten lobster tail beginning to harden on her plate like chicken fat. I knew it was her emotions I was feeling. I wanted to turn back and tell her not to worry, that she wasn't alone, that everything would be okay. I wanted to tell her I would always be around if she needed me. Mario rumped open the side door. I shook myself mentally like a dog coming in out of the rain. As I followed Linda into the parking lot, he handed me a homburg full of cash.

"Here you go, pal," he said. "Maybe this'll fit your head—who knows?" and we all laughed, I louder than the rest, in that goofy falsetto voice I fall into sometimes when I'm really nervous. It looked like a lot of cash. I tossed the hatful of money into the backseat. We all hugged and patted each other and babbled our goodbyes and then Linda and I folded ourselves like a couple of pieces of lawn furniture into her little car and started across the parking lot. It had rained, a brief steamy downpour. The air from the open window felt good. The streetlights lit up the puddles in the parking lot and gave the wet paving a satiny sheen. I watched him with affectionate gratitude in the rearview mirror as he stood edged in light from the lobby, holding the door and looking comical in his cutaway coat and dove-gray vest, waving goodbye till we turned onto the road and drove from view.

"What a nice guy!"

Still in her bridal gown and veil, Linda leaned over the wheel, her eyes narrowed in concentration and fixed on the dim patch of road in the headlights.

"Don't give him too much credit," she said.

Later that night we smoothed out and counted the crumpled bills on our bed. It amounted to just over five thousand dollars. The sight of so much money staggered me. It was a tremendous windfall—enough to live on for a year in those days. Almost enough for us to live on and pay for my last year at Bentham. What wonderful people, I thought. To put all that money in a hat for us and solve what was surely our most pressing problem—the business of paying for a roof over our heads and for a few cutlets on the table.

Phil wanted to pay for everything, but I was against it.

She was going to be my wife, I told him, and we would have to find a way to solve our own problems. I was fool enough at the time to think the hatful of money was providential. Later I learned that Phil had slipped most of it into the hat. We were married for five years before Linda told me. I could hear my voice tremble when I asked her why they'd deceived me like that. "Because we needed the help, silly. You were acting like such a jackass. It was the only thing Daddy could think of." I could feel my face burning with embarrassment. Over the years, I'd told the story of the lucky hatful of money to various people, as an example of how help usually turns up just when you need it most. I felt like such a pompous idiot. I couldn't understand why I hadn't figured it out on my own, when it was so obvious, now that I knew. The only answer I could come up with is that subconsciously I'd been in on the deception all along.

It didn't occur to me that anything was up the night before the wedding, either. Mario had organized a stag party for me at the same Italian-American Friendship Club where the reception was held the next day. I never stopped to wonder how suddenly, overnight, I'd become such a good poker player. I walked away from a tableful of my future in-laws with over $240 in winnings. I won the final hand of the night—a pot containing $65—with a pair of jacks. It didn't dawn on me till many years later that everybody but Arthur, who hadn't been clued in, was throwing in a lot of winning hands that night, to make sure that I walked away with plenty of cash in my pocket. I just thought my luck had changed. But at least I finally figured this one out on my own.

Before all that money fell into our laps, the plan had been that Linda was going to drop out and get a job and put me through my last year. I would work too, part-time. After I graduated and got a job, then I'd put her through. "We'll be like the Eisenhower brothers," I told her. "We'll put each other through school. Won't that be great?"

"I can think of better ways," she said.

"Keep your father out of it."

"I didn't say anything about him."

But that was before the hat showed up and solved our problems. That night in the Poconos, Linda said I was about the luckiest person she'd ever met.

"Things always seem to fall into place for you. Were you always this lucky? Or have you only been so lucky since you met me?"

"It's something new," I said, solemn as a donkey. "I never used to be this lucky."

What a jerk I was.

But Linda liked me that way. She smiled and gave me a kiss.

"What a lucky little boy," she said.

I think she thought it was cute that I was so naive.

The mountain of wedding presents we received took care of everything else. It was really obscene. We had enough linen and china to furnish a hotel. Phil gave us a suite of walnut bedroom furniture, ornate and massive enough to satisfy the pretentions of an Arab sheik. It was all out of scale and looked ridiculous in our apartment. Mario gave us the living-room furniture and the TV. Somebody I never heard of from the Catskills contributed the dinette set. One of the Uncle Tonys chipped in with a washer and dryer; not to be outdone, another Uncle Tony provided us with a double-door refrigerator, which we could never use at the apartment because it wouldn't fit in the kitchen. Phil rented a truck and had the relevant loot hauled to our place at school; the rest of the stuff, including the twenty-eight extra toasters we didn't need, he stored for us in two bays of his five-car

garage for over fifteen years, till we finally came to roost in a
house of own in Tallys Ford, with room enough to accommodate all kinds of depressing junk.

Besides ticking off our loot and counting our money, we
attempted to put together our matrimonial Erector set for the
first time that night. I suppose it is hard for someone in his
twenties or thirties to imagine how innocent people of our
generation were, before women's lib and Vietnam and the
birth-control pill; when being described as "gay" meant you
were carefree and happy, and "aids" was not yet capitalized
and still referred to people who emptied bedpans instead of
an epidemic tantamount to bubonic plague.

We were tired. It would have been better if we had waited
till the next day. But we were eager to get it over with so we
could go on and have a normal sex life afterwards:

"No, no. It doesn't go in *there,* dummy."

"Opps. Sorry. . . . Is this any good for you?"

"Yes, that's fine."

"Are you sure?"

"Will you stop talking? Let's just *do* it, for godsakes,
without all this talk! Jesus!"

And then later, a subdued review of the facts:

"You scared me, you know that? I thought you were having a convulsion or something when you finally—you
know."

"Well I was, sort of."

"Was it really any good?"

" 'Was it any good'! Well, I'll say! It was wonderful. . . .
Was it any good for you?"

"It was great. Are you really sure it was good for you?
You act sort of disappointed."

"Disappointed! Me? What a lot of hooey!"

Etc.

We managed to get through it all right, just as everybody

else did in our profoundly ignorant generation. With time, we improved and had a relatively satisfactory sex life, one that kept my low-grade fever in check for many years. It was nothing great, but it was certainly passable. I suppose we belonged to the last wave of American virgins. Men never talked about technique or admitted confusion back then (they still don't so far as I know), and Linda was part of the last generation of her gender to be victimized by residual but strong inhibitions inherited from their grandmothers, having to do with every imaginable topic from feminine hygiene to foreplay. It was an unfair time for both sexes. Out in the suburbs, where we eventually lived (and where I have spent virtually all of my life) I have the idea that the earth rarely moved for anyone in those days.

Even though it wasn't necessary, given our new found riches, Linda decided to drop out of school anyway. It was her junior year. She reasoned that she wouldn't be able to go on after I graduated in the spring, since I'd take a job somewhere and we'd move away. So she figured she might as well quit now and save her father's money.

The other kids treated her differently now that she was married. "They're a bunch of stiffs," she said. School was boring and they were boring, so she decided to pack it in. "Maybe I'll get a job," she said, but she didn't.

We lived in a nice one-bedroom apartment in a lovely old brick Victorian house on Buddleia Street. Occidental City, or Accidental City, as she called it, with the typical parochial sense of superiority of the born New Yorker, held little interest for her now that she wasn't in school. Admittedly the college was the town's main attraction. Although it was a pleasant little town. It just wasn't what she was used to.

She spent a lot of time on the telephone. She wanted to know how things were going back home. She missed the

Island, she said. There was always something doing on the Island. She was fond of the telephone. She had relatives in Ossining, Poughkeepsie, Buffalo, New Paltz, and White Plains. She had plenty of people to call, and she liked to stay in touch. I don't know what the bills ran. Phil had the telephone installed specifically so that she could call home, and the bills went directly to him.

At night when I tried to study she paced back and forth, from the kitchen to our bedroom in the back. I put the TV and the record player in our room, but she hated to go in there and close the door and watch TV or play records by herself. She said I always ruined it for her anyway, because whenever she went in there and tried to amuse herself, I inevitably knocked on the door and told her to keep it down. She liked to turn the volume up. She was one of those people who needs a certain amount of companionable noise around the place. It acted as a tonic. It soothed her nerves. Me, I liked everything quiet—or "dead," as she put it. My idea of a good time after I got through studying was to sit down with a book. This didn't go over big with her.

Some nights I did my studying at the library, but she didn't like that either. She didn't like being alone in the apartment. She was alone all day and that was enough, she said.

One night at dinner she suggested we go to a movie. *Look Back in Anger* had finally made its way to the local art theater and she wanted to see it.

"Not tonight. I have to study for a test."

"You always have to study for a test. Why don't you try studying to be a human being for a change?"

"I can't go," I said. "Besides, we don't have the money."

"Yes we do. Daddy sent me a check in the mail."

"I told you not to ask him for money."

"I didn't. He just sent it."

"Well send it back. We don't need it. Tell him to stick it where the sun don't shine."

That's when I found out when she really got mad she threw her food like a little kid. She let me have it with her plate of spaghetti. The plate hit my chest and landed in my lap. I got so damned mad that I nearly hit her. I guess she could see it, because her eyes got big and she cringed away from me. If I had, it would have been the end of it, right there. I wasn't going to bat women around. I wasn't going to have anything to do with that. I didn't want a marriage like Jack and Nola's. No way was I going to turn out like Jack in that respect. I got up and went in the bedroom and changed my shirt and pants and got my books and started for the door.

"Where do you think you're going?"

She was sitting at the table smoking a cigarette. She hadn't cleaned up the mess yet. There were splatters of sauce and strings of spaghetti everywhere, as if a little bomb had gone off at the table.

I didn't answer. I just kept walking.

She said, "If you go out, don't bother to come back."

When I got back from the library that night, I expected more trouble. But she ran to the door when I unlocked it and threw her arms around my neck.

"I was so afraid you wouldn't come back," she said.

She was only twenty at the time, so I suppose some of this behavior was perfectly natural.

That year, we spent the Christmas holidays at Bergen Cove. Fortunately, Nola had been invited to stay with the Wilhides at their farm in Virginia, from the middle of December till after the first of the year, so I didn't have that problem to contend with.

While we were at Phil's, she asked if I would mind if she stayed on and helped out in the restaurant for a while. She was good at doing the books and keeping the waitresses on their toes.

"They really need me around here. They're lost without Mama. You can take the car back to school if you want." She smiled. "You won't have me around to bother you. You can concentrate on your studies. Maybe get a little writing done—who knows? I'll be able to make some money too. That'll help out. I'll send you what I make. Then I won't feel so worthless anymore."

"You're not worthless."

"I *feel* worthless. What do you say?"

I said if that's what she wanted, it was all right with me. Frankly it was a relief not to have her around.

Shortly after I got back, I got a card from her telling me that they had gone down to Pompano Beach to open up the house for the winter. She stayed down there till the first of March. She was never one for the cold weather and always got out of it every chance she could. I was not upset by this development. I had plenty to do. Now that she was occupied, I could get it done. I recognized myself that this was not exactly the attitude of a man who was hopelessly in love.

When I graduated, she wanted me to take a job with her father, but I wouldn't.

"Look," I said. "Get it straight. I want to be a writer. I don't want to work in a restaurant. I don't want to work for a construction company. I don't want to work in the hotel-and-restaurant-supply business. I don't want to sell hair tonic. I just want to write. If I have to teach school to make a living—okay. But I'm not going to work for your father."

"All right. But will you at least get a job on the Island, please?"

"I'll look into it."

"Daddy will help. The principal at the high school is a friend of ours. Mr. Bleeder. He was at the wedding. Remember?"

"I can't say I do."

To make a long story short, Phil talked to the man, and I got the job, and we moved to Long Island. We rented an apartment in Robindale, two towns away from Bergen Cove. She was just a few miles from home and that seemed to suit her better.

I taught five sections of freshman English. I liked the kids and had a pretty good time. When I wasn't at school or correcting papers, I worked on the novel that I'd started down at Bentham. It began as a journal, which I commenced when Jack got sick. Gradually over time it took on a life and a shape of its own, and I began to think it might turn out to be a real book.

I worked on it whenever I could, for five years. I used weekends, holidays, vacations—whatever time I could find. I was either working on it, or thinking about it, or loathing the idea of it, every spare minute I had. I read a lot of fiction, hoping I could figure out how to do it by osmosis. Linda had a tough time understanding how I could still be at work when I was just sitting there, reading a book. She spent a lot of time over at her father's house so I could "be alone," as she put it.

I threw away twenty pages for every one I kept. I could hardly stand to read the stuff, it was so bad. It filled me with self-loathing. More than once, after reading a chapter, I went in the bathroom and chucked my cookies. Writing wasn't much fun. I began to think that I didn't have a talent for it after all. That idea put me in a real sweat. I had no idea what I was going to do with myself if I didn't turn out to be a literary genius. It never occurred to me to relax and enjoy myself. I wrote like a man driving a car with the gas pedal pressed to the floor while pulling on the emergency brake at the same time. Everything I wrote I worried to death. I read it over and over again and tinkered with it till I couldn't stand it.

Finally, after years of this, more out of exhaustion than conviction, I got together a slender little smudged-over manuscript of thinly disguised autobiography and sent it off to Leslie, who was still with Bergman & Childress. By this time, he was one of their associate editors.

I expected to get it back in a month or three, with a polite note attached. But he stunned me by calling one night three weeks later. He said he liked a lot of what I'd done. "You're *very* talented," he said, but I remembered he was theatrical, so I didn't believe him. He said if I was willing to rewrite the middle section, he'd try to work with me. He couldn't make any promises. But if I could fix it up to his satisfaction, he would take it to the editorial committee.

I said I thought I could do that. I held myself in till I got off the telephone. Then I beat the walls, and crowed like a rooster. I tried to call Linda over at Phil's, but no answer. They'd gone out to dinner somewhere. I got out my copy of the manuscript for company and put it on the coffee table, and sat down and had a couple of drinks, and just stared at it. I felt like a condemned man who'd just been pardoned by the governor. The manuscript made a nice neat little block of white paper sitting there on the table. I didn't dare pick it up or read any of it, for fear of ruining everything. I went in the bathroom after a while and talked to myself in the mirror.

"You punk," I said. "You poor sub-sub. Maybe you're not a dud after all."

I worked on it for another year. Leslie and I swapped chapters back and forth through the mail and sometimes we talked on the telephone. He was always very cautious. "I don't want to mislead you," he would say. "I don't want to give you any false hope." Oh no, I said. I didn't feel misled. My hopes weren't up. He felt obliged to say something like that every time we talked. A couple of times, if he'd been in the room with me, I'd have probably killed him.

Sometimes I felt I might actually get published. Other times I knew for a certainty that I'd never make it. But finally, one day, he called me up and said they were going to do it.

I suppose I would have gotten more excited if I hadn't been so worn out by all the work that had gone into it. I was happy, of course, but not as excited as I thought I'd be. Leslie had worked all the fun out of it for me. He had to do that. It was just an amateur manuscript before he took me in hand. But it wore me out. Still, I thought it would change my life when it was published. I didn't know how. Maybe it would sell a million, and make me rich and famous. I thought that would be a nice start.

Phil was very proud. He went around telling everybody about it. Whenever he introduced me to anybody after that, he always said, "This is my son-in-law. He writes books."

Nola's reaction was uniquely her own. When I called her up, I said, "Well, Ma, it's finally happened. After all this time, they're going to publish my book."

"That's nice," she said. "How's the weather up there? It's been raining cats and dogs here for days."

I was not popular with her at the time. She was still upset because Linda and I had moved to New York, leaving her alone with her elderly dogs in her little house in MacAbee. I had told her that I expected to teach in Pennsylvania when I got out of college. It was one of the reasons she'd chosen to stay there. When Linda and I moved to the Island, it put her in quite a snit, and she still wasn't over it.

When she heard the news, Linda wanted to celebrate.

"Let's go to Bermuda," she said. "You deserve a break. You've worked so hard, baby."

We had this conversation by telephone, and I could feel Phil hovering and cackling and rubbing his palms together somewhere in the background. It made me uncomfortable to discuss it over the telephone, but I told her the usual: we didn't have the money.

"Don't be silly," she said. "Daddy's so happy for you. You should see him. He's acting like such a nut. He wants to send us, Earl. He says after all the hard work, you deserve it. What should I tell him?"

I was too tired to argue. If he wanted to pay, okay. I didn't think I'd taken much from him over the years, although it was a lot more than I was willing or prepared to admit—or even knew about at the time. I thought it wouldn't hurt if I caved in this once and had a good time for a change.

So we went to Bermuda on Phil's money, and stayed at a ritzy little hotel that Linda found advertised in *The New Yorker.* I slept every morning till noon. We sunned ourselves by the pool in the afternoons. We dined in every fancy restaurant we could find. We danced every night in the lounge downstairs at the hotel. We got tan and sleek, and languid as cats.

When we got back, we found out she was pregnant. We were both a little surprised. She was supposed to be on the pill, but she'd always been a little careless about it. She had the packs with the dummies in them but she still forgot to take them from time to time. Anyway we were surprised, and I, for one, wasn't particularly pleased. I don't think she was, either. But Phil thought it was wonderful. He'd been after us for years to have kids.

When the book came out, hardly anybody noticed. It got a

handful of reviews, most of them favorable. The *Saturday Review* liked it quite a lot, calling it "an impressive debut." But the *Times* didn't like it. The reviewer said it was a book that a "wiser and more experienced writer would put in the bottom desk drawer and forget about." He had a good time with it. He said, "Albert Camus might have written something similar, had he been born tone-deaf and never left the family hearth."

It sold about a thousand copies and was remaindered fairly quickly. The big moment came when an author of small but estimable reputation called me up one summer night and told me she was a fan of mine. She thought my book was the best thing she had read that year.

It was lucky she wasn't standing next to me when she told me that. Likely I would have piddled all over her, like a puppy that gets overexcited when you show him too much attention.

After the book died its quick horrible little death, I had a collapse of my own at work. Everything began to irritate me about the place. I was tired of the chickenshit and the lousy pay. But mainly I was disappointed that the book I'd worked on, for so long and so hard, hadn't made a bit of difference in my life. Leslie told me not to be discouraged. "Write another one," he said.

I didn't think I had another one in me. I didn't want to go through it again. Besides, I thought I'd used it all up. I felt like a kid with a good fastball, who ruins his arm throwing in double A. I thought it was over. *Well, you tried,* I thought. *You're just no good at it. You might as well get on with the rest of your life.* At the moment, the long vista yawning in front of me looked pretty empty.

That review in the *Times* stuck with me. I couldn't get it out of my head. I knew the skunk was right. It *was* derivative; it *was* weak and feeble; it *did* stink. I don't know why I believed him, and not the writer who called me on the telephone, but that's the way it was. Since then, I've learned that most writers believe the bad reviews and not the good ones. Only most aren't destroyed by them—only wounded. I don't know who I thought I was. John Keats or somebody, I guess. Allegedly, a bad review *killed* him.

While I was going through these convolutions, Arthur had gone to law school, and then into partnership with his father. His father had a management consulting firm in Harrisburg. Frankenwood & Son, it was called. Only the "son" in this case was Arthur's father, who, in his turn, had gone into the business with *his* father right out of the Wharton School.

When he called me up and said they were looking for a writer, I jumped at the chance. He offered me fifty percent more than I was making as a teacher. I felt I couldn't turn it down. I was ready to latch onto a new life. I said to myself: Even if you're not the man you thought you were, at least you can make some money.

Linda wasn't happy about moving back to Pennsylvania. She said if she could have a new car to go back and forth, she'd go along with it. We were still driving the Ghia. Phil had wanted to replace it for years, but I'd held him off. This was a sore subject between Linda and me, but now she saw a way of getting at least a new car out of it. Phil handled it very diplomatically, though. He knew it was a sensitive issue. Mario had an Olds he'd only had for eighteen months that he suddenly developed an aversion for and wanted to get rid of. He made us a ridiculous deal one night at dinner, which we couldn't turn down. That's the way they got around that one, so little Early's pride wouldn't be hurt.

The three of us stayed with Nola—there were three of us now—till we could find a place of our own. It was only for a

few weeks—just long enough for them to become enemies.
The baby damned nearly drove her crazy. It was a small
house, and the baby was colicky. She woke up every time the
baby did. Which surprised me, because she used to be able
to sleep through anything.

She told me my wife was lazy. When I was gone, she said,
Linda let the baby lie in its crib and cry too long before she
attended to it.

"She leaves his dirty diapers soaking in the toilet," she
said.

This was true. I'd seen this for myself. I thought it was a
filthy habit.

In turn, Linda told me that Nola was a weird old bitch.
She said she couldn't wait to get out of there.

Keefer was born the same month the book came out. He
was a much bigger success. She'd had a tough time with
him—in and out of the hospital two or three times. When
the pregnancy started to get complicated, she moved in with
her father, so Anna could look after her full-time. It really
looked like we were going to lose him a couple of times. But
she made it all right.

HE came straight from the womb with a full head of shaggy
hair. When the nurse brought him out and showed him to
me, it really knocked me silly. I'd never held a baby before,
but I wanted to hold him right away. They had him wrapped
up in a receiving blanket. He was no bigger than the length
of my hand. He had a little red face, and little squinty eyes
like buttons, and all this shaggy black hair on his head. It
just knocked me silly.

When we got our own apartment, things fell into place for
a while. I'd given up the writing and had more time to spend

with her and Keefer. I bought my first ten-speed and went for rides along the river. I joined the Y and played some pickup basketball. I felt like a new man—much better and more relaxed than I'd felt in years.

I WORKED hard to learn the consulting business. I was pleased to find out that I was good at it. About three years into it, they offered me a partnership share if I could come up with the money. They wanted $65,000. It was really a bargain. After a lot of agonizing over it, I went to Phil and said if he'd lend me the money, I'd pay it back in five years with interest.

"Of course I'll help you," he said.

I said, "Let's have Vinny Palumbo draw up the agreement."

Vinny was Father Palumbo's younger brother and Phil's attorney.

"What's this? A business deal? Don't get so excited. I'm happy to do this for you."

"But I want it do it right. This is a lot of money."

"Don't be excitable. We'll do it any way you like. Are you happy now?"

I said I was and he laughed and patted me on the knee and offered me a cigar.

"Always such a serious boy."

Vinny drew up the agreement that weekend and we were able to sign it before Linda and the baby and I started back for Harrisburg.

When it came time to pay back the principal five years later, I took Linda and Keefer and drove up to Bergen Cove for the weekend. On Sunday afternoon I asked to speak to Phil alone in his study. When we got settled, I handed him the check. He got mad as hell. His face turned scarlet and then walnut like a little baby doing a number in its pants. He scowled at the check for what seemed like a full minute, and then tore it up.

"What are you trying to tell me with this, eh? That I'm not allowed to help my own children?"

"Not at all, Phil. I'm grateful for all you've done over the years. It's just I can afford to pay you back now. I've done very well, thanks to you. I just thought it was appropriate . . . after all, we had an agreement. . . ."

He stared at me till I shut up. Then his face softened and he patted me on the knee. He started to cackle and sat back and looked at me affectionately.

"Always the proud one, eh? I respect you for that. But listen: don't always push away my hand when I try to help."

"I don't, Phil. I really appreciate all you've done for us."

"You're my daughter's husband. My grandson's fahdah. You're like another son to me."

"I didn't mean any disrespect, Phil. I just thought—"

"I know, I know. You're proud of what you made of yourself. I don't blame you. You come a long way, eh? No more pot livin' in an attic somewhere. No more little teacher's salary, eh? A long way so fast. I tell you what to do with this money, it's so hot, it's burning a hole in your pocket."

"What's that?"

"Buy a house. You got enough for a good down payment. Reward yourself. You work hard. Now give your family a nice house to live in."

It was plain he wouldn't take the money. If I pushed, he would only get mad again. So I said, "Okay, Phil. Whatever you say."

That's when we bought the big house in Tallys Ford, where we lived till the marriage went belly-up.

WE weren't happy together. But we weren't unhappy all the time, either. We just weren't well suited for each other. It made us restless and impatient. We found each other annoying. From time to time we both longed for some change in our lives, but didn't know what to do about it. We had Keefer to worry about. For a long time, he was the glue that held things together.

Even a bad marriage is not bad all the time. We had our good moments. Occasionally I got splattered with a little meat loaf, or spaghetti sauce, or whatever else was handy, but not often. Sometimes we went for weeks without trouble. But in the end, what is bad is bad. You can't ever fix it, or find a real cure for it. We got on as best we could. I think I tried harder, to tell the truth. She had a careless personality. When she got mad enough, she didn't care what she said or did. She didn't expect me to take her seriously when she got like that. When it was over, she forgot about it. But I didn't.

It wasn't the life that I'd had in mind for myself, but it had its consolations. Keefer was the best part of it. We lived in a nice house, we had things pretty well fixed up. I liked the line of work I was in. It didn't mean a lot to me, but even that was good. It didn't hurt to do it. It didn't make me want to kill myself, the way the writing had. I could do it without a lot of grief and pain. And it paid well. That was the important thing. Reasonable compensation, I thought, for having ended up like this.

Part Two

Accidents

O n e

WE might have gone on that way forever, locked together in our tepid marriage, till death settled our accounts for us. Except during that curiously lackluster Bicentennial summer of 1976—the same year I'd tried to celebrate my independence by giving back Phil his money, and instead had ended up buying the house in Tallys Ford—we learned that Linda was pregnant again.

This upset us both. Keefer was eight, with all the difficulties of babyhood behind him, and we were in our thirties. I was closer to forty than thirty, although I still secretly thought of myself as permanently frozen in time in my midtwenties, the normal biological clock of humans forestalled by regular doses of bicycle pedaling along the Susquehanna and tennis matches with Arthur.

I felt no signs of aging or decay—why should I have? I had inherited Jack's capacity for fast healing, when it came to sore muscles and minor sprains, although I hoped not his susceptibility to cancer. To that end, I'd given up the coffin nails the year we moved to Harrisburg. All these natural gifts and good works inspired me to think that I was standing still on a hill in Darien.

I foolishly thought, no matter how much I dawdled and procrastinated, that somehow, in some way, someday, I'd be able to pull my life to rights and still have time left over to enjoy it. I guess I thought I was somehow saving it up in a metaphysical bank account that only I, of all earthlings, had access to; and when the signs were propitious again I could start drawing on it and then, and only then, would I begin to use up the allotted dribble of weeks and years again, having banked everything onward from about the day that I'd read that bad review in the *New York Times.*

I think both of us had the idea that when Keefer went off to college (in another ten years) it would be time to separate and see if we couldn't reinvent our lives—or whatever was left of them, putting aside my delusions. Subconsciously, we also might have been waiting for Phil to die before we made any moves.

Now this accident had happened, practically unthinkable, given the frugal amount of passion we spent in each other's arms. It threatened to wreck the vague plans either of us might have been hatching, and tack another eighteen years onto our sentence in each other's company. Under my breath, I cursed her for her carelessness.

Phil and Mario and Cousin Vito were happy to hear the news. And Keefer was delighted. When we told him, he hopped around the house singing, "I hope it's a bruth-thah, I hope it's a bruth-thah."

With nearly nine years separating them, I didn't think he and the baby would turn out to be playmates, but I didn't ruin his fun by telling him that.

When I called Nola and told her, there was a pause on the line. Then in a faint voice I heard her croak: "Oh no."

Since her reaction was the same as mine, it made me mad.

" 'Oh no'? What the hell is that supposed to mean?"

"I only meant that one child is probably enough in this day and age. What with all the wars and bombs and everything. I think we'll blow ourselves up before the end of the century—don't you?"

"Ma. For godsakes, you're supposed to be happy."

"I am, dear. I'm happy for you both. If that's what you want, then I think it's wonderful. I hope it's a girl this time. They're so much easier to bring up. Don't you think so? Of course . . ."

" 'Of course' what?"

"Oh nothing."

I knew what she was thinking: *Of course, why should it matter to me? I rarely see my grandchild as it is.*

When I visited her, I was usually alone. Linda wanted nothing to do with her, and Keefer ordinarily wanted to stay home and play with his friends. I didn't like insisting that he go with me, either.

"You go see her. Don't expect me to. I'll have her here for her birthday and Thanksgiving. But that's it," Linda said.

Rather than trying to explain why the family wasn't with me, I got into the habit of stopping in to see her for a few minutes during the week, on my way to or from the airport or some meeting that I was obliged to attend at one of the hotels out her way. It made it less awkward, although not much. Other than that, except for one of her occasional "emergencies," I didn't see much of her during this time.

After we were certain, and before we told anyone, we discussed the possibility of an abortion. It was never really an option. As I have said, Linda was not especially religious. But she was sufficiently superstitious to think that if she went against the church's teaching in so grave a matter, something horrible might happen to us.

"Besides," she said, "how would Daddy feel if he ever found out?"

Given my own close call as a fetus, I didn't like the idea anyway. If Linda had wanted one, though, I wouldn't have tried to talk her out of it.

She was thirty-four. Not exactly the ideal age for child-bearing. Especially considering the tough time she'd had with Keefer—or "Keeper," as Phil pronounced it. But this time the pregnancy sped along, smooth and uneventful.

The baby was due just before Christmas, according to Linda's obstetrician. Dr. Monaghan was an elderly gentle-man whom Linda admired for his courtly manners. He was flirtatious too, in a geriatric formal sort of way. His ancient nurse was rarely in the room when he examined her. It didn't bother her, though. She said if he tried anything funny, she'd give him a good punch in the nose—one that would make his head swim for a week. He listened to her tummy rumble through something that resembled a bugle. He made her put on a little examining gown that didn't close properly at the back and looked her up and down when she stepped on the weighing scales. From the back, she didn't look pregnant. This angle allowed his imagination freer play, she supposed.

"If it gives him a thrill to peek at my backside, let him. Why not? He's old and lonely. He hasn't got a wife or any-thing. Not even any kids of his own. I feel sorry for him."

She liked the old geezer. She was touched by his gentle, faintly prurient grandfatherly manner. She didn't mind it when he patted her knee or accidentally put his hand on her can as he escorted her down the hall. Often, as they sat in the quiet fugitive shadows of his inner sanctum at the back of the building, where the dusty blinds limited the light to a few golden strokes on the threadbare carpet, the muted

sounds of traffic from the distant street reminded her of the
sigh and caesura of the surf in the little cove behind Phil's
house. It made her feel so relaxed, so secure, so much at
home. The tottery old doctor—such a sweet old thingy, really—would look up from her file, smile dimly between the
stacks of unread medical journals collecting dust on his
desk, and gently wag his finger.

"Now now, my pet. We're gaining just a tad too much
weight, I fear."

She said every man should have such nice manners and
gentle ways with women. I took this remark as a reproof, a
slur on my own character, or lack of it. But I noticed the old
gentleman's kindly admonitions didn't affect her eating habits in the least. She put on a lot of weight with this pregnancy. Especially during the last three weeks of her term,
after Phil and Mario and Cousin Vito came down to lend
moral support and be on hand for the baby's arrival, and
"the boys," as she called them, took over the cooking
chores.

She developed a little double chin. With her round face
and pug nose and short-cut curly black hair, she looked like
a baby herself. Her belly swelled into the shape of a gibbous
moon: tight as a drum, heavy and uncomfortable with the
burgeoning lump of baby coiled inside. I watched her belly
button slowly disappear. It left behind a brown spot the size
of a silver dollar, like a bruise in a piece of fruit. When
instructed, I bent and listened to the gurgly waters. Once I
was kicked in the ear for my trouble.

I bought her maternity tops and dresses to replace the
ones she'd given away after Keefer was born. I helped her on
with those horrible slacks with the special elastic panel in
the front as she sat on the bed and groaned about her back
and swollen legs. I listened to her complain about her sore

nipples. I gave up sex. No sacrifice, I admit, since I lacked enthusiasm to make love to a woman who looked more each day like Babe Ruth at the end of his playing days. When nudged, I got up in the middle of the night. I fetched her ice water and the peppermint patties she kept hidden from Keefer in the liquor cabinet behind the bar in the study. I did everything I could, short of showing any real enthusiasm. If that wasn't behaving like a gentleman, I didn't know what was.

Phil and the boys took rooms at the PennDel AutoInn, about a mile from the house, much to Linda's chagrin. She wanted them to cancel their reservations and stay at our place.

"Come on, Daddy. We want you here with us, don't we, Earl? Don't insult us like this."

Over the years she'd picked up some of his rhetorical tricks. I made polite noises in my throat. Secretly I was glad they'd decided to put up at the motel. Generally the fewer people around, the better I liked it. I was fond of Phil and the boys, but having them underfoot for three weeks or more was not my idea of a good time.

She kept insisting at the dinner table on the first night of their visit that they stay with us. Phil made a face as if he'd bitten into something rotten and waved her off with a stalk of celery.

"Enough! Don't aggravate me with any more talk about this."

When he saw her eyes fill with tears, he laid the celery stalk on the tablecloth, patted her hand, and spoke more gently.

"Listen to me, eh? Be a good lil girl and listen to what I say. I know you'n' Ur like us here in the house wid you. Sure, sure, you do, I know. But I got a bad cough now, eh? I don't sleep so well at nights. Ever since your poor mother died, I don't sleep for nuthin'. I gotta sit up in a chair with this cough. Ask your brother 'n' Cousin Vito. Eh? Do I sleep anymore?"

Phil studied them severely. Mario and Cousin Vito obediently shook their heads no. He gave them a dismissive grunt and turned his attention back to Linda.

"Besides, we're gonna go to the track some nights. I don't wanna come and go disturbing everybody. How would it be to wake the baby every night, eh? Not so good."

Even though "Keeper" was eight, he still referred to him as "the baby."

"You want to go to the track in December? You'll catch pneumonia."

"Yaah." He waved her off with his celery again. "We stay in a warm pot."

By which he meant they would sit in the enclosed grandstand and not stand at the rail on the homestretch, where he liked to install himself in the good weather.

Even though it hurt her feelings, his decision to stay at the PennDel made little difference. Except for one or two nights, they were always at our house till one or two o'clock in the morning anyway.

I found myself wishing the baby would hurry up, so Phil and his entourage would go home. It had been nice having them around for a while. But it got old fast. I was tired of the company: the late hours; the cigar smoke; all the booze and the sumptuous meals that Mario and Cousin Vito insisted on preparing for us night after night; the endless gravelly table talk about horses and the New York Mets.

Certainly the visit had been good for her. She seemed happier than she'd been for months. It was not an unmixed blessing, though. Unused to wine with every meal and a steady regimen of after-dinner drinks, she was often crocked by seven o'clock. Back in those days, we were a much more ignorant lot. Few people were aware of the possible ill effects on the fetus that alcohol and smoking could cause, if indulged in too freely by an expectant mother. I don't think Dr. Monaghan ever said a word to her about it.

Linda made for a sloppy drunk. She slurred her words, spilled food down the front of her clothes, burned holes in the tablecloth with her cigarettes, and sat there with an elbow on the table, wearing a rubbery smile on her face. I knew better than to tell her to ease up, what with so much spaghetti sauce and so many pasta dishes ready at hand. She was more likely to let fly when she'd had a couple of drinks. I didn't fancy getting splattered in front of Phil and the boys.

Cousin Vito drove her to her appointments with Dr. Monaghan. She said the old guy was trying to get her to call him Dr. Tom. He said it was what he liked all his favorite patients to call him. She told him she wouldn't feel right about it. She didn't think it showed the proper respect.

He gingerly looped an arm around her. His hand strayed for a moment onto her swollen breast: the old innocent under-the-arm ploy of a horny adolescent. Of course he removed it at once.

"But I insist, my dear," he said with a courtly bow.

"Okay, I'll try."

But she could never bring herself to do it. She went on calling him Dr. Monaghan, but now with a smirk she could barely repress, and the old fool went on insisting that she should call him Dr. Tom.

"That's what all my friends call me," he kept repeating in a wistful voice.

"Can you imagine?" she told me with a shy smile that

made her lips tremble. "I think he'd like to fool around after I have the baby. I wonder if he gets this silly with all his expectant mothers?"

"If he's annoying you—"

"Oh no. If you said anything to him, I know it would absolutely crush him. He's perfectly harmless. I feel sorry for him. He must be awful lonely. I think he's kind of sweet, actually."

I shrugged and thought no more about it. I saw no harm in the man, if she didn't.

Poor Linda. She must have been so hungry for affection. I was spending next to no time at home. Always out on meetings, or on the road. Arthur and I and the rest of the staff were working hard. The business was thriving. It was taking us up and down the Eastern Seaboard, and as far away as Chicago and Kansas City. Work was a wonderful excuse to concentrate elsewhere. It was no wonder she didn't mind if his hand occasionally strayed to her backside. It was more attention than she got from me.

This didn't escape Phil's notice. One night after dinner, he said he wanted to talk to me privately. We went into the study under the pretext of having an ouzo together. Linda had wearily plodded upstairs to help Keefer get ready for bed. Mario and Cousin Vito were off cleaning up the mess they had made of the kitchen. From his point of view, the timing couldn't have been better for a little chat with me.

We settled back in our chairs and swirled the ouzo in our glasses till it turned cloudy.

"Well, well," said Phil, admiring his surroundings. "You come a long way. I remember when you were a pot. You didn't have anything like this, eh?"

"That's right. Now I've got all these books, and no time to read them."

"Yaah, books." He made a face. "But this house, eh? A big job. A beautiful baby boy. A good wife . . ."

I nodded my head, agreeing with everything he said. Yes indeed, I had it made.

He extracted a crooked black cigar from his inside coat pocket and lit it with one of the wooden matches he carried loose among the change in his pants pocket. Someday, rattling the change around in his pocket as he liked to do, he was liable to set himself on fire. The authorities might even put it down as one of those cases of spontaneous combustion that you occasionally read about in the papers. I would have to tell them about the matches mixed in with the coins in his pocket, and clear up the mystery. He scratched the match alive on his horny thumbnail. He cupped it between his petrified fingers and stiffly bent his face closer to the flame. The light from the lamp on the table behind him put his face in shadow. The match flared and dimmed in tiny duplicate pinpoints in the black shiny minus signs of his pupils, throwing into relief his flattened nose and deep-set eyes squinting against the match and the deeply scored lines that set in parentheses his wide mouth.

He got the cigar going and sat back in his chair with a satisfied growl. He puffed on it rapidly, as if keeping tempo with the thoughts percolating somewhere in the recesses of his brain.

He seemed nervous. He was a twitchy fellow anyway. Sometimes this twitchiness bothered him so much that for relief he felt obliged to ventilate a little spleen on Mario or Cousin Vito, or someone else close at hand. One day at Bergen Cove, I saw him practically run across the kitchen floor and kick Mario square in the seat of his pants. He was setting down some bags of groceries on the kitchen table. Phil's foot to his seat straightened him up and damn nearly lifted him off the ground.

"What did I do this time?" he asked in a plaintive voice, rubbing his backside.

I've seen Mario angry. I've seen him hurt and crestfallen. But in all the time I knew him, I never saw him flare up at his father. He didn't do it that time, either. It had been a direct hit on the tailbone. I imagine it hurt like hell. The rest of us sat there, looking stunned. None of us could figure out what he had done wrong.

"Nuthin'," said Phil darkly, looking a little ashamed of himself. "I'm just, ah—jumpy. Nervous. I hadda do *somethin'.*"

Sometimes he took his bad nerves out on Linda, although not often. She always remained his "lil baby girl." His feelings toward her were usually protective. But in all the years I'd known him, he'd never treated me with anything less than affection and respect.

Sometimes he turned his irritability against himself. This took the form of dissatisfaction with some item of his clothing. Either his shirt was too tight under the arms, or across his pigeon-breasted chest, or the shirttail wouldn't stay jammed into the back of his pants as it was supposed to. Now and then when he stood up fast, his underwear cut him in the crotch, making him cry out in a strangled voice as if an assassin had just stabbed him where it hurts the most.

I'd seen him take the little narrow-brimmed green Alpine-type hat with the little red brush in the hatband which he occasionally wore and airmail it across a room, because the hatband made his head sweat.

Tonight, it looked like his argyle sweater was the culprit. He kept plucking it at with his free hand. First under the arms and then at his breastbone, in a more less regular pattern of irritability, as if signing the cross in a particularly idiosyncratic manner all his own.

Finally he settled down. He took the cigar out of his

mouth. He stirred up the cloudy liquid in his glass and took a good swallow of the stuff. He smacked his lips and showed me all the yellowed ivory of his peg teeth in that piratical grin of his. As always, the muscles in his cheeks forced his narrow yellow eyes shut, as if he couldn't bear to look at me and smile at the same time.

"Linda says lots of nights you're out on business. A lot of travel out of town. Meetin's 'n' stuff."

"Yes." I shook my head as if it were regrettable. "We're really busy at the office. Business is up thirty percent over last year."

"Good, good. That's nice. You're becoming a big success. I'm so happy for you that everything is coming up flowers. Linda tells me you're thinkin' about writing another book."

A thin complicitous grin spread over his face from ear to ear.

"Whatsamaddah? You don't have enough to keep you busy?"

I gave it my best self-deprecating little chuckle.

"That was just an idea. I haven't started anything. I probably won't."

"How many hours a week you work now?"

"Me? I probably bill fifty or sixty hours a week. Of course, I can't bill for everything."

Phil favored me with one of his irrepressible cackles.

"Whatsamaddah? You wanna be rich or somethin'?"

I smiled.

"I wouldn't mind."

"Listen to me. Don't be offended if I give you some advice. May I share with you what's in my heart?"

"Sure. Of course."

"Thank you. I know how proud you are. That's why I ask. I know how hard you work. You could be my own blood son, and I couldn't love you more, or be prouder of you than I am. You understand what I'm saying?"

"Phil, you've been like a father to me—"

"Excuse me. If you don't mind shuttin' up, please. Just for a minute. I gotta finish what I'm sayin' before I forget it. Please don't take any offense by this."

"No offense taken."

"Good, good. Listen to me. It's nice you work so hard. But Keeper, he's growing up without a fahdah. Linda's lonely too, eh? Look at her face, you can tell. She says nothing. I can see for myself."

"I know I'm not spending much time with them—"

"Now a new baby is coming. What are you going do? Let your children grow up like weeds?"

He rumbled a little in his chest and coughed out a watery gasp or two, so I'd know he was trying to be funny.

"Listen to me. Work is good. Too much is bad. Always your family should come first. The country is going to hell because the people forget this simple truth. I wish I could go back 'n' spend time with my kids when they were little. I should have spent more time with my wife—may the Mother of God forgive me. Now she's dead and I'm alone. I can go to the track whenever I want. I got plenty of time now. I can go out to the cemetery and talk to her tombstone, if I want. You see how sorry you can be? I'm an old man. Excuse me, but I know what I'm talking about. I wanna be sure you understand."

"I do, Phil. I appreciate your concern."

He pointed his cigar at me sternly.

"The family, you understand? Take care of your family. Everything else comes second."

"Right, Phil."

His face softened.

"Don't worry." He smiled. "When God calls me, I'll make you rich."

I didn't know what to say. "Thank you" seemed inadequate. It didn't even seem appropriate. I nodded my head, returned his benevolent look, and waited politely for what he'd say next.

He let the promise of my future riches sink in for a minute.

"When the baby's old enough, take Linda away somewhere nice, eh? You know how she likes fancy places. It would be a nice thing to do for her, after all this. You can leave Keeper 'n' the new baby wid us. Who knows more about babies 'n Anna? It'll be like a second honeymoon. Only this time, with plenty of money and no worries. Maybe you wanna go back to Bermuda. What a nice time, eh? That's where you made your son—such a fine strong boy. Maybe all that sunshine did it for you. Maybe you wanna go back. Who can say? Maybe this time you'll make a couple of twins, eh? I'd be greatly honored to pay for such a trip. It would be such a pleasure for me. A lil anniversary present to give you kids early for a change."

I thanked him for his advice. I tried to be polite without outright refusing his offer. I told him I would talk things over with her and see if she'd like to go away sometime. (I already knew the answer to that one.) I promised I would see what I could do about my schedule and work out some way to spend more time with her and the kids.

I was tempted to say: Listen, Phil. Listen to *me*, for a change. A second honeymoon won't fix what's wrong with us. If we spend more time together, it'll only get worse, not better. Can't you see? We're living together in the only way we can.

But I didn't say any of that. Instead, I nodded my head

solemnly. I agreed that a little more time together ought to
do it—that, plus spending a couple of grand at some luxurious watering hole, where the food was fattening and the
golfing was good, where it never rained and the sun shone all
the time.

PHIL and the boys had been hovering on the scene like a bad
parody of the three wise men for nearly three weeks when
one night, at three o'clock in the morning, with snow mixed
with sleet whispering like sand against the windows, Linda
woke me with a powerful nudge in the ribs.

"Huh? Is it time?"

"Naw. I thought you'd like to play a hand of gin rummy."

"Ha. Very funny."

She snapped on the bedside light and we rolled out of bed.
At the same time, she reached for the telephone. I was out in
the hall, groping my way to the bathroom, when I heard her
say: "Hi, Daddy. I'm ready."

He had insisted that we call, no matter what the hour.

"But Daddy, what if it's late at night? What if the
weather's bad? You're not feeling well. You need your rest."

"You call! Don't aggravate me with this. I don't come to
Pennsylvania to sleep. I can sleep at home in my own bed if I
wanna sleep."

We were naming the baby after him: Philip or Philippa,
depending on the roll of the dice. He intended to be there
when it arrived, no matter what the hour or the weather.

I came back into the room, pulled a shirt and pair of pants
over my pajamas, and got her suitcase out of the closet.

"Turn on the porch light for Daddy."

"Boy, what a lousy night."

"I didn't *plan* it this way."

"Okay, don't get excited."

"Well don't give me any junk."

Downstairs, it was cold and damp in the hallway and the wind was booming against the front door. I got my overcoat and Bean boots out of the closet, put them on, and sat down on the stairs to wait for her. I hoped it wouldn't take Phil and the boys too long to get here. With the wind blowing like that, the roads were sure to start drifting shut in places.

She was in the bathroom for what seemed like hours. When she came downstairs, she was still in her robe and slippers.

"Aren't you going to get dressed?"

"Why bother? I'll only have to peel again. Isn't Daddy here yet?"

"Not yet."

"Good, I'm hungry."

"What do you mean, you're hungry?"

"Move. I want a dish of ice cream."

"For godsakes, you're going to have a baby. You can't go into this on a full stomach."

"Don't worry. Ice cream melts fast."

She was standing in the doorway to the kitchen, spooning in the last of the French vanilla straight from the carton, when Phil arrived. He cackled behind a spotted hand that looked like a garden claw.

"You love to eat, don't you, baby girl? Heh-heh. Come on, dahlin'."

"You'll get a fat ass, sis."

"You should talk, Tubbo."

Cousin Vito dug me in the ribs.

"Happy Fahdah's Day, Pops."

He had the baby-sitting assignment. Grinning sleepily, he crossed the living-room carpet, ground out his cigarette in the ashtray on the coffee table, stripped off his overcoat, and covered himself with it as he stretched full-length on the couch. He shut his eyes. His horse face took on an expression slumberous and tranquil, like a stone effigy atop a medieval sarcophagus. He seemed to fall asleep instantly with the same promptitude that worked for him in movie theaters.

"Come on! Come on! Let's go!"

At the sound of Phil's voice, Mario seized the overnight bag and led the way out the door. He hunched his balding head against the sleet as he stepped from the porch onto the walk, coated with snow that looked as slippery as soap powder. In the shafts of light from the windows and the doorway, the sleet came shawling down out of the darkness like showers of diamond dust.

Phil's big car was idling in the driveway. He and I followed Mario down the walk, helping Linda. She had her mink coat thrown over her shoulders like a movie star on the way to a premiere. Phil ordered me into the car first, so she could sit between us. By the time we got her in and settled, the hem of her robe and gown were soaking wet and plastered to her ankles. Her slippers were ruined too.

"It looks like those slippers have had it."

"Don't make a fuss about it. They're only cheap things anyway."

"Take them off and tuck your feet in the car robe. You don't want to catch pneumonia."

I was disgusted with her. She could have taken a second to put on a pair of boots, instead of going out into the snow like that. That airy carelessness of hers toward such mundane matters as possessions and property, so long as someone else was footing the bills, never sat well with me.

Phil snapped on the TV to have some noise for company. I

opened the bar, splashed some brandy in a glass for him, and poured some vodka over ice for myself.

"What about me? Aren't you going to offer me anything?"

"Linda: you're going to have a baby, for godsakes."

"Well . . . it's still rude of you not to offer me anything."

Phil laughed around the edges of the cigar between his teeth. "Umm-umm-urrh-urrh," he rumbled. A noise supposedly mirthful, but played at the wrong speed.

We settled back. We watched John Wayne being heroic on the TV. Mario cautiously manipulated the big heavy car through the swirling mixture of snow and sleet and the drifts forming in the streets. The wind was still blowing hard. No other cars were on the road.

Linda had her head on my shoulder and her hand between the buttons of my overcoat. When an especially bad contraction convulsed her, she let me know by digging her fingers into my side.

"Ow! That hurts."

"You should be on this end, bud."

Phil started to get nervous. He rattled the ice cubes in his glass. He puffed on his cigar. His eyes shifted from side to side. His forehead began to shine with perspiration, like a man suddenly trapped in an elevator.

"What's taking so long?"

"Pop, I've got to go slow on a night like this. Look at it out there."

"Hurry up, for godsakes! Before your sistah drops it on the floor back here!"

She patted his hand.

"Don't worry, Daddy. We've got plenty of time."

Finally the car crept up to the front door of the hospital. A little welcoming party was waiting for us. Through the glass doors, I saw Monaghan holding his white head erect, standing next to a nurse with a wheelchair, who moved forward smartly the moment the car stopped. She and I got Linda into the chair and in through the doors.

The nurse was about to take off with her across the lobby when Linda made her stop and turn the chair around.

"You guys wait for me, okay? No matter how long it takes. You wait right here. Don't go running off somewhere. Don't do the big male thing, and go off for a drink or out to breakfast or something. Okay?"

She said it with such childlike seriousness that it made us laugh, including Monaghan.

"Haw-haw. Don't worry, my dear. You're in my hands now. You can be sure I'll take good care of you."

"Don't go away," she said to me.

I kissed her forehead and assured her we weren't going anywhere. Then the nurse whisked her away.

When I introduced Monaghan to Phil he said, "You have a beautiful daughter, sir," and squeezed Phil's arthritic hand for emphasis.

He dawdled with us for a few seconds while we waited for Mario to come in from the parking lot.

"Well, sir. Duty calls. We don't want to keep your grandchild waiting, do we? Haw-haw!"

He set off slowly across the open stretches of terrazzo floor between the islands of orange and yellow Naugahyde chairs and sofas that stretched in a long archipelago across the lobby, from the entrance where we stood watching him to the polished black granite banks of elevators in the distance. Eventually he wandered out of sight.

"Funny duck, isn't he? Linda thinks he's wonderful. I think he's a damn fool, myself."

When Mario came in, we went upstairs. We were the only

ones in the waiting room that night. Somewhere down the hall, a radio full of static faded in and out, quavering out Christmas carols from two stations at once. It annoyed me to the point of lunacy. I was tempted to go down the hall and tell them to fix it or turn it off.

Phil was jumpy too. After a few minutes he began to growl at Mario.

"Why you breathin' so hard all the time? You got something wrong with your nose?"

"I'm just sitting here, Pop. Minding my own business."

"Look at you," Phil said in disgust. "You're gettin' fat as a pig."

"Come on, Pop. Lay off. Pick on Earl for a change."

We didn't have long to put up with each other, as it turned out. It seemed we barely settled in before I looked up and was surprised to see Monaghan hesitating in the doorway. He looked silly in his green cap and surgical gown, like an amateur thespian got up to play the part of the doctor in a French farce.

But his face was gray and troubled, and it brought me straight up out of my seat. He tottered two steps into the room, reached out uncertainly, and dropped a vague hand on my sleeve. Behind his glasses his pale-blue watery eyes, round as a parrot's, were shiny as wet shellac.

"I'm sorry . . . I'm afraid I have bad news. Your wife—"

"Oh my God—something's happened to Linda."

"Oh no no . . . she's fine . . . she's going to be all right. But I'm afraid we've . . . I'm afraid we've lost the baby."

I fell away from him in disbelief and horror. I turned and walked directly across the room into the telephone booth and pulled the door shut behind me. Mario followed after me and threw himself against the door and yipped like a puppy. I bent over and hid my face and rocked back and forth and cried. It caught me completely by surprise. She'd had such an easy pregnancy this time. I just hadn't expected anything to go wrong.

I know we acted like a pair of fools. But that's what we did. I heard a commotion outside. I looked up. Through the glass panel, I saw Phil and Monaghan. With terrific geriatric effort, they seemed to be dancing around the room.

But they weren't. Monaghan's mouth hung open in terror as he struggled to free Phil's grip on his windpipe. I opened the door and pushed Mario aside and tried to get them apart.

"Goddam you quack bastard! I kill you for this!"

Phil swung wildly and caught me a glancing blow on the ear. The three of us staggered, but didn't fall down.

"Let him go, Phil. He didn't do anything."

It only made him madder when I said that. He growled and shook Monaghan as a terrier might a rat he'd caught under the porch. Finally Monaghan and I loosened Phil's deathgrip on his throat; and with his gown in shreds, he fled the room.

I left Mario to calm him down and went after Monaghan. But he had disappeared somewhere in the maze of corridors. The hallway was empty and still.

I went down the hall to get away from Phil's voice. Mario was trying to settle him down. Phil was cursing him, calling him every name in the book. He sounded like a man who'd been cheated and was determined to make a scene till the management made it up to him.

I was standing just out of range of their voices in the foyer, resting my head against the wall by the elevators, when someone called my name.

"Mr. Dimes?"

A flustered nurse stood there, wringing her hands.

"Dr. Monaghan would like to see you, sir."

She led me down another hall and through some swinging doors with porthole windows into a cold barren general office area. He was sitting at a small metal desk, nursing a cup of coffee, trying to recover his dignity. He stood up when he saw me.

"This is terrible."

He offered me a khaki-colored stool with a perforated metal seat to sit on. He told me again how sorry he was. Then he looked at the floor.

"Nothing like this has ever happened to me in forty-four years of medical practice. I've never been . . . manhandled by a member of a patient's family before."

"I apologize for him. We were going to name the baby after him. Family is everything to him. He's very upset."

Monaghan shook his head sadly. He looked up at me.

"The child was perfectly formed."

He shook his head again.

"I don't understand it. Apparently it was dead for some hours, by the condition of the skin. I thought I had a heartbeat. I'm very sorry."

"I know you are."

"Will you explain to him that it was stillborn? There wasn't anything I could do."

"Yes, I'll tell him."

"He's very angry."

"Yes he is. I'll explain it wasn't your fault."

"Thank you. I would talk to him myself, but I'm afraid—"

"You're right. He'd only get upset again."

"It wouldn't do any good?"

"No, I'm afraid it wouldn't."

"This is very unfortunate. There was nothing I could do."

"I know. In a few days he'll understand that too."

"I don't understand it. Your wife has a beautiful body for childbearing. Beautiful big breasts and wide hips . . ." He gazed across the room at some private vision growing cold on the wall. He jerked upright in his chair as if recollecting I was still there.

"May I offer you a cup of coffee?"

"No thanks. Maybe I'd better see my wife."

"Of course. Surely. How stupid of me to keep you like this. I'll have the nurse take you right in. Will you authorize an autopsy? I recommend it. We should try to find the reasons for this."

Blindly, I scratched my name on the necessary papers.

"How would you like to handle the body?"

I was unsure of his meaning, and must have looked it.

"Sometimes the family wants a funeral," he explained. "Other times, they just want us to take care of it for them."

"Yes, you take care of it."

"That's what I would recommend."

"How—?"

"Cremation. . . . I'll have the nurse take you in now."

He stood up and shook my hand.

"You can call me Dr. Tom. All my friends do. I feel this tragedy has brought us together in a form of fellowship. Don't you?"

He flashed me a tremulous smile full of yellow horse teeth. He looked as though he was ready to cry. I didn't have the heart to do anything but agree with him. I nodded, returned the pressure of his handshake, and patted him on the shoulder. Just as he turned away, he showed me the saddest smile I have ever seen in my life.

I trailed down the hall after the nurse. I felt as if I'd been beaten with a broomstick. She was no taller than a high hurdle and built like the letter U upside down. Her feet

moved in parallel steps like a chimpanzee's, instead of crossing in front of each other. I watched her muscular calves,
clad in hose as deathly white as a mime's greasepaint, as I
followed her. The only sound in the passageway was the
squeak of her crepe soles on the polished floor.

Linda lay under a rumpled sheet on a gurney in one of the
cell-like recovery rooms. Her green gown was soaked with
sweat; her thick black curly hair was still pasted to her forehead.

As I hugged her she whispered, "Did you see him?"

"No."

"He was beautiful. He had a lovely straight nose like
yours. . . ."

She cupped her palms over her face and began to cry.
When I tried to hold her again, she shook her head and held
me off with her hands on my chest.

"I'm okay. Just let me get over this in my own way. Please
don't hug me again. I feel like I'm going to suffocate."

I squeezed her hand.

"Okay. Whatever you say."

"How's Daddy taking it?"

"Bad. He's already tried to throttle Monaghan. Mario's
trying to calm him down."

"Poor Daddy. You'd better take him home."

"I think I should stay with you. Mario can take him home.
He can come back for me later."

"No, you go with them. He'll just give Mario hell for
everything. He'll calm down if you're there."

"Are you sure?"

She gave me a brave smile.

"Yes, I'm sure. Come back this afternoon—okay? I promise I'll act more like a human being when I've had some
sleep."

It was midmorning before we got home. Keefer greeted us at the door.

"Where's Mommy and the baby?"

Phil emitted a grunt of sympathy and reached for his cigars.

"She'll be home in a few days. The doctors didn't have any babies for us this time."

"Darn," he said.

I bent down on my knees. Automatically he walked into my arms and laid his head against my chest. I loved him so much in that moment for his faith in the feeble answers we supplied to his unanswerable questions. I loved him for his big dark eyes and the imperturbable gravity of his round face. He had his mother's looks. He looked just like her.

Later that night we had a talk, just as I finished getting him ready for bed and was about to step out of his room. I was looking forward to going downstairs and having a couple of stiff drinks with Phil and the boys.

"Good night, son."

"Good night, Daddy."

"Sleep tight."

"Daddy?"

"What is it, son?"

"Who killed the baby?"

I closed the door to the hallway. I crossed the room and sat down on his bed. By the faint glow of the nightlight, I saw that grave baby face that he had inherited from his mother, looking up at me solemnly from his pillows. I smoothed his hair back from his forehead.

"Nobody killed the baby, honey. It was born dead. I told you that."

"Yeh but—how could it be born, if it was dead? Don't you have to be alive to be born?"

"Well . . . not always."

He took my hand and studied my knuckles with a puzzled expression.

"Was it a boy?"

"Yes, it was."

"Darn. I wanted a brother."

"Well . . . maybe you'll have one someday."

"What are you and Mommy going to do now?"

"What do you mean, what are we going to do?"

"Well . . . are you going to get a divorce or something?"

"No, of course not, baby. Everything's fine. There's nothing for you to worry about."

"Your voice sounds sad."

"I am sad. But I'll get over it. So will your mother. You'll have to help us, okay?"

"Okay."

"Good. Now go to sleep. And don't worry so much. Leave that for the grown-ups to do."

"Okay. I love you, Daddy."

"I love you too, baby."

T w o

THE day we picked her up at the hospital, she was wearing the black wool suit that I always thought looked so good on her. Her glossy black hair was pulled back into a chignon at the base of her neck. She looked morose and severely beautiful, and as she slid off the bed onto her feet, I tried to put my arms around her, but she held me off. Her face was white and trembling.

"How could you let them cremate him?"

It really caught me by surprise. I had no idea she'd feel that way about it.

"I thought I was doing the right thing," I said.

"How could you let them burn him like a piece of garbage? Get away from me."

Phil heard the last of this as he limped up in his bandy-legged rocking-horse walk. His sunken cheeks and stringy neck instantly mottled the color of burgundy wine.

"Whatsamaddah with you? Be nice to your husband! What do you think? Only you got a right to feel bad?"

"Daddy."

She held out her arms to him helplessly. Seeing it was a serious matter, he passed the stub of his wet cigar to Mario and gave her a hug that was all elbows. The back of his bald head gleamed like the knob on top of a walnut newel post.

"Whatsamaddah, lil girl?"

He patted her between the shoulder blades.

"Oh Daddy."

Her head dropped to his shoulder, as if she hadn't the strength to hold it up any longer. She began to cry—hard, racking sobs that shook her whole body. Phil patted her and waited. Mario slung his arm around me and gave me a consolatory thump or two on the shoulder.

When she raised her head again, her cheeks were muddy with mascara. She wiped away the dirty tears with the backs of her hands. She plucked at his lapels.

"Why did this have to happen?"

He laughed, a sound harsh and guttural.

"God don't tell me his secrets, dahlin'."

She hid her face again in the front of his coat, but she was calmer now. She was sniffling, trying to catch her breath. With his stiff gray fingers, he raised her chin.

"Come on, come on. You're making a big mess of your face, eh? You cry so hard, all the pencil marks run down your cheeks."

"Oh Daddy, I want to go home. I want to sleep in my own bed. Where's Keefer? Where's my baby boy?"

"Cousin Vito's watching him. We thought maybe the hospital would scare 'im."

"Dear, sweet Daddy."

We went down the corridor together and got in the elevator. While Mario and I attended to the billing and followed with the bags, she walked out of the hospital on her father's arm.

"Don't worry," said Mario. "She'll get over it."

I wasn't particularly worried about it. At that point, I just wanted to give her a good swift kick in the ass.

When we got home, she sank to her knees on the living-room rug and greeted Keefer with a silent ferocious hug. Over her shoulder he gave me a bewildered look. I tried to reassure him with a little encouraging nod.

"What's wrong, Mommy?"

Her eyes filled with tears as she held him away and smiled at him.

"Nothing, baby. Mommy's just so glad to see you, that's all."

She gave him another fierce hug. He looked utterly confused by this form of happiness. I thought she ought to try to buck up for his sake. But she was always very open with him when it came to her feelings. She considered it a point of moral superiority never to hold anything back from him. She called it being honest; but it wasn't being honest—not the way she did it. It was careless and irresponsible and self-indulgent. Nothing else.

Shortly afterward, claiming exhaustion, she went upstairs to rest in our room with the shades drawn against the afternoon light. I was happy to see her go.

That night, it was Cousin Vito's turn to make dinner. When it was ready, Phil shuffled into the hallway and shouted up the stairs.

"Linda dahlin'!"

No answer.

"Linda!"

"What, Daddy?" came the faint reply.

"You comin' down for dinner?"

"I don't think so, Daddy."

"Come on, baby. Cousin Vito make-ah duck special for you."

"I'm not hungry, Daddy."

"We got ice cream for dessert."

"Maybe I'll come down for ice cream and coffee later."

"Okay, honeybun."

As he turned from the stairs the targets of his yellow eyes met mine. He bobbed his head and smiled his crocodile smile.

"It's okay. You'll see. Coupla days, she'll be all right. She's young. Strong. Soon you'll make another baby together. She'll forget all about this. 's true."

He expected me to agree immediately, like an enlisted man acting on direct orders. He waited for some sign that, like him, I understood the way things were. When it wasn't forthcoming, he sighed and jerked his head, signifying that the least I could do was lead the way into the dining room.

Everything was simple to him—stark, but simple. He believed suffering was the natural lot of women, and that it was a foolish waste of time, and that men should have none of it. It was what women did best, and what men shouldn't do at all. When things went wrong, women wept and wrung their hands, and appealed to Providence for relief. It was altogether fitting for them to do so, part of the natural confederacy of ritual that existed between home and Father Palumbo's church, for instance, with all the nice statuary tucked away in the back garden. The women cried for the men, so the men didn't have to cry for themselves. The men were therefore freed to deal with each other: to seek redress for indignities; to assign blame; to make the appropriate acts of retribution. Even if sometimes it only amounted to grabbing an old fool by his lapels and spraying him with curses full of spittle and nicotine.

The dining room was humid and odoriferous with rosemary and garlic and other spices intermingling over the steaming platters of food that Cousin Vito, wearing a full white apron, was setting on the table. He bent stiffly from the waist as he reverently put them down, as if bowing in turn to each of his specialties.

The old man had outdone himself. He had food enough to feed even a fair-sized contingent of the Stephano family, should members of the clan suddenly descend on us, having heard of our latest disaster on the psychic web of metaphysical telegraph wires which seemed to connect them together all over the Eastern Seaboard.

"There!" He stood back to admire the loaded table and proudly wiped his hands on his apron. "Whaddya think of this, eh?"

A triumph of platters and tureens steamed on the cloth like a miniature industrial complex: *pappardelle,* a duck-and-lasagne dish, prepared in his secret game sauce; macaroni and sausage in tomato sauce; a big salad of lettuce and tomato and onions and green and red peppers, garnished with anchovies; a steaming bowl of broccoli and fresh mushrooms; tomatoes with fresh garlic and hearts of palm in olive oil and vinegar; pork chops in tomato sauce; a tureen of seafood chowder containing chunks of lobster, clams, mussels, and three kinds of fish.

Everybody murmured low-key growls of appreciation as Cousin Vito stood there beaming at us, with tomato sauce staining the bib of his apron.

"It's beautiful," I told him. "Truly beautiful. You've outdone yourself, Cousin Vito."

As Phil approached the table, he had another one of his hot flashes. But his fingers were too stiff to work the snap buttons on his plaid shirt and he was unable to get out of it by himself.

After thrashing about for a few minutes like a man in a straitjacket, he growled, "Goddam this ting! Somebody get it off me!"

He hunched on his chair in exasperated impatience, snarl-

ing and cursing, as Mario tried to unsnap and strip the shirt
off his stumplike torso and nearly useless arms.

"Vito! Let Cousin Vito do it. You don't know what you're
doin'."

"You don't need Cousin Vito. Hold still for a second."

"*Stupido!* Holy Mother, you give me a son like this!"

After the crisis was over, and with a smidgen of his dignity restored, he sat at the head of the table in his ribbed
undershirt, his arms propped on the tablecloth. I noticed he
was developing little conical mounds of flesh, like undiffer-
entiated nipples, on the ends of his elbows. They stuck out in
little tits even when he straightened out his arms. No end to
the indignities, I thought. They just keep coming, faster and
thicker, the older you grow. I remembered of a sudden something Nola had said to me a few weeks past, when I'd visited
her.

She had drawn my attention to her hands. The skin was
loose and waxen. She'd lost a good deal of weight in the past
year. "Look at this," she said. She pinched the skin on the
back of her hand. It stayed pinched up in a little soft ridge
till she smoothed it out again.

"Isn't that wonderful? God, I can hardly stand to look at
myself in the mirror anymore. I just droop in all directions.
I've got purple scribbly marks all over my legs, like somebody had a leaky fountain pen and used me for blotting
paper. I'll tell you, life is really something. If you're un-
lucky, they put you in a box and stick you in the ground
while you're still young and presentable. But if you're lucky,
you get to be old and ugly and useless like me." She gave me
a big sour grin. "Isn't life great?"

I allowed she might be right, but it didn't matter if she
was. It was better to be hard as agate, like Phil, instead of all
soft and boneless inside like Nola. I hadn't called her yet

about the baby, and I was dreading it. We passed the dishes back and forth. I watched Phil out of the sides of my eyes. Moodily, he relit his cigar, which had gone out in the ashtray during the struggle with his shirt.

"How about some duck, Pop?"

"I can't eat nuthin'. Maybe a lil salad. A lil glass of wine. Nuthin' tastes good to me no more."

We received this ritual remark in the usual silence and, as if that were the signal, we began to eat.

I had no particular appetite either, but I knew I couldn't refuse Cousin Vito's meal without giving insult. It would be like returning a funeral wreath and saying to the sender, "Thanks, but I don't care for flowers. Why don't you give them to somebody who does?" Phil, of course, was allowed to abstain from the feast. He could do anything he wanted. His authority superseded all the requirements of custom, even in matters dealing with death.

So I ate, as courtesy required. I ate the vast amount of food that Cousin Vito tenderly heaped for me on my plate. I told him everything was delicious, and he was pleased. I asked for seconds, requesting "just a little this time," since courtesy now permitted it.

And we ate together, passing the wine back and forth, and limiting our remarks mainly to compliments about the food and drink.

We found relief in fussing over Keefer. We tucked his napkin into his shirt so he wouldn't get anything on his new cowboy suit. We spooned the lobster out of the stew for him. We gave him the choicest bits of the duck. When he complained that it was too spicy, we wiped the sauce off the meat for him.

"How's that, my little prince?"

"Much better, peasant. What's for dessert?"

He rewarded us by singing a song that he'd learned in school. In a high trebly voice, with his napkin still tucked in his shirt, he sang to us:

> *"Oh, Señor Don Gato was a cat,*
> *On a high red roof Don Gato sat.*
> *He went there to read a letter,*
> *Meow, meow, meow*
> *Where the reading light was better,*
> *Meow, meow, meow*
> *'Twas a love note for Don Gato!*
> *'I adore you!' wrote the lady cat,*
> *Who was fluffy, white, and nice and fat.*
> *There was not a sweeter kitty*
> *Meow, meow, meow*
> *In the country or the city,*
> *Meow, meow, meow*
> *And she said she'd wed Don Gato!"*

Naturally he had to sing all the verses to us, including the part where Don Gato in his happiness falls off the roof and breaks all his whiskers and his little solar plexus, and how the doctors are sent for, but can't save the poor fellow, and how on the way to the cemetery as the funeral procession passes through the market square, the little caballero cat is miraculously revived by the smell of fresh fish in the air.

It was funny, at least the way he sang it, and it charmed us silly. We all laughed harder than we should have, for other reasons than the song. Then, flushed with success, he took his napkin out of the front of his cowboy shirt and made a droopy big bow of it and held it to the side of his head, and said in a helpless soprano:

"I can't pay the rent!"

He held the napkin under his nose, where it became a droopy 'mustache. He frowned and said in the deepest voice he could muster:

"But you must pay the rent!"

The napkin became a hair ribbon again.

"But I can't pay the rent!"

"But you must pay the rent!"

"But I can't pay the rent!"

The napkin became a bow tie.

"I'll pay the rent!"

A hair ribbon again.

"My hero!"

We all laughed at this performance too. What a relief it was to laugh. Having exhausted his repertoire of songs and theatrical set pieces, he slipped off with me to the living room while Mario and Cousin Vito cleared the table and fetched the coffee and dessert, and we put the Scott Joplin record on the stereo. It was one of his favorites.

To the music of "Sugar Cane," we began to dance-walk around the room on the outside of our imaginary spats, twirling imaginary canes and fluttering imaginary straw hats, and rolling our eyes like an old-time vaudeville team. Phil came to the doorway on his bandy legs and watched us slyly while trying to repress one of his helplessly sinister cackles behind his knobby wrist. A few seconds later, Cousin Vito stuck his horse face over Phil's shoulder and gazed at us with lunatic delight. Then Mario appeared with a broad grin on his fat face and filled in the rest of the archway.

"Heh-heh. Good boy, Keeper. Look at 'im dance!"

"You guys are good! Right, Cousin Vito?"

"Hey, I never saw better—not even in Union City!"

The happy music and silly commotion drew Linda downstairs.

Phil and the boys quieted down. Phil smiled and cackled and nodded in our direction, encouraging her to appreciate the spectacle we were making of ourselves.

Holding the collar of her robe to her throat, she stepped cautiously into the room and smiled wanly. We pretended not to notice and kept on dancing. But we rolled our eyes a little more, and lifted our legs higher, and danced a little more on the sides of our shoes.

"What are you two goons up to?"

We didn't dare answer, we just kept on dancing. Her face was glowing with a soft quizzical delight, and we didn't want to do anything that might break the spell. Keefer had all the instincts of a natural-born ham. He knew we had to keep dancing, that we shouldn't do anything that might shatter the mood. I never had to tell him anything, or show him a dance step, or anything like that. He just naturally followed my lead, knowing instinctively what to do next.

"Aren't they silly, Daddy?"

"Yeh. Heh-heh."

For a second I was tempted to bring her into the dance, but I was afraid to touch her and maybe ruin the effect the music was having. She looked so shyly happy that I didn't want to do anything to spoil it.

The record ended to a round of applause and laughter. Keefer took a deep bow and went off to watch the adventures of Ultraman on TV, a Japanese production, and one of the silliest shows in the history of the medium, but he loved it.

The rest of us gathered at the table, over coffee and dessert. Linda sat next to me. I took her hand and held it tightly, but she didn't return the pressure. I let it go, so she could use it to steady her dish, when I saw she was having trouble with her ice cream.

Phil cleared his throat.

"T'morrah, we're going back to the Island."

Linda winced as if she'd been stabbed in the side. Phil kept his eyes on his ice cream. He was whipping it with his spoon, turning it into soup, which was the way he preferred to eat it. After a pause, during which she stared at him pitiably, a stare he either did not see or choose to ignore, she said quietly:

"Please, Daddy. Stay just a little longer. We love having you and the fellas here. Don't we, Earl?"

I said, yes we did.

"Please, Daddy?"

"Naw, we gotta get back. The business, we gotta take care of business. Then we're going down to Florida for a while."

"I'll come down as soon as I'm feeling better."

"Good, good. When you come, bring Ur'n' the lil prince, eh?"

"Can't you stay a little longer, Daddy?"

"No-no, dahlin'. It's time for us to go home."

Meekly she nodded her head. She looked ready to cry. Shortly afterwards, she went back upstairs to lie down again.

I put Keefer to bed at eight, and the rest of us played cards and drank ouzo till midnight. When I went up to bed, she was sound asleep.

The next morning, Phil insisted on taking us shopping at the mall before he and the boys started for the Island.

He bought Keefer a creamy-colored ten-gallon cowboy hat, some leather boots, and a pair of black-and-white cowhide chaps, to go with his new cowboy suit.

"Next time, maybe I'll buy you the pony."

"Will you really, Grampa? I've always wanted a pony!"

Phil laughed and looked at me.

"Tell your fahdah to buy a farm, 'n' I'll buy you ten ponies."

Keefer thought this was a fine idea. He started begging me to buy a farm. But I told him to settle down and enjoy what he had and stop being a pain. He went off to sulk in the toy store. As he walked off, I told him to meet us out front of Wanamaker's in fifteen minutes, but he didn't answer me, and, with a reassuring nod of his bony head, Cousin Vito trailed after him to make sure that he didn't get into any trouble.

Phil conned me into going into a men's store with him, saying he was looking for a new hat, and then insisted on buying me a suit. Naturally he picked out the most expensive one on the rack. When I told him I didn't need a suit, he got angry and began to make a scene. He waved his arms around till I gave in and allowed the tailor to measure me. When we were finished and everything was paid for, I thanked him. He nodded coldly.

"Next time don't be so proud."

Then he and Mario dragged Linda into a jewelry store. She kept laughing and looking back at me to see how I was taking it. They were pretending to force her through the doorway. It was all supposed to be funny and lighthearted. I could see she was excited and wanted whatever he was ready to buy her.

That day it turned out to be an emerald ring set with diamond chips—really a beautiful stone.

When he demanded the price, the clerk stuck his nose in the air and said, "That one is five thousand four hundred dollars, sir."

In his dirty overcoat and open shirt and baggy pants, he didn't look as if he could afford a cup of coffee, much less pay for a ring with a price tag like that.

He cocked his head like a bird and squinted up at the clerk.

"Ain't you got nothing better?" he said. The rest of us laughed ourselves goofy at the look of surprise on the clerk's face.

In her way, she was a thoroughly nice person, but very spoiled. At the time I married her, it seemed like the solution to a lot of my problems. But now I know better; and I would never again marry a rich girl.

Three

EARL! Wake up! Wake up!"

She shook me, and I woke with a horrible sense of dread in the cold and dark. For a second I didn't know where I was. The suddenness of it sluiced through me like an electric shock and exited with a jolt through the soles of my feet. She was crying. I could hear the sleet against the windows again.

I reached over and snapped on the lamp. Everything sprang back in the reassuring light: the flowers in the wallpaper, the dresser, the bureau, the mirror, my tie looped over the knob of the closet door.

I lay back and held her against my chest. My heart kept jumping against my ribs and falling back and jumping again like a small frantic animal trying to break out of a trap. She had her cheek pressed against the place it jumped. I had to shift her, because it hurt. A shadow was beating on the ceiling above me. It opened and closed its wings like a camera lens. It took me a second to realize it was the pulse beating behind my eyes. I lay there and tried to collect myself.

When I could, I said, "What is it, Linda? What's wrong?"

Because it was beating so damned hard, you see. I had to wait till it settled a little, and I could catch my breath.

"Oh God."

"What's bothering you? Tell me."

"I had a terrible dream."

"What about?"

"It was about the baby. He was standing at the foot of the bed, smiling at us. He was all bathed in flame. Unharmed, perfectly formed. But outlined in fire. Oh God . . . it was awful."

The small hairs on the back of my neck stood on end. I held her tightly and smoothed the thick shiny black hair back from her forehead. She had a perfectly round forehead like a child's. I smoothed her hair back. We lay there, holding each other tightly.

"Listen to that. Like somebody throwing sand against the windows. God, don't I hate the winters."

"You want a cup of coffee? How about I make you some coffee?"

"Okay."

We got out of bed and put on our slippers and robes and turned on the light in the hallway.

"Let's look in on Keefer."

Quietly we pushed open the door to his room till the light from the hall sprang across the foot of his bed. He was sleeping on top of his covers again with his thumb in his mouth.

"Where's Bah Bear?"

"He must be on the bottom."

"Poor ol' Bah. He'll be flat as a pancake in the morning."

She put a hand to her mouth as we looked at him, lying there in his yellow pajamas on top of his bear and the covers, with his dark hair mussed up and his mouth open and his wet thumb still in it.

"He's got a lot on his mind, doesn't he? I wish I could sleep like that."

"He's beautiful. Isn't he beautiful?"

Downstairs we ate the last of the chocolate-chip cookies.

"You think he'll mind if we eat his cookies?"

"I'll buy some more at the store. He doesn't care, so long as they keep coming."

"That's right. He's a sport about his cookies. Let's have another."

Her face tightened when she smiled. It was enough to start the tears out of her eyes again.

"It's pretty bad, isn't it?"

"Yes, it's pretty bad."

"Maybe we ought to get away. What do you think? You think a couple of weeks in the sun would help?"

"I don't know . . . maybe. What about Keefer?"

"We'll time it so he can stay with Phil and the boys in Florida. They'll be going down to the house in another week or so, won't they? We'll drop him off and go somewhere by ourselves."

"Maybe we ought to take him with us."

"Maybe we should get away by ourselves. Come on—he'll have a good time with them. They'll take him to Disney World. Marineland. They'll spoil him rotten. He'll love every minute of it."

She picked a chocolate chip out of her cookie and put it on the end of her tongue.

"I'm not feeling very romantic."

"I know. We should wait anyway, according to your buddy Dr. Tom. We'll go away like a couple of old friends. We're old friends, aren't we?"

"Sometimes."

We laughed.

"That's good enough, isn't it?"

She smiled.

"Not always."

"Well, tonight it's good enough, anyway. I'll look into it tomorrow. Any place you want to go particularly?"

"Just so it's warm—so I can lie in the sun."

"I don't know what we can find this late. We'll find something, though."

"What about work?"

"It's all right. I'll work something out with Arthur. He owes me a few favors."

"Maybe we shouldn't."

"Oh yes we should."

So we went away. The travel agent said that the only place in the Caribbean that wasn't booked solid was Curaçao, and so like good, obedient children we went there.

We stayed in Willemstad, the only town of any size on the island, in the nice hotel they'd made out of the old fort at the mouth of the harbor.

The pool deck was on the roof. Sometimes I would mount the wide circular wrought-iron stairs with her after breakfast and sit in a deck chair and try to read while she sunbathed or swam languidly up and down the length of the pool. But the sun was always too bright, and after a few minutes I usually retreated to our room, where I could read in comfort.

We had the coffee shop and the pool virtually to ourselves. There was never anybody else around. It was the same in town. It had the uncanny emptiness of an amusement park out of season. You could sense everything had been arranged for your convenience and that the real denizens of the place were remaining discreetly in the background and would only come out of hiding after you spent your last dollar and went home. Then they would come out

and cautiously have a look around. Once they were assured
that the tourists were really gone they would blow a whistle
and have a party and real life on the island would start up
again.

Sometimes we wandered around on the roof of the place
and leaned out of the crenellations high above the waves and
gazed over the limitless plain of bright water that stretched
from the sheer wall of the fort out to the horizon.

The ocean lay in bands of brilliant color. At the base of
the wall it was an iridescent golden green. In the middle
distance it became a crude semicircle of magenta. Then it
cooled into an icy light-blue color that streamed outward
toward the horizon, where the ocean and sky joined together
without a seam.

It was all very pleasant and languid and uninspiring and
yet satisfying at the same time. We weren't looking for any
excitement, and certainly the place had none to offer.

On the Outra Banda heights, overlooking the bay and the
town, stood what had once been a small fort like an outcrop-
ping of jagged gray rock. Legend had it that it had once been
under the command of Captain Bligh. But this old sword had
been beaten into a plowshare. It was now a very pleasant
restaurant, and we dined there several nights during our
stay.

Iron grilles barred the tall narrow windows and divided
the twinkling lights of the harbor into grids, suggestive of a
star map on the ceiling of a planetarium.

Mild evening breezes streamed in the windows carrying
subtle fragrances of the island. These we enjoyed, but
couldn't identify. We stopped in the middle of dinner to gaze
out the tall narrow grilled window by our table at the harbor
below. It made for a very lovely restful scene. I sat there and
looked at the moon and the dark outlines of the harborside

buildings with their building-block-like Dutch facades and the glitter of moonlight on the disklike gleam of the harbor and wondered whether any of this was doing her any good. She seemed to be enjoying herself.

Sometimes in the mornings she induced me to put my book aside and go for a walk. There was a pedestrian bridge on pontoons which was supposed to link the two sides of the harbor, but it was out of order during our visit.

The thing had a three-bar railing, a humpbacked splintery wooden walkway, and metal arches overhead every few yards, encrusted with light bulbs, which made it look like a carnival ride.

It was supposed to swing on a hinge like a door. When it swung shut, people could walk across its wooden spine from one side of the harbor to the other. When it swung open, the cruise ships, the oil tankers, and the produce boats from Venezuela could swim in and out of the harbor's back rooms.

It was a wonderful proposition, but a purely theoretical one while we were there. The bridge was moored on the Outra Banda shore, where workmen tinkered with the little motor, which looked no bigger than a one-and-a-half-horse-power outboard. Meanwhile, everybody rode back and forth on the ferryboat, or walked the long way around.

Our walks often took us by the bridge. We watched puzzled mechanics in ribbed undershirts sweating over the machinery. The engine, it seemed, wouldn't work no matter what they did.

Once a dark man we took to be the foreman stood up from his painful crouching position over the engine as we stood watching against the railings above the bridge. Slowly he wiped his perspiring face with a red bandanna and looked at us. He was so black we couldn't make out his features in the dazzling sunlight, only the gleam of his eyes, but he seemed to be silently imploring us for advice. We didn't have any to give. When the man continued to stand there stubbornly, repeatly mopping his face with the bandanna and silently imploring us like that, we grew uncomfortable and decided to move on. It was funny the way he looked at us, as though we had the answers.

A few days later we passed the bridge again. This time the handful of ragamuffin mechanics was gone. Tools and various small pieces of machinery lay scattered on the gray splintery planks of the walkway, like artifacts left behind by a civilization suddenly overtaken and obliterated by catastrophe.

We never saw them again, although the next time we passed the bridge we noticed the tools and parts had disappeared.

One day we rented an orange Volkswagen Beetle through the car-rental desk in the hotel lobby and circled the island.

The road northwest out of Willemstad took us through parched countryside dotted with giant cactus. The car made a racket as we passed through the sunstruck landscape. A huge cloud of white dust rose behind us on the road and followed us everywhere like a specter. We didn't pass any other cars outside of town. We saw only occasional signs of human habitation along the road in the shape of shabby little pastel boxlike dwellings where inevitably a few red and blue rags hung limply from a washline in the front yard and a few scrawny chickens scratched in the dirt behind a low wire. Once we saw a goat tethered to a cactus.

We passed the moldering remains of what once had been farms built by the Dutch. The buildings with their red tile roofs and walled courtyards and cracked white plaster walls sat in the dust and silence. The broken windows were shuttered and the doors boarded over. We looked at the cactus and the arid land and wondered what the Dutch could have grown here to warrant building such estates, which you could see must have been lovely at one time. Whatever had caused them to settle here had obviously ended in disaster. The farms were so beautiful and yet so desolated that we didn't want to know the details.

We stopped for lunch at the restaurant at Westpunt, a clearing with a few houses on the western tip of the island. We were the only customers in the place that day. As soon as the young girl served the food, she disappeared. I wanted another beer, but she never came back. When it came time to pay the bill I went to the bar and shouted across into the open doorway that gave onto the kitchen. I could hear some people murmuring quietly to themselves somewhere out of sight. After a time they stopped talking and seemed to listen thoughtfully. Eventually a stout middle-aged man with a gray Fu Manchu mustache came into view and collected the money.

When we got back to Wilmenstad that afternoon, I was confused by the signs and the novelty of the traffic after traveling through the lonely countryside, and kept forgetting to drive on the left side of the road. All the rental cars on the island were painted orange—apparently so the natives could take appropriate evasive measures. I drove down a one-way street for several blocks before I realized what I was doing. In the meantime, the carts and wagons and other cars streamed past us unperturbed.

One day, walking along a chalky road on the Outra Banda, we found ourselves in the middle of a festival that materialized out of nowhere.

The music was provided by a few horns and many steel drums. A crowd of dancing islanders surged around us. Dark little children dressed in bright-yellow feathery chicken costumes, their heads peeping out below orange bills, peered solemnly ahead in the morning sunlight as they were pulled along on floats, surrounded by dancers and musicians.

"What's going on?" I asked some of the people passing by. But they were either oblivious or understood only the island dialect called Papiamento, and danced around us as if we were posts in the roadway.

"Is today a holiday?" I asked a man with bloodshot eyes and grizzled hair. But the man, like everybody else, appeared not to hear me.

The tide of people rose around us. We were submerged in the crowd and the noise. The fluty music and metallic drumbeats reached a crescendo. Overhead on the floats, the solemn feathered children passed by with great dignity. Then the sea of people and the music and the children got up like chickens suddenly receded and left us standing by ourselves like so much flotsam swirling in the chalky dust at the edge of the road.

The beautiful solemn children, their yellow feathers turned and flapping in the breeze, shrank away into the distance. The music grew tremulous and weak on the wind and then died away altogether. White sand, fine as lime dust, blew across the crumbling roadway as we watched the procession crest a hill and disappear from view.

"What was that all about?"

"Beats me. But I wouldn't have missed those kids in chicken feathers for anything."

Our room overlooked the ocean. Some nights we sat out on the balcony after dinner and had a drink. Usually we put in a call to Pompano Beach to find out how Keefer was getting along. He was always getting along fine, which disappointed us a little. We thought it would be nice if he missed us just a touch, but he didn't seem to. Nevertheless it made her feel better to talk to him every night.

"I know I'm silly. Do you think I'm silly?"

"No, you're not silly. Let's call, if it'll put your mind at ease."

"Geez, he doesn't even miss us, does he?"

"He doesn't seem to."

"The little brat. Daddy and the fellas are spoiling him rotten."

"I told you he'd love it."

She had trouble sleeping at first, so we each took one of the double beds. Things seemed to be going pretty well. I had explained the situation to Arthur, and he was very understanding, even though my absence meant a lot of extra work for him. But he wanted me to go. He told me to go away and stay away for as long as it took.

I decided we'd stay on as long as she wanted to. I didn't think it would be too long, anyway. But I thought it would be nicer to let her bring up the subject of going home first. When she was ready, she would let me know.

She got into the habit of rising early and going up to the pool by herself for a swim. By the time she got back, I was usually up and shaved and showered and ready to take her to breakfast.

One morning, no different from several others, I woke to find her bed empty as usual. I walked into the bathroom without giving it a thought and found her pale and naked, staring at herself in the bathroom mirror. Tears were streaming out of her wide dark eyes.

"Linda, what's wrong?"

"I don't know, I just feel sad."

She covered her face, made an effort at the same time to hide her breasts with her forearms.

I picked her robe off the floor and put it around her shoulders. With a grateful look, she wriggled into the heavy white terry cloth and tightened the belt about her waist.

"I'm sorry to be such a wet blanket."

"It's okay. I'm sorry I walked in on you. I thought you were at the pool. Aren't you having a good time? I thought you were having a good time."

"I miss Keefer."

"I know you do. You want to go home?"

"I want to go down to Florida with Daddy and Mario. I want to stay with them for a while. Can I?"

She tightened her belt again and smiled at me uncertainly.

"What about his schooling?"

"I can enroll him down there for a few months."

I looked at the floor.

"It's just that I don't think I can stand to be at home this winter. I just want to be somewhere where it's warm. Is it okay?"

"Jesus, Linda. I wish you'd get over this. This is no way to live."

"I know, I'm sorry, I can't help it."

She looked at me in the mirror. She was miserable about it, but that's the way she felt. She was still holding the ends of the belt in her hands, even though she was finished with it.

"I just need some time for myself. Please don't get mad at me."

"I'm not mad, I just wish you'd get over it. If you want to go down there, it's all right with me. How long do you plan to stay?"

"I don't know."

"Well it's fine with me anyway. Maybe when you come home you'll feel better."

"Don't be mad."

"I'm not mad. A little disappointed, maybe, but not mad."

Her eyes were glittering with tears again as she looked at me in the mirror.

"I still think about the baby."

"I know you do."

"I miss him—isn't that silly?"

"No, it's not silly."

"Some people would say he was never really alive. I never got to hold him in my arms or anything. But I miss him awful."

"Maybe you'd better not talk about it. It'll just make it worse."

"He was such a beautiful baby. It's almost as bad as if we'd lost Keefer—"

"Don't bring Keefer's name into it."

"You think it's bad luck?"

"I don't know what it is, but don't do it."

"I'm sorry."

"It's all right. You want me to get you some tissues?"

"Sometimes I think God took the baby away because I said I didn't want him. You remember that? When I first found out, I said I didn't want to get fat again. I said one kid was enough. I even talked about getting an abortion? You remember?"

"Don't be ridiculous."

"That's right. Don't be ridiculous. He won't hurt Keefer either—don't worry."

"I'm not worried."

"I'm sorry, I brought his name into it again."

"It's all right. Let's get off this subject. Let's go have some breakfast. Then I'll go see about the tickets. Is that what you want?"

"Okay. Maybe we can get out of here tomorrow."

"Sure. Why not? Maybe a few months down there will do you some good."

It'll be a relief to be alone, I thought. It'll be a relief to come home and not have to look at her. It'll be nice to come home after work to an empty house and not have to contend with her problems. I can eat out in restaurants and read the papers. I can get a lot of extra work done. Maybe it'll work out for everybody.

We got dressed and went down and had breakfast. Afterwards I took care of the tickets, and the next morning we got out of there.

F o u r

I *WAS* in Chicago for most of February, doing some work for a company called Royal Chicken Parts, Inc., a wholesaler of frozen chickens and pizza toppings. The company had quadrupled in size in six years. Morris Feldman, the vice president, thought he had detected a serious morale problem developing among the staff at corporate headquarters. They couldn't figure out whether they were still in the chicken business or whether they were really in the pizza business and just called themselves Royal Chicken Parts in order to fool the competition.

One thing led to another and kept me in town for three miserable weeks. Cecil Breeze, the old pirate who had founded the company, thought the real problem was that too many people were hanging about in the hallways.

"Too many goddam people!"

The old buzzard pounded his fist on the big half-moon of his burled walnut desktop and swiveled his black leather chair, so that he could glower at me properly.

"That's the problem! They got too goddam much time on their hands! Not enough work to keep 'em busy. That's when things go sour.

That's when they start to bitch and moan. Some mornings, I got to physically push 'em out of my way, in order to get out my office door. I literally got to kick and scratch, just to get down the hallway to the toilet."

He ordered us to work out some way of "flattening the organization," as he called it, and getting rid of all the "goddam deadwood around here." Having identified the problem, he took his wife out to their home in Palm Springs for a few weeks. The minute he left the building, morale around the place seemed to make a tentative comeback. The Founder, as he was called, was seventy-six, with no plans to retire. I could see Feldman had a problem.

It was one of those cold dark bitter Chicago winters. Blizzard after blizzard hit the city. Nightly, several inches of snow came sifting down out of the black skies. They couldn't keep the sidewalks clear. People bundled in fur coats and Tartar-style fur hats walked on slippery narrow paths between the frozen drifts that collected at the foot of the buildings. The snow in the streets was piled higher than the cars. Many of the side streets remained unplowed, closed for days at a time. The main thoroughfares were reduced to one lane each way. They were using power shovels to load the snow and ice into dump trucks and haul it off to the lake, but they couldn't keep up with it. People used up most of their energy just getting to and from work. Feldman told me that some days it took him four hours just to make the commute back and forth from his house in Wheaton.

"The minute I get to the office," he said, "I start worrying about how in hell I'm going to get home again."

One night I wandered out of the Palmer House in search of dinner. The wind was blowing off the lake, and it damn near froze me in my tracks. I should have turned around and gone back into the lobby and had my meal in the coffee shop.

But I'd been cooped up in the hotel for several nights, and I wanted to get out of the place. I staggered some two blocks, with multiple stops in doorways in futile attempts to escape the arctic wind, till at last I reached the Blackhawk, where, still numb and shaking with the cold, I consumed a mediocre dinner of roast beef and read my copy of the *Tribune.* It wasn't much of a victory.

Afterwards the wind blew me back to my hotel in record time. I spent the rest of the night huddling under the covers, trying to get my body temperature up to normal again. I finally got up and put on my overcoat and got back into bed that way. The next morning on the news, I learned it had been the equivalent of fifty below zero the night before. It had worked its way up to thirty-five below by dawn, but wasn't expected to get much warmer all day.

I have never been so cold in my life. It was like living above the Arctic Circle. After three weeks of this, I was tempted to tell Feldman to leave Cecil and the Ice Age behind and pack up the entire company and move it to another climate.

Ever restless, the Founder came back from Palm Springs before I could make my escape. That meant we had to spend another three or four days going over everything that we had done in his absence and change it all back again.

Feldman and I had come up with plan for reorganization that essentially broke the company into two independent operating entities with simpler and more meaningful charters of accountability at every departmental level. Under the plan, the pizza-toppings division would report to Feldman, and Feldman would report directly to a separate but interlocking board. The original chicken business we left in the hands of the Founder. We had also come up with what I thought was a quite meticulous and humane plan for streamlining the old chicken part of the organization, which truly was overstaffed, by means of attrition, early-retirement incentives, and, where feasible, retraining and transferring people to the toppings division, which was woefully understaffed despite the Founder's perceptions of the traffic outside his office door. As discreetly as possible, we had attempted to build a coop around the old man and keep him busy plucking feathers while giving Feldman a free hand in growing the rest of the business.

The Founder, of course, wanted none of it. Our plan for shrinking the staff on the one side was too slow and costly. Our projections for additional staffing on the other side were too generous. What was needed was some program that would cut costs now, not later, and show the corporate survivors of the bloodbath that we intended to "kick some serious ass around here and get those profit percentages back up there where they belong."

With regard to breaking the company into two operating entities and investing every parallel level of management with more autonomy and accountability, he said, "I am not ready to turn this company into a bunch of principalities where every little Bedouin in the organization is king of his particular sand dune. No, by God! Everybody in the place, from the janitor on up, ought to know very clearly what single man is in charge—in charge of everything, from pencils and stamps on up—and that he can go directly to that man and get a hearing, if he wants or feels the need for direction and advice. It was that way in Henry Ford's day, and back then the country never had it so good. That's the way it'll be around here for a while longer, so far as I'm concerned. Now let's start from scratch, shall we, and see if you boys can come up with some better ideas with a little help from me."

WE spent a lovely two or three days locked up in an office with him. Finally, on a Thursday afternoon at five o'clock, Feldman bade me a rueful goodbye and I was set loose.

I had taken my bag with me to the office that day, so I could catch the airport bus at the Hilton instead of going back to the Palmer House. It had been steadily snowing all day. Before the bus showed up, I checked with the airline ticket office in the lobby and was assured that O'Hare was open and flying. But when the bus finally got me there, only a few runways were open and everything was stacked up.

My flight to Harrisburg was delayed for six hours. I bought a membership in one of the airline clubs and spent most of the time in there, reading a copy of *The Eustace Diamonds* that I happened to have in my pocket for just such an emergency. *The Eustace Diamonds* is a wonderful old Victorian novel of well over seven hundred pages. By the time I got on the plane, I had it more than half read.

That night when I finally reached home, I gulped down two brandies and went to bed. At four in the morning the telephone rang. I had an idea who it would be.

A weak voice whispered in my ear.

"Early—is that you?"

I sat up and switched on the light.

"What's wrong, Ma?"

"I—I have to go to the hospital. I've got terrible pains in my abdomen. Ohhhh—"

"Did you call the ambulance?"

". . . No, no. Oh God."

Well, call a goddamn ambulance, I nearly said. But instead I said, "Try to get dressed. I'll be right over."

"Oh thank you, Early. You don't know how bad I feel. I think I'm going to die this time."

"Nonsense. You're not going to die. I'll be there as soon as I can."

Over the years, I had dealt with emergencies like this before. It was her season of the year for getting sick, and I was more or less used to it. It was good that Linda was away. These late-night calls from Nola used to drive her wild. She said Nola did it just to get my attention.

"She'll always do it, till you tell her to go to hell."

I told her I realized that. But some of these emergencies were real. The trick was learning when to help out and when to say no. That was the part I had never figured out.

It took me twenty minutes to get from my house in Tallys Ford to her house on Crooked Hill on the MacAbee side of the river. The last of her collie dogs had died off years ago, and she now lived alone with her old cocker spaniel, Tito. When she had sold the big house and bought the smaller property, she'd decided to downsize her dogs as well.

The house had a long low roof and sat at an attractive angle on a big lot with birch trees in the front yard. A row of hemlock and pine grew behind the three-board white fence that fronted on the sloping road and assured privacy. It was a nice little place, but she had never particularly liked it. It was *too* private for her. She couldn't see the lights of the neighboring houses at night. It had more lawn and shrubbery than she wanted. It was hard to get people in to take care of it at a price she could afford. She was thinking of selling it and moving to an apartment, but she couldn't make up her mind to actually move ahead and do anything about it.

I drove between the low white gateposts into her driveway and saw the house faintly illuminated atop its modest hill by the light from the lamp post at the bottom of the wide concrete stairs leading up to the front door.

The drapes at the living-room window were drawn. The house looked dark and forlorn. It sat in the cold wind on a little breadcrust of snow. Shadows moved on the roof, these made by the bare limbs of the clump birches on the front lawn. She or someone had shoveled a little path to the door.

The door was unlocked. I stepped into the dim hallway, which smelled strongly of the old dog. I could hear the thing panting at my feet. I could just make it out in the dim light from the living room.

"Hello, doggy."

I bent and petted the smelly old thing.

"Don't you stink awful, you poor thing. Doesn't your mother ever give you a bath?"

The dog gladdened its eyebrows and wriggled its backside and pushed against my knee as I patted it with growing repugnance.

It was so old it had turned a velvety suede gray from head to foot. What she would do for company when it died, I had no idea. She'd told me she didn't want another animal to take care of. Although what she did for him, besides dump a little dog food out of a can into his dish and push open the door to let him in and out of the backyard, I couldn't say.

A hoarse dry whisper came from the living room.

"Is that you, Early?"

She was curled in a fetal ball on the couch. Her feet were covered with an old afghan. The room was gloomy and cold as a meat locker. In the feeble light, I could see she was dressed and not in her bedclothes. At least she's dressed, I thought. That's a break.

She looked up at me.

"I think I'm going to die this time."

"You're not going to die, Ma. We'll get you fixed up."

I got her imitation leopardskin car coat out of the hall

closet. It was saturated with the smell of the heavy perfume she wore. I handled it with the same reluctance with which I'd patted the smelly dog. I took the coat and went back into the living room and helped her into it.

From the chair in the dining room, I fetched her pocketbook, which held her house keys and her Medicare and other insurance cards. I left on a light for the dog. She told me he didn't like to be left alone in the dark. Then we went out the door. I propped her up with one hand and locked the front door with the other. I helped her down the front walk and into my car, where she rested her head against the dashboard.

On the way to the hospital I discovered she hadn't had a bowel movement in fifteen days.

"Why did you let it go so long?"

She moaned.

"I don't knooow. God, don't ask me questions!"

Fifteen days. She'd been having intestinal difficulties on and off since September. She was sure it was cancer. I had taken her for a GI series in October, but they hadn't found anything. Fifteen days was a long time. Maybe she did have some kind of obstruction in her bowel, after all. The trouble with people like Nola was that you never knew when to take their complaints seriously. I began to ask myself why I hadn't kept closer tabs on her. What with the loss of the baby at Christmas, the Caribbean trip, and the Chicago business, I hadn't seen much of her at all since Thanksgiving.

I parked the car as close to the doors of the emergency room as I could get. I got her out of the car and across the parking lot, in through the automatic doors, and into one of the chairs in the waiting room. She could hardly sit up, the pain was so bad. Then I took her purse and went to the desk and logged her in. In a few minutes a tough-acting little nurse came out with a gurney and barked her name. She and I helped Nola onto the contraption.

"Oh my God."

Nola shut her eyes and squeezed my hand as she lay down. By this time I was really worried about her. I covered her with her tacky sweet-smelling coat and patted her on the shoulder.

"You'll be all right now."

"Keep my purse for me, will you? I don't want to take it in there with me."

The nurse disappeared somewhere, and we had to wait.

I cradled her purse under my arm like a football and alternately stroked her forehead and held her hand. She was lying in the same fetal position in which I'd found her when I entered the house. She was in a lot of pain.

"Oh my God."

"You'll be all right. They'll take care of you in a minute now."

A young black man swaggered through the swinging doors that led to the treatment rooms and stared at us boldly.

"This Miz Dimes?"

He wheeled her in feet first, so I wasn't able to flash her any last-second smile of encouragement, which made me feel bad. The doors flapped shut. I hoped they wouldn't find anything seriously wrong with her. Poor thing was all alone. Getting old. She'd never had much of a life: not much in the way of happiness or pleasure. She'd lost all the people who had really counted for anything. Strange: how everything seemed to pass her by, as if she'd been stranded in a spiritual and emotional Sargasso Sea all her life. She had told me more than once that happiness was a matter of luck. That it didn't matter what you did, how you struggled to change your life, or what you ate, or whether you exercised, or who you knew. It was all just a matter of luck, or fate, if you wanted to call it that. I was beginning to think she was right. But then, character *was* fate, wasn't it? Wasn't that what the ancient Greeks had professed? Character was what you made of your experience, not just simply what was handed to you by the gods. And so therefore weren't we responsible for almost any morass in which we found ourselves mired? I doubted if Nola would agree. I doubted if even I agreed. Having exhausted my talent for philosophy, I sighed and took a seat in the waiting room. I held her pocketbook on my lap and began to leaf through a dog-eared copy of *People* magazine.

I HADN'T finished glancing through it before a short balding intern with a pleasant smile came out and told me that she was impacted. I had never heard the term before.

"Impacted?"

"Yes. She's badly constipated. We'll have to clean her out, but she'll be okay. You'll be able to take her home afterwards. She says she's had trouble with constipation before. Nothing like this, of course. She's on medication for depression?"

"Yes."

"Sometimes constipation is one of the side effects. Both of some of the medications and of the depression itself. She doesn't sleep well, she says."

"No."

"It doesn't sound like she eats very well, either. We'll give you some instructions for some stuff she can take. She ought to be using a stool softener and taking Metamucil, or something like it, every day. But we'll talk about that later. Okay? We'll have you come back to see her as soon as we're finished."

Brisk and efficient, he had put his finger on the problem immediately. Poor Nola. Just full of crap as usual. Not a pleasant experience, but one that sure as hell beat cancer, or an intestinal blockage of some kind. I sat down in my chair and felt myself deflate with a sigh of relief.

Afterwards, they came back for me and led me through the doors to the cubicle where she sat on an examining table, listing woefully to the right. She was clad in a shorty hospital gown tied by one string at the back of her neck. Her short fat legs were scribbled with broken veins, just as she had described them to me once during one of her diatribes on the unfairness of life, as if, indeed, some malicious grafittist (if that is a word) had written all over her with a ballpoint pen. One dangling foot terminated in a cluster of corns and gnarled toes and rested on the purple instep of the other. She looked absolutely forlorn and stripped of self-respect, like some poor soul you might have found in a hospital charity ward before Medicare. I got her down off the table and quickly helped her on with her clothes.

As we stepped into the parking lot I put my arm around her and said, "Wasn't that fun?"

"Oh my God." She leaned weakly against me. "What a horrible experience."

"You just take the stool softener and the Metamucil, and you'll be all right."

"I don't ever want to go through anything like that again."

"Well then, take care of yourself, the way you're supposed to."

Now that I was back in town for a while, I made a point of calling her a couple of times a week. I tried to get over there at least once a week to see how she was getting on. She wasn't doing very well. Mostly she just stayed on the couch all day with that smelly dog by her feet. I urged her to get outside and get a little fresh air and exercise, but she said the weather was too bad. I suggested she drive over to the mall and walk around inside and get her exercise that way. But she said she was afraid to go over there by herself. She said people had been mugged in broad daylight right in the parking lot. To hell with it, I thought. If she won't do anything for herself, then she can just lie there and stew all she wants. But I couldn't leave it at that. She was getting so weak that she could hardly get off the couch. So I started going over there twice a week and getting her out to the mall for some exercise. I couldn't do it every week, but I did it when I could. It seemed to help quite a lot.

At Easter, I flew down to Florida to spend a long weekend with Linda and Keefer. When I arrived at the house Cousin Vito opened the door, arched his back, threw out his skinny arms, displayed all his teeth in a ghastly cannibal smile of greeting, then took my suitcase and led me through the cool darkened house to the sunny inner courtyard, where everybody was having a late lunch on the terrace by the pool. There was Keefer, dressed in a new cowboy outfit. When he saw me, he swept off his big ten-gallon hat with a dramatic flourish and hugged me around the waist. Everybody laughed.

"I missed you, Dad."

"I missed you too, son."

I went over and kissed Linda on the forehead and shook hands with Phil and Mario. They were both wearing aviator sunglasses and identical short-sleeved shirts with red palm trees on a white background, and white cotton slacks, and white basket-weave shoes. Phil had no socks on. Except for that, they were dressed like twins. Mario looked as if he'd lost a little more hair and gained a little more weight. He was tan and sleek-looking, but Phil was the gray color of an old ledger book. Linda had her hair tied back with a yellow-and-white polka-dot scarf and was wearing oversized sunglasses with white frames and a pair of lemon-colored shorts over a strapless red bathing suit made of some very tight shiny stuff. It fit her nicely. She had a tan and looked rested, and it appeared she had lost some weight. Something sharp as a blade turned over in me. I realized how long it had been, and suddenly I wanted her.

"How was the flight?"

"Fine. A little rough at first. Nice to step off the plane into all this sunshine. It's been a bear of a winter up north."

Cousin Vito brought me a cold beer and a plate of stone-crab claws and crackers and some mustard sauce to dip the crabmeat in. I ate the crab claws while everybody talked at once. Linda insisted Phil wasn't feeling good. Phil said he was feeling no better or worse than he had for years. Mario said he thought he was a little worse off this winter. Phil gave him a dirty look and told him to shut up. He turned to me with a pleasant smile and asked if I would like to go to the dog track later on.

"Sure. Sounds good. How about you, Linda? You going along?"

"You're kidding. Stand around all night and watch those dogs chase after a wooden rabbit? No way."

When we got home, she was asleep. But the next day we had a chance to talk about it. She said she wasn't ready. Okay, I shrugged. She wasn't ready.

"When are you coming home?"

"I don't know. Come on, you said you wouldn't push me."

"Sorry. You really love it down here, don't you?"

"Yeh, I love it. Daddy could find you a job down here, if you wanted."

"What?"

"I said Daddy could find you a job. He could probably get you a job as a stockbroker. He does a lot of business with one of the companies. The branch manager is a friend of his. We could all live down here. I think he's getting ready to sell out on the Island. He's getting too old for the cold weather and all the worries."

"That's nice, but I'm not exactly ready to retire."

"A stockbroker, I said. I didn't say anything about retirement."

"I'm not a stockbroker. I don't know anything about it."

"You've got a gift of gab. What else do you need?"

We stood there, several feet apart, looking at each other. After a while she shrugged.

"It was just an idea."

"Fine," I said and went upstairs to take a nap.

F i v e

I *WAS* out of town on business a lot that spring. There was plenty to keep me busy, both at home and on the road.

We were still a small outfit. We had resisted adding staff, despite the fast growth of the business. Arthur and I liked the idea of being in on everything—like that old buzzard in Chicago that I'd dealt with in February, nearly to the point of frostbite. Although I liked to think we were more reasonable and fair-minded than he was.

Arthur's father was a kindly old man with a lumpy forehead and a pallid complexion. His eyes swam around like blue amoebas behind the heavily magnified lenses of his glasses. At this point, he was pretty much window dressing. He was hard of hearing. He had tried a hearing aid, but it whistled a lot in various keys when he wore it, and he hated the thing.

He suffered from faint tremors, mostly noticeable in his head and hands. When he looked at you, the slight shake of his head sometimes gave the impression that he was repressing some deep emotion that was just about to boil over into the open. It made you hang on his every word, till you realized he was only talking about the mushroom sauce on the slice of London broil he'd had for lunch the day before, in the Harris Ferry Tavern at the hotel downtown. Sometimes he lurched when he started out to walk, as if he had suction cups attached to the bottom of his shoes. I'd heard Marty Briles, one of our consultants, refer to him under his breath as Mr. Frankenstein. I admit he walked like him a little bit. He was a nice man; mainly he came into the office in order to go somewhere in the mornings. Mrs. Frankenwood had died off some years ago.

Usually he lunched at the Penn Harris with one of his old cronies and then went home in the early afternoon to sleep off the effects of the single bourbon manhattan he allowed himself at lunchtime.

The main burden of running the business had long since devolved on Arthur and me. Besides Marty, we had two other associate consultants on staff—Barry Myers and Tony Shields. We were planning to hire a fourth, maybe even a fifth, if we ever found the time to get around to it. Arthur and I liked the idea of everybody being overworked anyway, and so we weren't moving very fast to do much about it.

One day, about three years previous to this, Arthur had made the mistake of attending one of the luncheon meetings of the Downtown Business and Professional Association. There he contracted a momentary seizure of civic spirit which had ended by causing us no end of trouble ever since.

The luncheon speaker urged those present to do what they could to ease chaos and poverty in the land by hiring the underprivileged. He had several success stories to tell—tales of young blacks and Hispanics on the edge of crime who had turned their lives around and become respectable taxpaying citizens.

Arthur was so moved by the rhetoric that afternoon that at the end of the talk, he rose to his feet and made a little impromptu speech about the special obligations of business to correct social injustice. Before he could clear the room and escape the consequences of his remarks, he had been cornered by the speaker, who happened to be the director of the local Job Corps Training Program. Arthur, with some embarrassment, agreed to consider one of the director's trainees for a vacancy we had in the mail room.

The old fellow with the toothbrush mustache and plaid shirt who had lackadaisically delivered our mail and run our errands for years—one Chester Flanagan by name—had had a second heart attack, which had forced him to start taking his naps at home instead of on the cot in the supply room at the office.

That was how Lionel Nightwine, a young man from the black ghetto bordering North Sixth Street in the city, had come to work in our office in the lily-white suburbs on the opposite shore of the river.

It had not been a particularly successful experiment. Apart from the handful of consultants, our staff consisted mainly of middle-aged suburban ladies who were frightened to death to go shopping in town. I don't know exactly what they thought was going to happen to them over there, but their fear undoubtably was largely racially inspired. Some of them hadn't crossed the river in years.

The ladies were apprehensive when they learned that a black man was going to take Chester's place. Suddenly there was a welling up of deep affection for dear old Chester, who for years had been regarded by everyone as nothing more than a sore tooth in the jawbone of our office politic. There was some vague talk among the women about forming a delegation to lay their grievances before us on the subject, but nothing ever came of it. Arthur was going through a sanctimonious patch and wouldn't have budged anyway. The agency had agreed to offset part of Lionel's salary with some federal grant money. So, besides getting to feel good about himself, Arthur figured we were getting a bargain. When I learned what salary he had hired him for, I told him he ought to be ashamed of himself. It was much less than what Chester had been making. Arthur defended it by saying Chester was "experienced." It took me more than a year to convince him that Lionel was entitled to a halfway decent wage, like anybody else.

In the early days of his employment, Lionel was exuberant and friendly. The women soon got used to seeing him bobbing around the office in his sunglasses, with the handle of his steel comb stuck in one side of his Afro like a metal feather, smiling faintly and singing to himself as he pushed the mail cart and listened by earphones to the portable radio he wore in the breast pocket of his shirt.

We had a policy that all the men on staff had to wear white shirts and ties in the office. This was a copycat notion that Arthur had picked up from IBM. He thought it projected efficiency and was good for business. Lionel complied by wearing short-sleeved shirts summer and winter with a tiny black tie at his neck that looked no wider than a string of spaghetti. He wore no undershirt. The color of his body showed through and darkened the appearance of the shirt considerably. It looked dingy—never crisp and white and efficient, which was what Arthur had had in mind when he had installed his white-shirt-and-tie policy. Although Arthur was a little dismayed by the effect, he never quite got up the courage to suggest that Lionel ought to wear undershirts so that his shirts would look whiter and brighter and more like ours. It was a good thing too. I doubt if Lionel would have taken kindly to the suggestion, although he put up with a lot from us.

He was six feet three, with the broad sinewy shoulders and big arms and tiny waist of a boxer. He was big and black and noisy, full of jokes and bubbly laughter, and most of the time he talked as if he had a mouthful of mush. There was no way we were going to scale him down to our size and make him look and act like just another white man, someone who'd merely had the misfortune of being born with a skin a shade or three darker than the rest of us.

I met him in the washroom one day, early on in his employment. He was bent over the basin, soaping his hands. Just that simple act made the muscles in his arms jump all over the place.

"Where'd you get those arms, Lionel?"

"These? Got these in a warehouse up on Seventh Street."

"You think they have any in white?"

He chuckled.

"No, I don't believe they come in white anymore."

I made my remark with the friendliest of intentions. Afterwards I decided it was as insensitive as some of the slurs I had heard around the office from time to time, such as Marty's affectedly casual reference to him one day as "the company nigger."

When the women found out that he intended to be friendly and harmless, they began to treat him with the vexed good humor they might accord an unruly child whose presence they were obliged to tolerate for the moment. Some of us tried to make him feel at home, but I'm afraid the whole affair was doomed to failure from the start. We were busy. Lionel took time and special consideration. We were low on both commodities.

At first he walked to work, trudging the distance in all kinds of weather from uptown in the city, across the Harvey Taylor Bridge, to the smoky glass box in Bridgeton, where we had our offices, on the opposite side of the river. It was about six miles one way.

Tony Shields lived on the East Shore, out in Lincoln Park.

After a few weeks, it was arranged that Lionel would meet him every morning on the corner of Sixth and McClay. Tony drove him into the office from there. The city bus line was at that time beginning to expand its suburban bus routes. After a few months, he was able to ride the bus back and forth instead of relying on Tony. The arrangement hadn't worked out particularly well anyway, since Tony was often out of town on business.

Once in a while he forgot to tell Lionel his travel schedule. Lionel would wait on the corner for him, sometimes for an hour or longer, before it occurred to him that Tony wasn't going to show up that morning. Then he would start out for the office on foot. He was often a couple of hours late to work. This was very irritating, since a business like ours relied heavily on the mail. Even after he started riding the bus, he was often late. Sometimes he overslept, or the bus broke down, or he made a mistake and got on the wrong one and didn't notice he was headed in the wrong direction for several stops. He called in sick a lot, too. I gathered he led a complicated life.

On the mornings Lionel was late to work, we took Tammy Jean Ray away from the offset press and had her sort and deliver the mail. She didn't like "doing his work for him," as she put it, while falling behind on her own. She grumbled about it a lot, saying nobody had to pick her up every morning in order to make sure she showed up on time.

Tammy Jean was a skinny little square-jawed nineteen-year-old with wiry red hair and freckles. She wore jeans and boots and favored checked shirts and hand-worked leather belts with big buckles. She liked country-and-western music. She couldn't stand the kind of stuff that Lionel played on the big boom box he kept on the bench next to him as he sorted the mail. Unfortunately for her, he used the little pocket

radio with the earphones strictly on mail deliveries around
the office. He was in and out all day long, what with deliver-
ing the mail, running errands around town in the station
wagon, and simply disappearing into certain reaches of the
building where nobody seemed to be able to find him when
he was needed. But whenever he was in the room with her,
he had the big radio blasting away. We couldn't hear it up on
the office level, and so we never gave it any thought. Tammy
Jean did not come to us about her frustrations concerning
the radio, although she complained bitterly to others in the
office. I suppose if she had come to Arthur or me, we would
have rolled dice or drawn cards to see if we ought to tell him
to keep the thing at home.

Tammy Jean lived in a little blue-and-white aluminum
shoe-box-like mobile home with a doorway trimmed and
lighted at night with a string of green and red Christmas
bulbs, beside a muddy creek that kinked through a trailer
park on one of the back roads off Route 83, down in York
County. She had an eighteen-month-old baby girl who had
been born with a heart defect. The doctors said it would
require corrective surgery someday soon. This had spooked
the baby's father, a moody boy by the name of Dean. Dean
had gone off to California on his motorcycle to try his luck
out there. She had tried to find out where he was, to get him
to kick in some support money, but his mother claimed she
knew even less about it than Tammy Jean. Tammy Jean
knew the old sow was lying. But what could she do? She
couldn't very well beat the truth out of her. Although if she
could, it would have made her feel better.

"Sometimes I'd like to taken a tire iron to that woman,"
she told me once. "Justa see if it mightna improved her
looks some."

In the mornings, she had to drop the kid off at the babysitter's, a stout woman named Estelle, who lived right there in the trailer park, with several kids of her own. Sometimes Estelle was sick with her kidneys, or had plans to go shopping at the outlet mall down in Reading, or to run out to Woolworth's, or Korvette's, or something like that. If so, Tammy Jean drove over to Cool Springs and left the baby with her mother. Sometimes her mother couldn't take little Tammy either, because of her bad back, and then Tammy Jean had to find somebody else.

She drove an old unreliable dual-exhaust two-door '63 Ford Fairlane Custom 500. The trunk was so big that you could put a ten-speed bike or even a cello or a bass fiddle in it and still close the lid. It was so rusted out that she'd been forced to fill in all the little holes with body putty "just so's the damn thang'll hold together." The faded blue car, which sagged to one side because the springs were bad, was so peppered all over with gray dots of plastic body filler that she'd nicknamed it Spot. Sometimes when she went out in the mornings, Spot would start, and some mornings it wouldn't. Spot was a persnickety creature with a mind of its own. Sometimes on a cold winter night, old Spot just seemed to expire from frostbite. It wouldn't even let out a whimper when she got in and turned the key the next morning. If it wouldn't start, she'd go over to the neighbor's and make him roll out and hook up his jumper cables from her car to his new Chevy pickup and bring old Spot roaring back to life again.

Despite these complications, she was never late to work: even though she had the sickly kid to worry about, and the unreliable collection of baby-sitters to deal with, and old Spot's personality problems to contend with, and lived twenty-five miles down the road in the puckerbrush, to boot. Tammy Jean said if you had a job, then by damn it was your responsibility to get there on time each and every morning.

"It don't matter if you're black or green," she said. "If you got a job to do, you're supposed to get there on time and do it. None of this wandering in when you will, expecting other folks to cover your butt all the time."

Lionel could expect nothing like sympathy or understanding from that quarter. Tammy Jean was worth her weight in gold and knew it. She was quick and efficient, churning out the considerable number of newsletters we were doing under contract for other organizations, as well as either printing or working with outside printers on our own reports, which were usually complicated by charts and illustrations. She also ordered the office supplies and kept track of the inventory and dealt with any day-to-day problems that came up with the janitorial service that we had out on contract. You couldn't go out every day and find someone who could work as hard and fast as she could and handle such a variety of duties. Lionel, on the other hand, delivered the mail, ran errands in the station wagon, and on occasion lugged heavy boxes around the office. I don't think he understood just how expendable he was.

Lionel's problems seemed to multiply like locusts in a plague year. One night in an uptown bar, he happened to run into his father, whom he hadn't seen in a decade. The reunion was not a happy one. They got into an argument over the elder man's treatment of Lionel's mother and Lionel ended up beating the bejesus out of him and got thrown in jail for his trouble. That night Myron Block, our attorney, and I got out of bed at three in the morning and went into town and bailed him out. A few weeks later, we accompanied him to the hearing before the justice of the peace. But Lionel's father didn't show up, and the charges were dropped.

He was out running some errands for us in the station wagon one day when he decided to swing by for a minute and see Sharmaine, the girl he was interested in. Sharmaine was sixteen and didn't yet have her driver's license. For some reason, Lionel thought she ought to have a quick driving lesson before he got along back to the office. In one of the alleyways uptown, she hit the accelerator instead of the brakes and knocked down, literally, one of the walls of a brick garage.

Fortunately neither one of them was hurt. The car was a total loss, though. We used the insurance money and some funds from the capital equipment account to get a new station wagon. We were due for a new one anyway.

Predictably enough, Sharmaine turned up pregnant and quit school. She said it was his. That was good enough for him. They got married.

That summer she accompanied him to the office picnic, which we held every year at Allenberry, in the pavilion down by the Yellow Breeches.

She turned out to be very shy. She had pretty eyes of a warm amber color. The light shining out of them made them look as soft and gentle as the eyes of a doe. She and Lionel sat at one of the tables closest to the woods. She didn't say much to anybody. She nodded when Lionel introduced us. Then out of shyness, ignored us all, as best she could. She chewed her hot dog and swigged her Coke thoughtfully, swallowed hard, and moodily gazed into the nearby woods, where big leggy rhododendrons grew in wild profusion in the emerald shadows under the pines.

That was the first and last time we ever saw her. A few months later she died, giving birth to Lionel's little boy.

"Imagine a young girl like that, dying in childbirth in this day and age," said Agnes Houser, the bookkeeper, in a tone of shocked disbelief when she heard the news.

She spoke for all of us when she said that. We knew it still

happened sometimes, but none of us had ever known anybody it had happened to, till then. Tony Shields got up a
collection around the office and was able to pass Lionel an
envelope containing about $250, which he said we hoped
would help out some.

Tony and I went to the funeral. It was a very emotional
service. Sharmaine's grandmother, who had raised her,
threw herself on the casket and had to be restrained. The
women wept and screamed, and a few of them fainted. The
minister said he was as puzzled by God's ways as the rest of
us, but we had to learn to carry the burden of suffering in the
name of Jesus Christ. Some people there seemed to find this
message comforting, although I'm damned if I know why.
Lionel sat in the front pew as tall as a tree through all of this
and never showed any emotion at all.

He was a father now, without a wife, but he decided to
raise the child on his own rather than give it up. He had
named the child Harrow. Or Harold—I wasn't sure which. I
tried to get it straight for weeks, but I was never sure which
it was.

"What did you say his name was, Lionel?"

"Harrow, man. I name him Harrow."

"Harold?"

"Yeh, man. Harrow."

"Harrow?"

"Yeh. Harrow."

He frowned.

"What's wrong with you? You starting to get deaf as Mr.
Peckerwood."

He laughed.

"Ain't that right, my man? You starting to go Peckerwood
deaf. Like that old man asleep all de time in his office upstairs."

At least he could still find something to laugh about. So Harrow it was, till someone told me different.

When Linda and I lost our baby, Lionel seemed to think it forged some kind of link between us. I happened to walk in on him in the men's room the following Monday. I knew he was in there, because the mail cart was parked outside with the undelivered mail still in it, even though it was nearly ten-thirty. In fact it was the main reason I went in there—to see if I couldn't get him to speed it up. Arthur had been bitching about him a lot lately. He said if he didn't get his act together pretty soon, we'd have to let him go.

"What's this 'we' stuff?" I had said to him.

"Well—you're part of management too, aren't you?"

Since everybody in theory supposedly reported to both of us, and in actual practice reported to neither of us, I had to admit that, indeed, I was part of the two-headed monster that went by that name around the office. If it really came down to it, we would probably flip a coin to see which one got stuck with the job. Maybe we would draw cards. Or roll dice. Arthur liked to play two-out-of-three. He thought it was more sporting that way. Some of the companies who paid us good money for our advice would have been appalled at the way we ran our own shop. Our practices at best were what you might call informal. We were strong in theory but cowardly in actual practice.

Lionel was leaning over the sink doing a whispered star turn before the mirror, singing to himself, as he nimbly picked at his cloud of wiry hair with his steel comb. The metal teeth plinked musically as they caught in the snarls of his hair. He straightened up when he saw me. He thumbed his sunglasses against his forehead and parted his plum-colored lips in a beautiful smile.

"Hello, Lionel."

"Say, my man."

Then he recollected my trouble. Immediately his face went somber and seemed to smolder with indignation on my behalf.

"I hear it about it, man."

"Well, sometimes—"

He grabbed my hands and interlaced his fingers with mine and raised them over our heads, reminiscent of the kind of affectionate gesture competing athletes sometimes accord each other at the end of a close race in the Olympic Games.

"Bad break, man. I coming to the funeral. I 'member what you did when Sharmaine pass away."

"There's not going to be a funeral, Lionel."

He let go of my hands, and our arms fell to our sides.

"No funeral?"

"No. We decided . . . see, the child was stillborn."

He looked as if he didn't get it. I saw him make a visible effort to shrug off the imponderable ways of the white man.

"I still feel sorry for you, man. Life is such a bag of shit. Lose a member of your family, man. Man, that's worse thing can happen."

"Thanks, Lionel. How are you and Harrow getting along?"

This was my attempt at a diversionary tactic, which turned out to be a little too successful.

Lionel shook his head darkly and pushed his sunglasses back on the bridge of his nose. He had repaired one of the sidepieces with surgical tape. The tape had turned gray and made it look as if a tiny hornet's nest was forming on the plastic by Lionel's temple.

"Shit, man. We got a bunch of problems."

"What's wrong?"

"The landlord trying to kick me 'n' Harrow out of our 'pahtment all de time. He say he gonna call the police and put us on the sidewalk with our furniture."

"Why does he want to kick you out?"

"He say we owe for the rent."

"Do you?"

"Hell, I gonna pay him! But I don't have no money! How can I pay if I don't have no money? He say he can't wait no more."

"How much would you need?"

"Seventy-five will buy that Jew mother till payday."

"Lionel!"

"Sorry, man. Forget myself sometimes."

"You can't go around talking like that. We have Jewish people on the staff. The Frankenwoods are Jewish, for god-sakes. Tony Shields is Jewish too."

"He is?"

He looked surprised.

"Yes, he is. Your friend Tony Shields."

Lionel looked away.

"I ain't got nothing against 'em," he said grudgingly.

"I know, but watch it, will you? People hear you talking like that, it could cost you your job."

"Yeh. Sometimes I forget where I'm at. You understand what I'm sayin'? I get tense with my problems."

I counted out some bills and handed them to him.

"You can pay me back. Twenty a month. Is that okay?"

"That's cool. I don't forget this, man."

"It's all right, Lionel. Now will you do me a favor?"

"What you need, my man?"

"Will you kindly get out of here and deliver the mail?"

He laughed and showed me his beautiful teeth.

"I do that right now, my man."

"Try to stay out of trouble, will you? Arthur's watching you like a hawk. A word to the wise. Okay?"

"I'm on it, man. Like a dog on a meatbone."

To be sure, the job had its moments of exasperation. But it had its peculiar consolations too. I didn't mind sorting through the mean-spirited pettiness and hypocrisy that permeated so much of our relations with each other in the office, as well as with our clients. It seemed necessary, in order to get things done. Accomplishing those tasks, which, among other matters, involved clearing the "deadwood" out of various corporate hallways, seemed important to me then.

I loved the mind-dimming beauty of the work. The problems were so simple in the abstract. Once you had worked them through, the solutions had the formulaic elegance of an algebraic equation.

I just loved it. Just loved to work on the problems. Just loved to write up the reports. I just swarmed all over my work, like a bee on a honeycomb.

Or, as Lionel might put it, like a dog on a meatbone.

S i x

I *WAS* in Atlanta on business during the first week in May. After it was finished, I made arrangements to fly down to Fort Lauderdale and spend a long weekend in Pompano Beach.

It was a soft warm tropical night when I arrived, The breeze ruffled my hair and searched the pockets of my flapping suit jacket as I crossed the tarmac. Cousin Vito was waiting for me by the gate. He was standing in the middle of a short stumpy group of Cuban women. His head and long neck stood out above them like a dried apple on a stick.

As always, he greeted me with a barely contained zany elation, like a young hunting dog out in the field for the first time. He punched me repeatedly in the seam between shoulder and chest where the armbone is closest to the surface, giving his knuckles a little corkscrew twist at the end each time, and asked me over and over again how I was. These subclavian punches hurt and put a little edge on my smile. Besides punching me and asking me how I was, he never knew what else to do or say to me, although he liked me a lot.

Despite my protestations, he insisted on car-

rying my bag to the car for me. He was forty years older than
I was, but he insisted, and I let him, rather than hurt his
feelings.

When I got to the house, Keefer was already in bed.
Someone had told Mario that he made the best margaritas in
southern Florida. He was throwing a little party in the courtyard by the pool to further his reputation in the field.

Linda held her drink away, so she wouldn't spill it, and
pressed her cheek against mine in a sort of distracted greeting full of bird cries of delight. She led me around by the
hand and introduced me to everyone. She was wearing a
gray silk blouse and an off-white nubbly shantung skirt, and
her shiny black hair was done up in a kind of geisha style
that was very attractive. Her rings threw off sparks as she
fluttered her hands about during the animated introductions
she was conducting on my behalf.

"And *guess* who this is! This is Earl! My *husband!* I told
y'all I had one!"

" 'Y'all,' " I said as we moved on to the next group.
"What have you been doing—reading *Gone with the Wind?*"

She laughed and pressed her hand to the gold medallions
glinting in the soft shadows at the opening of her blouse.
The silver and gold hoop bracelets on her slender arms
clinked together expensively.

"Oh my God! Did I really say that? Well, I suppose when
in Rome . . . Marvin, have you met my husband? I actually
do have one, you know."

The lighted pool was crystal-blue, like a giant tourmaline.
She walked me around to the other side, where Phil, looking
very uncomfortable in a tie and dinner jacket, stood in conclave with some of the guests, with a finger inside his shirt
collar in order to give himself some breathing room.

In his other hand, he waved a cigar with a red-hot coal at

the end of it. The men had their heads together, standing as close to him as they dared to, with that hot cigar in his hand. Phil darted glances at his attendant circle out of the sides of his glittery narrow eyes. He was relating some inanity with the air of confiding a valuable secret. He was speaking in a gravelly stage whisper that could be heard ten feet away.

Apparently we came up just as he delivered the punch line. They began to laugh as the circle broke apart to welcome us. One man, with white hair and shiny smooth pink skin like a baby's, threw back his cottony little goatee and showed us the fat underside of his throbbing throat as he crowed like a rooster. Phil shouldered him aside and gave me an embrace, ending with a little arm's-length shake by the shoulders.

"Ur! Where you been? I try to call 'n' tell you to come down last week. Whaddya doin'—out makin' money for Uncle Sam?"

He was smiling but his cheeks were mottled with a hot-looking flush. His eyes were glassy and he looked very tired. He didn't like parties, but he put up with them for the sake of Linda and Mario. They liked to entertain when they were in Florida.

He was glad to see me, but I could tell he was struggling with himself to keep from giving me hell for not coming down more often. He took me by the arm and turned me around.

"See this good-looking man? He's ah my son-in-law. Linda's husband. He's a smart boy, too, eh? Too busy workin' all the time to come see us. Heh-heh."

The jovial man with the goatee turned out to be a federal judge. The short thin dark nervous fellow, who had stepped back into the shadows at our approach and then stepped back into the light again when Phil introduced us, fixed us with a benign expression of penetrating calculation, like that of a savvy old tobacco merchant or cotton broker. His complexion was the sallow color of someone who had worked out of doors for years and now was forced to spend all his time inside. He was angular and sharp-edged, like a piece of sculpture soldered together with steel rods and snippets of tin. He owned orange groves and said he was thinking of buying a newspaper.

Vinny Palumbo was also among Phil's poolside circle of conspirators. He was down to attend to some complicated piece of family business having to do with real estate. He seemed surprised at first, and then inordinately pleased, to see me. He shook my hand and put his arm around me and told me what a long time it had been. I didn't remember that we'd ever been that friendly.

"How's your brother?"

He acted surprised that I remembered he had one. Everything seemed to catch him off balance.

"Oh—fine, thanks. He had a cyst so bad he couldn't sit down. But he's better now."

He gave Linda a kiss on the cheek and held her by the hands as if ready to skip down the length of poolside with her.

"You're looking very elegant tonight."

She bobbed in a mock curtsy.

"Well thank you very much, kind sir."

I met the new neighbors over by the bar, where Cousin Vito and Mario were holding court. Their names were Evita and Armando Goodman. They professed to be dear friends of Linda's.

"What a darling wife you have!"

"Yes! She is so vibrant!"

They said I would never know how delighted they were to meet me at last.

Armando was short and tense and prone to sudden outbursts of false laughter. He had short curly black hair. A luxiurant mustache swept along his cheekbones but didn't quite connect with his sideburns. He stood by his wife's side with the air of a boy going through the agonies of puberty.

She was an artificial but tastefully done blond. She had an exotic Mayan cast to her face, with full lips and a rather fleshy nose and almond-shaped eyes, which she had exaggerated with her eyeliner. She was not pretty in the conventional sense, but she was very striking. She was tall and stood very straight and showed off a lovely pair of breasts. I had the feeling she never forgot where they were. She did her best to make sure that Armando and I didn't either, by contriving to move her torso constantly as she talked, so we could appreciate the architecture from every angle. Armando was just tall enough so that if he stood on tippytoe, he could have hooked his nose in her cleavage.

We were standing by the bar. Armando happened to mention that he had never had a margarita. His family owned vineyards in Chile, he said, and he drank only wine, principally the vintage made and bottled by his family. Mario immediately took away his wineglass and insisted on fixing Armando one of his specialities. At first Armando protested. He held up the palms of his hands, buried his chin in his collar, and shook his head in protest.

"No, no, my friend. I couldn't possibly."

"Try one," said Evita. "Don't be such a piss all your life."

That seemed to settle the matter.

Armando took a cautious sip. He cocked his head and looked at his glass in surprise as if it had a false bottom or a trick compartment.

"Delightful," he said.

He tossed off the rest of it and smiled at us.

"*Magnifico,* my friend. That was like a short vacation."

"Careful," I said. "Those are sneaky."

I think he had two more. Within fifteen minutes he was asleep on the floor at the foot of his wife's chair. She reached down and patted his head.

"Poor Armando's exhausted," she said. "The experiment was too much for him."

She was very good-natured about it. After a while, she stepped over him and left him lying there on the tile floor and came over to me.

"Armando's liable to have a stiff neck in the morning."

"Never mind about Armando, darling. Linda didn't tell us you were such a handsome man. She said you used to be a naughty little boy. You climbed all over the outside of your house at night and spied in the windows to catch your parents making love. Is this true?"

"No. Not much of it. But I did climb on the house."

"Ah, now we're getting someplace! And did you spy on your poor mommy and poppy like that?"

"Yes, but not in the way you mean."

"*Caramba!* You *were* a naughty boy! And what are you now?"

"Pardon me?"

"I said, what are you now? Did you grow up to be a naughty man? Or are you tame, like my sweet Armando, who has two drinks and curls up and sleeps like a big dog at my feet?"

Linda came and rescued me at that point.

"I promise to bring him right back, Evita." She took me by the hand and started to lead me away. "I want him to see Keefer. He looks so cute in his bed tonight."

As we went upstairs I said, "I think she wanted to know if my monkey was at home."

"I know. Did it flatter you? She likes to break in all the new men."

"Well anyway, thanks for the rescue."

"Do you think she's attractive?"

"Attractive? I suppose so. She has sort of a Barrymore profile."

Linda snorted.

"You mean you could use her nose for a bottle opener."

"Yes, I suppose she'd be handy on picnics."

She turned and smiled.

"Don't agree with me so fast. It makes you sound guilty."

I fell into her like a meteor being pulled into the sun. She tasted sweet as a tangerine. I pushed up her dress and pulled down her panties, and not six feet from Keefer's door, we made love against the wall. Or rather we started against the wall. Slowly we slid down and ended in a tangle on the floor.

"Don't roll on me with all that jewelry. You're liable to give me contusions and puncture wounds."

"You silly. You're always so damned silly when you're supposed to be serious."

She covered her mouth with both her hands to keep the sounds from coming out. *Shh-shh!* I whispered in her ear. I think we made a lot of noise anyway. We were very excited. It actually hurt my plumbing a little bit, it had been so long.

Afterwards I said, "I hope you took your PEP pill today."

"My pep pill?"

"Yes, that stands for your Prevent Eventual People pill."

"Yes, I took it okay. I always take it now."

"I hope you haven't had any special reason to take it lately."

"No, I haven't. Not really."

"Not really?"

"I can't say I haven't been tempted. Vinny's been down here on business a couple of times."

"Oh no. Not that greaseball. Were you able to restrain yourself?"

"Would you forgive me if I hadn't?"

"Just say, 'Yes, I was able to restrain myself.' "

"Okay. Yes, I was able to restrain myself."

She thought for a moment.

"The last time I did anything like that was when Arthur and I had a little go of it."

"Really? When did this happen?"

"Oh, years ago. We were still in college. When your father was sick and you went home. Remember? Arthur offered to console me."

"Jesus. My friend, Arthur. Did you let him?"

"Almost. Close enough to feel guilty about it. Arthur said he'd die if I didn't let him."

"But you didn't."

"No. I shook him till he went off in his pants like a bottle of soda pop."

She laughed.

"I think I ruined half a dozen pair of slacks for him. I used to call him old sticky pockets. How is he, anyway?"

"Just the same. He's got some new poor little neurotic tootsie on the string. She lets him tie her to the bed with his neckties. He takes Polaroids of her. He showed me some at the racquet club the other day."

"God, he's weird."

"He keeps his tennis duds and a change of clothes at her place. She takes his tennis shirt to bed with her when he's not there. She says she loves the smell of his body. It really turns her on. She takes the shirt to bed with her so she can smell him in the dark and pretend he's there with her. Arthur was very proud of this when he told me."

"I'll bet he was."

"I asked him if he still had his bicycle. He got that silly little crease between his eyebrows. 'What's that got to do with it?' he said. 'Well,' I said, 'you could save some money and give her the seat for Christmas.' "

"What did he say?"

"He laughed like hell."

We lay there and laughed together on the floor.

"Daddy? Is that you?"

For a moment we were stunned.

"Just a minute, son. We'll be right in."

We scrambled to our feet and straightened our clothes. Linda shoved her panties down the front of her dress. Her mouth quickly skated over my face. In the process she pinched my lower lip with her tiny white teeth till my eyes watered. Then she slipped off to the bathroom and I went in to see him.

He was so happy to see me. "Dad! Dad!" he kept saying as if he couldn't believe it. He stood up on the bed and hugged me. I settled him down again. Linda came in and stood by the doorway with her arms folded and watched us, with just the faint wick of a smile on her face. I made Bah Bear do a dance on his chest and sing a few lines of "Don Gato":

> "*Oh, Señor Don Gato was a cat,*
> *On a high red roof Don Gato sat.*"

Out in the hallway she whispered, "Do you think he heard us?"

"No, I don't think so."

Just as we got to the top of the stairs, I heard him cry out jubilantly.

"Dad!"

"What is it, son?"

"How do you get love out of your body?"

We looked at each other.

"I don't know, son. How?"

"By kissing!"

"Okay, son. Settle down now and go to sleep."

We started down the stairs.

"I think he heard us," she said.

I shook my head.

"Not a chance," I said.

Seven

DURING the last weekend in June, the hardware dealers met in Atlantic City. We'd done a lot of work for them over the years. I went down to talk to the executive committee about doing some more.

At one of the cocktail parties, I met a pleasant young woman from Thailand. She told me that she now lived in Austin, Texas. I believe she worked in some capacity for the hardware association down there, but I never really got that straight.

Much of the time it was hard for me to understand what she was saying. She spoke in many different musical registers in order to make up for her difficulties with the language.

When I told her my name was Earl, she tilted her little cat-shaped face, pursed her lips, and blew it back to me in two notes as through a bamboo flute.

"Er-roo?"

I was utterly charmed.

"Er-roo? Is'n tha' awry?"

It certainly was. It always had been awry. Never quite the name I deserved. I wanted something better. Something altogether my own, instead of the leftover middle part of

Jack's name. In one of her weaker or more bitter moments, I don't know which, Nola had named me after him. It was a family secret. One I'm reluctant to reveal even now. I didn't discover it myself till I went to school and on the first day the teacher inadvertently called me by his name. In doing the paperwork, Nola had been obliged to cough it up, but she spoke to the school that afternoon, and I was never asked to answer to that name again.

It was a taboo subject at home. Nobody (only two alive still knew the awful secret: Nola and Linda) ever had the bad taste or termerity to link me with such certainty to my father by labeling me a Jack or—worse yet—a Junior. Certainly Jack hadn't been tempted. He had acted insulted when Nola told him she'd named a baby after him. Even Richie didn't violate the taboo, and he never played fair about anything. I know it seems impossible, but it leads me to wonder if he ever knew about it.

It is always an act of aggression to name a child after his father. Always a mistake, a curse, a misfortune. No innocent child ought to be treated that way: held up like a faint carbon copy of the original, if the father is admired and successful; or shrunk from in horror, if the father turns out a bull maverick.

But this little Thai woman, in the low-cut organdy cocktail dress, with the lovely freckles on her bosom, made the leftover fragment of my secondhand name as suitable-sounding to my ears as ever it had been, by immediately transfiguring it into the sweet fluty idiom that the mourning doves in the trees around my house used for calling to each other in the dark treetops at dusk and again in the early mornings.

Her name was Umporn. I said I was utterly charmed. I won't make a long story of it. I took her to dinner. After much conversation and wine, I took her to bed.

We woke early in the morning. Both of us wanted to prolong our pleasant time together. It was one of those twenty-four-hour love affairs that make you feel as though you're in the movies. We knew it wasn't real. But it was so nice neither of us wanted to end it right away.

I proposed we put on our swimsuits and go out and wade in the ocean. We could hold hands and feel the delicious chill of sea air and salt water on our bodies. We could watch the day strengthen on the beach for a few minutes. Then we would come back and have breakfast in my room.

She thought it was a wonderful idea. She went to her room to put on her bathing suit. I was to meet her in the lobby in fifteen minutes. It gave me just enough time to change and call home.

Yesterday, I had told Linda that I might be able to make it home that night. I said I couldn't be sure. It depended on business. She said in that case she wouldn't look for me. That's the way we'd left it. I thought I'd better check in with her again.

"So it ran longer than you expected," she said.

"That's right. Everybody talks too much at these meetings. We have another one this morning. I ought to be out of here by noon anyway."

"Drive carefully."

"Thanks, I will."

I told her I'd call again if there was another delay. I said I didn't think I'd need to stay down another night. She said she was happy for that.

She and Keefer had been home for three weeks. Without her saying so, I knew she was already bored with the routine.

I didn't know whether she and Vinny had been fooling around down in Florida or not. I wasn't sure. I wasn't even sure that I wanted to know. Maybe she had just cried on his shoulder—wetted his shirt with her tears till some of his chest hair showed through the fabric, like that time Mario had sopped his shirt front as he cried by his dying mother's bedside.

I wasn't particularly disturbed to find out about her and Arthur. After all, whatever had happened had happened long ago when we were all just kids. The way she told it, it sounded pretty ridiculous anyway.

Had anything been going on down in Florida, Phil would have known about it. It bothered me to think he would allow something like that to go on under his nose. It wasn't like him. Maybe he was tired of listening to her complain about me. Maybe he figured if she was going to divorce me, she might as well marry one of her own kind next time.

Whether serious or not both revelations, made to me while we lay tangled together like a pair of snakes on the floor only a few feet from Keefer's door, had had their disquieting effect.

They left me feeling—friendless. I don't know how else to put it. I suddenly realized nobody was left that I could trust. I don't know why it gave me such a jolt. It was something I should have known before. I suppose I had never thought about it. I suppose I thought there would always be somebody I could turn to, tell my troubles to, if I ever felt the need. Not that I had any appetite for that. But after Florida, I realized it wasn't even an option. It knocked me back a step or two.

That's how Linda found me when she came home. She thought I was mad at her. That my long silences were meant to be punishing or accusatory. But that wasn't what I was up to. The truth was, I was just feeling bad. That's all. Just down. But it certainly didn't help things between us. Her nerves were raw and close to the surface. She was like a person with a bad sunburn. You get irritable with people you feel you've wronged. Maybe she had a bad conscience.

Or maybe it aggravated her to feel compelled to sit around and wait for Keefer to grow up, so we could settle up and go our separate ways. I don't know what the problem was exactly. But whatever it was, it was just a variation of the usual one.

Marilyn told me I'd done the thing with Umporn to get even. I said I hadn't. I said it had just been an accident. Something that happened. I wasn't out for revenge. She said maybe that's what I thought. But probably the truth was that I'd done it because I was hurt. I said I didn't think so.

"Sometimes you're like your mother," she said. "You're good at hiding your motives from yourself. You're so numbed over, sometimes you don't know *what* you feel."

She was taking graduate courses in psychology at the time, so I was obliged to put up with a little of this kind of talk once in a while.

I went down and met Umporn and we walked down a flight of stairs and through the hotel tunnel which ran under the boardwalk out onto the beach.

The water wasn't as cold as we had expected. Pretty soon we were up to our necks in it, bobbing up and down on the waves, playing games with each other. She was only a little thing, but she had a beautiful body. I took her out where we could have some privacy. She had to dog-paddle to keep her chin above water. She took off the bottom of her suit and I took off my trunks and handed them to her. I smoothed my hands against her snowy thighs and slipped my cold fingers inside her. Despite the frigid water I felt myself getting hard. Her legs levitated buoyantly. She locked her feet around the small of my back. Her head went back. She closed her eyes and smiled as her long black hair spread in S-curves on the water. I drew her closer. I tried to get her seated on me. Even though I was partly anesthetized by the cold water, we managed it after a while. It wasn't much fun at first. I danced

back against the tide and pulled her closer. Gradually everything began to improve.

Over her shoulder I saw a tow-headed boy on a yellow
inner tube paddling towards us through the rise and fall of
the gentle swell. I stopped. When I did, she raised her head
out of the water to see what the matter was.

"Oh-oh. What we do now, Er-roo?"

"Nothing to worry about. It'll be all right."

"Quick now! Bettah tacky you pahts!"

She handed them to me in an underwater pass.

"Bettah I get in mine too!"

She struggled like a puppy in my arms, but the water was
too deep for her.

"Just wait a minute. He'll go away. Then I'll get you in a
little closer and you'll be able to get them on all right."

"Hokay."

Our heads bobbed like seabirds above the sawtoothed
waves. We watched the kid methodically paddle towards us,
looking up urgently between seas, to see if we were still
there.

I wasn't worried. In fact I thought it was funny. I thought
we were perfectly safe. The water was loaded with sediment
and fairly opaque. But she lowered herself a few more inches
into the water, till it slopped greedily about her chin and
lips.

"Don't worry so much."

"I no whurry wi' you, Er-roo."

Doggedly the kid paddled closer. He kept looking at us as
if he had something important to tell us, if only he could get
close enough. He had water goggles on and a big head like a
baby bird. The goggles were the funny ones, sort of like the
kind the old-time aviators wore, with round raised lenses
framed in bottle-cap metal and fixed in a strap of black
rubber with a buckle at the back of his head.

I let him get within a few yards.

Then I said, "Hello, son."

"Hullo."

He looked at me gravely. I thought he looked disappointed, as if we weren't the people he thought we were after all.

"Kind of deep out here for you, isn't it?"

He decided not to answer this. He didn't bother with me. He gave Umporn a final long last look as though giving up on her, rotated his inner tube, and sulkily began paddling for shore.

"Er-roo?"

"Yes?"

"Bahd news."

"Why, what's wrong?"

"I think I lose my pahts."

"You lost your pants?"

She bobbed her head. It was wet and dark and sleek as a sea otter's.

"I get ah-fraid when little boy come. I try get in. But ah—drop in watah."

"I'm sure they're around here somewhere. Let me get you in closer to shore where you can stand up comfortably. I'll put my trunks on and look for them."

"Hokay."

I felt around on the bottom with my feet. I looked all around, thinking they might be floating on the surface. I dove several times. I covered a pretty big area. I came up with a handful of kelp once, but no suit.

"Oh boy. Plenty trouble now."

"I wish we'd brought some towels along. I could wrap you up in one of those."

"What we do now, Er-roo?"

"I'll go up to the room and get my robe. You just wait for me. I'll be back in a minute."

"I sorry, Er-roo. You don't like me now, I bet."

"It's all right. Actually it's kind of funny. It'll give us something to giggle about at breakfast. You stay right here. I'll be right back."

"Hokay. Er-roo?"

"What?"

"I trusteen you."

I laughed.

"Don't worry, Umporn. I won't leave you out here without any pants."

"You bettah not!"

"I'll be right back."

"I ah waiting for you."

I waved when I got to the tunnel. She was just a dot in the surf. She didn't wave back. I'm sure she didn't see me. The sun was higher in the sky. More people were on the beach, more of them in the water. But she was easy to spot. She was bobbing in the waves a little off to the left of the lifeguard tower which lined up with the entrance to the tunnel leading to the hotel.

I hurried into the dank tunnel and came out into the sudden sunlit quietude of the hotel gardens. I went up the walk lined with sparse coarse grass and beds of barberry and mugho pines and cypress and some kind of tall ornamental grass with feathery tufts. The air smelled good, mixed with the strong clean scent of the midget pines and the faint peppery smell of damp sand. I went in the side door and mounted the stairs two at a time and crossed the lobby to the elevators. I pushed the button repeatedly, but I had to wait. It took a long time. The water ran off my suit and down my legs and made a little puddle on the marble floor at my feet.

When I got to my room, I had trouble with my key. I'd had trouble with it ever since I'd checked in. It didn't seem to want to work the lock. I fiddled with it till I lost my temper and began to swear to myself. I was about to go in search of the chambermaid when the lock finally relented and the door flew open so suddenly that I nearly fell full-length into the foyer. All it needed was somebody to swear at it a little bit.

I got the robe out of the closet and hurried back to the elevators. I had to wait again. Everybody was going down to breakfast or to meetings. The damn things were slow to begin with. It seemed like a long time. But really only ten minutes or so had passed since I had left her in the surf.

I was really anxious. When I reached the sunny gardens again I broke into a trot, passing with hollow footfalls through the cold dark tunnel out onto the warm sand. The lifeguard tower clicked rapidly into full scale as I ran down the beach carrying the robe. More people were in the water now. The surf had picked up a little in the few minutes I was gone.

I looked around for her, but I didn't see her. She wasn't where she was supposed to be. She wasn't to the left of the tower anymore. She was a little thing. Several bathers were in the surf in the same vicinity where she should have been, and I thought maybe I just hadn't spotted her yet.

I ran all the way down to the edge of the water. Still I didn't see her. I cupped a hand over my eyes against the sun. I looked back to make sure I was lined up with the right chair. It was number three, the right one.

I draped the robe over my shoulders and waded out into the surf about waist-deep. Kids and some older people were milling around in the water near me obstructing my view. I still saw no sign of her. I began to feel a tinge of panic. I looked around for the boy with the yellow inner tube. Maybe he would know where she was. But I couldn't find him either.

I walked up and down the length of the beach. I went into the water in line with every lifeguard's chair, just to make sure I hadn't somehow gotten the number wrong. Even though I knew it was the one lined up with the hotel tunnel.

Finally I had to go to the lifeguard.

"Pardon me."

He leaned down from his tower. He was muscular and very young and blond with an orangy look to his tan and a dab of white ointment on his nose. His bathing suit was about the size of a jockstrap. He was wearing a white pith helmet and a shiny metal whistle on a cord around his neck. The lenses of his sunglasses were black and opaque as a blind man's.

"Yeh, can I help you, mister?"

"I'm looking for a young lady. An oriental? Kind of short. She was standing over there in the water just a few minutes ago. You didn't happen to see her come out, did you?"

He was very polite about it.

"I don't keep track of the individuals, sir. We gotta keep the whole picture in front of us—you know? There's a pretty good riptide out there this morning."

"I think we may have a problem."

"What kinda problem?"

"I'm not sure. But she was supposed to wait for me right there."

"Maybe she got tired of waitin'."

"I don't think so."

He looked at me.

"See, the fact is, she didn't have any pants on. She lost them. I went up to the room to get this robe for her to put on—"

He stood up and blew his whistle.

"Hey, Gerald!"

He gestured to an older, patchily tanned man on the porch of the lifeguard shack up the beach. Gerald immediately started down off the porch toward us.

"You gotta talk to Gerald about this."

"Who's Gerald?"

"He's the captain. He handles the complicated ones."

I told my story to Gerald. His blue eyes twinkled tolerantly as I went through it. At the end he smiled as if he had just gotten the joke.

"She probably didn't lose them at all. She's probably back in her room at the hotel right now having a good laugh."

"No, Gerald. She lost them all right."

"How do you know for sure?"

"Because."

"Because?"

"Because we were fooling around."

"Fooling around?"

"Yes. Fooling around. You understand what I mean, Gerald?"

He blinked.

"Oh yeh, right. Now I get it."

"So she didn't have any pants on, Gerald. She got nervous when a little boy came too close. That's when she dropped them."

"Maybe she found them again when you went off."

"I don't think so—do you?"

Gerald scratched his whiskers.

"I guess not. Maybe we better talk to Macky."

"Who's Macky?"

"He's with the police. You sure of this story?"

"It really happened, Gerald."

"Okay," he said with a sigh. "Let's go see Macky."

Farther up the beach we found Macky sitting in a black-and-white cruiser.

Gerald and I sat in the backseat while I told my story again.

Macky wanted to know her name. I told him.

"She Japanese? Korean?"

"No. Thai. She's from Thailand. I don't have a last name. We didn't get around to that. But it might be American. I think she said she'd been married to an engineer. I think that's how she ended up in Texas."

"And you met this girl where?"

"Last night at a cocktail party in the hotel."

I told him the rest of it. When I finished, he suggested we drive over to the police station and continue the discussion there.

"You really think that's necessary?"

"Yes sir. We'll need a statement. It won't take long."

We went over to the station, which was three blocks back from the beach. I told my woeful tale to a Sergeant Mulholland. After I was finished, he seemed to want to hear it all over again.

"You say she was registered in the same hotel?"

"I think so."

"You sure she wasn't a prostitute?"

"No, no. I told you before. There was no money involved."

"But you bought her dinner, did you?"

"Yes, I bought her dinner and a few drinks. That was it."

"And then you took her back to your room?"

"Yes."

"And then what happened?"

"Look, do I have to go through all this again? I was supposed to leave this morning. My wife will be worried."

"Would you like to give her a call?"

"What I would like is to get out of here."

Mulholland pursed his lips thoughtfully.

"You didn't hurt this girl, did you, Mr. Dimes?"

"What?"

"I said, you didn't hurt this girl, did you?"

He was giving me his professional deadpan look. I suppose he'd learned it at the police academy.

"Listen," I said. "I came to you, remember? I reported this because I think she's missing. I didn't do anything to her. If I had, do you think I would come to you?"

"Some people do, sir."

"Well, I'm not one of them. May I go back to my hotel now? I've really got to get home."

"Sure. I'll have Officer Macky give you a ride over. Sorry to keep you so long."

"Forget it. Will you kindly have somebody call me when you find out something? This thing has me upset."

Mulholland lowered his eyes and pursed his lips again.

"We'll certainly let you know. Soon as we know something. Thanks for coming in."

When I got to my room, I called Linda. It was after two o'clock. I explained I'd been delayed because a woman had disappeared in the surf.

"You?" she said. "What happened? Why are you involved?"

"Because I saw it. Or at least I think I did. One second she was there, the next second she was gone. The lifeguards didn't see anything. I was the only one who saw it. I just finished telling my story to the cops."

"You sound shaken."

"I am shaken. I think she probably drowned. I'll be out of here as soon as I can check out and get the car out of valet parking."

I drove across the marshlands toward Philadelphia. I got on the turnpike and started west through the rolling countryside. The sight of the stone farmhouses and the dip and rise of white board fences along the edges of the neat green fields and the pretty sight of sleek horses with nicely curried manes and fat haunches in the pastures helped to smooth me down. The long drive home gave me plenty of time to think about it. I couldn't get it out of my mind.

Poor girl. She probably had gone out a little deeper. Nervous about being caught. Maybe a wave knocked her over. Likely she couldn't even swim. I felt terrible about it. Just terrible.

When I got home, Linda wanted to know the details. She gave me a little time first. I went upstairs and took a nap. But when I came downstairs and the three of us sat down in the kitchen to a dinner of waffles and bacon, one of Keefer's favorite meals, she wanted to know all about it.

I could see she had her antennae up. She had that curiously calm manner that some women affect when they suspect their husbands of funny business. I tried to get out of telling her. I felt awful. I didn't want to talk about it. The other thing was, I didn't want to have to lie through my teeth.

"You really think this a topic for the dinner table?"

"I'm just interested to know what happened."

Keefer was sucked right in by this, only he genuinely wanted to know the grisly details.

"You really saw someone drown-ded? Stevie Dietz saw a police diver pull a lady out of the river. He said an eel wiggled out of a hole in her stomach and jumped into the water."

"Keefer! That's enough of that talk."

"I'm only saying what Stevie said."

"Well, can it. I don't like it."

"Right. Put a lid on it, Keef. You know how squeamish your father is."

"Geez. Other people get to say anything they want around here. I don't know why I can't."

"Because you're a very short person. When you get taller, you can say what you want."

She turned back to me.

"What happened?"

There was no getting out of it.

I'd gone down for a swim. I noticed this oriental woman in the surf not too far away from me. I noticed her because she was so short. She was in pretty deep water. She didn't seem very sure of herself. She looked like a nonswimmer to me. I looked away. A pretty good wave came along. It just about knocked me over. When I looked back, she was gone. She couldn't have gotten out of the water that fast. She was just gone. I looked all around for her. When I couldn't find her, I went to the lifeguard. That was it; that was my story.

Linda lit a cigarette and blew the smoke down the front of her blouse. She looked up at me and picked a piece of tobacco off her tongue.

"Was she pretty?"

I knew I was in trouble. I couldn't figure out how she'd caught on to me so fast. I decided to play for time. I thought maybe indignation would work.

"What kind of a question is that? I see a woman drown. And you want to know if she was *pretty?*"

She picked up her plate of waffles and hit me with it.

"Have some more," she said. She pushed my plate off the side of the table. I'd just finished putting the syrup on. It landed upside down in my lap.

"You'd better fill up," she said. "Because it'll be your last meal around here."

"Hey, you guys."

Keefer's eyes were going fast back and forth between us as if watching a tennis match.

"You fucked her, didn't you?"

"Linda—what the hell—"

"You fucked her. She called here about an hour ago. She said she'd tried to reach you at your hotel. But you'd checked out. Something about some friends coming along. Finding her. What did you do to her? Where did you leave her? I couldn't understand half of what she said. She talked like goddam Charlie Chan. 'I solly. I no know he mahrried.' I said, that's all right. Forget about it. Go have yourself a fortune cookie."

"Keefer, you'd better go out and play."

"No. Let him stay. Let him find out what a big prick his father is. Going out of town on business trips. Fucking everybody he can lay his hands on."

"Don't talk that way in front of him."

"I'll talk any goddam way I please. Here, have some syrup on your waffles."

She started to pour the pitcher of syrup into my lap. I took it away from her. She reached around and grabbed the telephone book off the counter and smacked me alongside the head with it. I grabbed her by the front of the blouse and picked her up out of her seat and drove her against the kitchen wall.

"Don't hurt her, Dad!"

He had a piece of waffle on his fork. His face was streaming with tears. It was all scrunched up like a little old man's.

Her eyes darted from side to side, looking into mine. Excited, as if dealing with a dangerous and unpredictable lover.

"Go ahead. Hit me. I'll tell Daddy. He'll goddam have you killed. If he doesn't, I will."

I turned her around and grabbed her by the scruff of the neck and the seat of her pants and ran her out of the kitchen into the dining room. I gave her a shove and let go. She stumbled against the table and fell down on the rug. I went back into the kitchen.

"Get out!"

I heard a crash. She'd pulled the tablecloth off the table and a vase of flowers came down with it.

"Get out! Get out!"

Keefer sat there with his fork in the air staring at me. I extracted a piece of waffle from the placket of my shirt and set it on the table. I could hear her screaming and tearing the drapes down at the dining-room windows.

"I've got to go, son."

"Why's she so mad? What did you do?"

"Listen, Keefer. No matter what happens, I want you to remember that I love you. Okay? I'll see you in a couple of days."

"Are you going?"

I gave him a kiss on the head.

"Yes. Just for a couple days. Don't worry. I'll see you in a couple of days."

Linda came back into the room and swept the dishes off the drainboard by the kitchen sink. I started for the door.

Keefer cried out.

"Dad!"

Just that one syllable, in fright and bewilderment. It damned nearly broke my heart. But for everybody's sake, I thought I'd better keep moving.

E i g h t

I *WAS* in the driveway, about to get in my car. The windows were open and I could hear her raving like a madwoman upstairs, followed everywhere by Keefer's wailing. Doors and drawers opened and closed with sounds like pistol shots.

My clothes started flying out the windows.

Suits, shirts, socks, sweaters, underwear tumbled down on the azaleas and rhododendrons below. Some things snagged on the branches of the dogwoods, making it look as if we'd hung out a line of washing in the front yard.

The hard stuff followed—shoes, bottles of shaving lotion, my tennis racquet. It had no real pattern, of course. Soft stuff was mixed in with it, too. A can of shaving cream followed by a pair of socks. I wasn't anxious to get in there and start pulling my shirts and underwear off the bushes and trees till most of the hard stuff was out of the way. I kept a jar of pennies at the bottom of my closet. I didn't want to get in there and get cold-cocked by that. There was no sense in getting killed over this.

Finally the jar of pennies flew out and

smashed in the periwinkle at the base of the shrubbery. I took that as my signal. I got the suitcases down from the overhead storage in the garage and began to pick my clothes off the bushes and the trees.

I had to leave some of my underpants dangling from the higher branches. I wasn't going to shinny up a tree in a three-hundred-dollar suit to retrieve a two-dollar pair of underpants. Three hundred dollars was a lot to pay for a suit in those days. Sending it to the dry cleaners to get the syrup off my fly was one thing. But splitting out the seat of my pants or tearing out the sleeve of my suitcoat or even falling out of a tree and breaking my neck was quite another. Besides, I was in a hurry. I wanted to get out of there before she took it into her head to come out and start beating me about the head and shoulders with the telephone book in front of the neighbors. I didn't want to play the fool in front of anybody who might be watching me out his window for any longer than was absolutely necessary.

I stuffed into the bags what I could reach on the trees and bushes and grabbed my suits and whatever else I could find on the ground (including my Rolex, which I never wore on trips and which she'd thrown out, box and all; I found *that* under one of the azalea bushes) and threw everything into the trunk of my Delta 88 and got out of there.

I stopped for a few drinks at one of the expensive local watering holes along the river. If I kept my coat buttoned when I walked in, I didn't think anybody would notice the syrup on my pants. Besides, I needed a few moments in a nice quiet bar to gather my thoughts. I thought I ought to give myself more time for collecting them than I'd allowed for collecting my underwear and socks. A martini or two, I decided, might serve as an aid to clarify and soothe my mind.

I was glad Umporn was still among the living. But I had mixed feelings the way I'd found out about it. I wondered how she'd got my number. Then I remembered giving her my card at the cocktail party, early on, when I was trying to impress her. On it was printed:

EARL DIMES
Executive Vice President
Frankenwood & Son, Inc.
Consultants to Business and Government

It had the number for the office as well as my number at home.

Doubtless she was busy calling my room while I was at the police station telling Mulholland my sad story. Friends. Friends had found her, Linda said. They probably had a towel or a beach robe with them. It was as simple as that. If I remembered right, she had told me she was going to New York for the rest of the week. Probably she had called the house from there, as soon as she arrived at her hotel. Concerned that I'd be worried. Why in hell hadn't she just left me a note at the desk in Atlantic City?

I sorry, Er-roo. You don't like me now, I bet.

They used big olives in their martinis. Not the usual soggy little bar olives you find around everywhere. When I was in town I always stopped in this place for that reason. I fingered one of them (I always asked them to put in two) out of my drink, popped it into my cheek, and sucked on it suspiciously. Somewhere I'd read recently that they'd begun to stuff olives with artificial pimiento in order to cut down on the costs. I always looked forward to the olives in my martinis. But ever since I'd read the article, I could never eat one without a sense of grievance. I sucked on my olive and considered how everything in general was going to hell in a hand basket.

I sorry, Er-roo. You don't like me now, I bet.

You're right. I don't like you. The tariff is altogether too damned expensive. I'm glad you're not dead. But I wish to hell I'd never met you. In a few days I suppose Linda will calm down. We'll talk this over like reasonable people. But whatever happens, it'll never be the same again. Not that it was that great to begin with. Still, I can't blame it on you. I didn't have to find those damned freckles so attractive.

I took a good pull on my drink.

Cheer up, I thought. You're not dead yet.

I bought a newspaper. I went down the road to one of the best restaurants in town for dinner. I thought I saw the maitre d' glance dubiously at my trousers when he seated me but to hell with him. I was going to have a nice meal even if I choked on it. I didn't intend to suffer over this any more than I had to.

When I came out again, a hatch had come off the river. The car was covered with little pale-bodied nymphs or may-flies or whatever they're called, and it was starting to get dark.

Instead of buying a book and getting a room at a motel, I decided to go over to Nola's and ask if I could park myself in her spare room till I worked things out between Linda and me.

What possessed me to do this, when going to Nola's was always a bad idea, I can't say. But that's what I did. I suppose the naturally depressive effect of the drinks and my sumptuous repast was making me feel sorry for myself. I must have been looking for sympathy. Although why I thought I'd find any at her house is another one of those mysteries about myself that I'll never solve.

The place looked dark and deserted as usual when I pulled in the drive. I was sure she was at home. She never went anywhere anymore after dark. It bothered her eyes to drive at night.

I went up the dark walk. I rang the bell. Nothing. Through the heavy curtain at the door, I couldn't make out if there was a light on in there or not. I couldn't hear the TV set either, although she always kept the sound on low and mainly seemed to use the light from the thing as a way of finding her way around in the dark. I rang the bell again.

I thought maybe it was broken. It would be like her to have a doorbell that didn't work.

I tried the screen door. It was locked. I rang again. I was about to start hammering on the doorframe to see if that might work when I heard Tito begin to bark halfheartedly.

It took her a long time to get to the door. Without opening it or turning on the outside light, she spoke in a high thin querulous voice through the wood in what sounded like a mixture of fear and exasperation.

"Who is it?" she asked in that voice which suggested she'd rather not know.

"It's Earl, Ma."

An incredulous pause followed.

"Who?"

"For Christ's sake, Ma! Open up!"

Bolts shot back and chains rattled feverishly. I stood waiting in the darkness. She had the place locked up like a fortress. Finally the door opened a crack.

"Early? Is that really you?"

"Yes, Ma. It's really me."

"What are you doing here at this hour?"

"Linda threw me out. Can I come in?"

"But Tito and I are leaving for Maine in the morning. We have a cottage all rented and everything."

"I know. I won't screw up your plans. I promise. Will you kindly unlock the screen door, please?"

She did so with a good deal of reluctance. I entered the dim and doggy-smelling hallway, put my bag on the carpet, and gave her a peck on the cheek. It was plain she wasn't especially pleased to see me. She was still worried that I was going to mess up her plans.

"What a surprise," she said without particular enthusiasm.

"See? It's really me. It's not the bogeyman after all."

"She kicked you out? What did you do? No. Don't tell me. I don't want to know. You're too much like your father. Besides, I never liked her anyway. She always treated me as if I had leprosy or something. I don't think I've been in your house ten times since you got married. What are you going to do now? I hope you're not going to leave your child in the care of that woman and her family. Oh—her father!" She shuddered. "What's that horrible man's name?"

"Phil. Can we go into the living room and turn on a light? I'd like to sit down. This thing has me worn out."

"I'm sorry. I didn't mean to keep you standing in the hall. Do you want a cup of tea or anything? I can't offer you much. There's nothing in the refrigerator except a little dog food and some canned milk for my coffee in the morning."

We settled in the chairs by the fireplace.

I said, "It's possible this thing might blow over in a few days. Do you mind if I stay here in the meantime?"

"But I've already told you, I'm going to Maine. I always go to Maine at the end of June. You know that."

"If you give me a key, I'll just stay till I'm able to work something out. I won't make a mess. I'll leave everything just as I find it. In fact, probably better. You know I'm a pretty good housekeeper."

Tito backed into my legs for some attention. I leaned down and scratched him along the spine. He smelled awful. He looked over his shoulder at me with what can only be described as a smile on his face. He wriggled his little stump tail for all he was worth, humping his back voluptuously as I patted him. Finally he sank in satiated ecstasy onto my feet and out of reach of my fingers.

"I only have one key. I gave the extra to Mrs. Blondell. She said she'd look after my cactus while I'm away."

"I can get it from her and return it when I leave."

"Oh."

She seemed surprised by the simplicity of this solution.

"Well . . . that sounds all right, I suppose. Provided you don't lose it out of town somewhere on one of your trips around the world."

"I won't lose it."

"Would you like a cup of tea now? I wish I'd saved you a tollhouse cookie. Tito ate the last one just a few minutes ago for his bedtime snack."

"A cup of tea sounds fine."

She was gone a long time. It always took her a long time to prepare anything. I remembered the air of bafflement with which she confronted the kitchen in the mornings when I was a kid, as if overwhelmed by the idea of preparing breakfast. We had all ended up making our own meals, doing our own laundry, making shift on our own. It had turned out to be good training for later on. Linda wasn't much for housekeeping either. They were so different. Yet in many ways, they were so alike. Which was likely the reason they didn't get along.

I bent down and patted the dog again for something to do.

His tongue hung out of his mouth like a piece of boiled ham.

"You poor thing. Doesn't your mother ever give you a bath?"

For an answer he sat up and breathed in my face. He nudged my hand with a nose as dry as a piece of cork.

"God, what a nasty fish breath you have, little dog."

Finally she came back with my cup of tea.

"What a time for this to happen. What's that on your pants?"

"I spilled a little syrup on them. Don't worry, I won't louse things up for you."

"I'm not worried about that. I just feel bad about leaving you."

"That's all right. I'm a big boy now."

"The cottage is all rented and everything."

"I know. Stop worrying about it."

The dog leaned against my legs as I drank my tea. Likely I would have had to send my suit to the cleaners anyway to get the smell of the dog out. I put down my cup and bent to him again.

"Here, let's have a look at you, silly."

I pried his mouth open and looked down his throat. I saw a glob of white behind his tonsil.

"Have you had him to the vet's lately?"

"Why?"

"He's got some kind of a growth in his throat. Maybe that's why his breath stinks so bad."

"What? Where?"

"I'll show you, if you come over here."

She rose from her chair with a sigh and came over to my side.

"What do you want me to see?"

"See this?"

I held his jaws open. Deep in the back of his throat on the left side was the wet glimmer of a small white mass.

"See that white glob behind his tonsil?"

"Well, no. Honestly I can't see anything."

She began to pet him lavishly.

"Are you Mommy's good boy? Yes, you are, sweet little doggums."

"Look again," I said.

She had gotten him excited and I had to hold him down.

"Look in there. Can't you see it? Christ, it's about the size of a golf ball."

"I'm sorry. I don't see anything."

"Put on your glasses."

"Well, I suppose I could do that. If I could find them. Everything has me in a dither tonight. You didn't see where I put them, did you?"

"No, I didn't."

"Well, I'll need them." Her voice became high and plaintive. "I won't be able to see to drive tomorrow without them. I had them just a minute ago—"

"Forget it. Just take my word for it. He's got some kind of a growth in his throat. He ought to go to the vet."

"But we're leaving tomorrow. I can't do that till we get back. Can I, baby dog?"

The dog gladdened his eyes and wiggled his backside as she talked to him, but stayed where he was.

"Why don't you take him to a vet in Maine? There's probably one in Bath or Brunswick."

"Oh, I couldn't do that. Dr. Perlmutter is his doctor. I couldn't take him to some stranger."

"Well, you do as you think is right. But I don't think you can afford to fool around with this. By the time you get through messing around, he could be dead."

She sat back with a shocked expression on her face.

"How can you talk that way? It's bad luck to talk like that. What are you trying to do—frighten me?"

"Ma."

"What?"

"Cut the histrionics. Take your dog to the vet."

"Well . . . I suppose I could. If I ever get a minute. I had hoped to go up there and relax a little. Now I have you and the dog to worry about. I suppose the Wilhides will know of somebody."

She put her hands on her knees and bent forward and spoke to the dog again.

"Do you want to go to the doctor's? No, no. Of course not. Going to the doctor's isn't any fun, is it?"

Tito polished my shoes with his backside as she fussed over him in that special wheedling voice she used for talking to him. She kept it up for so long that he finally decided it was worth his while to get off his can and go over to her. She kissed his nose and laid his gray velvety muzzle against her cheek and patted him elaborately as a reward. Although how she could stand to kiss and hug the poor smelly thing I couldn't say.

Shortly thereafter she went into the hall and called Mrs. Blondell on the telephone to say that I would be picking up the key in the morning.

"I didn't know he was coming either," she said in a low confidential tone. "He just broke up with his wife. Children: you never know what kind of heartache they'll bring you next."

Shortly afterwards she went to bed. She apologized. She said she hoped I wouldn't think she was rude, but she was very tired and needed her rest. She thought probably the excitement of my unexpected visit had something to do with

it. And of course she had that long trip to begin in the
morning. She was going as far as New Haven to stay overnight with some friends. Nevertheless, just the thought of
two days on the road and a trip of nearly six hundred miles
was enough to wear a body thin.

"Stop talking. Go to bed. It's okay. Really. I'm going to
turn in myself in a few minutes."

"Well . . . all right, then. Good night, dear boy. I feel so
sorry for your troubles."

This expression of pity annoyed me more than I can say.
Even allowing that I had come looking for something very
like it, it always bothered me whenever she affected concern
for me. It always seemed so artificial and forced. Yet pity
was probably the deepest emotion she had left to give to
anyone. She had loved Jack to distraction, till he had
smashed her heart repeatedly. She remembered her parents
with great reverence. She had certainly loved Richie. She
had fussed over a series of fawning neurotic animals. But for
the most part, she was done with deep emotion. It cost too
damned much. It was a young person's game—all that hysteria and messiness, involving helpless feelings of depen-
dency. These days, when moved by the difficulties of people
she liked, or thought she ought to like, she doled out drib-
bets of pity like small gifts of money. Hoping it would do, so
she could be left alone and undisturbed by deeper tremors.
After what she'd gone through with Jack and Richie, I
couldn't blame her. All she wanted now was peace and quiet
and sufficient income to spend her summers in Maine.

But I couldn't accept her niggardly little gift of sympathy
with anything like good grace. It was such a cheap coin. I
pushed it away almost before I knew what I was doing.

"Don't waste your time feeling sorry for me. I'm sure
everything will work out for the best."

She stiffened slightly as the warning tone in my words registered.

"I certainly hope so, for your sake. I hate to see another Dimes make a mess of his life. Come, Tito. Time for bed."

The dog struggled to his legs and gamely trailed after her.

I was glad to be left alone. Our conversation had produced an unsettling effect on me. I could never talk to her without feeling a certain amount of agitation. She always irritated me. I wasn't sure why. I wanted to sit there and relax for a few moments and pretend she didn't exist.

I finished my tea. I carried my bags back to the makeshift guest room off the kitchen. I began clearing the junk off the bed—boxes full of receipts and various worthless documents; piles of washed but unfolded clothes. The room was furnished with a few pieces of the big dark furniture left over from the old house. It was too big for the room, which was small, even tiny. The clearance between the bureau and the bed was less than a foot. I pulled down the bedspread and discovered there were no sheets on the mattress. I had no idea where she kept the linens. To hell with it, I thought. I can sleep without sheets for one night.

I unlocked the window and tried to pry it open. It was stuck, swollen shut with humidity and long disuse. Tito's odor was strong in the room. I had an idea I had appropriated his sleeping quarters. I balled up the smelly bedspread and threw it into the corner. I lay back on the bed. A spring twanged like an untuned guitar string. I turned over and bumped my knees against the big bureau which towered over the bed. A film of cold perspiration popped out on my forehead. I can't sleep in here, I thought. I'll suffocate to death.

But I was too tired to move.

Don't be a baby. What do you care where you sleep, or

what size the room is, or what it smells like, or whether you can get the window open or not?

But I did care—about all of it. I was already beginning to miss my own bed badly. It was king-size, with a firm mattress and a soft blanket on it that I liked to pull up to my chin even on hot nights. Linda used to make fun about how I always needed my blanky about me. At home there was a good light to read by on the nightstand beside the bed. This room had nothing but a dim overhead fixture. Damn the way she lives, I thought.

Gradually a sweet heaviness stole into my limbs. The drowsier I got, the less the size and smell of the room mattered. I was grateful that at least this was not going to be one of my nights of insomnia, although even at best it always took me a long time to fall asleep. But at last I did, still fully dressed, lying on a diagonal across the striped ticking of the mattress with my shoes still on and my feet still on the floor in the little allotment of space between the bed and the bureau.

When I woke in the morning, my legs were asleep up to my hips and Nola and the dog were gone. It took me a while before I got the circulation moving in them again and could stand up. I scratched my belly and wandered into the kitchen. I thought maybe she'd left me a little coffee. Instead I found half a dozen dirty cups glued to the kitchen counter. I was surprised that a hardened ring of coffee could have that much adhesive power. They must have been sitting there for weeks.

When I opened the refrigerator, dust balls shot out from under the door and danced across the floor. I discovered the milk was sour when I poured some of it into my instant coffee. There was no orange juice or grapefruit juice. Only some prune juice that was so thickened with age that it gagged me when I tried a sip of it. I spat it into the sink. I gave up on any attempt at breakfast altogether when I found one of Tito's gray hairs clinging to the yolk of my fried egg as I transferred it on the spatula from the frying pan to my plate.

I decided to scrape the half-eaten crater of hardened dog food from Tito's bowl on the floor by the sink before doing the dishes. Apparently she never washed his dish, but just kept refilling it over and over again. Layer on layer of food had hardened on the sides like plastic wood and had reduced the usable diameter of the dish by about fifty percent. I found I couldn't pry the dried glop off with a tablespoon. I considered attacking it with a knife. Only then did it occur to me to hold it under the hot-water tap till the stuff softened up.

You really have a lot of Nola in you, I thought. You always try everything the hard way first.

The flow of hot water released a smell almost as nauseating as the dog itself. I asked myself again how anybody could live this way.

At last I got it clean and stuck it out of sight in the cabinet under the sink. I covered the bottom of the sink with a little hot water and scrubbed it clean. Then refilled it, put the dishes in, and squeezed the last little bit of detergent out of the plastic dispenser which sat on the windowsill.

I looked all over the place for some more dish detergent. There wasn't any. Instead I found a pail of garbage, the source of the faint non-dog-related smell that had been troubling me since I had begun my work at the sink. I carried the pail at arm's length, holding my breath all the way, to the big garbage can she kept at the bottom of the stairs off the back porch.

It was stuffed full. It smelled worse than the pail I'd just removed from the kitchen. Evidently she had let it go till it had gotten too heavy for her to carry out to the curb. I wondered how long she intended to let it sit there before she asked me to come over and take it out to the street for her.

I'd had enough for one morning. I dropped the pail next to the big can. I fled back up the steps into the house. To hell with it, I decided. I'll deal with it later.

I couldn't bring myself to take a shower till I used some bathroom cleanser to scrub off a little of the mildew on the tiles and grotting around the bathtub. It seemed everything I attempted in that house opened up a Pandora's box of filth and disorder.

I should have laughed it off. But the truth was, it disturbed me all out of proportion. It reminded me too much of my dreary childhood—all the disarray and dust and dirt and dim lighting and general household malaise that had pervaded our miserable incarceration together as a family. I couldn't wait to grow up and get out. That morning, in the grip of a grisly recapitulation of those old adolescent loathings, I couldn't wait to get dressed and get out of there, either.

I called Florence to let her know I was running late.

"Mr. Frankenwood has been asking for you all morning. We've had some trouble here."

"What happened?"

"I'm afraid Lionel tried to strangle Tammy Jean."

"Good God," I said. "I'll be right there."

N i n e

THE office was in turmoil when I arrived. Margaret was not at the reception desk and the switchboard was ringing.

"Will someone please get that?" I said in a large voice as I crossed the lobby toward the elevator.

The door leading to the general office area opened. Margaret skittered for the switchboard with a simpering smile on her face, her high heels clacking with a lot of self-important noise on the tile floor. In the lightning flash of the open doorway, I saw a knot of anxious white faces hovering above Agnes Houser's desk. Agnes was of Pennsylvania Dutch stock—stolid, reliable, grimly unflappable. The other women always flocked around her in times of crisis.

The men were gathered in Marty Briles's office. Tony was leaning back in his chair uncomfortably, with one leg wrapped like a vine around the other, nervously biting his nails. Barry stood by the bookcase lighting his pipe. His bald head had a solemn jesuitical air about it. When I passed the door, he kept his eyes lowered as a precaution against anybody seeing into his soul that morning. But Marty looked up and smiled cherubically, which convinced me he'd been about the devil's work. We could always count on him to make a bad situation worse. He had a gift for rumor and innuendo unsurpassed even by some of the people we did business with in Washington.

Only Florence seemed unaffected by the general stir in the office. She was at her desk, typing up the notes I'd given her for a report on a visit to a client in Cincinnati the week before. She looked up from her work, nodded as if to say, "Ah, there you are," and smiled sweetly.

"He's waiting for you," she said.

I opened the door to Arthur's office. He had swiveled his chair around in order to look out the window. His elbows rested on the credenza behind his desk, his knuckles were buried in his long pale cheeks. His dark melancholy eyes gazed down the long expanse of green lawn, past the picnic benches we'd had set out under the locust trees for the employees (which nobody ever used), at the sight of the slow brown ugly river at the foot of our property. He had the tragic air of a man who'd rather be at home, taking pictures of somebody tied to the bed.

It was his morning to play tennis at the club. He was still in his tennis whites. Apparently he'd got the call about Lionel and Tammy Jean while still on the court. A magnifying glass and one of the leather-bound volumes of his stamp collection lay open on his desk. He kept it in the safe in his office and took it out to look at in times of crisis. He'd been collecting since he was a kid. He told me once that it was worth upwards of half a million dollars.

He swiveled around and beamed.

"Thank God you finally made it. I was afraid I was going to have to go through this on my own."

His reddish mustache positively brightened at the sight of me. It was much lighter than the color of his thinning dark hair, which I often accused him of dyeing. I used to tell him that the dye on his mustache didn't match the dye on his head. I told him he ought to mix up one big batch of the stuff in a bucket and dunk his head in it. That way, I said, he'd get the color of his hair and mustache to match, plus a nice little tan to boot.

Arthur was subject to mood swings. I kidded him a lot to keep him loosened up. I ragged him regularly about his string of girlfriends. I said he used mud packs at night to keep that youthful look. I told him he was the only the man I knew who was six feet three and found it necessary to wear elevator shoes. I claimed he wore panty hose under his tennis shorts so his legs would look nice. I jabbed him all the time, and he loved it. He told me once that some days he didn't "feel real" unless I poked fun at him. I'd been accommodating him for years in that respect. I'd found it also made good business sense.

When he fell into one of his abysmal passages of helpless melancholy, he wouldn't come near the office for weeks. He canceled his trips and appointments and stayed home; and as a consequence, business suffered. He insisted on signing all the paychecks himself. When he was in one of these moods, it sometimes resulted in delays. Once he was signing them in the bathroom at home and accidentally dropped them all in the toilet. Agnes had to write a whole new batch that time. But he was very bright and got on famously with his clients. When he was in his manic phase, nobody could keep up with him. He could work twenty hours a day for weeks at a time.

I was concerned how the Lionel–Tammy Jean crisis would affect him in the long run. When it was all over, I'd have to let him take me out to the club and beat me silly at tennis. That always seemed to cheer him up.

"I thought you might not show," he said. "You know . . . what with all the trouble you're having at home and all."

"She called you."

He nodded his head. It was little for his size. It looked even littler since he'd taken to having it closely trimmed, now that his hair was beginning to thin. His orange mustache prickled like a fuzzy caterpillar as he stretched his rubbery face in a grimace of commiseration.

"Last night," he said. "Melody and I had been asleep for an hour. Suddenly the phone rang. It was Linda, raving like a maniac."

Melody was a redheaded hairdresser of considerable reputation around town. She'd been rumored to have gone down on a state senator during a late-night dinner party at one of the local restaurants. She did him up while he affected nonchalance and hummed and looked around at the other diners and up at the ceiling and fought with himself to keep from stuffing the tablecloth in his mouth so he wouldn't start howling at the moon outside the window. She'd been his girlfriend away from home for a couple of sessions of the legislature, but lately had taken up with Arthur.

Shortly after the beginning of this affair, Arthur had dragged me out to dinner to meet her. She was just what I'd expected: attractive, even pretty, in a cheap flashy way. It was the senator, she told me, who had developed in her a taste for Dom Pérignon. She shrugged and gave me a fetching little pout of her wet-looking lips. She snuggled against Arthur.

"Now I can't drink anything else, can I, Frankie-poo?"

All Arthur's girls called him Frankie. Frankie-poo was something new, however.

He set her up in her own business downtown in a place called Tresses. He wanted me to get all my haircuts there. I said no thanks. I didn't want to come home smelling like a whorehouse. The woman must have bathed every morning in Shalimar.

"Wonderful," I said. "She called you."

"She certainly did. She also called Dad. She said she thought we ought to know what you really did on business trips. She said you were a bad boy at the beach." He grinned. "Were you a bad boy?"

"It's too complicated to go into."

"I don't believe it. Nice little Early boy turns bad in middle age. Will wonders never cease. You think this blowup is permanent?"

"I don't know. I'm going to give her a couple of days to cool off."

"Well, try to get her to stop calling people. She's not handling this in what I would call a discreet manner."

"You know Linda. She couldn't give a damn what other people think."

"You don't have any client lists lying around the house, do you?"

"No, I don't think so. Why?"

"She might take it into her head to start calling them."

"Jesus, you think so?"

"Why not? You'd better get her under control in a hurry."

"Right. How do I do that?"

"Threaten her, what else? Have the telephone disconnected. Turn off the water. Whatever it takes."

"That's easy for you to say."

"Well, you'd better do something, before this gets out of control."

"I'll give it some thought."

"Are you ready for this morning's real problem?"

"Lionel and Tammy Jean."

"Right."

"What happened?"

"We have to get rid of that crazy son of a bitch. He grabbed her by the throat. Backed her up against the paper cutter. He said he'd cut her head off if she ever gave him any more shit. When she came in here she was trembling all over. Although I don't think she was scared so much as good and mad. She said if we didn't do something about it, she was going to go home and tell her new boyfriend and he would."

"What started it?"

"What?"

"I said what started it?"

"I don't know. They were sorting the mail. Or rather she was sorting it and he was jiving around, listening to the tunes on his boom box. She got exasperated and called him a name. No doubt one that was accurate. That's when he grabbed her."

"What did she call him?"

"What does it matter? He *assaulted* her, for godsakes! The guy's got to go."

"Where is she now?"

"I sent her home, gave her the rest of the day off. I told her we'd handle it. We can't afford to lose her. If we lost her, we'd be up the creek."

"Don't you think we ought to find out how this happened? What if she laid some racist epithet on him? Are we going to let her get away with that?"

"We told him if anybody gave him any trouble, he should come to us. You told him that, didn't you? Wasn't that the text of one of your recent pep talks?"

"Yes, it was."

"Well, he didn't. Instead he dragged her around the room and threatened to cut her head off. We've got to can him. I called the police. They're sending somebody over."

"You called the police? What for? Is she pressing charges?"

"I don't think pressing charges is something that would occur to Miss Tammy Jean, the raccoon queen. Her idea of due process would be to salt your backside with a load of number-six birdshot. No, I just want a cop here when we go downstairs and tell him he's through. I don't want that jerk to grab me by the throat."

There was a discreet knock at the door. It opened just wide enough so that Florence could thrust her tidy gray head through the opening.

"Officer Shuey is in the lobby, Mr. Frankenwood."

"Thanks, Florence. Tell him we'll be right down."

He turned to me again.

"You in on this? Technically he works for you."

"Sure, I suppose so. Poor guy. I feel sorry for him."

"Save it. He's been nothing but trouble since we hired him."

"Correction. Since *you* hired him."

"Okay, so rub it in. I made a mistake. Did you ever make a mistake? You want to flip for this?"

"No thanks."

"I didn't think you would. You have no sporting blood at all."

We took the elevator to the lobby and introduced ourselves to Officer Shuey. He was a burly, grandfatherly-looking man with a pleasant expression on his face and a pair of blue eyes which matched the color of his shirt. He was standing by one of the potted ficuses making notes with a pencil stub in a small grubby pad and looked up with his mouth open when we stepped off the elevator. He shook hands briskly, moving from foot to foot the way someone might who comes to your door on a cold winter morning, only it was the first of July. His big rough hand made me feel ashamed of my small soft one. He was dressed in a light-blue short-sleeved shirt with a black tie which matched his pocket flaps and epaulets. His shiny trousers were black too. Except for the wide heavy gun belt strapped below his belly, he might have been a bus driver. His hat was under his arm. He had a big round head and a brown wrinkled face like a fisherman's. He wore his graying blond hair in a crewcut. He glowed rosily with apparent good health and had a bustling way about him even when he stood still.

He frowned and wetted his pencil with the tip of his tongue and hugely scrawled a few words in his pad as Arthur briefly explained the situation.

Arthur finished by saying, "We're going to have to fire this young man, officer. Normally in a situation like this we would tell the person he was through and he would leave. But we don't know what to expect with this guy. He's violent. He thinks hitting people solves problems. He beat up his father once. We had to bail him out of jail that time. Remember, Earl?"

Although it was hardly the right characterization, I didn't think it was the time to argue about the details.

"Now he's gone after one of our girls. Choked her, threatened her. So we have to fire him. Obviously he has a violent nature. We don't know how he'll react. So we'd like you to come along to the mail room while we tell him. Okay?"

Officer Shuey adjusted his gun belt, scratched his cheek, and grimly considered the matter.

"I guess I could do that."

"Thanks very much. It'll be a big help to us."

"Arthur, are you sure we have all the facts?"

He turned to me impatiently.

"What do you think we should do? Wait till he kills somebody? Come on, let's get it over with."

We took the elevator down to the basement level and walked down the hall to the double doors of the mail room. Outside the doors, we could hear the rhythmic threshing of the offset press, accompanied by the driving beat of music from Lionel's big radio. He carried it blaring on his shoulder in and out of the building, morning and night. I sidled up to the doors and peeked through one of the porthole windows. I saw the radio on the bench by the pigeonholes, but no sign of Lionel.

"I can't see him. I guess he's still in there."

"He's in there all right," Arthur said. "He's been skulking down here all morning. Didn't even try to make amends by getting the mail delivered."

"Maybe you gentlemen should go in first," said Officer Shuey. "Then I'll kinda, you know, back you up if there's any trouble."

"Excellent idea."

Arthur looked at me.

"You probably ought to go in first. You're the one with the special relationship."

"Right. Let him nail me."

"Okay, chicken. I'll go first."

"Never mind, I'll do it."

"This is ridiculous. What are we arguing for? Officer Shuey ought to go in first."

He smiled confidently at Shuey. Shuey blinked his shirt-blue eyes as if to say: *Who, me?*

"See, he might hit one of us over the head and talk later. But one look at your uniform . . ." Arthur looked him up and down in apparent admiration. "That ought to make him think twice before he starts anything."

"He's probably right," I said. "You're the authority figure. You probably ought to go in first."

Shuey looked dubious.

"What is this guy? A nut case?"

"No, no. He's got a little bit of a temper, that's all."

"Maybe he's a tad crazy," I said.

"What—are you crazy? He's not crazy."

"Is he armed or something?"

"Look," said Arthur. "The guy's a mail clerk. He's not a psychopath, for godsakes. All you have to do is go in there and tell him you're a policeman."

"That's it. Just go in there and show him your badge."

Arthur's expression warned me to behave myself.

"Really, he's not a bad guy. When he sees your uniform, I'm sure he'll calm down and listen to reason."

"Okay," Shuey said. "I'll go in there. Then you guys come in."

"Right. Go in there and tell him you're a policeman."

"Will you shut up? This is serious."

"You have to admit it's pretty bizarre."

"Later with that stuff. Are you ready, officer?"

Shuey nodded. He adjusted his gun belt, straightened his hat, and pushed open one of the swinging doors. The sound of the radio flared and fell back as the door swung shut behind him.

Through the door we heard Lionel say, "What you want, pig?"

"I'm a policeman . . ." faltered Shuey.

We pushed open the doors and stepped into the room like a pair of gunfighters entering a saloon.

Lionel's nostrils flared at the sight of us. Then his eyes

narrowed as he realized the full extent of the conspiracy against him. He smiled at me bitterly.

"You call the cops on me, my man?"

"Lionel—"

"You call this fucking pig, my man?"

"Calm down, Lionel."

Lionel turned on the cop.

"You going to 'rest me, chicken fat? Come on, do your stuff. Come over here 'n' 'rest me."

He picked up a hammer from the work table and planted his feet wide apart. He showed his white teeth. He was all muscle and sinew and looked about seven feet tall.

"Come on, my man. Do your bidness."

"Now son . . . no sense making this any worse than it is—"

"Lionel, you're fired," I said. "I'm sorry, but you're fired."

"*Fired!* You fire me 'cause that white bitch call me a dumb nigger again!"

"No. I'm firing you because you grabbed her by the throat and threatened to kill her."

"Kill her! I didn't threaten to kill her! She lying at you, man. Can't you see that?"

"It doesn't matter, Lionel. We can't have this going on in the office."

"It don't matter? Why am I fired, if it don't matter?"

"Because you can't go around choking people."

"Somebody lie and you fire me 'cause they white."

"That's absolute crap and you know it."

"She call me a dumb nigger to my face, man! What was I suppose to do?"

"You were supposed to come to me."

"Shit-shit. I ain't no pussy. I handle it my own self. That's de way it is."

"Sorry. This isn't the Wild West. I warned you to watch yourself. We bent over backwards for you. But this was the last straw."

"Last straw, huh? What's me 'n' Harrow going to do now?"

"I don't know. I'm sorry it came to this."

"They's after me now, people at the Welfare. They trying' take Harrow away from me, say I ain't fit for a daddy. Now I got no job."

"Sorry. I wish things were different."

Suddenly he winged the hammer across the room. It hit the metal door of the supply cabinet with a loud crash. All three of us jumped straight up in the air. Shuey reflexively went for his pistol, then hestitated, with his hand still on the pistol grip.

"That's right, pig. Shoot me."

Lionel turned away from Shuey and glared at me.

"I'm telling you something, my man. I'm making you a promise. If I lose Harrow 'cause of you, I gonna make you pay. You hear, my man? I fix you good for it."

"Don't make any fast moves," said Shuey.

"Fas' moves. What you talkin' about, pig?"

"Get out, Lionel. Take your things and go."

"I'll get. But I don't stay got. This pig ain't going to be around all the time with his fast moves. Is you, pig?"

He picked up the blaring radio. He paused again, staring long and menacingly at me. He looked at Arthur.

"How come you so quiet, big man?"

"I'm an observer, Lionel. Just making sure office policy is carried out."

"Office policy, huh? Shit. Peckerwood policy, that's what."

He flashed his teeth at me and stage-whispered:

"You 'member what I say."

He hoisted the radio to his shoulder. With slow arrogant deliberateness he strutted to the door and slammed it shut behind him. For an instant we heard the loud throbbing of his radio in the passageway outside. The music ceased abruptly and he was gone, as if he and the radio had disappeared in a puff of smoke.

Arthur looked worried.

"You think he might try anything? You know, like come around the house at night? Maybe we ought to hire a security agency for a few weeks."

"Don't worry, Arthur. He won't hurt you. Get a big dog. Chain Melody in the front yard."

He doubled over. My jokes sometimes affected him like an attack of appendicitis. I figured I was on a roll.

"Is that a real shine? Or are they the plastic shoes you ordered through *Popular Mechanics?* Don't they make your feet sweat?"

He straightened up and gave me an affectionate shake by the arm.

"Good old Early boy. Where would I be without you?"

T e n

THE smell of the ghastly old dog assailed me that night as I swung open the door to Nola's house. I stepped into the dark hallway. As I did, I experienced a hot stinging sensation on my shins and ankles. I thought it was circulatory; a nervous reaction of some kind. Later that night, when I peeled off my socks in the little guest room, I discovered that my shins and ankles were dotted with a dozen or so itchy dime-sized welts.

A rash, I thought, scratching myself. A nervous eczema, brought on by the mere thought of crossing the threshold and entering my mother's dismal house.

Every night, on stepping into the hallway, I had a repeat episode. I began to think I really *was* having some kind of psychoneurotic reaction to the filthy place. At bedtime, I would see that the rash had spread some more.

It took me three days to figure out the real answer—three days longer than it should have. When Tito went north with his mistress, scores of fleas had been left behind in the carpet.

In the evening, the frantic little creatures swarmed into the hallway to welcome me home.

They pounced up my pant legs, biting my ankles through the thickness of my socks, stinging me to the height of my kneecaps.

On the night I finally figured it out, I had stopped at the liquor store on my way home to buy myself a bottle of Tanqueray. I wanted to get into bed with a little gin to keep me company as I read *Keys of the Kingdom*. It was one of the few novels left on Nola's bookshelves. In the main, they were given over to volumes of inspirational poetry and treatises by Rabindranath Tagore, Lin Yutang, Kahlil Gibran, H. A. Overstreet, and others of that variety who had been popular thirty or more years ago. I don't believe she had bought a book in all that time. Certainly not a good novel. I didn't think Linda would let me back in the house to get at any of my own books. She hadn't as yet thought to throw them out of the window, so I couldn't go over there and collect them out of the front yard, as I had my shirts and underwear.

I was going through another one of my bouts of insomnia. I desperately needed something good to read.

We had talked several times by telephone. Talking only made the situation worse. She didn't want to talk anymore. She told me if I wanted to talk, I should do it through her attorney, Clyde Swink.

I knew Clyde. He was the best divorce man in town, albeit a regular grease gun. Nobody liked to do business with Clyde. He made you feel like burning the sheets and showering with a Brillo pad afterwards. He was the kind who left spots on the wallpaper when he sat in a chair and leaned his head back. But he was good, no question. She told me I couldn't see Keefer again till we worked out at least some tentative agreement through Swink.

It looked like that might take some time. In a word, she wanted everything: the house and all the furniture; the stocks and bonds; a paid-up membership in the country club of her choice; half my income till Keefer got his Ph.D. or reached his thirtieth birthday, whichever came last; plus a million-dollar insurance policy on my life, should I try to get out of the arrangement by up and dying on her.

Under the circumstances, I thought a little gin was in order that night.

I was lying there, propped up on my pillows, sipping the gin straight, without ice, out of a coffee mug, and wallowing in A. J. Cronin's prose, when something bit me hard in the armpit.

I extracted a little black dot that seemed to be the source of the offense and examined it. It made me sit up in bed fast when I realized what it was. I cracked it between my finger-nails and combed through the bed for more. A dozen or so had found their way into the sheets with me. I killed them all.

Fine, I thought. Isn't this just fine.

It was nearly two in the morning. Still, I was tempted to give Nola a call at the cottage and tell her just what I thought of her and her dog, but I didn't.

By seven o'clock that morning, I was on an airplane bound for Memphis, Tennessee. At one o'clock that after-noon, I was due to present recommendations for a new salary administration program to an affable group of bright young men and women who were busily squandering their lives and energy on behalf of a midsize company down there in-volved in the manufacture of filtering devices for air condi-tioners and furnaces. It was a job that would keep me in a nice clean flea-free environment for at least three nights running.

I thought they might all starve to death by the time I got back. I was dog-tired when I got in from the airport at about eight-thirty. Curiously, I had forgotten all about the fleas. The only thing on my mind was a good night's sleep. I was so exhausted that it didn't seem possible anything so trifling as insomnia could keep me awake that night.

When I stepped into the hallway, I experienced the now familiar hot stinging sensation, as if the veins and arteries from my knees on down had suddenly been bathed with a warm acid infusion of blood.

I don't know what I said. I shouted some horrible epithet at the ceiling. I remember throwing my suitcase across the living room.

Still muttering imprecations to myself, I retrieved my bag and got out of there. I went directly to the local Marriott and checked in. No more nights of martyrdom in Nola's house. At least not till I had it fumigated.

In the morning, after a sleepless night, I went back over to the house and left the key in the mailbox.

When I got to the office, I called the exterminators. I told them I'd pay them twice what they usually got if they would go to the house that day and rid me of those damned fleas. The man I talked to—one Boyd Coolidge by name—enthusiastically agreed to do just that.

That night when I got back to the house I stood in the hallway and savored the difference. No hot stinging sensation. The fleas were gone. A masked trace of what smelled like a powerful chemical hung on the air but was hardly noticeable. I inhaled what, for all I knew, was a poisonous draft of cancer-causing pesticide and smiled with satisfaction at the ceiling. Lord, Lord. What a pleasure. If only to have beaten back a minor pestilence for just a few days.

It turned out to be my only triumph of the summer.

After weeks of futility, which involved calling my house from various locations around the country and being hung

up on each time by Linda, I gave in and hired Lloyd
Schwanger, an attorney every bit as greasy as Clyde Swink
himself. Within twenty-four hours, I had access to Keefer
again. Linda agreed he could stay with me for the weekend.
She called it a gesture of "good faith"; but I knew the only
reason she agreed to it was that Schwanger had somehow put
the squeeze on through Swink.

I arrived early to see if she would talk to me—at least
stand in the doorway and talk to me. I thought if we could
talk, we could save a lot of time, money, and grief. It was
even possible we might work out a reconciliation, if only for
Keefer's sake. I didn't quite realize that it was over. I was
thinking what a horrible effect a broken home would have on
him. I didn't really care much about her feelings—or my
own, for that matter. She was a bad habit I was used to. I was
willing to put up with her, for his sake. I wanted him to be
happy. I didn't want him to replicate my unhappy childhood.
Obviously, I wasn't using my head.

When she opened the door, she said, "You're fifteen minutes early."

"I know. I wanted to talk to you."

"If you have anything to say to me, tell your lawyer. Get
off my porch. Get your car out of my driveway too. You can
wait at the curb till it's time to collect him."

"Linda."

"What?"

"How long is this going to go on?"

"How long is what going to go on?"

"I mean, aren't we ever going to give it another try?"

She looked as if I'd taken leave of my senses.

"You must be kidding. I'm relieved to have you out of the
house. The only time I miss you is Thursday night at six
o'clock when it's time to take the garbage cans down to the

curb. This has been a time of revelation for me. I finally found out what's been wrong with me for the last fifteen years. It's just this simple: I'm tired of living with a sneaky dick like you. I want honest people around me. People who want to have a good time. People who live at home during the week instead of in hotel rooms in Kansas City and Detroit. I want people in my life who want to do something besides read books. Or sneak around on the side. Goddammit, I want some *fun* out of life for a change!"

She slammed the door in my face. I stood there for a moment, staring at the brass knocker with my initial pretentiously engraved on it in Olde English script. Then, considerably shaken, I groped my way back to the Olds and backed it down the driveway and waited meekly at the curb for the fifteen minutes to be up.

When it was time, I started up the driveway—rather I began to totter up the drive, feeling as though I'd aged a year for every minute that had passed.

I looked at my house with its nice yard, its freshly painted shutters, the dogwoods near the front porch. For the first time I knew I would never see the inside of it again. We would probably have to sell it and give the money to those craphouse rats we'd hired to do our wrangling for us. I nearly swooned at the prospect. What would happen to everything? What would happen to my books and records? What about the stereo and the TV? What about my new speakers? Everything we'd done, everything we'd assembled so carefully over the years, was now about to be changed into nickels and dimes on the dollar and scattered to the wind.

Under the pressure of these thoughts I wobbled, but did not fall, in the middle of the driveway. The front door opened. An invisible hand pushed Keefer, clutching Bah

Bear, out onto the porch, along with a shopping bag holding his pajamas and a change of underwear. The door closed against his fanny, nudging him forward like an encouraging hand. The paper bag fell over. Out fell his pajamas with pictures of airplanes all over them onto the flagstones. I righted the bag and stuffed the pajamas back in. I picked him up and kissed both him and his bear. I set him down on his legs again and patted him on the head. I didn't trust myself to say anything. It was as if it were the first time I'd seen him in fifteen years. I knew what I was feeling was ridiculous—a mixture of love and outrage, a sense of injustice and deprivation all out of proportion to my actual grievances—so I kept my mouth shut and took him by the hand and led him down the driveway to my car.

We were quiet on the drive back to Nola's. We kept counsel with our private thoughts for most of the trip. Finally he broke the silence.

"Are you ever coming back to live with us?"

I decided to fake it. I was still operating under the delusion it was he, and not myself, that I was trying to protect.

"I don't know, son. Your mother and I still have to talk about that. I don't think we've really decided anything as yet."

"She's really mad at you."

"I know."

"If you don't come back, will you get your own house?"

"Well, I suppose so. Probably an apartment."

"Will I come and visit?"

"You certainly will."

"And maybe you'll get a dog? So I can play with him when I come over?"

I was offended by his sudden tone of enthusiasm.

"Well . . . a dog, you know . . . that really presents a

problem. I'm away a lot on business. You know that."

I hated the look of disappointment on his face.

"Nobody would be around to take care of it. I don't see how I could do it, Keefer."

"Aw gee. That's what I wanted for my birthday. I always wanted a dog. Mom says I can't have one."

"Well, don't get discouraged yet. Maybe we can work something out."

"What do you mean?"

Hope kindled in his voice again.

I had no idea what I meant. I had only intended to soften the blow a little.

"I don't know exactly. I'll talk to your mother about it. Maybe she'll change her mind. It'd be a lot easier for you guys to have a dog. She's home all day. The two of you could take care of it together."

"Yeh! That's what I told her!"

"I'll talk to her about it, see what she says."

"Would you, Dad? Thanks a lot!"

I knew I shouldn't have done it. I felt guilty about it afterwards. It was taking advantage of his innocence to pretend that I had any influence left with her, when I knew that anything I said would just cause her to dig in her heels all the more. But I had promised, and so I did talk to her about it—briefly—when I took him back on Sunday afternoon.

"No dogs," she said. "That's out."

"He really wants one, you know."

"Fine. Get one. Let him poop all over your mother's floors."

"You know with my work that's not possible."

"Too bad. I guess that settles it then."

"His birthday is coming up pretty soon."

"That's right."

"How are we going to handle that?"

"I'm taking him down to Daddy's for a couple of weeks."

"You mean, I don't have anything to say about it."

"That's right. You don't have anything to say about it. You can celebrate with him before we leave. Or after we get back. Whatever. One more thing. If that kid comes home with a puppy some weekend, I'll have it put down. I'll send the bill to you and that bozo you have working for you."

"May I ask a question?"

"Certainly."

"What does your father think about all this?"

I said it because I thought I was holding an ace, and now was the time to play it. It did have an effect. It made her mad as hell. Her face got red. Her little pug nose puffed up as if she'd been stung by a wasp.

"It's none of his business! Nobody tells me what to do anymore! Get off my front porch!"

Again the door slammed in my face. This time when it closed, the first sick sensation came over me finally that it was truly over.

A few weeks later, Phil called on the telephone and woke me up in the middle of the night. When I picked up the receiver, he was already shouting incoherently, in the middle of some apoplectic rampage that sounded as if it had been going on for ten minutes at least. I had no idea what he was saying at first. Or whether in fact he was saying it to me or to someone in the background, like Mario or Cousin Vito, who had irritated him by some word or deed just as he'd picked up the telephone to call me. The only thing I knew for sure was that it was Phil. That harsh gravelly voice of his I would have known anywhere.

I listened to him cuss for a few minutes.

Then I decided to interrupt, so he'd know I was on the

line. We hadn't really established that yet. "Hello?" I said.

Either he ignored this or didn't hear it. He kept on with his tirade, half in English, half in Italian. Gradually I understood that he was talking to me—had been all along—and that he was telling me to go home.

"Go home! You hear me? What's wrong with you? You give up you family for a piece of skirt somewhere? You dumb goombah! What's your son gonna do, eh? What's he do now for a fahdah? Eh? Go home! Listen to me! I'mah sick man. Don't aggravate me like dis."

"She kicked me out, Phil."

"Whaddayou talkin' about! Are you a man or whaddayou? Go home! What are you trying to do—kill me?"

"Believe me, Phil—"

"Goddam you! Listen to me! I love you like a son, you son of a bitch! Better than that *stupido* God gave me! I don't talk to hear myself. Go home! Before I drag you into the street and break your legs, you son of a pig! I beat you with a stick like a dog! I flatten your head so you can play checkers on it! I—"

"Phil, don't work yourself up. You'll have a stroke."

"I'mah sick. Sick! You hear me? I'mah nolman. Don't do dis to me!"

"I'm sorry, Phil—"

"Go home!" he shouted and slammed down the receiver.

He had always believed in making his point and hanging up. He hated telephones. Even in the best of moods he shouted into them as if he were talking into a tin can. It was a mark of his deep love for Linda that he suffered her to call him once or twice a week and keep him on the line for as long as she did.

I expected him on my doorstep the next morning. Maybe holding Linda by the ear with one hand and grasping Keefer

with the other. He would smile and smile his crocodile smile
till his head seemed in danger of falling off his knobby
shoulders and rolling to a stop on the doormat at my feet.

He would talk fast. He would shower money around like
confetti.

Whatsamaddah? he would say, holding Linda out by the
ear. *You don't like each other no more? What if I break your
legs? Better yet, take a vacation! I send you to Bermudah!
Hawaii! Sicily! Eh? you wanna go to Sicily? Mario, Cousin
Vito 'n' me, we take care of Keeper while you guys go. Two,
t'ree weeks—good as new! A coupla lovebirds again, eh? Eh?
Maybe dis time you'll make a couple of twins! I give 'em all
cowboy suits 'n' lil matchin' ponies to ride.*

He would follow this speech with a gravelly laugh. It
would rumble around in his chest till it activated his emphysema again, forcing him to stop mixing threats with bribes
and concentrate on spitting into his handkerchief.

But he never showed up.

I knew something must be very wrong. I thought he had
finally given up on me. I thought Linda had told him that I
wasn't worth it, and he had shrugged his shoulders and said
something like "Okay, honeybun," and that was that. I was
sorry to lose him. He was the closest thing to a real father
that I'd ever had—or at least the closest approximation to
my notion of what a father ought to act like. But it didn't
occur to me that I should do anything about it, except to bear
the loss stoically.

WHEN Nola came back at the end of summer, she was surprised to find me still in her house. Somehow between the
job, the legal wrangling, and the weekends with Keefer
(which had resumed after Linda brought him back from

Florida) I hadn't got around to finding an apartment, even though it was clear that I should.

"My goodness, I don't see how we can all live together in this little house."

I had no intention of living all together in her little house.

"Don't worry. It's just taking a little longer than I thought to work things out. I'll be out of here in no time now."

"No hurry. Stay as long as you like. You don't mind if I put the suitcases under your bed, do you?"

I didn't mind. I didn't mind that she wanted me out of her place either. I took it for a sign that she was still feeling fairly well. When she was feeling well enough to manage on her own, she took a certain pride in treating me as a nuisance.

On the night of her return, I took Tito aside with some foreboding and peered down his gullet. There was the tumor, glistening back at me from behind the left tonsil. A slick glossy little balloon, it was now the sickly color of cooked cauliflower.

"You didn't take him to the vet, did you?"

Recriminations, even mild ones, never worked well with her. They either puffed her up with righteous indignation when she was feeling well, or crushed her outright when she wasn't.

"No, I did not. I wasn't going to turn him over to some stranger out of a telephone book. Now that we're back, I'll call Dr. Perlmutter."

"You probably killed him by putting it off."

I was scratching the dog's head. I didn't mean to say it. It was in my thoughts and it just slipped out. The dog was gazing up at me, its brown eyes glazed over with a ridiculous expression of devotion. Poor fool, I thought. To put your trust in the likes of us.

She was sitting in the chair opposite before the fireplace. Under the powder and rouge, her face blanched. She stared at me for some seconds with an expression of shock.

"What do you mean?" she asked finally in a voice hardly above a whisper.

"He was sick when you left for Maine. You said you'd take him to a vet as soon as you got there."

"I said no such thing. I didn't know he was sick. It's fine for you to sit there and say anything that pops into your head. Tito's just a dog so far as you're concerned. But he's my friend. He's the only real friend I have—"

She began to cry.

"Ma—"

She glared at me.

"I wasn't going to entrust him to a stranger!"

"I told you he was sick before you went away. I said he had a tumor—"

"You *never!* You never told me any such thing!"

"Yes, I did, Ma. That's why I wanted you to take him to the doctor right away."

"You never told me that. I think it's horrid of you to say so now. It's cruel and perverse of you to come up with it now and worry me sick. How do you know what's wrong with Tito anyway? Where's your medical degree, I'd like to know?"

"Ma, this is so typical. You always want to argue when you're feeling well."

"I don't either. I *hate* to argue."

"Well then, get on the phone and call the vet. Let's tend to the animal instead of all this nonsense."

She got up, started for the hall, then stopped. I could hear her snuffling, trying to hold it back. She turned and stood in the middle of the room, looking from me to the dog, wringing her hands. Her baby-blue eyes were starred with tears.

"I'm afraid," she whispered.

My heart went out to her.

"That's all right. Come sit down and drink your tea. I'll make the call for you."

Dr. Perlmutter was well acquainted with her devotion to her animals. He had been the family veterinarian for many years. He agreed at once to examine Tito the next day. In the morning, she was too tired from the long trip and too apprehensive to take the dog into his office by herself. I called Florence and told her I'd be late. We took the dog over to Perlmutter's clinic in my car. He looked in the dog's throat, frowned, took a biopsy, and told us he'd call as soon as he had something to report.

Two days days later, he telephoned just as I came in the door.

"Oh yes! Just a minute, doctor. Early's right here. He understands these things better than I do. I'll let you talk to him."

She held the receiver against her bosom and looked at me anxiously.

"You talk to him. If I talk to him, the news is bound to be bad. You talk to him. You have better luck than I do."

He suggested that I bring her and the dog in to talk about the test results the next afternoon. He said he would explain everything and recommend what he called "an appropriate course of action."

Nola was out in the kitchen making herself a cup of tea. She was rattling teacups and saucers, making a determined effort to make sure she didn't overhear anything I said. I decided it was safe to ask him a few questions.

"How does it look?"

"Not good."

"I'll let you tell her that tomorrow."

"I know she adores the animal. I'll do what I can to make it easy on her."

SHE was holding Tito on her lap when Perlmutter entered the office, bringing into the room momentarily the distant frenzied barking of another of his patients. He greeted us pleasantly, shuffled a few papers on his desk. He was a bear of a man with burly shoulders and a big bald head and a bristly dark beard that hung down on his breast and looked like a beaver's pelt. He was wearing a lab coat with several ballpoints clipped to a plastic liner in his breast pocket. The beard and the faux-tortoiseshell frames of his thick glasses gave a fierce aspect to his expression, but he was a very kindly man. He glanced at me uneasily, and then said gently to Nola:

"I'm sorry to tell you this, Mrs. Dimes. I'm afraid Tito has a carcinoma."

Nola looked bewildered.

"Did you say, 'Tito is a Casanova'?"

"No, Mrs. Dimes. I said he has a carcinoma."

"Oh." She smiled weakly. "I thought you said—"

She shielded her eyes as against a bright light and began to cry. She was one of those people who smile when they cry. She sat there in her polka-dot dress with a little straw pillbox on her head, holding the old dog on her lap. She had put on a nice dress for the occasion. She said dressing up was always good luck.

Perlmutter lumbered out from behind his desk and pressed some tissues into her hand from the dispenser on the wall.

"I know this is very bad news for you."

She looked up. She searched his face to see if he was capable of understanding.

"Tito is my friend. My only friend."

Her voice broke and she pressed the tissue to her lips.

Perlmutter sat back on the edge of his desk and solemnly nodded his head.

"If you like, you can leave him with me. I'll see that he doesn't suffer anymore."

"You mean—have him put to sleep?"

"Under the circumstances, that would be best. He's going to suffer a lot otherwise."

"No." She shook her head. "I could never agree to that."

"For godsakes, Ma. You heard what he said."

But she ignored me. She was dealing with an expert now.

"Can't you operate? Aren't there drugs? You must be able to do something."

Perlmutter opened his thick hands to show he wasn't hiding anything. He slowly shook his head.

"He's riddled with cancer, Mrs. Dimes. It would be a blessing to put him out of his misery."

She looked down at Tito, who lay on her lap, motionless and bleary-eyed.

"He's not suffering. Are you, Tito?"

She looked up at the doctor.

"I'll take care of him. I couldn't have him put to sleep. Any more than I could have someone in my family put to sleep."

"Really, Mrs. Dimes, it would be much better for Tito—"

But she had struck upon what she considered the moral high ground and she refused to surrender it.

"No. I could never do that. Any more than I could smother a baby with a pillow."

I could have kicked her. I knew anything I said would just stiffen her resolve, so I said nothing when Perlmutter looked to me for support. When he saw none, he surrendered.

"I'll give you something to deaden the pain."

On the way home in the car she said, "Doctors—they don't know everything."

She looked at me for confirmation. I kept my eyes fixed on the road and said nothing. I didn't want to start in with her. I was afraid if I started, I wouldn't know how to stop. She was seventy years old. She would never change now or be any different than she was. She'd never been able to take care of anything or anyone. She was only good for managing a few petty pleasures. It was much too late to call her names or make accusations. It would only hurt and baffle her. It certainly wouldn't change anything. It would only end in setting off another one of her spells of depression.

She was cuddling the dog on her lap and scratching his floppy ears.

"They don't know about the power of love. We'll show them what love can do. Won't we, baby dog?"

That afternoon, I began my search for an apartment. Two weeks later, I moved into Waterbury Place, a new complex just renting out in Lincoln Park.

She buried Tito in the local pet cemetery. I attended the ceremony. She would never have forgiven me if I hadn't. The inscription on the headstone was simple. *Tito,* it read. *Always Loyal.*

As it happened, the pet cemetery was only a mile from her house. It was relatively easy for her to go over there in her old car once or twice a week and raise what I imagine was an impassioned prayer or two over his grave.

E l e v e n

I*T* was strange to wake in the mornings and find
myself in my new apartment. Sometimes I lay
there wondering where I was and how I had got
there. Half awake and reluctant to be anything
more than that, I made determined attempts to
remain a part of the sleepy warmth of the mattress for as long as I could.

It usually worked for ten minutes or so.
When I couldn't play possum any longer, I
opened my eyes and took inventory: my shirt
and tie on the bedpost; the light seeping in
below the drawn shade at the window; the low
burble of the fish tank I'd bought for Keefer as
it muttered insanely to itself in a dark corner.

I played a game with myself. The shadows in
the corner where the fish tank was created an
optical illusion of sorts. Some mornings I lay
there and watched what I knew to be a burbling
aquarium metamorphose into a solid block of
serpentine marble mumbling to itself. But the
trick always failed when the tank's air filter
began to choke and gag like Phil having one of
his attacks of emphysema.

I got up and dusted the furniture with the
underwear I'd worn to bed. I thought of it as
killing two birds with one stone. Or "killing a

bird with two stones," as Marilyn put it one day many years
later, after she had walked in and altered my life for the
better, and was telling me about some clever time-saving
device she'd come up with at school. Marilyn had a great
talent for innocently fracturing boring old adages. I have the
impression that all Yoopers do. It must be all the iron in the
drinking water up there or something.

I used my shorts for the little jobs, like the end tables. I
dropped my T-shirt to the floor. I used my foot to dry-mop
the hall and the strip of hardwood floor around the shag rug
in the living room. When I was through, I threw my combination underwear and dusting rags in the hamper and took a
shower. I thought a trick like that saved a lot of time.

I stood in the hot downpour stolidly as a cow, trying to
think as little as possible. Nevertheless, it often occurred to
me that my nice hot shower might turn out to be the high-
light of my day.

Lately I'd been getting a series of semithreatening telephone calls from Lionel. I said they were semithreatening.
He couldn't make up his mind which to do: call me up and
threaten me, or call me up and just chat for a while.

"You move, man. You think by moving you can hide from
me?"

"Don't flatter yourself. My wife and I broke up."

"You did? How come?"

"It wasn't working out."

"Seem like a lot don't work out where you concerned, my
man."

"Maybe so. What's on your mind, Lionel?"

"Money. That's what's on my mind. Say you loan me
three hundred dollars. How that sound, Whitebread? Then
if you nice, maybe I won't come over there and bust you in
the mouth."

"Sorry. I'm a little short on cash myself."

"I ain't got no milk for Harrow."

"I'm sorry."

"You sorry. You sorry a lot. How 'bout I jump out of the bushes some night and see how sorry you be then?"

"I wouldn't advise that. These days, I carry a gun. I travel a lot, you know, and crime is up. It's a .357 Magnum. You've heard of those. It's a *big* gun. If you jump out of the bushes, I'm liable to get scared and blow a hole in you the size of New York City."

He laughed, long and low and sly.

"Shit, man. You ain't packin' no gun."

He was right. I had no talent for handling tools of violence. Had I one, I probably would have ended up blowing the toes off my feet. I only knew about the gun because it was featured in a Clint Eastwood movie I'd seen in Cleveland one night when I had nothing better to do. I thought maybe the caliber would impress him.

Sometimes he'd call and just breathe on the line. Other times he would describe to me how I'd ruined his life. I listened to his diatribes. I tried to insert helpful suggestions. He kept asking for money. Once he said he'd become a Muslim if I didn't send him some. After several such calls, I lost patience and started hanging up on him.

"Sorry, Lionel. I'm sorting my sock drawer. Why not call back tomorrow?"

Sometimes Keefer was in the apartment with me when Lionel telephoned. He was able to deduce what was going on by listening to my side of the conversation. When he told his mother about the calls, she was concerned.

"Maybe I shouldn't let Keefer come over, with that black guy creeping around the place."

"He's not creeping around the place. He just calls on the phone once in a while. Don't be silly."

"I don't know. If I were you, I'd watch out."

I did take extra precautions when Keefer was with me. I made him wait in the car with the doors locked till I made it to the door of the apartment house with his paper bag of clothes. When I was sure the coast was clear, I signaled for him to follow. I felt a fool for doing this, but thought it better to be safe than sorry.

Keefer didn't seem to find the situation particularly frightening or unusual. So much had changed in his life over the past few months that the notion somebody might be stalking his father seemed a natural part of it.

By the end of summer, Linda and I had worked out the final terms of our settlement. Almost simultaneously, I decided to leave Frankenwood & Son.

Arthur was shocked and tried to talk me out of it. When I told him I'd still be available to work with him on special projects from time to time, it mollified him somewhat.

"We're still going to be friends?"

"Absolutely."

"We can still play tennis?"

"Certainly."

"Twice a week when we're both in town?"

"Sounds fine."

"And I can still call you up and talk about my problems?"

"Yes. But stay off the topic of sex till I find a woman friend."

He laughed and shook me by the shoulder.

"Jesus, Early. What am I going to do without you?"

I was tired of all the travel. I wanted more control over my life, so I could spend more time with Keefer. I was also tired of Arthur's unpredictable mood swings and his tiresome stories about the ever-changing string of vacuous sex fiends in his life; and of Marty Briles and his pernicious slurs against all and sundry; and of old Mr. Frankenwood, bumping around the place in the mornings and asking Florence to type a letter for him just as I was getting ready to give her a bunch of work. I still loved Florence, whom I'd had the good luck to hire during my first year at Frankenwood. She and I understood each other. Our relationship had some of the flavor of a longtime marriage. We went about our work quietly and peaceably without the need for much conversation or fuss. Both of us valued peace and quiet and harmony. We didn't understand why the rest of humankind didn't get along better. I would miss her. But I thought I could do without the others. I wanted to be on my own. I thought I might as well clean out my closet entirely while I was at it.

Officially, I was resigning from the firm "to pursue other interests"—the usual time-honored lie. My name would continue on the stationery as "partner emeritus." Arthur thought it had some business value. I was flattered, but doubtful.

Arthur was very generous. I got a nice sum of money based on my share of estimated future earnings for the contracts and accounts in-house and a cash settlement representing my share of the company's net assets, including the building at its current market value. In return, I surrendered all future equity rights with respect to the corporation and its activities. I signed a covenant promising to keep my paws off the client list for a period of eighteen months.

I left the details to the attorneys—Lloyd Schwanger, to whose standard of living I was becoming indispensable; and the firm's general counsel, Myron Block, an honest, reliable man of outstanding integrity. Within a surprisingly short time, I found myself without a good reason for getting out of bed in the mornings.

I felt no special pressure to undertake any work on my

own, beyond a few days a week. Without the distractions of the office, I had plenty of time to plan my weekends with Keefer.

I read the literature on the National Zoological Gardens. I studied the membership bulletins concerning the exhibits at the Smithsonian Institution. I was interested to know what was going on at Hershey Park and whether the Phillies or the Orioles were at home. I read the local paper, as well as the *Post,* the *Sun,* and the *Inquirer* on Sundays. I looked in the appropriate sections of those pages for entertainment suitable for an nine-year-old boy. I took notes. Weekly I found fresh inspiration. For instance, what about a tour of the U.S. Treasury? He'd never been there, I was sure. On his visits over the years, Phil had taken him virtually everywhere within a three-hundred-mile radius of Harrisburg. But never to the Treasury, I didn't think.

I had a lot of time on my hands. I found myself calling Linda and offering to do favors.

"How about I take Keefer out to dinner tonight and give you a break?"

"How about forgetting it?"

"Listen, anytime you want to go out or something, just let me know. I'll be happy to baby-sit."

"What are you—trying be a smart-ass or something?"

"No, I'm serious. Hey. I'm going over to the Gateway Mall this afternoon to do some shopping. Can I get anything for you? I could drop it off on my way back."

I tried to get her to be a bit more flexible. But she held rigidly to the court-sanctioned custody terms which our creepo attorneys had worked out.

"Really, we can do anything we want, so long as we both agree."

"It says you get him on the weekends, buster. Starting at

nine A.M. on Saturdays and ending at six P.M. on Sundays, period."

"True, but we don't have to—"

"Yes, we do, wiseguy!"

If I knocked on the apartment door (by this time the house had been sold) a few minutes early, she still insisted I go back and wait in my car till it was exactly the time stipulated in the agreement.

Precisely at nine, the door of the apartment building would fly open. Out would tumble Keefer on the dead run, hugging a grocery bag full of his clothes for the weekend with his scruffy old teddy bear riding on top of the pile. I see him still—running across the lawn toward the car, waving wildly. Always beaming from ear to ear. A happy kid, it seemed to me at the time. But that was purely wishful thinking on my part. The divorce did him great damage. It planted little tiny time pills of neuroses that went off in him like little bombs when he reached adolescence.

"Where we going today, Dad?"

He always wanted to know the plan as soon as he got in the car.

"We going down to see the white tigers? Aw, you said we could! We going to the ballgame instead? Huh? Aw come on, Dad! They're playing at home tonight! Philly's not so far!"

How could I nurse my grievances in the face of this smiling boy? My own pallid mug bagged into a wan and reluctant smile as he clamored into the car, making life lively again, eagerly repeating his weekend war cry: "Where're we going today? Huh? Huh?"

That fall, when the crabgrass began to die, and the sun began to sink lower in the sky, and the days began to grow short and crisp, Linda suddenly became less difficult to deal with. She decided of a sudden that it was all right for me to pick him up on Friday nights, rather than wait till nine on Saturday morning.

The master hearings were over. Our final papers would be coming through any day. Now that everything was settled, I thought she was beginning to relax. She *was* beginning to relax. But not for the reason I thought. Keefer disabused me of my mistake one night on our way over to the apartment. I remember it was the weekend that I'd bought the goldfish for him as a surprise.

"Mom's got a boyfriend."

"She has?"

"Yeh, you should see him. He's about a hundred years younger than she is. He's got a motorcycle. You should see her on it. Boy, does she look funny."

"What's his name?"

"Michael."

"Michael." I began to laugh.

"What's so funny?"

"I don't know. It just sounds funny, that's all. Your mother with a boyfriend named Michael."

As I put the key in the door I said, "I've got a surprise for you."

"Where is it?"

"In my room."

He streaked down the uncarpeted hall to the bedroom. He was really excited. I followed after him, afraid I'd raised his expectations too high. He wants a dog, I told myself. He wants a new bike. You should have warned him that it's only a couple of goldfish.

When I got to the door of the room, he was on his hands and knees looking under the bed. He hadn't noticed the fish tank gurgling in the corner.

"Where is it, Dad?"

"Right behind you."

He turned around and spotted the tank. All the air seemed to go out of him. Immediately he straightened again and covered up as best he could.

"Fish."

He got to his feet.

"Oh boy."

"You like them? I know it's not a dog. But it's a little something I can have around here for you when you come over."

He gave me a quick smile and looked away fast. He fixed his eyes on the fish tank again.

"Yeh. Boy, they're really nice."

He went up to the lighted glass and peered in. The fish looked like fat chocolates wrapped in gold foil. They were all head and practically no body and trailed long fins as sheer as negligees. He tapped a finger on the glass. They ignored him and kept swimming in circles.

"Want to feed them?"

"Sure."

"Here's the box. Don't put in too much. Just a little does it. These fish are kind of finicky, you know. Not to mention stupid. Feed them too much and they'll eat themselves to death. Sort of like Uncle Mario."

He took off the lid and sprinkled a little of the powdery food on the water. The bug-eyed fish rose to the top. A few air bubbles formed like pearls and broke the surface as the fish swam around gulping down bits of the dirtlike food as it slowly diffused and sank toward the bottom.

"I thought you'd enjoy having them when you came over."

He nodded and swallowed hard. I felt I should explain further.

"I would have gotten you a puppy, but when I really go back to work, I'll be out of town a lot. A little puppy would starve to death. I can get the fish a two-week feeding tablet and just drop it in the tank. I already bought some, in fact."

"It's okay, Dad."

He kept his eyes on the fish.

"I like them. I think they're pretty neat."

He looked up.

"Thanks a lot."

"Maybe later on . . ."

He had that deadpan expression on his face—the one that became so characteristic of him later on.

"I guess you're not ever coming back, are you?"

"Probably not."

"I wish you would. I'd really be good if you came back."

I kneeled down and gave him a hug.

"Hey, you're the best boy in the world. It doesn't have anything to do with you. Your mother and I just don't get along."

"I wish you did."

He looked as if he was ready to cry.

"Well, look at it this way. Now you have two homes instead of one. You get to have two birthday celebrations. Not bad, huh? You'll probably end up with twice as many presents at Christmas, too. See how it works out? You get two of everything. When I go back to work, I'm not going to take any jobs that'll keep me out of town on weekends. You'll always be able to come here on Saturdays and Sundays. I'm going to take vacations, too. When you're not in school, maybe your mother will let me take you on a couple of trips. We'll stay in hotels. You can swim in the pool and order up room service. That'll be fun, won't it? How's that sound?"

"Okay, I guess."

"Atta boy."

I took him on my lap and hugged him silly—more for my benefit than his. I was really feeling bad for us both. He was such a good kid. He was doing a good job with this, making the best of it. I held him tight. I inhaled the scent of his hair. It was chestnut brown like his mother's. He smelled like a bird dog who'd been running in the woods all day—a good clean animal smell, full of the scent of fresh air.

It took him about a month to lose interest in the goldfish. At first, he wanted to clean the tank all the time. I would look up from my book or paperwork and he would be standing there by my chair with all the stuff we'd bought: the rubber siphon, the tiny strainer, the plastic buckets, the new package of gravel.

"Can we clean the tank, Dad?"

"Okay. Sure."

It didn't need cleaning, but I didn't want to dampen his enthusiasm. We unplugged the filter and took it out and laid it on some newspaper. If there was any gunk on it, we cleaned it off. We put some water in one of the buckets and netted the fish, using the little cloth strainer, and dumped them into the bucket. (We had to watch to make sure they didn't jump out onto the floor, but they never did.) We siphoned off some of the water into the other bucket till I could carry the tank into the bathroom without slopping water all over the place, and I emptied it into the toilet. Then I drained off the blue gravel at the bottom onto some newspapers that I spread thickly on the bathroom tiles.

Then it was his turn. He put the tank in the bathtub and swabbed the glass sides with the natural sponge we'd bought especially for this purpose at the pet store. After he was satisfied it was clean, I handed him a new package of gravel and he laid down a new floor at the bottom of the tank. (Later on, when we got smarter, we used to rinse out the old gravel in a strainer at the sink.) I stood there through all of this because he liked me to watch—to make sure he "did it right," he said. When he was finished, we put it back on the stand in the bedroom. We used the buckets to fill it up again. Then he put the fish back and we reconnected the filter and put the top on and plugged in the light, and he was happy for a few minutes.

But after a while he lost interest, and the aquarium became a night-light of sorts. When I entered the room after the eleven-o'clock news I would find him asleep on the cot, his face bathed in the green reflection of the light from the quietly burbling aquarium. Above his head the fish, almost companionably it seemed, kept up their silent reconnoiter in the glowing green block of water.

I developed an affection for the fish. When he wasn't there during the week, I sometimes talked to them. I tapped the glass and said things like:

Keefer's coming. He'll be here pretty soon now!

By this time, I'd taken up with a woman named Gloria— more in reprisal than for any other reason, reprisal for what I considered the unreasonable haste with which Linda had taken up with Michael. I met her at a dinner meeting of the public relations society. She was in her early thirties and quite attractive, I thought. She had never been married. She told me she was more interested in "getting someplace than in settling down."

She was making good money as director of communications for an insurance company. She had her eye on New York, Chicago, Los Angeles—places like that. She thought geography was exciting. Just the names of places, any place she hadn't been, excited her. I had an idea the best place to make love to her would probably be on an airplane. In a way she was perfect for me at the time, since obviously she was just passing through town on her way to more important places. This was good. I certainly wasn't looking for a permanent relationship.

She would come over to the apartment once or twice a week, when we both happened to be in town, and I would fix her dinner. Afterwards, we would watch an old movie on TV or make love. Once we did both simultaneously—although we did our movie-watching covertly. We were on the couch. We got into it before I had time to get up and shut off the set. I remember she asked me to please remove the newspaper underneath her about halfway through. I'd folded it and thrown it on the couch when I came in that night. She had lain back on it and now she said it was uncomfortable. She arched the small of her back. I pulled the newspaper out from beneath her while she looked away with a vague smile and pretended not to watch the movie.

When we made love in the bedroom, she insisted I disconnect the aquarium's air filter. She said she hated the sound of it slurping and burping lasciviously in the background, as if giving vent to involuntary commentary as it watched us.

"Oh I hate that!" She shivered. "It makes what we're doing sound so disgusting!"

I thought her reaction was funny, and I kidded her about it. I said, "Think of the poor fish. Having to hold their breath all that time, while we make love."

But later on, it annoyed me. There wasn't anything wrong with the sound of the aquarium. Actually it was very soothing.

"You're into some weird stage of divorce, darling. Perhaps you and your fish tank would like to be alone."

She was like that. She was insistent about her place in the scheme of things. She felt insulted because I never invited her over when Keefer was visiting.

"What's the matter? Are you ashamed of me?"

I tried to explain that it wasn't good to confuse him. When he was around, I wanted to give him my undivided attention.

"I see so little of him, you see. Just on weekends."

But she didn't see. She didn't see that at all. So gradually I stopped calling her. It was much better that way.

I needed some time off. Work was beginning to fill in my weeks again. Weekends were reserved for Keefer. Otherwise, I really wanted to get away from people. I wanted to read in bed. When I slept, I wanted the bed to myself. I didn't want somebody's arms and legs in my face. I didn't want somebody shaking me awake with urgent needs I was too sleepy to understand or do much about. For now, I just wanted to keep it simple.

Keefer's coming! I'd tell the fish, and sprinkle a little food in the tank.

ONE weekend in late October, one of Linda's countless Uncle Tonys and his family came through town on their way to Williamsburg, Virginia. They had children around Keefer's age, and they wanted to take him along.

Linda called to ask if I would mind giving him up for the weekend. She said she'd make it up to me in some way later.

"He really wants to go," she said. "But he's too polite to ask you if he can."

This particular Uncle Tony was in the banana business and reputedly had connections with the mob in Queens.

"Does he have to wear a helmet and a bulletproof vest?"

"Very funny."

"Okay," I said. "Maybe I could have him for a few extra days at Christmas."

"We'll talk about it," she said.

I had a few martinis that Sunday afternoon and fell asleep on the couch in front of an old William Powell–Myrna Loy flick on TV. It was a slow gray rainy day. When the telephone rang it woke me up. I threw the papers off and fumbled for the receiver. It was Linda. Hers was the first actual voice I'd heard all day.

"Remember what you said if I ever needed any favors?"

"Sure. What's up?"

"Well—I need you to come over to the hospital. I'm still covered by the Blue Cross plan, right?"

"Yes—both you and Keefer."

"Daddy's going to get me my own coverage, but he's been so sick . . ."

I sat up.

"Linda, what's wrong? Did you hurt yourself?"

"Well—Michael and I had a little accident. On his motorcycle. We hit a tree."

"Jesus. Are you okay?"

"Actually they say I broke my leg. I got a little bump on my head. Otherwise I'm fine. Michael's okay too. You're okay, aren't you, Michael?"

A sleepy voice mumbled in the background. She laughed, but I couldn't make out what the answer was. She put her hand over the receiver and said something else to him. It was one of those rude interludes newly infatuated couples indulge in, in front of other people. I waited for it to be over. She wasn't doing it to make me jealous. Fat chance. Besides, she wasn't like that. She might be thoughtless, she might be rude, but she was perfectly guileless. I thought of Florida and Vinny Palumbo. Then I remembered her little episode with Arthur. I began to wonder if I really had grounds to draw any conclusions about her at all. She finished her parenthetical chat with Michael and came back to me.

"Michael's a little out of it right now. He broke a leg too."

"I'll be right over," I said.

"Do you mind bringing me a pack of cigarettes?"

"Be happy to. Still smoking Winstons?"

I found them in the emergency ward, propped up like dolls on beds across the aisle from each other. His bed was a little closer to the door, but I didn't notice him right away.

"Michael, say hello to Earl here."

I had walked right past him, although they were the only ones in the room. I looked over my shoulder, smiled, nodded: *We're all friends here* was what I intended to convey. A bearded youth with a bandaged nose and a cast on his leg looked at me out of black glittering eyes. They were as bright and soulfully sad as the eyes of a dormouse. He managed a feeble wave. It was followed by the limp collapse of his hand onto his chest. He was suffering. Either he was near death or in a state of despair, I couldn't tell which.

I turned back to her and held out the cigarettes. She tore open the pack and lighted one up and sucked greedily on the noxious thing. I tried to suppress it, but I felt the usual pinch of distress deep in the pit of my chest. I hoped my face didn't show disapproval. I didn't want any trouble. She carefully blew the smoke against the wall and away from me—more than she used to do when we were together. Our manners were beginning to improve again, now that we were no longer married.

She raised the cigarette to her parted lips. It was a pretty gesture—far more so than the reason warranted. I saw the bandage on her wrist. Her leg was raised and splinted. Otherwise she looked unharmed. Her color was good. She looked rested and happy. That's what love does for you, I thought sourly. It works better than a face-lift.

She pushed some ringlets off her forehead with the back

of her hand and shook her head to make her thick curly hair fall into place. She had great hair.

"Fractured tibia." She smiled shyly. "Some fool, huh? Riding around on a motorcycle at my age."

"Why not, if you're having a good time."

"You talk to them about the coverage?"

"It's taken care of."

"Thanks. It was nice of you to come right over."

"How's your dad?"

"He's bad. Real bad. I'm worried about him. He's lost so much weight. You wouldn't recognize him. Mario is thinking about putting him back in the hospital. You really ought to call him. He still thinks the world of you, you know."

"I didn't think he wanted to talk to me."

"He was mad at you for a while. But he's over it now. Call him."

"I will."

But she didn't seem to hear me. She was gazing into one of the far corners of the room, with that open-mouthed look she got on her face when she was thinking of something.

"I was going up, to be with him. Now this."

"You can still go up, can't you?"

"Yeh, you're right. I can get Mario to send Cousin Vito down with the car."

"That's a good idea."

"Yeh, I can still get up there. No problem. What do you think of Michael?"

"What do I think? I just met him. He's got a nice wave."

"He looks like a kid, doesn't he?"

"Not that young. The beard helps. How old is he?"

"Twenty-five. I could be his mother."

"How old are you now? Thirty-seven? Borderline, at best. Anyway, you look as young as he does."

"You really think so?"

"Absolutely."

"He feels awful. He keeps telling me he's sorry. Isn't that just like a kid? Maybe you could cheer him up on your way out."

I saw no reason not to stop by his bed. He really did look miserable. He was lying on his pillows with a thin forearm, like the bare branch of a young sapling, resting just above the thrust of his bandaged nose. He was suffering tragically, in the fashion of young people everywhere.

"How are you feeling?"

Startled, he withdrew his arm and blinked his uncanny bright eyes. He was going to have a nice pair of shiners in the morning. He seemed stunned that I would even speak to him. For some reason I shook his hand, which added to his confusion, but afterwards he didn't seem to want to let go. I stood there holding his hand while he told me how bad he felt.

"I just feel awful."

"Are you in a lot of pain?"

"No, no. I mean I feel awful about *her.*"

His face contorted and he looked away. He stretched his jaws as if trying to relieve a pressure bubble in his ear. He touched his heavily taped nose. I wasn't sure what was going on, till I saw a heavy tear slide down his cheek and disappear into his beard. He swiveled his head again on the pillows and looked at me earnestly.

"She's such a wonderful person. I took her out on that bike and ran her into a tree. I never even tipped over on it in three years. Then I take her out and do this. I might have killed her."

"Don't be so hard on yourself. She's all right."

"I can't believe it. I take her out and nearly kill her. It's like my whole life is cursed."

"Think of it as luck. You could be a lot worse off."

"If anything ever happened to her I'd kill myself. I really would."

His eyes turned blind and shiny as bits of mica. He squeezed my hand and turned his face to the wall again. He was certainly an emotional fellow. I wondered what he did for a living. I thought she'd told me he was a schoolteacher. An art teacher—wasn't that it?

He let go of my hand.

"I feel like a fool."

"We're all fools when we're in love."

I meant it as a joke, but he took it straight.

"She's the greatest woman I ever met. All the rest were just kids next to her. This sounds bad, but I'm glad she kicked you out. Little Keith is great too. Just great. I'm really crazy about them. Now I guess I've ruined everything."

"Not at all. She thinks you're great too."

"She does? You mean she's not mad at me?"

"No. She thinks it's funny. It's been an adventure. How many people can say they ran into a tree together on a motorcycle? It'll give you something to talk about."

"Oh, I don't know," he said darkly. "I don't think it's that simple."

"Are they keeping you overnight?"

"I think so. Why?"

"Get them to give you something to knock you out. I'm sure everything will look better in the morning."

"I will. Thanks."

So much for emergencies, I thought. I went home and finished my nap.

T w e l v e

LINDA telephoned on Wednesday to say she was taking Keefer out of school for a few days so they could go up and see Phil. Cousin Vito was coming down in the car to get them.

"We should be back by Saturday. Sunday— better make that Sunday. We'll be back by Sunday for sure."

"You're cutting into another weekend. This is getting to be a regular habit."

"His grampy is deathly sick, wiseguy. Don't you think a little exception might be in order?"

"Is Michael going with you?"

"Is that any of your business?"

"I was just curious."

"Yes, he is, if you want to know."

"I thought he was a teacher."

"He is. But he's a substitute. He's not on contract or anything. It makes it nice. We can get up and go whenever we want. I want him to meet Daddy. When are you going up?"

"I've got to be in New York at the end of the month. I thought I'd go out and see them then."

"Good. If he has to go in the hospital again, he should be home by then. Well . . . see you. Take care of yourself."

"Okay, Linda. Have a nice trip. Give Phil my best. Give me a call when you get back, okay?"

"Okay."

I wasn't surprised when I didn't hear from her on Saturday. But when she didn't call by Sunday noon, I took a ride over there.

Her car wasn't in the parking lot. That gave me a bad feeling right away. Maybe she was having it serviced while she was away. But I didn't think so. I went to the door and knocked. The hollow sound told me the place was empty. Really empty: devoid of people, furniture, draperies—everything. They're gone, I thought. They've moved away.

No, I must be wrong, I decided. I knocked again. I waited for her to open up and tell me to go back to my car and wait there till nine o'clock next Saturday. Again the sound echoed through the apartment. I tried the door, but it was locked.

I went to the manager's office. Of course it was closed, but her apartment number was posted on the door. She lived in the unit directly above the office. I went up and rang the bell.

She was an affable woman in her fifties, with lots of blue eye makeup. She wore rings on all her fingers and had an intricate beehive of platinum hair coiled high on top of her head. She was corseted and big-busted and stored her glasses on her bosom by means of a chain around her neck.

"Oh yeh, hon. Her and her boy moved out last week. She give a month's notice, which was up Saturday a week."

"She didn't leave an address, did she?"

"Oh yeh, sure. Leave me get my keys. We'll go downstairs 'n' look at the files."

We went downstairs and she opened up the office.

"Sorry to put you through this trouble."

"Oh, I wasn't doing nothing anyways. Lemme see. Oh yeh, sure. Here it is. You wanna copy it down?"

It was Phil's address on Long Island.

"No thanks. I'm familiar with it. Thanks a lot."

"Oh sure, hon. Don't mention it."

I stopped at the UniMart up the street and got on the pay phone.

"Yeh?"

It was Mario, answering the telephone in Phil's time-honored style.

"Mario, this is Earl. Is Linda there?"

"Hello, Early! How are ya?"

"Pretty good, Mario. How have you been?"

"Aw, not so good, what with Pop and everything."

"I know. I was sorry to hear about it. How's he doing?"

"He's bad, Early. Real bad."

"I'm sorry. I'd like to come up and see him sometime. You think that would be all right?"

A pause.

"I guess so. I dunno. Yeh, I guess it would be all right. I don't know for sure, though. Maybe I better ask him. He was pretty mad at you, y' know."

"I know. Please ask and let me know. I'd really like to see him. Mario, where are Linda and Keefer? I just checked at the apartment. The manager says they moved out."

"Yeh, that's right. They moved out."

"Well, where is she?"

"Sorry, Early. I'm not supposed to say. The truth is, I'm not even sure. That's the way she wanted it. She was afraid if I knew, I'd blab it to you. I probably would, too. I don't think what she's doing is right."

"What's going on? Come on, Mario. Be fair."

"Sorry, I can't help you. I'd like to, but—"

"I'm coming up there, Mario. I'll bring the cops if I have to. This is the weekend. I've got a right to be with my son—"

"Hey, who's stopping you? Bring the army, if you want. They're not here."

"Where are they?"

"I tole ya, I don't know for sure."

"Sorry. I can't believe that."

"Looka. All I can tell ya is they don't live here."

"Where are they? Why did the manager give me your address?"

"She had to have her mail forwarded somewhere. Right?"

"Oh. Well—is Phil there? Let me talk to Phil."

"He can't come to the phone. He's too sick."

"Come on, Mario. Be a pal."

"He couldn't talk to you anyway. They took out his voice box two weeks ago."

"His voice box? Jesus, what's going on? I didn't know he was that sick."

"He's got throat cancer. Didn't she tell you? They don't think he's got a chance. But they said he oughta have it out, so I said okay. You know what got him? Not the cancer. He coulda fought that off with a coupla cigars. I think it was you and Linda. That's what really got him."

"That's awful. Ask him if I can come and see him. Let me know as soon as possible, will you please?"

"He can't talk, but he writes stuff on a pad. I'll ask him and let you know."

"And you really can't tell me anything about Linda and Keefer?"

"Only what I know. Right after the ceremony, Cousin Vito drove 'em to the airport. They were goin' to California. That's all I know for sure. She said they'd be in touch as soon as they got settled."

"Wait a minute. Wait a minute. What ceremony? What's this about California? What are you talking about?"

"Didn't she tell you anything? She and Michael got married here at the house on Thursday. She wanted Pop in on it, so they had it here at the house. Then they left for California."

"On their honeymoon?"

"No, no. They're gonna live out there. She sold everything. Her car. All the furniture. Him too. They're makin' a fresh start out West."

"Jesus, Mario. This comes as an awful shock to me. I didn't know about any of this."

"Yeh, me too. Seems like a big change, don't it? Movin' West and all? Especially with Pop being so sick. But you know Linda. Once she makes up her mind—"

"What about me? I'm supposed to have Keefer on weekends. I don't even know where they are."

"She said she'd give you a call once they got settled."

"But she took Keefer with her."

"You didn't expect her to leave him behind, did you?"

"This is incredible. I can't believe this is happening to me."

"Believe it," he said and hung up.

TEN days later, among the bills and circulars from grocery stores in my letterbox, I found a card postmarked San Francisco, with a picture of the Mark Hopkins on it. On the back, it read:

Keefer wants to talk to you. We're all fine, so don't worry. We'll call at 8 P.M. on Sunday night, the fifth. You'd better be home if you want to talk to him.

Linda

It arrived on Tuesday, the seventh. Two days too late.

I clutched my head and groaned. What had he thought when the telephone went unanswered? That I'd casually forgotten to be home in time for the call? Or did he allow that I might be out of town on business—just too busy to be home?

Damn her, I thought. She probably mailed it late on purpose. "8 P.M." What did that mean? Eastern or Pacific time? If Pacific, it meant the call had come at midnight. Wherever she found herself she was likely to think it was that time all over the world. She probably meant Pacific. At midnight I had been in a taxicab, coming in from the airport. On my way back from a trip to Columbus, Ohio. One I could have easily postponed till the following week, had I known about the call. I felt like cutting my throat.

A week later another card came.

You weren't there, you bum. He was heartbroken. It was a good lesson for him to learn about you. We'll try again at 8 P.M. on the 18th. If you're not there this time, forget it.

Luckily it arrived a few days in advance, so I was able to reschedule a trip to Boston and be home the night she said they'd call.

Eight o'clock came and went. To be on the safe side, I dialed the operator.

"I'm expecting an important call, operator. It was supposed to come through at eight o'clock. I wonder if you would call me back to make sure my telephone is working."

"You couldn't call out, sir, if your telephone wasn't working. Unless it was off the hook."

"It was on the hook all right. I checked it. Maybe it's just not ringing. Would you mind very much trying it?"

"Okay, sir."

Probably she had to put up with a lot of fools during an evening's work. On the other hand, I was paying for the phone. I had a right to know whether it worked or not.

"You see, my son is calling from California. I haven't heard from him for a while. I sure don't want to miss the call because the phone doesn't work."

"Certainly, sir. I understand."

"Well, thank you. I appreciate it. You'll call me back?"

"Yes sir, I will."

"Thanks a lot."

I replaced the receiver and watched it impatiently. It seemed to take a long time to handle such a simple request. Maybe it *was* broken. In order to ease the tension, I decided to freshen my martini. Sometimes all you need to do is move away to make it ring. It did, just as I tilted the bottle. I managed to spill gin all over the front of myself. I dried my hands on my shirttail and hurried into the living room.

"Hello?"

"This is the operator, sir."

"Oh, good."

"Your telephone works, sir."

"Yes, it does, doesn't it? Well, thanks a lot, operator."

"You're welcome, sir."

"I know you think I'm a pain in the ass."

Fortunately the line was dead when I blurted this. They take your telephone away for saying things like that. Why I felt compelled to say it, I don't know. Except I was spending a lot of time alone. Perhaps I was beginning to lose the knack of civil intercourse. I went back to the kitchen and took a short intense swig of my drink.

Ah, the second Mrs. Tanqueray, I said to myself. How lovely you are this evening.

It was thirteen after eight. I decided she was, as I suspected, operating on Pacific time. That meant I had nearly four hours to go.

I picked up a book of Ruskin's essays and settled in for a long read. Maybe I'd take an hour's nap around ten. I wanted to be fresh when I talked to him. The nap would take care of the martinis. Then a little splash of gin in the bottom of a glass would set me up and I'd be ready for the call.

Just then the telephone rang again, harsh and stupefying, like a rock lobbed through a plate-glass window. Quarter past eight. I shook my head. Just like her. Never on time for anything.

"Hello?"

"Yeh, man. Hello your ass too."

"Lionel! Get off the phone! I'm expecting an important call."

"Sure. You always too busy, ain't you?"

"Sorry it seems that way. I've got to keep the line open tonight. So bug off."

"They took him, man."

His voice went hushed and low.

"Done took him. Say I ain't fit to be his daddy. Shit, man. I'm his daddy, whether I fit or not."

"You're not the only one. My *wife* took my boy. I don't even know where they are. The lawyers say she has custody. She can take him anywhere she wants. I don't care what *she* does. I just want him back. That craphouse attorney who works for me says I can file for dual custody in the California courts, if I want. The *California* courts, for Christ's sake. He says frankly he doesn't think I would stand a snowball's chance. Besides, what would a custody fight do to my kid? He's been through enough already."

"Done took him. Shit. I'm his daddy, whether I fit or not."

"I'm supposed to get my son on weekends. She married some guy and moved to California. Can you beat that? I don't even know where they are."

"Shit, man. If some bitch do that to me, I slap her so silly she be up in the trees singin' wid de birds."

"So get off the phone, will you? I got a postcard saying they might call tonight. Maybe they're trying to get through right now."

"Okay, man. Later."

In a few minutes it rang again.

"Hello?"

"Just 'cause you got troubles don't mean I'm through with you. 'Cause of you, me and Harrow ain't together—"

"Lionel! Get off the goddam phone!"

"I'm just lettin' you know, man—"

I slammed it down, hoping it would bust his eardrum.

Time passed slowly. Occasionally, between sips, I glanced at the telephone, expecting it to do something besides just sit there.

I couldn't concentrate on Ruskin. He was too much water to carry after a couple of martinis. I put him aside and turned on the television on top of the bookcase opposite the couch.

It was so little and so far away that I had to squint to see it—which was the way I liked it. Be damned if I wanted one I could actually see. Gloria always despised the thing. She told me I ought to get a decent one so we could watch the movies without straining our eyes. I was glad I hadn't wasted the money. It was bad enough having one at all. I used it mainly for the news and the noise it made anyway.

I sipped my drink and looked around the room. I tried to read the titles in the bookcase. I could identify most by the book jackets. At least I had my books. At least she had let me have those when she'd sold the house. I could hardly see across the room—nearsighted from spending so many hours over the fine print in corporate reports. From time to time I squinted at the TV, to see if I could figure out what it was squawking about.

Somehow the time passed. At ten, I turned off the set and got the clock down out of my shaving kit on the closet shelf in the bedroom. I set it for eleven and lay down on the couch for a little nap.

I didn't think I would be able to sleep at all. I lay there for what seemed a long time. The clock ticked tinnily, with industrious malevolence, like a little time bomb getting set to go off.

It stung me awake like an angry hornet. I woke groggy and irritable. I slapped it around till it shut up. I staggered to the bathroom and splashed some cold water on my face. I didn't look very good in the mirror.

You drink too much, I told myself. Altogether too much.

I splashed some more water on my face. Then I went into the kitchen and poured myself a beer.

At five of twelve, the telephone rang.

"Person-to-person call for Mr. Earl Dimes."

"This is Mr. Dimes. Go ahead, operator."

"I have a person-to-person call for you from Linda Malloy, Mr. Dimes.

"Thank you, operator."

"Go ahead, ma'am."

"Hello?" My voice was actually trembling.

"Hello, Earl."

"So it's Linda Malloy now. You didn't waste any time, did you?"

"Fuck off, wiseguy. You want to talk to him or not?"

"No offense. I was just—"

"What I do is my own business. I don't have to explain myself to you. You got that straight?"

"Right. I've got that straight."

"Okay. Now he's been bugging me to call you. I don't think it's such a hot idea, but he's been driving me crazy about it. He's got his own ideas, I'll give him that. So okay. Here's the deal. You don't ask him where he's calling from, where's he's staying, or anything like that. You respect our privacy, understand? I'm going to be on the extension, so no tricks. Get it?"

"Linda—"

"That's the deal. Take it or leave it."

"I'll take it."

"Okay. You've got two minutes."

"I haven't talked to him for a month."

"Two minutes. Take it or leave it."

"Okay, okay."

"Remember, wiseguy. I'll be listening."

The next words I heard were "Hello—Dad?"

It cut through me like a spear. I was surprised how much it hurt.

"Hello, son. Boy, it's good to hear your voice again. How are you?"

"I'm fine, Daddy. How are you?"

"I'm swell, baby. You sound so grown-up. I really miss you."

"I miss you too, Daddy. When can I come home?"

"I don't know. Your mother and I will have to talk about it."

"Can't you come and get me? I wanna come home. I don't like it out here."

"Hey," Linda said.

I couldn't stand it.

"Baby, I would come and get you in a second—"

"Hey!"

"—but I don't know where you are."

"Okay, wiseguy. You blew it. Hang up, Keefer."

"Daddy!"

"Write to me, Keefer! Call me again, baby!"

"Dad!"

"You're just like him," Linda said. "Give me that phone."

I heard him yell, "I wanna talk to him! I wanna talk to my dad!"

The phone went bonk-bonk in my ear, apparently shaken loose from his hand. He was bawling angrily. "Lemme talk to him! I wanna talk to him!"

A chair dragged across the floor, followed by the thump of something heavy. "You little brat," Linda said. In the background, a man's voice began to murmur. Michael, the peacemaker. "I warned you!" Linda said. "Neither of you knows how to play fair!" Followed by more bawling.

I shouted into the phone.

"Keefer! I love you, son!"

Gradually their voices trailed off into the distance. It sounded as if she was forcing him down a hallway into a room at the back of the place—the hotel, the apartment, wherever they were staying. Michael's voice still murmured, counseling restraint. I stood there with the telephone against my ear like a compress. I was damned if I would hang up. Even if she forgot to put it back on the hook till the next day. Maybe he would sneak out of bed later that night. He would see the telephone was still off the hook and sleepily speak into it.

"Daddy?" he would whisper, and I would be there.

"Yes, son. Tell me where you are, and I'll come get you."

Somebody picked up the line.

"Still there, Earl?"

"Michael? Is that you?"

"Yes, hi. Sorry about the uproar. How are you?"

"Pretty lousy, frankly. Where are you people?"

"We're not quite settled yet. Don't worry. As soon we get straightened out, we'll let you know where we are."

"You took off without telling me."

"Well—that was Linda's idea."

"He's my son, Michael. I've got some rights."

"I know that. We just want to get a head start out here, so we can be a family."

"Michael, he's my son."

"I know, I know. But he lives with us. Here, I'll let you talk to Linda. She's calmed down now. She can explain it better than I can."

A pause. Then Linda came on the line again.

"Earl?"

"Linda, what the hell—"

"Please, Earl. Just shut up and let me talk for a minute. Okay?"

"Okay. But make it good."

"Well, it's very simple really. Michael and I thought we should make a fresh start. I've always loved California. Michael's originally from here. His family is out here and everything. I thought, that's it. It's perfect. So that's why we came out here. I didn't tell you because, honestly, I knew you'd put up a squawk. I thought you'd get your cheesy lawyer after me. I didn't think he could stop us. Neither did Swink. But I didn't want to chance it, so we just took off."

"Jesus, Linda. Thanks a lot."

"You want to know something really stupid?"

"What?"

"I didn't tell you I was getting married because I was afraid you wouldn't approve. Isn't that stupid? It's like you're my father or something. I've always hated that about you. That feeling of disapproval you radiate all the time."

"When do I find out where you are?"

"After Christmas."

"Christmas! That's another six weeks."

"I'm sorry. I truly am. I just feel we need some space to get established as a family. Keefer's having trouble accepting the situation. Michael plans to spend a lot of quality time with him."

"I'm not surprised he's upset. You practically kidnapped him."

"Hey, watch your language, wiseguy! I don't like that kind of talk."

"Okay, okay. Don't hang up on me. When are you going to call again?"

"We'll call around Christmas. I'll let you know."

"How about Thanksgiving?"

"That might be a little soon."

"Give me a break, Linda. This is awful hard for me to take."

"Well—I'll talk it over with Michael and we'll let you know."

"What about your father? You picked a hell of a time to move, so far as he's concerned."

"Don't lecture me, wiseguy! I've always *hated* that about you! I'll hang up quicker than you can spit."

"No, no, don't hang up. I'm sorry. Talk to me a little while longer."

"That's better. Besides, you don't know the story, buster. You always think you know everything, but you don't. Daddy *wanted* me to do this. He said if I was going to move

to California, I should do it. I shouldn't wait, I should do it
now. That's the way Daddy is. That's the way he always ran
his life, and that's the way he wants me to run mine. He says
I can always fly back and see him. Just before his operation
we were up there visiting him and he said to me"—and here
she imitated Phil's gravelly voice and gruff manner to per-
fection—"he said, 'Whaddayah think you do, eh? You
gonna sit around 'n' wait for me to die before you live your
life? Don't be stoo-pid. You could wait forever. Anyway, I go
when God wants, no maddah whutchu do, honeybun.'

"Oh Earl, he's been so wonderful and brave through all of
this. I can't stand the thought of losing him. He's always
been there for me, all my life. I can't stay with him all the
time during this. I can't. It's just too hard. I don't have the
courage. Mario can take it, but I can't. I plan to fly back
every week or so to see how he is. But, God. It's so painful.
My father, weak and sick. Phil Stephano, without a voice!
God, life is awful sometimes, isn't it?"

"When you fly back, will you be bringing Keefer with
you?"

"What—so you can hang around Daddy's house and try
and snatch him when we show up? Not likely, pal. Besides,
it's no good for him to see his grampy like that."

I thought maybe if she was bringing him back East with
her, she might agree to let me have him some weekend. But
since she already had her mind made up on the subject, I
saw no purpose in trying to argue the point with her. Instead
I said:

"I want to go up and see your father sometime. Mario is
supposed to let me know if it's all right. In fact, I'd better
call him again. It's been a while since we talked."

"Oh good! Please go up, Earl. Daddy always thought the
world of you. It would mean so much to him."

So we ended our conversation on that rather conciliatory and melancholy note; and I hung up the telephone feeling even emptier than before.

Apparently Michael didn't think it would do any harm, and they called again at Thanksgiving. This time we were all careful and the conversation went along smoothly.

They said I could write to him if I liked. Swink would see that the letters were forwarded. I did that, but I didn't hear from him in reply, except for one three-line, cautiously worded note on tablet paper. He said he was having a good time and liked the weather out there. It was just like being at Grampy's down in Florida.

When I consulted Schwanger on the question of Linda's refusal to reveal their whereabouts for another six weeks, he told me again that we could petition the courts and see if we could "show cause" why Swink should be ordered to turn over the address to us.

He said he thought we stood a slightly better chance on this than on the issue of dual custody (which I'd already dismissed as too slight, too complicated, and too hard on Keefer). He also said he thought it would take the courts longer than six weeks to decide the matter. Swink could throw up enough of a smoke screen to delay the process that long alone with no trouble at all, without even taking into account the natural inertia of the court system.

"Probably you'd be better off saving your money," said Schwanger. "That is, if she really is going to tell you where they are in a few more weeks."

My sentiments exactly. Why line his pockets, since it wouldn't speed things up and would only serve to make Linda mad and a little more spiteful? I backed off.

I suppose I could have hired a private detective. A private investigative agency might have had ways of finding where they were quicker than it was going to take for Linda to tell me. But once I knew, what was I going to do? Go out there and confront her? Try to get the court to slap her with a restraining order to keep her from moving again while I made a long-shot attempt at gaining custody? This didn't look like such a good option either; although later on, in light of some forebodings I had about Keefer's well-being, I wished I had tried it. At least I would have known where he was. But instead, I decided to stew in my own juice for six weeks and wait it out. I thought such forbearance on my part might work in my favor in dealing with Linda.

I had a lot of time on my hands and decided to do Keefer's Christmas shopping early. One night I was out in one of the malls looking for presents, and I heard his voice.

"Dad?"

A high voice, definitely his, over the general noise of the crowd. Quavery, as if unsure and frightened.

I wheeled around.

"Keefer? Where are you, baby?"

I made my way through the shoppers in the direction his voice had come from. Maybe they had spotted me and spirited him into one of the shops. I peered in the windows and doorways of the stores. What would they be doing back in Harrisburg, anyway?

"Keefer!"

"Something wrong, mister?"

A security guard had crept up on me. An old guy with imperturbable cloudy-blue eyes and shaggy eyebrows, who looked more in costume than in uniform, despite the pistol on his hip.

"I'm looking for my son. I thought I heard him call me."

"You think he's lost?"

"No, he's with his mother. I thought I heard him call me, that's all."

"Well, if he's with his mother, he can't be lost, can he?"

"No, I guess not."

The old geezer laughed.

"You guess not?"

"Right. You're right. He's not lost. Thanks anyway."

I went home. I couldn't get the sound of his voice out of my head. I didn't like the way I felt. I had an awful feeling something bad had happened to him.

I couldn't sleep that night. I told myself no amount of worry would solve a thing, but it didn't do any good. Sometime before dawn, I finally fell asleep.

In the morning, I boarded an airplane for Indianapolis. Between planes in Pittsburgh, I called Schwanger.

"Lloyd, I feel something's happened to Keefer."

"What, did you get a letter or something?"

"No, I just have a bad feeling. Listen, will you get in touch with Swink and make sure everything is all right?"

"Sure, if it'll ease your mind."

"Thanks. I'll be in Indianapolis today and tomorrow. I'm staying at the College Inn. Maybe you could call me there, leave a message—"

"I'll call you. I don't know how soon I can reach him. I should have something for you by the time you get back."

"Try to find out as soon as you can. This thing's got me. I can't sleep or anything."

"Take it easy. Just sit tight till I get back to you."

"Thanks, Lloyd."

When I didn't hear anything that night, I called the next morning. He said he hadn't been able to get through to Swink. He was still working on it.

"Just go about your business. I'll have something for you as soon as I can."

"I'm about crazy. Try to find out as soon as you can."

"I will, I will. Stop worrying."

When I got home Tuesday night, the lock on my door was broken. The pillows on the couch were slashed. The bookcases were overturned. Books lay everywhere with their pages creased and bindings split. The draperies were torn down at the windows. The rod had been wrenched out of the plaster. At first I thought it might be the work of thieves. But nothing was missing, from what I could see.

I went from room to room and surveyed the damage. The mirror in the bathroom was broken. The shower curtain had been pulled down. He had finished off his work by shitting on the floor.

In the bedroom, the fish tank lay on its side. It was resting on the rug on top of a pile of slushy blue pebbles in the middle of a dark water stain about the size of a small duck pond.

Fragments of dishware littered the floor in the kitchen. The sink was full of broken glass. Every dish, every glass, had been smashed.

I found a message written in mustard on a paper towel on the kitchen table. The crude yellow letters had been extruded from the plastic squeeze bottle I kept in the refrigerator door. It read:

Diner in the ovin

In the broiler, I found Keefer's goldfish laid out tail to nose and charred black.

List of suspects down to one.

I didn't report it. I didn't see the point. What would they do? Lock him up for a week? I cleaned up the place and had the locks changed. Except for the shit on the floor, I lived in the middle of the mess for several days before I could muster the energy to clean it up.

On Wednesday, Lloyd Schwanger got back to me. Swink had assured him that Keefer was perfectly fine.

"Relax. Stop worrying."

"Thanks, Lloyd. I appreciate your help."

"Anytime."

But I knew I was right. The voice at the mall had been his. He was crying out to me. Trying to hold on against the tide of time and separation that was pulling us apart.

When you break up with a barnburner like Linda, you pay for it with everything sweet thing in your life.

That's what I saw in the kitchen that night, as I stared at the charred bones in the broiler.

Thirteen

THE following Saturday, I drove up to the Island to see Phil.

I had talked to Mario again. He told me it was okay. Phil wanted to see me. He also gave me fair warning.

"If you wanna see him, you better come now. I dunno how much longer he's gonna last."

With that black-bordered remark tolling in my head, I decided I'd better not wait till the end of the month.

It was dark and cold when I stepped out of the apartment building that morning and got in the car to start for Bergen Cove. The darkness made me shiver. It was charged like a sponge with the impenetrable black ink of cold winter mornings. The first light was not encouraging either. The sky turned the color of pond ice. But by the time I reached the Berks County line, it had warmed into a brilliantly blue enamel and had given a special texture like impasto brushwork to the corn stubble in the farmers' fields. I pulled off my jacket. I turned the heater off. It became one of those soft warm days full of shadow and sunlight that sometimes fall to hand like ripened fruit at the end of autumn, just as we get ready for the short dark days at the end of the year.

When I got to the house Cousin Vito was out in the driveway under the trees, looking like Lon Chaney in makeup for his role in *Phantom of the Opera.* He was polishing Phil's big car. He smiled a ghastly smile in greeting.

"Gettin' it ready in case he wants ta go for a ride," he said in a hoarse voice, gesturing at the car with the polishing rag in his bony hand.

Mario was coming down the steps from the house as Cousin Vito said this.

"You dumb goombah! How many times I gotta tell ya? He's not goin' for any rides. He's dyin', for Chrissakes! When you gonna wake up?"

"Well—we could ask. You never know. You know what I mean?"

He appealed to my sense of the fantastic with a faint shrug of his thin shoulders.

"What can it hurt? He always liked ta go for rides. Maybe it'll make him feel better. Maybe some fresh air . . . maybe if I drove him out to Montauk Point . . ."

"Sure. Right. Maybe if you drove him down to Disney World. He'd probably feel like a million bucks."

Cousin Vito lifted the chauffeur's cap he wore cocked over an ear as large and pendulous as a bat hanging from the ceiling of a cave. He scratched his head. His thin greasy-looking hair was parted in the middle. He was at least as old as Phil, but there wasn't a gray hair among the sparse black threads on his head. He shrugged his shoulders again.

"Who knows? You might be right. He always did like drivin' over to Disney World when we was down at the house in Florida. He was big on Mickey Mouse. He bought me a hat with ears once."

"Awww—why do I waste my time talkin' to you!"

Mario made a violent dismissive gesture—not unlike Phil in the old days. He took my elbow and guided me up the flagstones toward the house.

"That dumb goombah. He still thinks Pop's gonna make it."

Mario told me to ready myself. He said Phil looked awful. He had lost some more weight during his latest stay in the hospital, and was now down to a hundred pounds. He was so thin that when they brought him home this time, his pants fell down as they were getting him out of the car to take him into the house.

"I stood him up and his pants fell down. Right on the ground. There he is, standing there with everything waving in the breeze. When they dressed him at the hospital, the dumbos forgot to put his underwear on. So I lift him out of the backseat and lean him against the car, you know, so I can reach in for the suitcase. And his goddam pants fall down. He's standing there in his shirttails. I figure I'm really gonna get one for this!"

Mario said he was reaching into the backseat for the suitcase. Perfectly positioned for a drop kick to the tail section. From long experience, he automatically shut his eyes and braced himself, expecting to feel the point of Phil's shoe in the seat of his pants at any second. When nothing happened, he opened his eyes and backed out of the car. He thought maybe Phil was waiting for him to turn around so he could give him a few rapid slaps across the face, as if applying a little after-shave for the bracing effect it might have on his complexion.

But then he realized Phil was just standing there, hogtied by his own trousers. They lay in the dust down around a pair of dirty-looking legs so skinny that his knees looked little

more than a double bulge in a horseshoe-shaped length of
firehose. With one vague hand, he was touching the handkerchief at his throat. With the other, he was holding himself against the car so he wouldn't fall down in the dirt along
with his pants.

He was looking around in bewilderment, as if uncertain
where all the fresh air was coming from. For a second, Mario
thought Phil was squinting at him, as if trying to recollect
who he was and where he had come from. But no: he was
peering over Mario's shoulder, at the sight of his house, with
a vague sense of mistrust in his eyes, as if he'd never seen it
before. His own house! Which he'd caused to have built for
his young family in the first flush of prosperity nearly forty
years ago, after the style of a country villa, with its long
rambling lines and low mansard roof, its custard-colored
stucco walls, its French doors flanked by tall green shutters,
opening onto flagstone terraces shaded by the poplars and
other trees that he and Cousin Vito had planted with their
own hands. Looking at it as if he'd never seen it before! As if
he dreaded to cross its very threshold!

Mario said he never wanted a kick in the pants or a slap
across his face so bad in his life. It made him feel like
bawling to see his father standing there looking around
meekly with his pants in the gravel. Instead, he started hol-
lering at Cousin Vito. The old dope was still sitting in the
car, having taken this moment of all moments to recomb his
hair in the rearview mirror. He combed it forward. Then he
combed it straight back. Then he parted it and combed it to
either side. Mario stood there and watched him in amaze-
ment.

"You dumb goombah! Whaddaya doin'? Ain't you beautiful enough already? Get over here 'n' help me! He's standin'
here with his pants down, for Chrissakes!"

He set the suitcase on the driveway. He pulled up his father's trousers and told him to hold on to them. Phil did so, while still staring at the house mistrustfully. Then he held him under the arms and told Cousin Vito to grab his feet. Together they carried him up the steps like a folding lounge chair and into the house, where Anna helped them put him to bed. He had remained there ever since.

"He's never gettin' out of bed again. It's hard, but I gotta accept it. For him, it's the end. Stupid, out there polishing the car: telling me I ought ask if he wants to take a ride out to Montauk Point. He's got rocks in his head the size of cannonballs. We got nurses for him twenty-four hours a day. What's he think? He's gonna come out on the steps someday and say, 'Yoohoo, Cousin Vito. I grew a voice box over the weekend, 'n' I wanna go for a ride.' That dumb goombah! He oughta be on a farm somewhere."

For the first few days, Mario told me, Phil seemed to make a rapid recovery. He started acting like his old self again. He sat up in bed. He pushed the nurse away when she tried to change the handkerchief and clean his whistle gadget. He wrote incessant messages with the pencil and paper kept at the ready on the nightstand by his bed. FOOD, he scrawled in big letters, trying to make the paper bark with his old voice of authority. DRINK, he demanded. TV, he wrote when he wanted entertainment. Sometimes he would scribble FUCK OF; by which Mario understood his father wanted to be left alone. Mario would take the pretty young nurse by the elbow and leave the old man to himself for a few minutes as he wished.

"He don't always spell so hot, but he gets the message across."

Gradually the onslaught of his furiously scribbled messages began to subside. He had no particular fluency when it came to words on paper. He had always depended on voice inflection and gesture to give his orders the proper shading. He scribbled and slashed at the page. He tried to supplement with grimaces and furious nods and shakes of his head. When Mario or the cute little dumb nurse misunderstood what he wanted and brought him the wrong thing, he threw whatever it was on the floor. The bigger the mess, the louder the crash, the better he liked it. It was as close as he ever came to having a voice again.

Slowly, however, his tantrums gave way to sullen indifference, loss of appetite, and long snoring naps. This was the state he was in now. Except for a few hours each day, when he roused himself to glare like a wounded hawk at the friends and relatives who timidly streamed through his room every afternoon between the hours of three and four to pay their respects.

My special midmorning audience didn't last long. Mario had rented a hospital bed. The head of it was cranked up partway and the railings raised. The bosomy nurse had propped him up on his pillows for the occasion. He lay on the high hard shelf of his bed with his pad and pencil in his lap, his bony knees draped in the sheeting wound around his legs. Secure behind his railings, he looked like some awful scrawny wizened baby—a recently hatched-out California condor. His glittery eyes darted in my direction for a second when I entered the room, blinked as if shocked at the sight, then fixed stubbornly on the drawn draperies of the windows opposite his bed, which, if open, would have given him a view of his fallow garden and grape arbor. I thought this would be his revenge for my desertion: that he would not look at me from his deathbed. But no. That was apparently not it. He just needed to look away in order to collect himself. He could do that more easily by avoiding my eye.

Mario indicated a chair a few yards from the bed. I sat down and waited. Mario stood by my chair to act as interpreter.

Phil attempted a few messages. He closed his gnarled fingers around the pencil stub. He couldn't hold it very well. He kept dropping it into the chasm of his lap. The young nurse kept retrieving for him. She giggled the third time it happened.

"You just like me to tickle you."

He stabbed at the writing tablet impatiently, hopelessly, trying to make it speak for him. The dots and slashes on the paper looked totally unintelligible to me, as they passed from the nurse's hand, over my head, to Mario. But he made sense out of them somehow.

"He sez: You don't look so hot."

"Probably not, Phil. I've been working hard."

More frantic stabbing with the pencil, till the point snapped off.

The nurse giggled again.

"You're just a little devil today, aren't you?"

She pushed back the chair at her little desk by his bed, came around the front. With a tinkly laugh, she fumbled the pencil stub out of his emaciated lap again. She resharpened it at the pencil sharpener screwed to the edge of her little desk. When she held it out, he grabbed it from her roughly. He scribbled some more. He tore off the sheet and passed it to the nurse, who passed it over my head to Mario with a smile.

"He sez—" Mario looked at me darkly. Big grapey shadows darkened the sockets of his eyes as he struggled with his emotions.

"He sez . . . he sez he loved you like a son. Like an old man with only one son. A child given to him in his old age.

But you let him down. He sez: You broke my heart."

"I'm sorry, Phil. I wish things had worked out."

More scribbling. He paused to give me a sidelong look out of his narrow glittery eyes. It was a look of utter hatred and contempt. He ripped the paper from the pad and thrust it at the nurse, who glanced at it this time before she passed it over my head to Mario with a flirtatious little smirk. Phil patted the handkerchief at his throat to make sure it was still in place. He raised his hip in the air and heaved himself onto his side, turning his face to the draperied wall. The interview was over. I had been dismissed. I was to leave the house now. Condemned, I assumed, to mull over in perpetuity the full extent of my sins against the family. There was no need for Mario to translate the final message, but he did anyway.

"He sez—oh yeh." The disk of Mario's dark face brightened. He seemed considerably cheered by the runic scribble on the crumpled scrap of paper he clutched in his hairy fist. He tried to suppress the flicker of a shamefaced smile as he looked up at me to deliver Phil's final volley, but he couldn't manage it altogether. I recognized the anguished ambiguity in that twiching grin of his. It was a smile long familiar to me. It was the smile of a benchwarmer son. "He sez: You're stupid, and that you should go away now, so he can die in peace."

I stood up.

"I understand, Phil. I'd probably feel the same way if I were in your shoes."

I started for the door.

"Wait a minute! Wait a minute! He's tryin' to say somethin' else."

Phil was flailing at the bedcovers, in a terrific tangle of sheets, struggling to turn over and face us again. The nurse rushed forward to help him. I heard a bubbly aspiration of impatience escape his lips. Around the edge of her starched white sleeve, I saw his eyes were on me again. He made a violent gesture. I thought he was giving me the finger.

"He wants you over by the bed."

Phil watched my approach avidly. His skull looked fragile as an eggshell. He kept his shiny eyes on me. He looked very severe and unforgiving. He had about him something of the fanatical glitteriness you see in the old photographs of Rasputin. He made another violent gesture, which I didn't understand.

"He wants you to get down on your knees," Mario said. And added in a choked voice, "I think he wants to give you his blessing."

I did as I was told.

He gestured again, for me to come nearer to the bed. I moved a few paces closer on my knees.

He grabbed me roughly by the ear and used it to crank me up so he could take a good look at me. His eyes slowly filled with tears. He shook his head and smiled sadly. He made a vague despairing gesture in the air. I suppose it was the sign of his benediction. He took my head in both hands like a bowling ball. I felt his dry lips touch my forehead. Then he pushed me away and faced the wall again.

In the hallway, Mario gave me a doleful look.

"He always liked you better 'n me. Don't it seem a little unfair to you?"

"He loves you, Mario."

"I know, I know. It's just that . . . I wished he *liked* me too. Ya know what I mean?"

I knew what he meant. Knew it chapter and verse.

Outside on the gravel, he said, "Come back 'n' see us sometime, okay? What happened between you 'n' Linda, that's history. It's got nothin' to do with us, right? So come back 'n' see us. Me and Cousin Vito, we're gonna be lonelier 'n shit when that old crook in there kicks the bucket."

"I will."

Something in my voice caused him to raise his head. Whatever he saw in my face made the light go out of his eyes.

"No. No, you won't."

"Sure I will."

"Naw. You'll never come back. That's the way is. Right? People have their own lives to live. To hell with everybody else."

"I'll come back. I promise."

"Yeh, sure. Take care of yourself. Okay?"

We shook hands and left it at that. I got in my car and circled the drive and drove out through the gates, while he stood at the top of the steps leading to the wide front door, and waved.

I never saw him again.

A WEEK later, I had a card from him telling me Phil had died. I was glad he had slipped his keepers so quickly. On the card, Mario wrote that he and Cousin Vito had gone to the track following the funeral, but neither had won a dollar. He said he guessed he and Cousin Vito just didn't have Phil's kind of luck.

AFTER Phil died, Linda relented and told me where they were living—just outside of Santa Barbara, as it turned out. She had decided life was too touch-and-go to hold out on me any longer.

"Who knows?" she said. "You could drop dead tomorrow."

I was glad for the change, whatever her motivation. I was busy that fall, trying to establish a client list for myself. But I managed to get out there and visit Keefer in the middle of December. I took him down to Disneyland for the weekend. He'd already been there several times, thanks to Michael, but he was happy to go back again and give me the guided tour, since it was my first time.

He was pleased to see me, but not beside himself by any means. He was making the adjustment. Michael was being exceptionally good to him, it was plain by the way Keefer talked about him. He told me Michael had promised to buy him a motorcycle when he got old enough. They were going to tour up and down the coast—maybe even travel into British Columbia. Michael said it was the most beautiful place in the world. He said nothing could match travel by motorcycle.

"I thought probably he'd had enough when he ran your mother into a tree and damned nearly killed her."

Keefer looked shocked at the brutality of my slur against the great and noble pastime of motorcycling.

"Oh no. He says it's safe if you know what you're doing—safer than a car."

Other than that single outburst, I kept my opinions to myself. I admit I was jealous he was taking to Michael so quickly. But six weeks is a long time in a boy's life—probably like six months to an adult. It wasn't a comforting thought. I was already beginning to feel like an outsider, someone who might manage an avuncular relationship with him, but not much else.

Work has always been the answer for me. I made sure I had plenty of it in the weeks leading up to Christmas. I got out the notes and a fragmentary draft of an old story I'd begun while waiting for the book to come out, back when Linda and I lived in the little apartment in Robindale, just a few miles from Phil's house. I read it through carefully. It was much better, much more promising, it seemed to me, than I remembered. I decided to work on it in my spare time.

The season came on quickly. My shopping list was short. I found myself visiting a new band of clients in New York, Chicago, and Boston. I was able to finish off in some very nice stores. Nola was planning on spending the holidays with the Wilhides on their farm just outside of Charlottesville, Virginia, so I wouldn't have her to worry about. I was looking forward to a few quiet days alone in the apartment. A time when I could hole up, do a little reading for pleasure, and generally avoid my fellowkind for a few luxurious days. I had no desire to go anywhere or to see anyone. If I got bored with my own company, I could always turn on the football games.

I did go out and buy a tree, to make the place look a little more festive. I had a time getting it to stay upright in its stand. I was not particularly handy in those days. I only took an interest later, when Marilyn and I bought the house.

After several minutes of squatting and fumbling with the crude turning screws that were supposed to dig into the tree's pitchy trunk and hold it steady, I uncramped and stood up to catch my breath and look at the results.

It looked a little crooked, but it was a nice big tree. Nice and full. No raggedy bare spots, not scraggly at all. It would look just fine when I got the red and blue bulbs and garland on it. I considered wrapping some boxes in gift paper and sticking them under the tree to take away the bareness. If I was going to do this, I thought, I might as well do it right.

As I stood considering this, the tree fell over suddenly and jabbed me in the eye. I bent over and clapped my hand over it. I felt something warmly wet on my fingers. Oh Christ, I thought. It's bleeding. It isn't bleeding, is it? Make it not bleeding. Jesus, Jesus, not my eye. I drew my hand away and squinted at it. It was daubed with blood. Blood all right: bright and plentiful.

I made it downstairs to the parking lot and got in my car. I cocked my head to one side in some fool notion that it might slow the bleeding and drove to the emergency room at the Pressman Clinic. They took one look and sent for Dr. Moffet, the ophthalmologist. He was not long in arriving.

"Take your hand away," he said.

"I can't."

"I can't work on it if you don't take it away."

Reluctantly, I removed my hand. I was in no humor for him to be fooling around with it. It hurt too much.

"Now open it."

"I can't."

"We'll give you something to numb the pain."

Holding my lower eyelid out, he inserted a hypodermic needle very carefully below my eye. At the puncture, I damned nearly fainted. Almost immediately the pain began to subside. He was able to shine his penlight in there and start to work without causing me any real discomfort.

"You damaged it, all right. Scratched the cornea pretty bad. Clipped a little piece of meat out of the white part. Cut your eyelid pretty good too. You had quite a wrestling match with that tree."

"It was stupid. I don't know how I did it."

"You'll be all right. I don't think you'll ever see out of that eye as well, of course. What we've got to watch out for is infection. Mainly we just have to let it heal. I've bathed it. Take these pain pills. You'll be pretty ouchy for a time. Put this ointment in it three times a day. Just take the bandage off and lower the bottom lid and squeeze in about that much. Don't touch it with the tip of the applicator. It won't be comfortable. It'll be very sensitive to any light. But you'll manage all right. Now I'm going to bandage it, because I want you to protect it from any nasty bumps or strong light for ten days and give it a chance to heal."

"You think it's going to be all right?"

"Yes, I think so. If you take care of it, I don't know why not. Infection is the main thing. We'll keep a watch on it. Don't go poking anything else into it for a while. Come over to my office tomorrow and see me. I'll have them call you with a time. We'll change the bandage. We'll have to change it every day, till it's ready to come off."

"Thanks."

"Glad to oblige. Now go home and rest. Take the next ten days off."

"I'll be happy to. I'm feeling really punk."

"I shouldn't wonder," he said.

I was headachy and feverish. I couldn't wait to get home and take a pill. The pain came and went in spasms and seemed to replicate the original trauma each time. At its worst, I had to pull over onto the shoulder of the road till it let up. Feeling faint and sweaty, I lay across the front seat and held my head, hoping some dumb cop wouldn't come along and ask me to explain myself.

I went directly to the bedroom and turned on the electric blanket. I got into bed. I shivered till the heat finally penetrated my bones and nudged me into a state of fitful sleep. I stayed there for fourteen hours, waking only from time to time to reach out and swallow another pill.

The next morning, I woke with a fiery pain in my good eye. The first thing I remembered was the doctor's remark about infection. Was it possible it could spread from one eye to the other so fast?

I felt my way to the bathroom. The eye didn't want to

open when I tried to study it in the mirror. It smarted and watered as I squinted at the glass just long enough to understand that I had a rash which ran from my hairline across the right side of my forehead, down into my unpatched eye. It trailed off halfway down my left cheek. The path it made was shiny—purply-red and pimply. It stung as if I'd stuck my face into a patch of nettles.

My eye watered copiously as I worked my way down the hall to the telephone by the sofa in the living room.

"Now you've gone and bunged up the other one," said Moffet in disgust. "You'd better come right in and let me look at it."

"I can't. I can't see. There's nobody here to drive me."

"Hmmm—you couldn't crawl over here, could you? Just head north when you get to Second Street."

"That's very funny."

"Well, all right, young fella. I'll make an exception in your case. What's your address?"

He didn't keep me waiting long. He seemed to get everywhere he was going in a fine hurry. I sat on the couch with my eye shut while he got the tools of his trade out of his black bag and fussed with the lampshade. I had a tremendous headache.

"Put your head back."

"I got it back."

"Well, put it back some more."

I grew tired of him squinting down his ocular scope and breathing into my face.

"What is it this time?"

"Looks like you got yourself a lovely case of the shingles."

"The shingles? I thought they went around your waist like a belt, and you died if the two ends touched."

"Old wives' tale. But they can be nasty. You've got your-self one of the nastier versions I've ever seen."

"What causes it?"

"Nobody knows for sure. Inflammation of the nerves. Viral in nature. Not sure what causes it. Often associated with stress. You're not going to be very comfortable for the next few days."

"I don't feel very comfortable now."

"Cheer up. It'll get worse. Stay in a dark room. I want you to get to bed and stay there except for office visits. Can somebody help out for a few days?"

"I don't think so."

"Nobody at all?"

"Well—there's my mother."

"Better give her a call. First thing you can do is get her to get this prescription filled. Now I'll take a look at that other eye. A man could build a practice around you."

I called Nola. I was not happy about it, but I did it.

"I hate to bother you, Ma."

"Don't be silly. I certainly owe you one for all the times you've helped me."

"Really, if you'd rather not . . ."

"Stop being stuffy. Tell me what you need."

She got the prescription filled and did some grocery shop-ping. She made a stop at the liquor store. I had decided to switch from gin to vodka, thinking it might go easier on the stomach lining. When she got back, she made a great show of lining up the vodka on the coffee table in front of the couch where I was resting.

"Here is your indispensable booze."

I sat up with a hand over my eyes.

Evidently she was going to read me a temperance lecture as the first installment on the debt I'd incurred by asking for help. She no longer approved of drinking, having given it up many years ago.

"It goes in the cabinet over the refrigerator. You can just put it on the kitchen table for now."

"I thought you might like to admire it first. Look how much there is. It ought to keep you going for three or four days."

"I get the point, Ma. Just put it away."

"It didn't do your father much good, did it?"

I agreed it had done him nothing but harm. But then again, I didn't get like him when I drank.

"My, my. It's so funny, isn't it?"

I couldn't see, but I could imagine the smile pursing her lips and the faraway look in her eyes.

"What's so funny, Ma?"

"Oh, everything."

"Come on, out with it. Now that you've started."

"I was just thinking how funny it is when you're young. How things like sex and liquor seem so necessary. When you reach my age you realize how stupid it is."

I opened, then shut my mouth, and decided to let it go. Her observations about human nature often arose oddly, like suddenly visible smoke from undetectable Delphic fires. When they came, they rarely bore directly on the subject at hand. If they did, it was in some elliptical way and beyond my depth.

"I would rather have my old dog back anyday than some dirty man."

"I'm sure you would."

"What's that supposed to mean?"

"Nothing more than I said."

"Well, I don't care. People put too much emphasis on sex these days. They'd be better off if they didn't. I don't think

Mother and Daddy ever slept together again from the day I was born. They had more important things on their mind."

I wanted her out of there. She thought she ought to tidy up the apartment as part of her errand of mercy. She was full of sighs as she stood in the middle of the living room trying to decide where to begin. I told her it wasn't necessary.

"I'll get to it when I'm feeling better. No big deal."

"I'd like to be of help. It's just I don't know where anything is. It's so much simpler to work at home among your own things."

"Forget it. You got the groceries and the booze. That's enough."

She brightened at this, like a child being excused early from school.

"Really? Are you sure I can't do anything else?"

"Positive."

"Well, I *do* have work waiting for me at home."

It was a relief to us both when she left. The silence rose in my rooms. I welcomed it like a healing balm. It hurt my head even to speak or listen to sounds.

For a week she ferried me to the doctor's office to have my dressing changed.

"Oh God!" she said on the second day, just as we reached the car.

"What's wrong?"

"I forgot to take the fish out of the freezer. Now I don't know what to have for supper. Oh well. I'll manage."

It was clear she was beginning to make sacrifices. I was sorry I had burned so many bridges. I might have been able to call on someone else.

We didn't talk much on our trips to the doctor. I had all I could do to deal with the nausea that gripped me whenever I left my dark apartment.

I was as good as blind. With her help, I negotiated the
various stages of the trip: down the stairs to the front door;
down the walk into the parking lot; and into the passenger
side of the old Rambler. She always parked it dead in the
middle of the lot, usually blocking in two or three other cars
in the process, just in case the transmission acted up and she
couldn't get it into reverse.

"Jesus, Ma. You didn't park in the neighbors' again, did
you? Why don't you get this thing fixed?"

"Oh shut up."

She tried not to rock me around. Every sudden movement
hurt my head. But she was a bad driver. Her mother had
been a bad driver. So had her father. It was in the blood. I
held my head, kept my unbandaged eye shut, as we swerved
in and out of traffic. My main consolation was that I couldn't
see the stop signs and red lights she ran through.

From time to time she would say in a thoughtful or out-
raged tone:

"What is that man shouting about?"

Or:

"Who does that fool think he's shaking his fist at?"

The lot at the doctor's was small and crowded. She pulled
into the no-parking zone out front, left the Rambler babbling
in various zany registers to itself at the curb, and walked me
to the waiting room. Then she went outside and drove the car
around and around the block till I appeared again on the
front steps. She would then repeat the maneuver: leave the
maddened Rambler jibbering to itself at the curb, come
fetch me, lead me to the car again, and drive me home. It
was a trial for us both.

Inside, the vaguely restive medical tech who presided
over the outer reaches of Moffet's universe could never seem
to guide me through the warren of hallways to the particular

cubicle selected for my examination without running me
onto a chair or pushing me into the weighing scales.

"Careful there," she would say.

Then followed the examination itself. I supposed I was
taking it all like a baby, and said so once.

Moffet flipped up his goggles.

"That's right. You *are* acting like a baby. I get people in
here with real problems. Much worse off than you."

Humbled, I sat there meek and uncomplaining, as the son
of a bitch hurt me again.

When it came time for the bandages, it was all I could do
to keep from whimpering with gratitude.

On the way over on the third day, she said: "I hope you
get over this fast."

She had no aptitude or patience for nursing. Neither did I.
I suppose I could have taken care of Keefer no matter what.
You like to think there are some exceptions.

On the drive home, she confessed her real worry. She was
afraid she wouldn't be able to go down to Charlottesville for
the holidays.

"If you don't get better soon, I'll have to cancel my
plans."

"Don't be silly. I'll be okay by the weekend. You just go.
There's no reason to change your plans."

"Will you really be better by then?"

"I'm positive."

"Promise?" We both laughed at her little joke.

"Christ, you're awful," I said.

I confess my heart went out to her as she sat there looking
as pleased as if I had just paid her a compliment.

On Christmas morning, I lay on the sofa taking comfort in
the steady murmur of the television set. As yet it still hurt to
watch it. I thought I might have a drink by way of acknowl-

edging the holidays. I got up and switched channels to catch the news.

I shuffled about the apartment, squinting no more than I had to out of the eye with shingles. I had just settled back on the sofa when the story came over the TV.

"Doctors at the Pressman Clinic are looking for people who have an infection called shingles, in order to make a serum to save a boy's life. Perfecto Rivera, six years old, of Lebanon, is suffering from a rare case of internal chicken pox. He is listed in critical condition. Only an antigen taken from the blood of someone suffering from shingles at the right stage of infection can provide the life-saving help that the Rivera child needs. The hospital has made several public appeals. If you think you can help, please call . . ."

By God, I thought. Maybe I'm the turkey they're looking for.

"Yes, we're still searching for a donor," said the doctor they put me onto when I dialed the number mentioned on the news. His name was Levis. He sounded tired. "How fast can you get here?"

"I can't get there. I can't see well enough to get there."

"You can't see?"

"No. I've got shingles in one eye and I jabbed the other with a Christmas tree."

"I'll send somebody. Sit tight."

When I walked into his office, he looked at the crusty mess on my face and broke into a smile.

"You're beautiful. Absolutely goddam beautiful."

He rushed me down the hall, where they hooked me up to some transfusion equipment.

"I can't get hepatitis from this stuff, can I?"

"Of course not."

The nurse was insulted by the very idea.

"Good. I can do without that on top of everything else."

I was rolling down my sleeve afterwards when Levis poked his head around the curtain.

"Somebody out here wants to see you."

"Who would that be?"

"Mrs. Rivera. The boy's mother."

"Oh no. Let's not have any of that."

"Oh come on. Let her say thank you. What do you say?"

He disappeared without waiting for an answer. In a minute, a small dark woman in a cloth coat, wearing a bandanna on her head, appeared around the edge of the curtain and beamed at me. She was carrying a brown paper sack.

"Perfecto's pajamas."

"Pardon me?"

She showed me the paper bag.

"My son's pajamas."

"Oh, yes. Well . . . I hope he gets better soon."

"Thank you. Thank you so much, I can't say enough many times."

Her eyes shone with such heartfelt gratitude that it embarrassed me.

"Well . . . I hope it does some good."

I was afraid of queering the kid's luck by sounding too confident.

"Oh, yes. God watches over us."

"No doubt he does."

"Because of you, my Perfecto will live."

"I'm sure the doctors will do everything—"

She shook her head impatiently.

"No, no. Not doctors. You. You come from God."

If I came from God, I had certainly picked a circuitous route.

"Actually I heard about it on TV," I said, and immediately felt foolish.

"I will pray for you."

I don't know why I felt offended, but I did. She was too fervent or something.

"Now really. There's no need for that."

"No, no. I have promised God."

"Well—thank you."

"At St. Teresa's always a candle will be burning in your name."

"Thank you. I hope your boy grows up to be president."

She showed me beautiful teeth.

"If so, we will invite you to the White House."

"Oh no. I'm not settling for that. I want to be Secretary of State."

I got away from her as quickly as I could.

IN the old days, plenty of good doctors thought bleeding a patient did much to regulate the spleen and bring a person's system back into proper balance. Dillard told me once when I was a little boy that bloodletting had been given a bad name by fools who didn't know when to quit. He had himself bled twice a year by some old quack who lived in the woods near the abandoned quarry just up over the ridge from his house in Dunnocks Head. He said it did him worlds of good. "Worlds of good": that was his expression for it.

The next morning, I wondered if there wasn't something to it after all. My temperature was back to normal for the first time in days. My rash was all but dried up. I took the bandage off my Christmas eye. I found I could stand the light tolerably well. All that week I improved steadily. By New Year's morning, I was pretty much back to normal.

Always a bad sleeper and an early riser, I got up at dawn to shave. As I lathered up, I happened to glance out the bathroom window. There, in the pearly early-morning light, a red fox trotted along the escarpment of tilled fields which abutted the excavated parking lot in back of the apartment house.

His ruddy coat flamed against the snow as he moved along, his black nose close to the ground. He broke into a trot against the frieze of broken cornstalks, as if onto a scent. I watched him till he loped out of view.

A few snowflakes blew sideways outside my window, like fine ash drifting on the wind. The snow was bright on the hillside as if lighted from below.

He was gone that fast. It made me wonder whether I'd seen a fox or a spirit.

I finished shaving. I glanced out the window again as I patted my face dry with the towel. I would have liked to see him again—trotting along, all business, with his nose to the ground.

I went into the living room and turned on the TV for the sake of the noise. Then I went into the kitchen and fixed myself a drink.

"Ah," I said to my glass. "Truly you come from God."

Part Three

A New Life

One

THERE followed what I call my anacreontic bachelor years.

My business flourished in a modest way. I kept it small, so I wouldn't have to hire anybody. When PCs became feasible, I bought one. I've always managed to keep the work under control. It's the other stuff that has given me trouble.

I went through a series of women friends. I can't say practice made me any better at picking them.

For a while I took up with an artist from Washington, D.C. Her name was Tenley Moore. When I knew her—nearly ten years ago now—she was painting what she called a "hydrocycle" of drowned women based on characters from literature and mythology. The canvases were huge. They extended from the floor to the pipes just below the ceiling in her studio, which was located on the top floor of a dreary building on P Street, just a few blocks from the University. The corpses which peopled these pictures were handsome and of epic proportions. Silver-and-black water and lettuce-green lily pads figured in the paintings as well. She finished one or two a year and sold them for substantial sums. The income, however, was not sufficient to support her. For this she relied on her father, who was someone of importance at ARCO. Although he was a powerful presence in her life, I never met him during our six months of friendship.

Tenley liked to cross her legs. She would pull her skirt up above her knees and caress her shins as she talked. She leaned forward over her long legs and told me charming stories about her lack of aptitude for boring tasks of any kind.

She had a walk that affected men much as an underground spring affects a forked stick in the hands of a water witch. My grandfather Dillard was a water witch. One day in the woods when I was six I saw the stick he was witching with dip and pull down so hard that the bark peeled right off in his fingers. Tenley's walk had the same effect on men. Some tried hard not to look, but nearly all twisted around in spirit, and a few peeled off a layer of metaphysical bark in the process too.

One day she took this walk into a garage. She didn't go into the office, as she would have had she been giving it any thought at all, but took it right in through one of the wide doors opening onto one of the bays where they pulled the cars in for repairs.

She took it right up to a fellow in a pair of greasy overalls with a cigarette screwed into one side of his mouth and a look of astonishment on his face as if a squirrel had just run up his pant leg.

"Hi," she said. "I'd like to get my front end realigned. Can you help me?"

Whistles and catcalls rose from every corner of the shop. Mechanics lifted their heads from underneath engine hoods. Others rolled out from under automobiles and sat up with happy crooked grins on their faces. When she realized what she had said, she pressed a hand with long red fingernails to the bosom of her blouse and laughed along with the rest of them.

Amid more catcalls and whistles, the manager hastily quick-stepped out of his office and led her up the three concrete steps to the relative safety of the customer service area with its tire displays and shelves of replacement batteries, lest she say something else that might possibly set off a full-scale riot among his employees.

In many ways she was delightful company. We went to Boston one weekend to see an exhibit of nineteenth-century American painting. I can see her still, absolutely naked, jumping up and down on the bed in our room at the Plaza, trying to touch the high old-fashioned ceiling with her outstretched hand.

Her coppery hair was soft as the feathers on a baby chick. She had green eyes and the complexion of a six-year-old child. She wore the reddest lipstick she could find. She had sharp little white teeth like a puppy. She used to bite me all over my body—quick sharp little puppy bites, just to make me yip.

She liked to make love in the car in the parking lots of restaurants after dinner. At the table, she would lean over and tell me what she was wearing under her dress. She said we would have to do it in the parking lot again because she couldn't contain herself till we got home. But it wasn't really passion she was feeling so much as it was the danger and excitement she liked, the possibility of getting caught.

When I called her on the telephone during the week, she would say things like "When you come down here this weekend, I'm going to ride it till it falls off. You'll have to take it to your doctor in a handkerchief."

I didn't find this as thrilling as she intended. Making love to her required a talent for gymnastics. She had read the *Kamasutra* at a vulnerable age. It had ruined her for normal sex. She liked to get tangled up and then crawl around on the floor a lot, like those double-jointed people who tie themselves in knots and walk around on their elbows.

Sometimes we started in bed. Sometimes on a chair or against a door. We might end up under a pile of clothes in the closet. Or in a tub of Jell-O in the bathroom. After a weekend with her, I had brush burns all over my body. "You're turning my strawberries to blueberries," I told her once.

I liked her a lot. She was mischievous and unpredictable and intelligent and talented. She was better-read than most women I knew. It was true she was immature in some ways. She was easily bored and had no idea of the value of money. But I thought we were getting on very well, and I began to take her seriously.

In July of that year, I took her along to Fog Mountain. On the strength of a book of mine that had been published the year before, Leslie Crowthers, unknown to me, had submitted my name and had managed to wangle me a fellowship to this illustrious old conclave of scribbling adulterers and alcoholics. The conference had been taking place in an old hotel on a mountaintop in the Berkshires in the middle of every summer for the past several decades. Leslie was always doing things like that—working benevolently behind my back to turn me from a weekend dabbler into a real writer, fully committed to my craft, so I could starve to death like the rest of them. I both resented and loved him for it. It frightened me that he thought so highly of my work.

At any rate, I went to the conference and took Tenley along. I introduced her to everybody I met as my fiancée.

Privately, we joked and made light of this slightly old-fashioned, slightly absurd characterization of our relationship.
But we both knew behind the solemn mockery of these introductions lay the potential for real seriousness.

I saw how the poets swarmed around her immediately at
the cocktail parties that were held on the lawn in the evenings, when I went off to fetch her drinks from the bar. They
gazed at her with such sad, if covert, longing. When I returned, drinks in hand, they smiled me back into the magic
circle of her presence with faint, albeit friendly, contempt. I
think they disapproved of me. They thought I treated her too
casually; that I was careless, that I didn't really deserve her.
They would drift away and leave us to our own devices (although they returned fast enough whenever I wandered off
again). Their parting glances seemed to say: *My my, you fool.
Have you no idea of the magnitude of your good fortune?*

Through the bleary eyes of a handful of paunchy old
poets, some half in the bag and many long past their prime, I
began to see her in a new light. I realized again with a fresh
burst of enthusiasm what a vivacious, attractive, and truly
charming woman she was.

It was a romantic setting. The dark mountain brooded
over our heads; the air was remarkably crisp and bracing;
the shadows of the charming old ramshackle hotel lay long
in the grass at our feet; handsome, intelligent people murmured all around us, many with their arms tenderly locked
around each other.

We both realized then if I got gooned enough at one of
these parties, I might at any moment suggest that we run off
and do something rash. But the conference drew to a close;
and with it, the immediate danger passed.

We loaded our suitcases into the car and I drove her
home. We agreed it had been a lovely interlude.

Fortunately she took up a nasty little habit just in the nick of time, before the danger had a chance to build up a new head of steam. It was minor, really, but it set off a complete and sobering reconsideration in my mind.

Sometimes, when I leaned forward to kiss her, she would suddenly lick my face and fall back, giggling at my look of surprise.

"Don't do that," I'd say.

But it only made her laugh all the more. *Such a solemn prig!* her expression seemed to say.

The worst part was that her saliva was above average in viscosity. Having been lapped by a few babies and several dogs in my day, I know I wasn't imagining this. Her tongue wasn't merely wet. It was sticky as a toad's.

I asked her to stop, but fortunately she persisted. Those occasional vile catlicks woke me to the fact that I was trying hard to make another serious mistake. She would have made my life every bit as miserable as Linda ever had. Probably worse.

I said goodbye to Tenley and with a feeling of relief went back to my books.

But not for long. It seemed I could never stay out of trouble for long.

There was Phyllis, for example: a pretty brown-eyed brunette with high color in her cheeks and the kind of peppy personality that I associate with the Jack Russell terrier who lives next door to me.

When I knew her eight years ago, Phyllis had been married three times. She could be up to five or six by now. The fact that she had been married several times should have made me cautious, or at least curious, but it didn't. I accepted it on face value when she said that she'd had no luck with men till I came along. Didn't I have the same problem

when it came to women? The only untoward thing I noticed
about her in the early stages of our relationship was that
when I took her out to dinner she tended to treat the waitresses very coldly, as though they had affronted her in some
way.

We got along so well that I asked her to move in. It turned
out to be a terrible mistake. Afterwards, I couldn't look
across a room if a woman happened to be in my line of
vision.

"Why are you staring at her?" Phyllis would say. "What
are you trying to do? Mortify me in front of everybody?"

She went through my address book and altered the num-
bers opposite any female name she found listed in it, including that of my dentist. She also altered Leslie's number,
assuming from his name that he must be a woman. She
developed the habit of calling me late at night—sometimes
as late as three in the morning—when I was out of town on
business, to tell me that she loved me.

"That's very nice, Phyllis. But couldn't you have waited
till morning to tell me that? I don't want to hurt your feelings, but I have an important meeting tomorrow. I really
need to get some sleep."

"It's just that I miss you so much," she would say.

She often insisted on unpacking for me when I came home
from a trip. Once I happened into the bedroom as she was
getting the clothes together to do the laundry and caught her
sniffing at my underpants. I turned and left the room without
a word. I suppose she was checking for signs of semen,
another one of her surveillance techniques to see if I was
cheating on her while I was on the road. Whatever the reason, it made me shudder with repugnance.

One night, around the holidays, and shortly after the episode with my underwear, we ran into Arthur and one of his

friends in a restaurant. We invited them over for drinks and dinner on New Year's Eve.

On the day of the dinner, I called Arthur at the office and arranged to meet him for a drink beforehand late that afternoon, ostensibly to talk over old times, but mainly to get out of the apartment, so I wouldn't be around when Phyllis got home from work.

I also wanted to warn him about Phyllis's curious reactions when it came to references about the women in my past. I would tell him to make no cute innuendoes or lewd remarks about my heretofore bad taste in females in an effort to ingratiate himself into Phyllis's good graces. In that way lay disaster. I'm sure, too, that I would have told him some of the awful things I had to put up with, including the story about the underpants, so that he could tell me I was living with a hairball of a monster and ought to find some way of getting her out of my apartment, pronto.

I needed reassurance that I indeed had another disaster on my hands. Over the years, Arthur had had plenty of trouble with a series of dingbats himself. I wanted his advice about what to do. Naturally I desired to take this up with someone who suffered from much the same difficulties as I did and therefore was probably the unlikeliest person to be of any real help. That's the way I operated in those days.

As it turned out, Arthur brought his date for the evening along to the cocktail lounge where we had agreed to meet, so I had no chance for the kind of consultation that I had hoped for. His friend's name was Rusty—at least, that is what she went by. It was not the same young woman we had seen with him in the restaurant a few weeks ago. Apparently she had been replaced—although the new girl was of the same type: too much makeup, overdressed, hopeless at conversation, and very attractive in a cheap, flashy way. Arthur led a very active social life, and it had always been accompanied by a very high turnover rate when it came to the women.

He and I swapped the usual collection of tried-and-true insults. I told him the adult bookstore down the street was having a sale on feathered dildoes. I said he ought to stop in and buy a new one instead of going through the bother of getting the old one refeathered all the time. He asked me why I wasn't carrying my little doughnut pillow with me that night. Did that mean my hemorrhoids were better? Rusty thought we were hilarious, which only served to egg us on.

Not surprisingly, we were a little late getting back to the apartment. We were full of apologies and giggles when we came in the door. Arthur, smelling pleasantly of scotch, offered a complicated and, I thought, reasonably funny explanation for our being twenty minutes late. But Phyllis didn't think so. Even under the best of circumstances, she didn't have much of a sense of humor. She came from German stock. Like most of them, she was very literal-minded. A joke had to be stupid and bawdy or else she didn't get it.

She gave us a frigid reception, then returned to the kitchen to heat up the oyster stew again. I put some Bach on the stereo and fixed some drinks.

"Phyllis, would you like a drink?"

Silence.

"Phyllis. Would you like a drink?"

"No. I would not. Thank you."

I made a face and shrugged my shoulders. Rusty giggled. Arthur told a long pointless joke about an amorous moose that climbs into a canoe after a hunter who is playing a trumpet.

When he got near the end, he looked blank and gave his forehead a slap. "My God! I've forgotten the punch line!"

We cackled like a bunch of idiots; we were utterly shame-

less. It was more than Phyllis could bear. No doubt she
thought we were laughing at her, playing the martyr in the
kitchen, and she wasn't far from wrong. We heard a crash. A
moment later, she stalked into the living room. Her face was
red and her fists clenched. She looked as if the top of her
bouffant was about to blow off. She stuck out her bottom
teeth at me and said:

"You can lick it off the floor!"

She flew down the hallway and slammed the bedroom
door. For a moment we sat there stunned.

"Well," I said, getting up. "Let's go see what Phyllis has
made us for dinner, shall we?"

"Good idea," said Arthur.

We went to the kitchen doorway and peered in. There
were oysters all over the place and a large steamy buttery-
looking puddle of milk on the floor.

I said, "Do you really want to lick this stuff off the floor?"

Arthur pretended to think it over.

"No. I don't think so. I've never liked this method of
preparation. It always tastes too much like floor wax to me.
Unless, of course, you add paprika. We could add lots of
paprika. Then we wouldn't notice it."

"Let's not chance it," I said. "The three of us will go out
to dinner. Right after Phyllis finishes with her act."

We went back to the living room. We could hear Phyllis
throwing things around in the bedroom, making as much
noise as possible. In a few minutes, she came out carrying
her suitcase.

"I'd like my Christmas lights, please."

The little tree we'd bought for the holidays was still up
and decorated.

"I'll send them to you."

"I want them *now.*"

She started tugging at the string of lights. The tree fell over. She kept tugging on the lights, reeling them in by holding onto the free end and wrapping the cord over her elbow and through the natural hook made by her forefinger and thumb. As she reeled in her lights, the tree spun on the floor, accompanied by the soft plopping sound of breaking bulbs. When she was finished, she put the lights around her neck and picked up her bag. She shot me a final murderous look and went out the door, slamming it behind her as hard as she could.

"Well," I said. "It looks like we really have something to celebrate."

Arthur shook his head and smiled.

"Tell the truth. Where do you find these women?"

"It's a disability, Arthur. You shouldn't make fun of somebody's disabilities. It's like being tone-deaf or color-blind."

"I've never known anybody who got mixed up with a crazier bunch of women," he said.

I thought I could name one other. But I decided to keep it to myself.

After that, whenever Arthur and I met around the holidays, I would say to him, "How about coming over to my place on New Year's Eve? We'll have a couple of drinks and throw a kettle of oyster stew against the wall. What do you say?"

He would say it was surely a wonderful way to bring in the New Year and that we really ought to do it again sometime.

If we had women with us—and usually we did—they naturally found our conversation baffling.

I would explain, while Arthur nodded in vigorous agreement, that having friends in and throwing a pot of oyster stew against the wall was an old Celtic custom. It was the

way my family had always brought in the New Year. I said I
was surprised they hadn't heard about it, since it was a very
common practice in certain parts of Wales and Scotland.

I'm sorry to say that this explanation satisfied most of
them.

AFTER Phyllis, I took my act on the road. I decided it wasn't
good to have close relationships with women in the town
where you lived—and certainly not wise to invite them into
your home.

I suppose I was going through yet another stage of divorce. I thought I was acting of my own free will, not going
through any stage. But doubtless even a thrown stone hur-
tling through the air thinks it is operating under its own
volition.

It was good to be done with the Glorias and the Tenleys
and the Phyllises and the handful of other less remarkable
women of shorter duration who had made a mess of my days
and nights in recent months. I decided I really preferred the
company of perfect strangers.

The phrase "perfect strangers" has an aptness beyond its
commonly accepted meaning. Because strangers, I discovered, try hard to be perfect with each other. The novelty of
just meeting someone puts a person on his or her mettle.
Everything is fresh, everything is new, all of it is potentially
exciting and rewarding. Both man and woman in these situa-
tions carefully manage their weaknesses. They recognize the
propriety of withholding unpleasant information about
themselves. This lack of candor usually turns out to be an act
of kindness. In the opening hours of such a friendship, mu-
tual sympathy and diplomacy reach their highest levels, only
to degenerate as people truly get to know each other. Disappointment sets in, intolerable disappointment. How sad, I

thought. Intimacy must have its consolations; but at the moment, I couldn't think of any.

So I adopted a new strategy which I thought was better suited to life on the road. I called this "the moving-target principle." I entered into a series of relationships with women in various cities along the great-circle route of my commercial wanderings. I had no intention of taking them seriously, nor did I expect them to take me seriously. My sole purpose was to enjoy their company, express admiration for their looks, their good taste in music, their ideas, and the way they wore their hair. I intended to be charming if I could, to give pleasure at no inconvenience to myself, and to move on before anything bad happened. I did this well. Now that I no longer took them seriously, they seemed to like me better. I found I could speak my thoughts, for example, without running much risk of giving offense. This I couldn't do with people like Phyllis or Gloria.

I met these new people at the Chicago Art Institute and in places like the Twin Tablets in Minneapolis. The Twin Tablets is frequented by young business and professional women from the Minneapolis–St. Paul area. It is probably the best place in the country to meet a nice, good-looking, semi-well-educated Midwestern woman. But generally everywhere I traveled, the women I encountered were well-dressed and attractive and held responsible positions in business. We had drinks together. We found a quiet place where we could have a good dinner and talk. As to restaurants, I relied on their advice, since I was the out-of-towner. Sometimes we went out dancing. Afterwards I escorted them home in taxis to tall sedate buildings of brick and glass with doormen and good security systems. Sometimes I was invited in, sometimes not. Always we parted on the best of terms.

On occasion I called them when my travels took me to

their particular city again. They greeted the sound of my voice on the telephone with a gratifying note of surprise and enthusiasm.

Some of them had estranged husbands. A few of these men went through their ex-wives' trash, offered doormen bribes for information about their comings and goings, and rang the telephone ceaselessly from three in the morning till dawn. I have lain in the darkness next to more than one beleaguered woman and listened with her to the telephone wailing like a lost soul. These poor creatures didn't even dare to take the receiver off the hook. They were too frightened, too scared, to reveal even that much information to their callers.

But they were the exceptions. As sympathetic as I felt for their situation, I did not hang around and wait to get shot or beaten to a pulp outside their apartment houses.

Most of the women I met had boyfriends on hold somewhere. The men either bored them, or made them restless, or had disturbing habits. In any event, my women friends were having second thoughts about them. They found me a sympathetic listener and good company. They told me it was a relief to get away for a few hours from all that ponderous smothering business that passed for serious attention between the sexes.

If I had no female acquaintance in the city and had no desire to find one, I filled the hours pleasantly by drinking vodka martinis, usually at the bar of the hotel where I was staying (the safest place for this kind of indulgence when out of town on business), and talked to the bartender about sports.

In this way, I found out that a team doctor once performed a hemorrhoidectomy on Joe Cronin, the great shortstop of the Boston Red Sox in the '30s, right on the trainer's table in the Boston clubhouse; and afterwards the doughty shortstop went out and played both games of a doubleheader. I also learned that Yogi Berra once went into a pizza joint and ordered a pie; when the counterman asked him if he wanted it cut into eight slices, Yogi is reputed to have said, "Naw, I can't eat eight pieces. Better make it six."

These are things you can't learn anywhere else.

I drank at a slow steady pace calculated to produce a pleasant buzz; but at a regulated level, so as to avoid that awful sluggishness I felt in the mornings whenever I indulged too freely.

These activities tended to keep me up late. But if I were up in my room, I reasoned that I would be reading the book I had packed in my overnight bag till the early hours. Or watching one of the old late-night movies on TV that I was coming to enjoy more and more the older I got—lovely old films, starring people like Ray Milland, Humphrey Bogart, Gene Tierney, Susan Hayworth, Tyrone Power. They were like old friends. I enjoyed their company better than that of most of the people I knew. Now that most of them were dead, I felt I knew everything there was to know about them. But I could always do these things at home. I was on the road. So I used my road strategy.

When my acquaintances found out that I suffered from insomnia, sometimes not sleeping for more than an hour or two out of twenty-four for weeks at a time, they were impressed. Some even professed envy.

"Boy, I wish I could do that. I'd get so much done . . ." Tell me about it. It would drive you crazy in a month.

After several months, the late nights and the booze began to have its effects, despite my seemingly endless capacity to run without normal amounts of sleep. I found myself beginning to fade by noon. A drink or two at lunch usually picked me up and allowed me to keep pace with the best of them in the afternoons. Of course, I never drank at lunch unless it was also my clients' habit to have a cocktail. Most of them sagged a bit after a drink or two, but not me. Alcohol had the opposite effect on me. It exhilarated me. It gave those tired blood cells of mine a booster shot.

But I knew I couldn't just work, read, drink, and indulge in what was known then as "casual sex" (what an innocent, even old-fashioned sound the phrase has today, given the dangers now; although even back then there was nothing "casual" about it, when you considered all the time and energy it took).

I became subject to sudden cold sweats and nausea. I got sick a few times in clients' offices—broke out into a sudden gluey perspiration, got dizzy, had to take off my jacket, loosen my tie, and hold my head between my knees. Once they sent for the company doctor.

"Any numbness in your arm? Pain in your chest?"

I remember the man had a toothbrush mustache and a lot of hair up his nose. I told the other anxious executives in the room that it was probably caused by the antihistamine I'd taken that morning. They all sat back, relieved. In a few minutes, I was able to get back to work. But I knew it was time to give up the moving-target principle and find a new strategy for the road.

I added yoga to my bag of tricks. On the floor of my hotel room I practiced exotic exercises. I stretched my neck. I grimaced and looked very fierce into the mirror—something called "The Lion"—to tone the muscles in my face. I scraped the coating off my tongue with one of the tongue depressors I carried in my shaving kit, thereby ridding my-self of layers of old dead epithelial cells and freshening my mouth and probably my attitude as well.

I did something called "The Cobra" and listened to my vertebrae crack one by one. This was accompanied by a pleasant relaxing sensation all along my spine.

Here's how I did it. I lay on my stomach with my forehead resting on the floor. Hands palm down, forearms about parallel with my shoulders. After some slow breathing—much of the benefit of yoga had to do with slow, measured breathing—I raised up my head slowly, rolling my eyes upward toward the ceiling. Gradually I began to press down with my hands and raise myself off the floor. I made sure that my hips remained inert to keep the pressure of this levitation centered along my spine. The exquisite pressure, just short of pain, flowed serpentine, from vertebra to vertebra, all the way down to my lower lumbar. Wonderful.

I repeated the exercise three times between intervals of controlled breathing. When I was finished, I was so relaxed I could hardly get off the floor.

I followed this with the next-to-last exercise in my nightly routine. I squatted on my heels, my toes curled under so that the ligaments were stretched to the maximum. My arms rested lightly on my thighs. I stared heavy-lidded at the wall of my hotel room and concentrated on relaxing the muscles in my face. I slowed my breathing; I tried to feel the air passing across the membranes of my nose. I tolled the universal mantra: *Oooooommmmmm!* The vowel filled the room, making the atmosphere suddenly solemn and templelike. Then I vibrated the ending consonant through my sinuses. It made all the bones in my head hum as if I had entered a bell tower just after the bell had been struck.

I repeated the mantra several times. What the people in the next room thought of this sound I never stopped to consider. Or what the chambermaid would have thought had she chanced to open the door with her pass key at that moment on her nightly room check and found me dressed in my underwear making that strange noise while squatting in the middle of the floor.

For my grand finale, I shifted the weight of my torso forward to the heels of my hands. I extended my neck, widened my eyes, and stuck out my tongue and tried to touch the tip of my chin. I held this position for two full seconds, eyeballing the wall like a catatonic. I forget the name of this exercise. Then slowly I subsided back onto my heels and exhaled.

Ah, wonderful. And mighty good for you too, I suspected.

Curiously, although the sense of well-being persisted when I got into bed, I found that I slept no better with exercise than without it.

I considered giving up booze, but I wasn't ready to surrender one of my few remaining pleasures. Instead I dropped red meat from my diet, as recommended by the author of the book on yoga that I'd read.

In the middle of winter the year after Phyllis (February, I think it was), I was in New York on business. I was staying at the Highlander over on Sixth—or the Avenue of the Americas, if you insist—a deplorable choice of hotels but located near to my clients' offices. In my little shoe box of a room before bedtime that first night, I overdid a spine-stretching exercise. With my hands placed behind my knees, elbows crooked out, I had tried to touch my kneecaps with my head. I felt a warm pleasant suffusion along the length of my spine, but no immediate ill effects.

The next morning, I couldn't straighten up. I had to go around that day using the kind of walk I have always associated with Groucho Marx. My client also thought I walked like Groucho; he mentioned it several times during the day. "What is this?" he said. *"A Night at the Opera?"*

Later he apologized for making fun of me. "I'm sorry, I don't mean to laugh," and he laughed again. "But you look so funny."

Actually it made him fond of me. I don't think he particularly liked me at first. But when he saw that ridiculous things happened to me, and that I could look as big a fool as the next man, it softened his heart toward me. Over the years I suspect it resulted in a lot of extra business I wouldn't have gotten had I been able to walk right that day.

The Germans have a beautiful word for it. They call it *Schadenfreude*—which means malicious pleasure obtained from the miseries of others. Although my back problems, especially my story about how I got them, amused my client, the situation left me feeling depressed.

I decided to revert to my old practices for one evening. I thought it might cheer me up. So that night, after having dined with my client and his associates, I went off to the hotel bar for a solitary nightcap. I wanted to listen to a few of the bartender's stories, if he was feeling sociable. Then I was going to bed. Or upstairs, at least. I was already snookered, having had five martinis at dinner. But I felt the need for one more drink and a little conversation that had nothing to do with business for a change.

I met a well-tailored woman with short, thick, nicely cut red hair and a charming accent who, to my surprise, turned out to be a prostitute on a visit to America from Amsterdam. She was here as a tourist, but not averse to earning a little change to help cover her expenses.

"My back is very bad, as you can see."

"Oh, I'll be very careful. I'll do all the work. You needn't do a thing."

"I hurt it doing exercises in the room last night."

She gave a little whoop of laughter and grabbed my arm.

It was a wonderful sound and it made me like her automatically. She had high coloring and very blue eyes and a round pleasant face.

"Oh my dear," she said, covering her mouth as if with embarrassment. "I thought you were a humpback. I'm so relieved."

Actually, she *was* relieved. She offered to knock ten dollars off the price. That made me laugh in turn. This time she wrinkled her nose and snorted before she gave in and whooped again. We had another drink together. We became so companionable that it seemed rude to turn her down. So off we went to my room, where I had a devil of a time getting in the proper mood to consummate our friendship.

My back was still killing me, which didn't help. Nevertheless, through all of my bumbling ineffectuality and her equally ineffective assistance, we had a good time. We giggled a lot and thumped around against the walls and furniture. Finally we fell down in the middle of the floor. She held on to my neck as we went over. When we landed, she cracked my back as expertly as any chiropractor.

"My God! You fixed it! I can walk like a normal person again. You've saved me a trip to Lourdes."

Afterwards I tried to give her all the cash I had. It amounted to $127 and some silver.

"Here, take it all. I wish I had more to give you."

Which provoked another outburst of charming laughter.

"I couldn't. You won't have a penny. How will you have breakfast in the morning?"

"I'll put it on my credit card—add it to my room bill."

"What about the taxi to the station?"

"I'll walk. Besides, I can cash a check in the morning. Go on, take it. It's really all right."

"We'll split it. How will that be?"

We settled on that finally. I did have another day and a half in New York to get through. I never carried much cash on me when I traveled. It was a good thing too. Because if I'd had five hundred dollars or even a thousand, I would have tried to give her all of that too.

She was good enough to leave shortly after that, even though it was three o'clock in the morning—hardly the time of night for a woman to be wandering alone about the city.

I was working on a letter to Keefer. I hoped to have it ready to mail in the morning. I was only a quarter of the way through *The Woodlanders.* I wanted to finish it before I boarded the train for Harrisburg the day after tomorrow. So it was just as well that she decided to leave. Although I told her she was welcome to stay, if she didn't mind sleeping with the lights on and with me moving about the room for the remainder of the night. She declined the invitation and left, quite rightly deciding that I wanted to be alone, now that she had restored me to health.

About four in the morning, the telltale lasitude of sinew and muscle that I waited for every night finally stole over me as I sat writing at the little desk. Such signs usually meant I was ready to sleep for an hour or two. I got into bed. The sheets still smelled of my chiropractor's perfume—a strong sweet scent not unlike the smell of raspberry jam. I soon drifted off. But at first light, I woke in one of my patented cold sweats, not unusual in itself, but this time accompanied by an excruciating pain in my chest.

My left arm was numb. When I got up to go to the bathroom, my legs turned rubbery. I sat on the floor abruptly with my back against the wall. Cold sweat poured icily off my forehead. It streamed out of the hair at my temples and down my neck and chest. The crown of my head was soaked, as if I had just stepped out of the shower. I was shivering uncontrollably. Slipping sweatily down the wall, I lay on the floor, my knees pulled up to my chest.

Maybe this is it, I thought. *Maybe this is the heart attack I've been counting on to get me out of this before I get too old.* I considered crawling over to the telephone and calling the front desk to ask them to send for a doctor.

But I had a strong dislike for the idea of being paddled and prodded by a strange professional man in a hotel room in New York City, a fellow no doubt with horn-rimmed glasses, bald-headed and beetle-browed, smelling powerfully of camphor or vitamin B-12 as he bent over me, frowning and breathing hard. I had no desire to have the Haitians who worked in the hotel gawking in at the door while my beetle-browed doctor tried to crack my breastbone with his fist or used my fountain pen to perform an emergency tracheotomy. I wanted to avoid the hospitals too. I'd seen the film, starring George C. Scott. I didn't want to end up dead in a dark corridor someplace, or with one of my legs amputated by mistake. I decided if I was dying, I would do it right here, where I could do it quietly in the privacy of my own room. Besides, the pain was letting up. Or so it seemed.

I remembered I hadn't finished my letter to Keefer. If this was a real heart attack, I certainly wanted to finish the letter. It would be my last chance to "talk" to him. Even though, by this time, it was evident that he didn't really think of me as his father anymore—Michael was his father now. Nonetheless, maybe he would keep the letter. Maybe in a few years he would be happy he had it.

I crawled over to the writing desk by the bed. I had to rest on the floor a couple of times. When the pain came back, this time it was like an animal biting me from the inside. I curled up into a ball and held myself when it bit and waited for it to go away again. After a while I reached the desk and pulled myself up into the chair.

I started with a story I thought might amuse him.

"When Daddy went out of town last week, he packed his bag in a hurry. On the last day of his trip, he reached in his suitcase for his last pair of underwear and what do you think? They were a little pair of yours! How did they get in Daddy's bureau? They must have been in the back of the drawer. Left over from the days when you used to come and visit him and sleep on the cot under the goldfish tank. Remember the goldfish? Poor goofy Daddy. He didn't have any clean underwear to put on. . . ."

Then I got maudlin and scrawled out what amounted to my epitaph in the guise of my hopes and aspirations for him.

"When you grow up, try to be a mite smarter than I was. Use your time wisely. It runs out faster than anybody suspects. Don't, for God's sake, become a writer or a management consultant. Don't waste your life. Do something useful. Even if it's only building birdhouses or cutting sugar cane. But for God's sake don't sit behind a desk and call it living. Or fribble your days away engaged in endless useless meetings with people who don't otherwise seem to know what to do with the hours between breakfast and dinner. . . .

"I know we don't see much of each other anymore. We probably won't ever again. But I want you to know something. I want you to carry it with you wherever you go. I want you to remember that I love you. I always have, from the moment they brought you out of the delivery room, and I always will."

The telephone was on the nightstand by the bed. It took me what seemed like half an hour to reach it and ask for a bellman. But it only seemed like a minute before he reached my room. Although that may have been because I was concentrating so hard on crawling from the telephone to the door.

"Yes?"

I was surprised by the sudden knock.

"Bellman, sir."

I slipped a ten under the door and called his attention to it. Then I slipped the letter under the door.

"I want you to put a stamp on that letter. Mail it for me. Can you get a stamp somewhere at this hour?"

"Yessir. There's a machine downstairs in the gift shop. It'll be opening up in a few minutes."

"Good. Put a stamp on it. Drop it in the mailbox. Keep the change. That's your tip. It's very important that the letter is mailed. As soon as possible. Can you do it for me?"

"Yessir, I can do it. No problem."

"Good. Thank you."

"Okay, sir. Sir?"

"Yes?"

"Are you okay in there? You don't need a doctor or anything, do you?"

"No, no. I just—hurt my back a little. I'll be okay if I spend the day in bed."

"Oh." The bellman sounded relieved. "You had me worried there for a second."

"No, I'm fine. Just mail that letter."

"Don't worry, sir. I'll take care of it."

Exhausted by this effort, I fell asleep on the floor in front of the door. At nine, I woke feeling very weak and used-up, but the pain was gone for good. I made my way across the carpet again, scaled the side of my bed, and gratefully settled under the sheets.

Before I fell back to sleep, I called my client's secretary. I told her my back was much worse and that I would not be in that day. I said I was going home to consult my doctor. She was very sympathetic.

"Yes, that's probably the best thing."

I told her I would call again as soon as I could to set another appointment.

"Please give him my apologies."

"Oh he'll understand, I'm sure, Mr. Dimes. You can't be expected to work with a back like that."

That day I lay undisturbed in my room and, wondrously, slept long and hard. I'd had the good sense to hang out the "Do Not Disturb" sign when I put out my friend the night before, and the chambermaid did not bother me. I left her an extra five on the bureau for any trouble or inconvenience I may have caused her.

That night, feeling very much better, I caught the train home.

T w o

I *DID* not see Keefer much over the years, given my faltering sense of paternity and the intervening three thousand miles of geography. I came to think it was better if I stayed in the background.

He said to me once when I was out visiting him, "You're not my father anymore."

They had been out there for about a year.

"Oh?" I said. "Who is?"

"Michael. He's my father now."

"Let me ask you a question. What's your last name?"

"Dimes."

"What's your middle name?"

"Earl."

"What's my last name?"

"Dimes."

"What's my first name?" (He wasn't in on the secret about my real first name.)

"Earl."

"Don't you think there's a reason for these remarkable coincidences?"

My feeble attempt at irony had no effect. I was upset by this more than I let on. I told myself it was just a phase he was going through.

But I couldn't convince myself that we weren't at a critical crossroad in our relationship. I took it up with Linda.

"I can't help it if he thinks of Michael as his father. After all, Michael does everything for him. Keefer has his own feelings. He's allowed to express them."

"Well, I hope you don't encourage him to think that way. It makes me feel like the forgotten man."

"Frankly, I do encourage it. I don't know why you think I wouldn't. I want him to feel that he's part of a real family. Not just tagging along on my second marriage."

I thought she had a point. As the years went by, I stepped more and more into the background.

He came East to stay with me for a month when he was fourteen. He had long Christlike hair down to his shoulders and was into heavy metal.

It had been a year since I'd seen him. I hardly recognized him. That is to say, I hardly recognized myself in him any longer. I suppose I was expecting a clone—somebody who had the same ideas and interests as I did.

I thought we could play tennis together in the late afternoons. But he was not very good at it and he didn't enjoy playing. He wasn't interested in books either. He said, "Books are for twerps." Then, looking around the room at my bookcases, he added, "No offense." He was bored by the kind of music that I liked. "Mozart really eats it," he said.

" 'Eats it'? What does that mean?"

"I mean—I know you're really into him 'n' all. But don't you think he's really kind of a priss?"

When he was three years old, I taught him how to draw. I showed him how to use a rectangle, circle, and triangle so that he could draw anything. I demonstrated by drawing a rhinoceros. We drew rhinos all afternoon. He looked like Winston Churchill in those days. He had a wet droopy lower lip and a mixing-bowl haircut. He sat on my lap in his short pants and bent his big head to his work and drew and drew and drew.

I have always liked rhinos since then—big clumsy lugs, ugly armor-plated leftovers from the age of dinosaurs. I was in Kenya not long ago. I saw a park ranger drive one down a dusty lane one day by jabbing the meek brute in the hindquarters with a rifle and pelting him with stones. I brought back a wooden carving of the animal. I keep it on the desk in my office. Sometimes when I look at it, I think of Keefer and the day I taught him how to draw.

The visit was not a success. We went up to New York for a weekend and I took him to see *Amadeus,* but it bored him silly.

There were no children allowed in the apartment complex where I lived. At night, he stayed in his room and listened to his Metallica tapes. One morning I found a roach clip under his mattress when I was cleaning his room. I asked him if he was smoking pot.

This made him angry, although he didn't answer the question.

"I don't want you using dope in this house. I don't want you smoking in bed either. If you fall asleep, you could burn the place down."

He wouldn't talk to me for the rest of the day.

One night, after I went to bed, he got up and took the keys to my car and drove to one of the malls where the local kids hang out, and backed my car into a light pole in the parking lot. When I went out in the morning, I found the rear deck and right fender pushed in. When I asked him if he'd taken the car, he denied it. I don't know why I was so ready to suspect him, rather than conclude that somebody must have run into it in the parking lot, as he suggested.

When he saw I wasn't going to buy into the anonymous hit-and-run theory, he knitted his dark brows and looked at me thoughtfully.

"You never believe anything I say. You automatically think everything wrong around here is my fault. I really fuck up your little routine, don't I?"

"Watch it, young man. I don't go for that kind of talk. Save it for your heavy-metal friends."

"Sorry. I mean, I *interfere* with your program of Mozart and martinis. You don't get enough reading time. Your tennis game suffers when I'm around, right?"

The parody was close enough to my real feelings to cause me to smile uncomfortably.

"Something like that. I'm sorry you find me such a stuffed shirt. I'm not used to having someone else bumping around in the apartment with me."

"I'm your kid. I'm not 'someone else.' "

I felt a hot rush of anger. No, I almost said. You're not my kid. Don't throw that at me. You resigned that position five years ago. You told me I wasn't your father anymore, remember? You can't go back on it now. Not when I've worked so hard to get used to it.

But I didn't say any of this. Likely I didn't have to.

I still see the way he looked that morning. I see his long hair, the sparse stubble on his chin, the frowning dark eyebrows; the sudden clearing of perplexity on his young face just before he looked away and muttered:

"You don't give a rat's ass about me. I can't wait to get out of here."

I took it for another one of his attempts to manipulate my feelings. But I was wise to him. I handled it very coolly, I thought.

"That can be arranged. If that's what you really want. I'm

sure your uncle won't mind if you turn up a few days early."

"Yeh, sure. Right."

"I could call him. Is that what you want?"

"Yeh, that's what I want. At least around him I can be myself."

I nodded grimly. Good riddance, I thought.

I called Mario to let him know his nephew was on the way. The next day I put Keefer on the *Broadway Limited* for New York. We had our breakfast, we drove to the station, and we waited for the train in utter silence. I had tried to start a conversation with him a few times early that morning. But when he refused to answer, I gave it up.

"Okay," I said. "If that's the way you want it, it's fine with me."

When it was time for him to get on the train, he did not say goodbye. He picked up his duffel bag and slung his guitar over his shoulder by the strap and walked down the stairs to the platform without a word. I did not follow him. Nor did he look up before he got on the train to see if I was still there at the top of the stairs watching him. I left the station feeling very angry.

I never saw him again—not till Linda called me four years later to tell me that he had set himself on fire, and I flew out there to do whatever I could do, which essentially amounted to nothing.

They let each of us go in separately to see him for a few minutes. They took me aside before I went in and told me he was dying. But I didn't believe it, till I saw him.

They had a kind of tent made of sheets suspended over him and just his face showed. His long hair and dark eyebrows were gone. He had little bubs on the side of his head instead of ears. He slid his eyes carefully to the side to look at me when I entered the room. Then just as carefully, without moving his head, he looked away.

As I said at the beginning of this, he wouldn't speak to me. I knew he could still talk because they said he had asked the doctor for something to get it over with fast. But he wouldn't speak to me, or to his mother, or to Michael either, for that matter. I suppose he had done with us. We had turned out to be pretty much useless in helping with his other difficulties. Now he was at a place in his sufferings where we were utterly irrelevant.

I began to babble about a trip I wanted to take him on. I was going to make everything up to him by taking him on a nice trip.

"Kenya. We'll go to Kenya. We'll go out to the game parks. We'll fly out to a different one every day. We'll go see the rhinos. Remember the time we drew the pictures? Well, now we'll go and see the real thing. Okay? We'll go and we'll have a swell time for a change."

When it was time for me to go, I didn't want to. They said I had to. I said I would just sit there and be quiet. I wouldn't bother anybody. I just wanted to be there. I didn't want him to be alone anymore. It was an awful thing to be alone, especially if you were sick, and I didn't want him to be alone.

No, no, they said. You must go out in the hall again. But I didn't want to. Please, they said. You don't want to upset him, do you? I said of course not. I'm not upsetting you, am I, Keefer? Let me stay, for Christ's sake.

But they said no; and finally I did as I was told and went outside again.

T h r e e

I*T* has been three years since he died. For two of those years, Marilyn and I have been married.

I tried to get along without her. I told myself it wasn't fair to call her, now that I had such a burden of grief to carry. But in the end, I called her anyway, and she came back immediately after school was finished without any preconditions.

On the telephone I said, "If you still want to get married, let's do it."

"No, that's one thing I learned out here: what I need and what I don't. I should never have left you, Booby. I was going to call."

"I'm glad. But I had to call you now. I was worried when school let out I would lose track of you. I wouldn't know where to find you."

"I would have called you. I would have told you where to find me."

"Should I come out there? Maybe I'd better come out there right now. Are there any planes into that place? Maybe a ski plane that could land on the tundra or something?"

"No, let me finish up. Let me get out of here. I'll see you in a couple of weeks. I'll never leave you again, Booby. I promise."

"Get here in a hurry. Will you please?"

"Yes, don't worry. I'll be there as soon as I can."

"How are you coming? By car? I'd better come out there and drive you back."

"It's not necessary. I'll be careful."

"I know all about careful. I'm coming out. Let me know when you get things ready. Okay? Really, I would like to come out. I don't want you driving all that way alone."

So I went out and got her and drove her back. I really got lucky that time, because she came back to me; wanted to come back to me; was so ready to come back to me. I don't know what I would have done if she hadn't.

For two months I didn't tell her about Keefer. I don't know why I didn't. I just didn't. She knew something was wrong. I was having that dream about him and waking up in cold sweats, but I wouldn't tell her what was wrong. I told her it was business. I was just worried about business.

"Well then you'd better get a new business," she said. "This one has you about frightened to death."

I didn't think it was her problem, you see. I just wanted to keep it to myself and work it through on my own. She had come back to me and that was enough. I didn't want to burden her with my problems.

Then one day it just came out. We were in the kitchen having lunch. When I told her, she tried to get out the door. She wanted to get away from it. But she missed the doorway and ran into the wall instead. She hit it so hard that it knocked her down. She sat in the middle of the kitchen floor and cried as hard as anybody I've ever seen. I got down on the floor with her. I held her in my arms and rocked her back and forth. I smoothed her hair and held her.

There, there, I said. It's all right.

She cried so hard, I felt something tight begin to ease in me. It was as if she was doing something for me that I couldn't do for myself. I think she was crying for all of us.

Not only for a boy she never knew who had incinerated himself in a flash fire of rage and self-hatred because, at the age of eighteen, he thought he had reached the limits of his capacity for pain and despair. But for all of the people she loved—her poor father, who had ruined everything and died alone in a rented room. For her mother, her brothers and sisters, and me—all still burning in the swift invisible fire that consumes our lives.

I STILL dream about him. I see him two or three times a month down by the river with his lighter and can of gasoline.

I holler in my sleep, but he can't hear me. He goes about his work so determinedly. I struggle with him. *Here, give me that goddam lighter! If you want to torch somebody, try me. Pour the gasoline over my head. But you!—Christ, you haven't even lived yet. Jesus Christ, please don't do it. Don't do it! Please!*

"Booby! Wake up!"

It is so real every time. I've got the shakes and the darkness makes me frantic.

"Turn on the light! Turn it on!"

Because I've got to have a light after that. Marilyn's cool hands feel good on my sweaty face.

"Was it really bad?"

"Yes, the bad one all right."

"It's over now. You're back in bed with me. The light is on. You can see everything. It's not scary now."

Sometimes, after such childish reassurances, I'm actually able to sleep again—so long as the light stays on and I lie in the arms of my young wife. She looks about twelve when she is asleep. Yet she is a teacher of children. She put herself through college by working in a veneer mill in the summers, wearing steel-toed boots, heavy gloves, a hard hat and surgical mask. She worked in a room where the air was full of dust and the temperatures reached 115 degrees, lifting and grading sheets of veneer all day long and putting them into the right storage bins. She is my child now. I watch her. I love her shallow breathing and the absolutely untroubled look on her rosy face.

But three o'clock in the morning is a bad hour; and more often than not, I get up and go downstairs and make myself a little drink and read something till it gets light again outside. Then, usually just as Marilyn is getting up for school, I go back to bed and find I can sleep for a few hours.

It is not bad. Not bad at all. Not the way it used to be.

Sometimes, long ago, on those rare occasions in the old days when Phil felt himself briefly foiled by some temporary breakdown in the smooth operation of the universe, he would turn to me with a frown and growl: *Howdycouldbe?*

Howdycouldbe.

Meaning, "How could it be?"

As if life made any sense at all. Or as if someone like me could explain its occasional delays and inconveniences to a practical man of business like Phil. He surely didn't need my advice. He already had a formula that worked: live your little portion, take what comfort comes your way, and stay clear of the imponderables as much as you can.

Sometimes when Marilyn starts out the door for school on a snowy day, or calls up the stairs to tell me that she is on her way to fetch in some groceries, or is leaving for her aerobics class, I bolt out of my office and down the stairs and grab her before she can get out the door.

I kiss her. I tell her I love her. I say, "You're beautiful. I love your face. I love everything about you."

"Oh Booby," she giggles. "You're so romantic. I just love it."

But I am not romantic. I am just old and scared.

We English-speaking people have such a paucity of words for love. We need as many words for its variations and gradations as the Eskimos have for snow. I need all the assistance I can get in defining my feelings for her. They are so complicated and the available vocabulary is so vulgar. We nickel-and-dime people have no particular talent for the subject in the first place.

We were in London last year. We were in town for only a day or two when Marilyn found out one of my secrets: I have no sense of direction whatever. I have traveled a lot. I have groped my way in and out of cities all over the country. I have traveled to other countries and passed through them as dazed and hopelessly lost as an amnesiac. Despite this handicap, I have enjoyed my travels but, in the main, I have made a mess of them. When Marilyn realized that I was not the sophisticated traveler that she thought I was, she thereafter took me by the shirt front and led me around everywhere we went. This was a much better arrangement. I began to relax and enjoy myself, knowing that I would eat at regular times and be able to find my hotel again. If I acted too feebleminded, she called me Uncle Ferd and we pretended I was home from the institution on a weekend pass. In this capacity, I saw the Victoria and Albert Museum and many other edifying sights.

One night we were on the Underground, making our way back to our hotel after traveling some distance to an outlying district of the city—to see a musical production of *Moll Flanders,* of all things. We were standing near the door in the nearly deserted car, getting ready to change to the Piccadilly Line at the next station, when we were accosted by a snaggle-toothed young tough dressed in black leather and rivets, with a shaved head and a swastika tattooed on his forehead. He sidled up to us and insinuated great violence to my person unless I found it in my heart to hand over five pounds in a great hurry.

He was very jolly about it and rather drunk, and quite hopeful, I think, that I would refuse him so that he could have the fun of kicking in my ribs in front of Marilyn. There was nobody else in the car. We were alone with the thug, except for a frail-looking derelict swaying in a duplicate stupor against a negative of himself in one of the dirty windows.

When the skinhead sidled up to us and threatened me with his parodic fawning posture and broken-tooth smile and suggestively dangerous voice, Marilyn began to tremble against me like a rabbit scared into a state of paralysis. For some reason she kept sliding around to the front of me, she kept getting in between me and the troublemaker. I kept pushing her behind me, out of harm's way, while I pompously lectured the grinning brute.

"Listen here. You'd better leave us alone, or I'll have you arrested."

Or some such twaddle. Where I thought I was going to find a cop at that hour and place I hadn't yet considered.

He made a sudden grab for my arm and growled, "Look 'ere, Oncle—"

That is all he managed. Because in that instant, Marilyn kneed him in the balls. She followed with an uppercut to his nose (large, like an inverted teapot spout, a real bottle opener of a nose), using her handbag full of junk for a truncheon. I know from experience (since I often hold it for her outside of department-store rest rooms) that it must weigh in the neighborhood of fifteen pounds.

Looking shocked, the young man staggered backward, holding on to various parts of his anatomy. He reached for, and missed, one of the overhead straps and sat down hard in a puddle of piss in the middle of the aisle of the swaying car,

with a look of disappointment on his face as if, through some
deficiency of character, we had let him down. He was still
sitting in his puddle, nursing his nasty-looking nose, when
we got off the train at South Kensington.

Immediately on the platform, Marilyn's legs went woggy
and we had to sit down on a bench till she recovered herself.
Her eyes were still big and scared-looking and she looked
like she was holding her breath.

"Oh Booby! I was so scared he was going to hurt you!"

When I was sure she was all right, I said, "For Christ's
sake, Marilyn. Don't ever kick me like that. That poor son of
a bitch will never walk right again."

Rescued, you see. Where is the love word for that? She's
rescued me—or what is left of me. Not the other way around
(although she says I've rescued her, too). Not the way it's
supposed to be, according to the movies. She's rescued *me*.
Like Jack regularly came and rescued Nola and Richie and
me when we ran away from him in the old days and found
ourselves stranded and out of gas in some godforsaken motel
somewhere.

"Will you love me forever?" she asks me sometimes.

She is so damned fervent about it. It seems to me on that
question I ought to be the anxious one. But I do my best to
reassure her.

"Yes," I say. "I'll love you forever. You don't have to
worry about that. I'll never leave you."

"Oh good!" she says. "Because I'll never leave you, either! I love you, Booby. I'll love you forever too!"

Given the helplessly perfidious nature of human beings,
this kind of talk sounds as wonderful and yet as goofy to me
as it did four years ago. But it is the truth—or as close as
people like us ever get to it.

Sometimes when we are in bed at night she whispers in

my ear, popping sounds of whispered words, the sudden inspiration of breath: so delicate and intimate a sound at midnight. A whispered string of sounds like the spluttering of a candle flame in the wind. I don't hear the words. I hear the sounds. I know what she is saying and she, in turn, knows what my listening means.

These days, and at my age, my prayers are simple. Leave me a little hair and a few teeth for my vanity's sake. Keep my brain intact so I can work till I fall through my appointed doorway into the earth. And keep this lovely woman beside me. I ask only that she stay for so long as it is good and does her no damage. But, please, don't let her leave me any time soon.

Four

NOLA told me once, when she was feeling especially bad, that the only reason she could see for living was so when you got to the end, you wouldn't want any more of it.

She might turn out to be right about that. In my case, the deposition is incomplete as yet. But in hers, all the outstanding evidence has been returned, and the last little bit of it doesn't look that gloomy to me—considering who we are talking about.

This is what happened. She finally made up her mind to sell her little house and clear out of central Pennsylvania. She always said she despised the place, and finally she got up enough gumption to get out. All this was done with Dwight's advice. Or Mr. Fister, my former stepfather, as I like to refer to him.

She bought a condominium and she and Dwight (or Mr. Fister) moved to Fort Myers. Dwight was of the opinion that the Florida sunshine would do her wonders. He was a charter member of the American Academy of Fine Ideas, and this was one of them. Apparently he had others, too. Because two months after they moved down there, they got married.

Afterwards Nola sent me a somewhat embarrassed and apologetic note in which she attempted to explain everything.

> I know you will think me a foolish old woman. But Dwight simply insisted. He says there are no barriers where love exists. Doesn't that sound like something he found on a greeting card? But I suppose even an old woman is entitled to some happiness—particularly if it just falls into her lap. I hope you approve, dear boy. If not, I hope you'll forgive me and keep an open mind. I know it'll be difficult for you. You've always had such strong opinions about everything, ever since you were a little boy. Of course, it'll no longer be necessary for you to go on paying Dwight's salary. Not unless you particularly want to. He can always find a little work. In the event, we can get along just fine on my little income. . . .

I immediately wired my congratulations and good wishes. Having just married Marilyn myself, I was hardly in a position to call her names for marrying a man some forty years younger than she was.

She died last spring—a happy woman, I presume—and left everything to Mr. Fister.

When he came north last summer to visit his cousin Jeffrey, I arranged to have lunch with him at the Friendly's in the Gateway Mall, which was where he wanted to meet, since it was close to his cousin's house.

I was still after answers, although, by this time, I should have known better. I wanted one last chance at penetrating the long-standing mystery of my relationship with Nola. I thought Mr. Fister, my stepfather, might be able to help me. The fact that she hadn't left me a saucer or a spool of thread troubled me. It wasn't that I needed anything. It just seemed like the final repudiation.

Dwight and I beat around the bush for a while, pretending

to be amiable. Dwight told me he had started writing a novel. I had inspired him, he said. It was all about a young nihilist by the name of Abner Gation and how he is saved from despair by an older woman. They meet in the hospital. She is in for varicose veins. He is one of the practical nurses. I told him it was a wonderful idea and wished him luck with it. Then we got down to cases.

"She didn't leave me a thing, Dwight. Not that I expected anything. Why do you think she cut me off?"

"Oh Arrow, this is so embawwassing."

"I'm not trying to embarrass you, Dwight. I'm just curious to know what you think."

"She wuved you, Arrow. She wuved you vewy much."

"Yes, I'm sure she did. But why do you think she didn't like me? Was she still mad because I wouldn't take her to Maine that time?"

We had arrived at the dessert. I was having coffee and Dwight had just started in on his banana split. He began to fiddle with the walnuts in his whipped cream. I could see my questions were disturbing him, but I couldn't help myself.

Almost five years ago, in the very same restaurant, Nola and I had had a serious falling-out. She had just returned from a month with the Wilhides in Maine. She was not feeling well that summer, and she had come back in the middle of August instead of waiting till after Labor Day as usual.

Marilyn and I were just getting ready to leave on vacation. We had rented a cottage at Five Islands. She had never been to Maine, and it was my first trip back in years. I wanted to show her some scenes out of my checkered childhood: Fatima and Dillard's old house on Nichol Street in Dunnocks Head; the empty lot where the house I was born in once stood, before it fell into the gully, and left me without a birthplace; the stony little cove where I had learned to swim while trying not to step on the horseshoe crabs.

The idea of the lunch was to welcome her back. But Nola had her own agenda. She said coming back to Pennsylvania, with all its heat and humidity at this time of the year, had been a serious mistake.

"I've been thinking," she said. "I'd like to go back to Maine with you and Marilyn."

Marilyn immediately fixed her gaze on her stuffed avocado.

"Of course I wouldn't stay with you two. I'd stay with Fran and Stanley Martin. They said they'd love to have me."

"I'm afraid we can't."

"You can't? Why not?"

"Because we've made plans. We're not going straight through. I want to stop at Fog Mountain for a few days. I haven't been back since I was a Fellow. Leslie said he'd be up there this time. There are a couple of other people I'd like to see. I've made reservations at the Blueberry Inn. I'm afraid we got the last room."

I'd had another book published the year before. It had sold better than anything I'd written to date, and I wanted to go up there to Fog Mountain and see Leslie, my editor, and bask in the admiration of my colleagues.

"I could stay in another motel. I'd pay for myself and go my own way."

"The conference attracts a lot of people, Ma. I doubt if there are any more rooms available in the area. Besides, it just isn't a good idea. Not this time."

"Marilyn wouldn't mind if I came along. Would you, Marilyn?"

"It doesn't matter what she thinks, Ma. It's just not a good idea at this time."

I didn't want Marilyn making a show of good manners against her own interests. She had only a few weeks left before school started again. She had been looking forward to the trip all summer. I didn't want to put it in jeopardy by bringing Nola along, given her difficult personality and unpredictable health problems.

"Well, I don't see why not."

"I'm sorry, Ma. It's just not a good idea."

We ended it there. I was mad at her because she'd been so persistent, and she was mad at me because I'd held my ground. The conversation cast a pall over the luncheon and we parted company as soon afterwards as we could.

Before we left for Maine, I gave her a call.

"We're starting out in the morning. I just called to say goodbye. We'll see you in a couple of weeks."

"Is that all?"

"Yes. That's all."

"Fine," she said and hung up.

Well, to hell with you, I thought.

I didn't call her when we got back. I thought: Let her stew in her own juice for a while.

Three weeks later, she called in a panic to tell me that her refrigerator had broken down. Could I come right over, because she didn't know what to do.

"I'm sorry, Ma. I'm on my way out the door. I've got to be in Cincinnati tonight."

"Oh my God. What am I going to do?"

"Well, first, get a grip on yourself."

"Oh my God. All my food will be ruined."

"Listen to me for a second. Who do you deal with?"

"Deal with?"

"Yes. Don't you have a place where you buy your appliances?"

"Well, I don't buy them every day."

"Yes, but when you do, who do you deal with?"

"I don't know. Friedman and Wallace, I guess."

"Get in the car and go down there—"

"I can't."

"Why not?"

"The car won't start. I tried it yesterday. I don't know what's wrong with it. I think the battery is dead."

"You belong to Triple A. Get them up there to start the thing. Get it to the garage and find out what's wrong with it. I told you to get rid of that heap years ago."

"Please don't yell at me."

"I'm not yelling, Ma. I'm trying to reason with you."

She was beginning to moan softly between short gasps of breath. The dread anticipation of any possible exertion on her own behalf always made her breathless with anxiety when she was suffering from depression like this.

"Now look, Ma. It's really no big deal. Don't get worked up."

"Oh God."

"This is a part of everyday life. Just a minor problem. Call Friedman and Wallace. Tell them you want a refrigerator delivered today. Tell them you'll be down to pick it out. Then call your neighbor, Mrs. Whatsis—"

"Mrs. Blondell."

"Yes, Mrs. Blondell. She'll take you down there, I'm sure, if you explain the situation. Okay?"

"Oh God."

"Now listen, Ma. You do these things. Then you call me right back. I'll wait ten minutes for your call before I leave for the airport. So you call me. All right?"

"All right," she said meekly and hung up.

I waited the ten minutes. Almost exactly to the second she called me back and told me that the refrigerator—*mirabile dictu!*—was running again. "It just came on again somehow. I don't know how, it just did." She reported this in an extremely weary voice and said she was going back to bed, having been totally worn out by the emergency. I left for the airport that day feeling very satisfied with myself. At least the crisis had been postponed for the moment. I knew I could not hold back the floodtide of her bitterness for long. I would have to pay the price for disappointing her. Was this what the Bible meant by the sins of the father being visited upon the son? I had to wonder.

The following week I had another call from her.

". . . can you come right over?"

"What's wrong, Ma?"

"I don't know, I'm confused. I can't get dressed. I can't write a check. I need to write a check today. I haven't been able to take my medicine or anything."

"Ma, take the medicine. You don't want to get any worse with this thing."

"I can't, I can't. I'm too confused. Will you come over?"

"All right, Ma. But see if you can't get dressed in the meantime."

She was dressed in a pair of checked slacks and a navy-blue middie top when she answered the door. Thank God for that, I thought. At least I won't have to help her on with her clothes.

"Hello, Early."

She gave me the timid smile she used in times of crisis. She had a remarkably soft and girlish voice for her age. On the telephone, salesmen still often mistook her for a child.

"Hello, Ma. How you doing?"

As if this were the password, she opened the door wider and let me into the dark, musty-smelling house.

"Why don't you open the drapes and let some sunlight in here?"

"The drapes help keep out the cold."

"It's not that cold out. It's nice. The sunlight might do you some good, cheer the place up a little. I don't know how you can stand to live in the dark like this. You live like a damn mushroom. No wonder you feel lousy all the time."

"If I opened the drapes, it would just show all the dirt and dust. I don't want to see it."

"All right, suit yourself. I don't get it. But that's the way you want to live, so do what you want. You will anyway. Where's your medicine? Are you dizzy or anything?"

"No, I'm just confused. I can't seem to do anything for myself this morning. I can't think straight."

She stood in the middle of the hallway batting her violet eyes at me, helplessly wringing her little marsupial-like paws. She really did look helpless. It always made me feel both mad and guilty at the same time to see her act so damned feebleminded. Sometimes I suspected it was all a put-up job. But even if it was, it only meant she was truly sick; because no normal person would act like that. *S'true?* as Phil would say. Wasn't that the way all these machinations of hers ought to be interpreted, according to what I'd read on the subject? So I threw off my mean-spirited thoughts and put my arm around her and gave her a hug. It was awful to get old and not have anybody around to hug you now and then. No doubt that alone accounted for a lot of her strangeness.

"Don't you worry about it," I said. "It's perfectly normal. I get confused all the time. You know, when I get tense and under a lot of pressure? Hell, the same thing happens to me. So you stop worrying about it. It's perfectly natural. You just have to learn to relax, that's all. Don't take everything so seriously, okay?"

"I'll try."

"Good. That's good. You try. Where's your medicine?"

"In the kitchen."

"Let's go take care of that."

"Okay."

Several prescription bottles cluttered the shelf by the sink. She changed doctors and prescriptions frequently. She always had. The only doctor she had ever stuck with was little dapper Dr. McSherry, the one who had supplied her so freely with the "pep pills" back in the old days, but he had been dead for a long time. She had little faith in doctors. Like Diogenes in search of his honest man, she was still looking for a doctor she could believe in. We'd been to a half-dozen different ones in the last three months.

She fumbled among the pill bottles for what seemed like several minutes. Her hands were slow; her face, powdered and rouged and seamed, had the open-mouthed, droopy-eyed expression of a sleepwalker.

"Is that it? I can't see without my glasses."

I read the label. It was the antidepressant.

"That's it. Sit down here."

She sat at the table in the small dining room. Behind the drawn curtains, a wide window ran nearly from floor to ceiling. It looked out on a small wedge of grass, some trees, a bank of myrtle. It was a pleasant shady scene, often active with birds and chipmunks. To sit here at the table and have a cup of coffee and gaze out this window was almost as nice as being outdoors. But here, too, the draperies were closed. She had always kept her houses as dark as possible, whether or not she was in one of her funks.

The fixture over the table cast a funnel of light on the piles of unopened mail—heterogeneous stacks of bills and outright junk, threaded occasionally with a real letter here and there, judging from the pastel envelopes; numerous catalogs from mail-order houses; copies of magazines, *Modern Maturity* and *National Geographic,* with the brown wrappers still on; supermarket circulars printed on mealy-looking paper.

The circle of light falling on this blizzard of junk was as

dim as the rays cast by a kerosene lantern. I had been trying to get her to sort through this trash for weeks, but so far without success. I supposed sooner or later I would have to give in and do it for her.

I stood in front of the open refrigerator and poured her some orange juice while she sat hunched and forlorn and silent at the table. I heard her fingers frittering nervously among the crepitant envelopes and magazines. I put the carton back, shut the refrigerator, and carried the juice down the length of the narrow kitchen to the dining room, where she sat with the patient and downcast air of a poor dumb beast left out in a rainstorm.

"Here's some juice, Ma."

I handed her the cup of juice and put the two brown dots of medicine into the soft waxen palm of her free hand, one by one, with the emphasis of punctuation.

"Take those."

She tossed the pills into the back of her throat with a sudden gesture like an Indian getting ready to hoot. With her head thrown back in a posture of exhaustion, slowly, with much pumping of her Adam's apple, she swallowed the pills and drank off the orange juice.

"There, don't you feel better already?"

She looked at the table.

"No."

"That was a little joke, Ma. Don't be so serious. Now you want to write a check today. Is that right?"

"It's for this bill." She held up a crumpled envelope.

I took it from her and removed the bill. It was the renewal notice for the auto club. Her checkbook was among the litter on the table. I put it on the placemat in front of her. There were pens and pencils on the table too. I put one of the pens into her hand. Sick or well, she always lived like this, surrounded by dim light and clutter with nothing in its rightful place. It irritated me, always had, for as long as I could remember.

I opened the checkbook.

"Now this is a bill for twenty-six dollars. Write that down. No, write that on the second line, Ma. Write down 'AAA' on the first line."

Laboriously, sighing all the while, she wrote out the check and did the rest as I instructed: made the notation on the checkbook stub; separated along the perforation that part of the bill that was to be enclosed with the payment; put it and the check inside the envelope provided; wrote her return address on the envelope; sealed the envelope; tore with great painstaking a stamp from the book of stamps also found among the debris on the dining table; and licked it and stuck it slovenly onto the envelope with the heel of her palm.

"There. That wasn't so bad, was it?"

"It was horrible."

Indeed, it had been horrible for both of us. I had stood there, a witness to the amount of effort and energy it had taken her to perform the simple task. I felt as if we both needed a nap after that.

"Come on, get on your coat."

"Oh no. I can't go anywhere. Look at my hair."

It was matted and dingy and looked like she hadn't combed it for a week.

"You can cover it with a hat. Come on."

"Where are we going?"

"Over to the mall. You need a little exercise. You can't lie around all day and feel good. You can get your hair washed and curled and blow-dried while we're there. That'll make you feel better."

I went into the hall. She trailed after me reluctantly. I opened the sliding door to the closet and got out her ratty-looking coat. It was still saturated with that awful perfume she wore.

"Jesus, Ma. What the hell do you call that perfume?"

"It's called Fascination. Why—don't you like it?"

"You could use something a little subtler."

I watched her literally sag under the criticism. I was instantly sorry for it. I should have known better. She was in no shape to take any criticism just now.

"It's nice," I corrected myself. "Just a tad strong maybe. Where'd you put your hat?"

"Up on the shelf."

I got down the fuzzy khaki-colored hood, lined with red material.

"You want to wear this again?"

"Yes."

It came to a peak over the crown of her head and tied under her chin by means of two red strings. I fought with myself to withhold comment while she put this on. It was still a little early for this incredible hat. If she was sick all winter, and it looked as though she was going to be, then I would have an awful long time to look at the thing, whenever I got up the nerve to drag her out of the house and take her on one of our periodic excursions to the mall. This was my standard treatment when she went into one of her swoons: get her out among people; make her get a little exercise at least, and look in a few shop windows. Not much, but better than nothing. It worked at least as well as the medicine she was taking. But I couldn't keep my mouth shut about the hat.

"What is that, Ma? North Korean Army issue?"

"What?"

"Your hat. It looks like something that comes with bugles and overruns American positions."

"Don't you like it?"

She looked at me so shyly, it made me feel ashamed of myself for kidding her. I gave her a squeeze. When I did, a wave of the repugnant perfume seemed to waft out of the coat and irradiate into the close atmosphere of the dark little hallway.

"I adore it. It's you, Ma. Don't change a thing."

Looking up at me, she smiled suddenly, pleased as a child.

"You're kidding."

"Well, maybe a little. It's a nice hat, though. It really is."

On the way over to the mall, I asked her how her bowel was behaving. When she was depressed, it was usually the first thing that gave her trouble.

"Not good. I had diarrhea again yesterday."

"What did you do—guzzle another a bottle of lemon citrate?"

"Well—I hadn't been to the bathroom for two days."

Over the years I had learned to question her closely. She was a great believer in the Fifth and never willingly gave any evidence against herself. I always had to pry it out of her.

"Then I suppose you took some Kaopectate."

"I had to. I woke up with cramps in the night."

"Really, Ma. You lie around all day. You don't eat right. You swill Kaopectate and get plugged up. Then you guzzle lemon citrate and get diarrhea. It's no wonder your bowel is messed up."

"Well, I don't want to end up in the hospital again, like that other time. That was a horrible experience."

As we shuttled past the shoppers in the aisles of the men's department at Wanamaker's and headed for the doors that gave onto the mall proper, I attempted a little conversation.

I had the silly idea that conversation might be good for her. I thought if I could get her to take a momentary interest in something besides her pills and the vagaries of her intestinal tract, she might start to get better. I should have known it was doomed to failure from the start.

Nevertheless I started in. I had been reading Ouspensky. Have you ever heard of Ouspensky? No, she had not. She had never heard of any of the obscure people I read. Philosophers and historians and foreign novelists and such. She never read anything anymore anyway. She couldn't get interested, she said. Besides, it bothered her eyes. Back when she used to read, she liked books about the Duke and Duchess of Windsor. Nicholas and Alexandra—interesting people like that (all big-time leeches, I noted). She also liked the inspiring writers, people who had something nice to say, like Kahlil Gibran and Lloyd C. Douglas. She would sooner throw up than read any Dostoevsky. Sick, sick stuff. And who was that one you used to read so much in college? D. H. Lawrence, that was the one. Everybody said he was a homosexual. Or a sex fiend, she forgot which. No, if that's what people meant by good literature, she didn't want any part of it.

Well, Ma. This Ouspensky guy is a wonderful wacko. He thinks ants were probably once a superior race. They developed such a rigid and perfect system of social organization that it led to the destruction of their intelligence. How about that? Isn't that a wonderful crazy idea?

He also believed in reincarnation. But reincarnation that took you backward instead of forward in time. He thought you repeated the same life over and over again, lived through the same events over and over again, till certain bad tendencies in your character either overwhelmed and utterly destroyed you and you were snuffed out like a candle, or you overcame them and then you went on to a higher plateau in your next incarnation and your life kept getting better and better each time you lived it, till you achieved—

"I feel faint. I think I'm going to fall down," Nola said and sagged against me.

We had walked a quarter of the length of the mall. I put my hand on her forehead. She was cold as a frog. I looked around for a bench.

"Over here, Ma. Let's sit down for a minute."

We sat down on the free end of a bench occupied by two elderly gentlemen. On our trips to the mall, I had noticed that lots of older people in sneakers used the place to social-ize. None of them looked too happy about it. They acted as if they had come to a sad pass in their affairs to be sitting around a shopping mall every afternoon.

She sat there panting, unable to catch her breath.

"Here, take off your coat, Ma."

I helped her off with her tatty coat.

"You feel any better?"

"In a minute maybe."

"I wonder why you—hey, wait a minute. What did you have for breakfast this morning?"

"I didn't eat breakfast."

"What did you have for dinner last night?"

"I didn't eat dinner."

"Jesus, Ma. No wonder you're dizzy."

It turned out she hadn't had anything to eat since the Meals on Wheels people delivered her lunch the day before: chicken, spinach, pineapple, roll, juice, and a half pint of milk in a waxed cardboard carton.

The meals the agency delivered were about as interesting as the kind you find in a school cafeteria. But at least I could be sure she was getting one meal a day, five days a week. That is, if she would eat it. No doubt she planned to fast till they delivered another meal on Monday. I decided we had better stop at the store on the way home and get her some groceries. Nothing hard to prepare. Deli stuff, like pasta

salad and lunch meat and cheese. Maybe half a broiled
chicken. She wouldn't cook anything for herself. She
wouldn't even heat a can of soup when she got like this.

I looked at her. She slumped on the bench in an attitude
of pathetic defeat, the hood still tied by its red strings under
her jowls. Sitting there with her hood on, looking small and
diminished, and blinking narcoleptically at the floor, she
looked for all the world like a poor little dwarf who'd been
slipped a mickey.

I took up her coat and stood up. I held out my hand.

"Come on. Let's go get you something to eat."

Obediently she stood up and took my hand and paddled
off with me to the lunchroom in the back on the ground level
of Penny's.

The young girl who waited on us smiled and greeted us
pleasantly as she handed us the menus. After an hour with
Nola, I felt unusually grateful to see somebody who was
sufficiently animated to hazard a smile. I was no good at this.
No good at this at all. I just wanted to take her home and
leave.

When the waitress came back with our coffee, Nola ordered the meat loaf. I asked about the soup of the day.

"Sausage and pasta," said the waitress. "It's good."

"Fine, I'll have that."

By the time the food arrived, I had run out of small talk. I
had talked, and she had looked at her hands on the table.
After a while, I said to hell with it, we can both do with a
breather.

Silently, I ate my soup, which was good, just as the waitress had said it would be. Nola, with her eyes averted, quietly and steadily worked her way through a small tossed
salad, mashed potatoes, and a slab of meat loaf covered with
a gravy that was as thick and dark-brown as chocolate sauce.
At least there was nothing wrong with her appetite.

After lunch, we rode the escalator up to the beauty shop on the second level.

"What's your first name?" shouted the fat girl at the desk. She had lank greasy hair and a pockmarked moon face and looked about eighteen.

Nola had an air of nebulous impenetrability about her that often caused store clerks to bark at her as if she were a stranger from a distant gallaxy.

"Nola," said Nola.

"Okay, Lola. Take a seat. We'll call you. It'll be about twenty minutes."

"Oh, I don't think—"

"You can wait twenty minutes, Ma. What's your hurry? You have a train to catch or something?"

She acquiesced meekly and shuffled toward the director's chairs with backs and seats of royal-blue sailcloth in the little alcove where the customers waited. On the platform across from us, the operators were busy with customers. The place was all neon and chrome, a harshly lighted kitschy display of somebody's idea of Art Deco.

Nola stared at the carpet and drifted off into one of her meditative trances.

I nudged her.

"Are you having any good thoughts?"

"No."

"Then get out of yourself. Watch the girl work on her customer. Look. She's got pretty hair, hasn't she?"

"Yes," she said and looked at the floor again. That was about all we could manage.

She went into a very bad tailspin. I took her to another doctor, a prissy young psychiatrist who had pretty lips and talked like a girl. He changed her prescriptions. When that didn't work, he put her on a new combination of pills. When that didn't work either, he increased the dosages. Nothing seemed to do any good. She lost a lot of weight that winter. She was too listless to do anything for herself and lay on the couch in the living room all day.

One day, after a visit to the new doctor, she told me she didn't understand the schedule for increasing the dosage of the antidepressant that he'd given her.

The first ten days, she was to increase dosage from fifty milligrams to fifty-five milligrams. The next ten days, from fifty-five to sixty milligrams. After that, she was to take sixty-five milligrams.

In order for her to do this, he had written her prescriptions for ten- and twenty-five-milligram pills. He wrote out on a slip of paper the combination of these pills that she needed to take in order to achieve each level of the graduated increase in dosage. Somehow she couldn't get any of this through her head.

"Think of it in terms of making change. You only have dimes and quarters. Now what combination of quarters and dimes does it take to make fifty-five cents?"

"Well, let's see. I'm taking five pills now. So I suppose if I took six . . ."

"No, Ma. You're taking ten-milligram pills. They're dimes. Six of them make sixty. You're supposed to take fifty-five milligrams. Start with a quarter. What does a quarter equal?"

"I don't know."

"Jesus, Ma. Of course you do. You know what a quarter is, don't you?"

"Twenty-five cents."

"Right. Now you have twenty-five cents. How much more do you need to make fifty-five? Remember now, you only have quarters and dimes."

"I suppose another quarter . . ."

"That would give you fifty, Ma."

"... and a dime ..."

"No, Ma. That would give you sixty. You want fifty-five. Now start with a quarter again."

"Why do they have to make it so confusing!"

"It isn't confusing, you're fighting it. You want to take one pill and be done with it, so you don't have to think about it. But they don't come in the size dosage you need, so you have to combine them. You have to combine the quarter- and dime-sized ones to get the dosage you need. Understand now?"

"I can't think. My mind must be going."

"Your mind is *not* going. You just don't want to deal with it. You've got this block about it's being difficult. But it isn't. It's simple. You just have to accept it and think it through."

But I couldn't get it through her head, and I couldn't go over there three times a day to make sure she took the right combination. That's when I went out and hired Mr. Fister, my future stepfather.

"Is that why she was still mad at me, Dwight? Is that why she didn't leave me a nickel or a thread? Was she still holding a grudge because I wouldn't take her back to Maine that summer?"

"I think the difficulty was the other way awound, if you weally want to know."

"What do you mean?"

"She said she could never talk to you, Arrow. You always made her feel uncomfor'ble about herself."

He squirmed in his seat. He didn't like any of this. It made his eyes water to have to look at me directly for so long.

"I wuved her, Arrow. I wuved her vewy much."

"I know, Dwight."

"You scared her. I think she resented you a widow bit.

She said you had aw the wuck. Nobody else in the family had any wuck because you had it aw. She said you never needed anything she had to give. That's why she weft everything to me."

"That wasn't my point, Dwight. I'm glad she made you her beneficiary. It was only right. But wouldn't it have been nice if she'd left me a small token of remembrance? Like Tito's old dog dish or something?"

"She said you never needed anything. Not even when you were widow. She was stwange when it came to you. When your wast book came out? Evewybody in the condo was talking about it. She didn't even tell them she was your muvva. I said, 'Aren't you pwoud of him?' She said, 'Yes, I'm pwoud. But I think I would enjoy his success more if I thought he wiked me.' "

Dwight went very red in the face, like a baby filling his diaper. He was very upset.

"Okay, we won't talk about it anymore. You'd better eat your banana split. It's melting all over the place. How about another Coke?"

"Oh Arrow! I am sowwy you and Muvva didn't get along better."

"That's all right, Dwight. Some people aren't meant to get along. She and I never spoke the same language."

That's where we left it. Dwight had to rush off to the rest room. I think all the excitement made him spit up his bananas.

I waited for a few minutes. When he didn't come back, I paid the bill and left. It was not a nice thing to do to one's former stepfather. After all, he had taken an aged parent off my hands. But I was pretty certain Mr. Fister and I had nothing left to say to each other. Adieu, Dwight. Good luck, wherever you are.

F i v e

I should explain something else. Three months after Phil died, I got a check in the mail for $250,000. Mario had attached a note to it. He explained that Phil's will had finally been probated and this was the check for the money that Phil had left me.

The final paragraph read:

> I know you always put up a stink when he tried doing you a favor. Well, do *me* a favor this time. Don't argue. Try to be graceful for a change. If it makes you feel better, think what he would of done if he wasn't still pissed off at you. Linda says take it and be happy. Maybe it'll make up for some of the bad times she gave you.
>
> —Always,
> Mario

For a long time I kept Phil's money in the bank. Over the years, it has distressed me by growing substantially in size.

When Marilyn came along, I finally relented and used some of the appreciation to make a down payment on the house that I bought in my futile attempt to settle her down and keep her quiet on the subject of marriage.

But I couldn't bring myself to use any of the original principal. I still thought of it as Phil's money, entrusted to me for some purpose as yet unrevealed, to be held in perpetuity if necessary. Or till some duly anointed, heretofore wholly anonymous deputy of his turned up on my doorstep some morning with further instructions. Maybe he would demand the key to the safety deposit box which held the CDs, and finish by saying something like:

"He sez: Okay. Now you're tru doin' him this lil job, you should maybe go out to a nice park somewhere 'n' drop dead. Or go to your favorite restaurant 'n' choke on a chicken bone. Do us all a favor, huh? Make it snappy."

Lately Marilyn and I have spent some of it on travel. It is what we used to go to England last year. But I think I will take the balance and help establish a chair in his name in the English Department at Bentham. Wouldn't that be a gas? Having a chair of literature named after Phil? Indeed, why not? He spoke some of the most telling English I've ever heard in my life. If he knew about it, he might smile at me and say, *Howdycouldbe?*

I don't think it would make him mad. Although maybe it would. You can never tell with Phil. *"Whatsamaddah for you,"* he might say. *"You spend all dat money I give you on a* chair? *Whaddayou—crazy or somethin'? You coulda bought an apahtment buildin'!"*

I have a further word to say about Arthur, too. My melancholy old friend, that affable old snake-in-the-grass, who once tried to seduce Linda when I had my back turned and he thought she might be vulnerable to lewd suggestions.

She and I have stayed in touch by telephone off and on since the accident. Our conversations are desultory and far-ranging and far more open than they were when we were married. I suppose it was inevitable, given the cozy latitude of these discussions, that I would ask her one day why she had done those things with Arthur when, as I remembered it, she didn't even particularly like him.

"When I tried to get fresh, you punched me in the nose."

"That was different. I was serious about you."

"Maybe if we had broken down and had sex, we would have spared each other a lot of grief later on."

"Oh no." She knew just what I meant and she wasn't having any. "We would have gotten married anyway. I'm sure of it."

"You think so?"

"I'm positive. Maybe you don't remember. But I really loved you. You were the handsomest, smartest boy in school. You really knocked me out."

"You didn't act like it very often."

"I had to play it cool. Otherwise, you would have probably walked away. You didn't seem to be very impressed because I was rich. Besides, Daddy thought you were wonderful. That clinched it. I always did what Daddy thought was right in those days."

"An arranged marriage, almost. Too bad your father wasn't a little better at it."

"Oh, he was good at it, all right. We were the ones who weren't so good at it. If we'd been born in Sicily, I bet we'd still be married today, and probably no worse off for it. This country isn't a good place for sticking things out anymore. Like, if the tires on the car show a little wear? We want to trade it in. We don't want new tires. We want a new car. If we're unhappy with our friends or family, we trade them in and get a new bunch. Why waste time trying to work things out? Isn't that the way things are today?"

"I guess so. But it still doesn't explain why you used to jerk off Arthur on the steps outside your dormitory."

She laughed and laughed when I said that. But she never did explain. Maybe the reasons are too obvious for me to understand.

Anyway, after the elder Frankenwood died, my friend Arthur (or Old Sticky Pockets, as he was known in some circles) sold the business to Cuspid, Seabold & Fryers, an international consulting firm with home offices in Philadelphia.

He took a partnership in their Chicago office. From there, he went to Melbourne, and I simply lost track of him. Arthur and his stamp collection had gone international. For all I knew, he still was snapping Polaroids of nubile Aussie beauties tied with neckties to his bedstead down under. That should be the end of the story, but it isn't.

Last winter Marilyn and I flew down to Grand Cayman for ten days. I was sitting on the beach reading the *New York Times* when a small headline on the front page of the second section caught my eye.

It was about Arthur, of all people. He had been in Cleveland on business. Apparently he had moved back to the States some years ago. According to the article, he had approached a couple in an automat and offered to pay a sum of money if they let him watch them perform certain sexual acts. They agreed. They went to a motel to carry out this arrangement. There the couple robbed and beat him and strangled him to death, using the cord from the telephone.

They stuffed his body into the trunk of his rented Lincoln and drove out West, using his American Express card to pay the expenses. They dumped his body in a cornfield in Nebraska somewhere.

They were finally apprehended by local police in Phoenix, Arizona, while trying to cash a check with Arthur's name on it in a convenience store. They were returned to Cleveland to stand trial. The jury had just brought in a verdict of guilty.

Poor Arthur—that he should have to pay with his life for the misdemeanor of asking for a peep at scenes from which he felt himself excluded, except as a paying customer. He did not know how to love people properly. It is a common malady, one that hardly should be punishable by death—or else most of us would be up on charges sooner or later. How unhappy he must have been. How sad and frightened, with nobody to talk to, except hired strangers, about the sordid little tableaux of men and women playing hide-the-salami in his fantasy life.

I had a glimpse of his torment, had I only realized it at the time, when from time to time he showed me those silly Polaroid shots of his compliant girlfriends tied to his bedpost. I laughed at him. I think it made him feel normal. I made up jokes at his expense, and it reassured him that he really was a party to the daylight, not the horrible loathsome creep that he thought he was. I did him the small favor, but never the large. I never let him tell me how awful he felt.

I also lost track of Lionel, but I've never read about him in the papers, thank God. His semi-threatening phone calls all those years ago petered out in a series of stupefied and perplexed silences, as if he'd forgotten his reasons for calling. Finally he gave them up altogether. We never mentioned the time he trashed my apartment and zapped Keefer's goldfish. No bragging on his part. No recriminations on mine.

As I said, Linda and I have kept in touch since the accident. We don't talk about Keefer very often. We don't call each other on his birthday or around the holidays. We try to stay away from the most difficult and painful remembrances. But we call each other from time to time. We check in, as I imagine people do who have been hijacked together on an airliner by terrorists. People—otherwise complete strangers—who have cried and pleaded for their lives and shat their pants together and therefore understand certain things about each other that nobody else ever can.

Over time, I have gradually learned more about Keefer's unhappy life, and I understand more about what motivated him to do what he did. Even as I write the words they produce in me a sense of revulsion and self-hatred. For I have had to be tutored in the basic facts in order to know something again about the son I am grieving for.

Here are the facts which explain nothing. About a year after he visited me for the last time, he was involved in a shooting accident at home. Linda said she didn't call and tell me about it because it was their problem—"a family problem," I think she called it. Something they had to work through on their own. She didn't want to worry me with it, she said. There was nothing I could do about it anyway. And besides, she wasn't anxious to discuss it with anybody outside of the immediate family. I didn't resent it when she told me that, for by that time, by anyone's definition, I was most assuredly outside of the "immediate family."

They bought him a rifle. It was part of a plan to get him away from a set of bad friends he'd taken up with in the neighborhood—kids from good families, of course. But spoiled, with too much time on their hands, and too much money in their pockets. She suspected this was where Keefer had picked up the pot-smoking and the back-talk habit.

At any rate, they were going to change all that. Keefer had recently taken quite an interest in guns. Michael decided he would teach him how to shoot at the rifle range and then take him elk hunting in Montana in the fall, if he got off to a good start in school.

"The year before, his grades really stunk," she told me.

"He got expelled for a week for smoking in the boys' john. He was in trouble all the time. We didn't want to go through another year like that. So we decided we'd do some things together. Like a family."

That's where the rifle and the elk hunting was supposed to come in. One day, Keefer took some boys into his room to show them his new gun and shot one of them by accident. Michael had just pulled into the driveway and heard the gun go off.

Through the open window he heard one of the boys exclaim, *Oh my God, Keefer! Why did you shoot him?*

Michael ran into the house. He rushed upstairs and found the boys crowded around another boy whom he had never seen before. He was on the floor, propped up against the bookcase which Keefer used to display his model planes. He sat there with a bewildered look on his smashed face, bleeding profusely. A chunk of flesh on his arm had been shot away too.

Michael asked them where Keefer was.

"He's calling nine-one-one," they said.

"Get me a towel," he told one of them.

He folded the towel into a pad to stanch the flow of blood from the boy's face. The boy was very brave. He couldn't swallow very well. His jaw was shattered and his throat kept filling up. He asked Michael to prop him up higher, which he did. He was afraid of choking. Of filling up and choking to death.

"Don't worry," Michael said. "I'll hold you. I won't let anything happen to you."

Michael held the boy in his arms till the ambulance came.

"Where's Keefer?" he asked the other boys.

"He's in the hall," they said. "He won't come in."

Michael rode in the ambulance to the hospital with the

boy. He stayed in the waiting room while they took him into surgery. The boy's family had assembled by that time. The grandfather gave Michael hell all the time they waited, for not keeping the gun locked up, the way he should have.

Fortunately, the boy survived.

There was a lawsuit, of course, and a big settlement made by the insurance company. But the boy survived. Before it was all over, he had three operations to repair the damage. But if the bullet had hit him square by another half inch, it would have killed him outright.

"Keefer took it hard."

"Very hard. You know how cruel kids can be. When he went back to school, they wanted to know if he'd killed anybody else lately. He told me if Kip didn't make it, he'd kill himself."

"Of course, there was never any question of that. The boy was out of danger after the first operation. He had a long, difficult recovery, but there was never any question about him dying. Still, that's what Keefer came home and said.

"He wanted me to scrub the carpet in the room. He wanted me to get the bloodstains out right away. I scrubbed it with everything I had, including club soda, which worked about the best. That's what they use on airplanes, you know, when you spill something on yourself. I got most of it out. You couldn't tell it was there.

"But he said it kept coming back. He would take me up in his room and show me where the stain had come back. You could maybe see just a faint outline of something, if you looked real hard. I scrubbed it some more. But I couldn't satisfy him.

"Finally, we had a new rug put in. But he didn't like the room anymore, so we did the guest room over and moved him in there. It was a tough time for him."

The following year, he dislocated his hip in a motorcycle accident. As promised, Michael had gotten him a two-stroke for his sixteenth birthday. He had it about two weeks and smashed himself and the motorcycle all to hell in one of the canyons during what he called a hill climb in competition with half a dozen other kids.

The surgeon was concerned that the blood supply might have been cut off to the femoral head. He said the bone might begin to die. Keefer went back every six months for regular checkups. He'd had his last one just two weeks before his accident.

Linda asked the doctor how long it would take to know for sure whether the bone was all right or not.

"You know what that jerk-off told me? 'Duh. It's hard ta know. I seen cases where it didn't go bad for seven years.' Seven years! God. That was reassuring, wasn't it? The turkey. He said it right in front of Keefer, too. I could have killed him."

She said he was very upset the hip might go bad and leave him with only one leg to stand on someday. She did her best to reassure him that it was unlikely. Very unlikely. Still, she worried about it as well, and, she said ruefully, "It probably showed, too."

Not long afterward, the girl that he'd been seeing for two years broke off with him. They were "too young to get serious" was the way she put it. Besides, he was still laid up in bed at home and there was almost a month of summer to go. The deprivation was too much for her to bear.

"She picked a bad time for it," said Linda. "His self-esteem was shot, as it was, without that little twit pulling up the last floorboard under his feet."

That seemed to do it, she said. After that, he became even more difficult and withdrawn.

It was a sad, sad litany that seemed to go on forever.

I wanted to shout, "What did you *do* about it? What did you do to help him? To stop this inexorable slide toward the pit? Couldn't you see what was coming?" But I checked myself in time before I added that particular brand of self-righteous rhetoric to my calendar of sins and omissions. I had been a stranger by choice and absolutely worthless to him while he was alive. The least I could do was hold my tongue now that he was beyond my capacity either to help or to hinder any longer.

She had been there, at least. I had done nothing for him at all. Not even written or called. Holding back. Holding out. As if he owed me an apology, before I could resume any sense of responsibility for him, however tenuous. I was shocked to think how much I'd behaved as Nola would have done in a similar situation. Niggardly nickel-and-dime sort of stuff. Afraid of giving, without assurance of getting back full value. It made me sick to think I had acted like that.

Certainly I was in no position to make accusations. I had my own sense of complicity to live down.

"We failed him," she had repeated over and over again at the hospital, and we surely had. Horribly. With great complacency and selfishness. It is something we both will live with for the rest of our days.

The police showed up at the house the following spring. It seems a pistol had come into Keefer's possession briefly. He had traded some motorcycle parts for it and then, in turn, traded the pistol for a skateboard.

It turned out the pistol had been stolen in a burglary, one in a recent series that had plagued the expensive residential community where they lived. Keefer wouldn't tell the police where he had got the pistol. He said he wasn't going to "narc" on anybody.

Linda said the police didn't want him. They wanted the name of the next kid in the chain leading back to the burglaries. But he wouldn't cooperate. As a consequence, they said they would have to charge him with illegal possession of a handgun and sale of stolen property.

Linda and Michael called a lawyer friend of theirs who talked him into a little sensible cooperation. It was just enough to get the cops to drop the charges.

"I don't know," she said. "It was just one thing like that after another with him. I'll never understand it."

When they discovered he was still smoking pot and decided to put him in a detoxification program, he stopped talking to them, too.

The program was supposed to be for ten weeks; it was operated out of a beautiful estate on the Monterey Peninsula.

"Just the place I would want to go if I had that kind of a problem," she said. "But he busted out of there in just three weeks. He didn't come home. He went to Los Angeles and lived on the streets for three more weeks before the cops found him and brought him back. You can't imagine how hopeless I felt. I had no idea what to do for him after that."

These facts came out gradually, over the period of several conversations. Neither of us could stand to talk about it for long. Since that subject was so painful and imponderable, we mainly talked of other things.

We talked a lot about Mario.

"He's going with that nurse that took care of Daddy at the end. Remember the dingie with the big jugs and the silly laugh? He's going with her! I think it's the first girl he's had since high school."

She was very excited about it. She was hoping that he'd get married, have kids, settle down. Even the prospect of having the dingie for a sister-in-law didn't faze her. It was the idea that counted, not the particulars.

"He's been a bachelor too long. He's really getting weird. He's acting more like Cousin Vito every day."

"How is Cousin Vito?"

"Oh hell. He's fine. Just as loony as ever."

Two years ago, she and Michael sold the house and moved to Sonoma County, way up in the wilds of Northern California. They were tired of suburbia. They were looking for something slower and more temperate. Something more old-fashioned, with changeable weather and more sky and less bustle. They bought a lovely old B&B up there, which they call the Vintner's Revenge.

"Michael was always the one for country living, you know."

"How about you?"

"Me?" A thoughtful note came into her voice. a bit sad, too, I thought. "I like it all right. It's peaceful up here. You know? You can sit out on your porch at night. You can see the stars. I like that."

ALL my teachers are dead now.

They didn't live giant lives. They are as anonymous and futile in death as ever they were in life. When Linda looks at the night sky from her porch out in Northern California, she does not see the outlines of their shapes wheeling in pin-pricks of starlight in the constellations above her head. But here in the East, my nighttime skies still swim with thoughts of their follies and futilities.

I watch Marilyn's face on the pillow beside me. The corners of her mouth turn up in a natural smile; it is part of her anatomy, for godsakes. She sleeps on, undisturbed by the light from the lamp on my night table. I watch the rise and fall of her untroubled breathing, and try to make sense of it all.

It is a futile business. I feel I should know so much more than I do. I ought to be a far wiser and better man after all this, shouldn't I? Else what has been the purpose of our joint foolishness and suffering? Only for the sole account of making us not want any more when we get to the end of it, as Nola once said in one of her Delphic moments? The poor woman followed the teachings of a sad oracle. I, for one, would rather not believe in them. Surely there must be something better.

I am on my own now.

Except for Marilyn, the world seems a dark and shrunken place.

IT has been six months since I last talked to Linda. In the course of our usual digressive conversation, I asked her about Mario and the nurse. She told me they had broken off long ago. All of her dreams and aspirations for something good coming of the affair between her brother and the dingie nurse with the big jugs were now, as she put it, just a matter of "ancient history."

"He didn't seem too upset, the jerk. He just shrugged it off. 'Aw,' he says, 'we just got bored with each udder.' "

Her imitation of him was perfect.

Last year, he sold everything on the Island and moved to Connecticut. Linda told me he owns a wildly successful seafood restaurant in Hartford called the Jolly Lobster.

Cousin Vito decided not to go along to Connecticut, although he was invited. He cleaned out the converted toolshed at the bottom of Phil's long-neglected garden,

where he had lived for over forty years. He packed the suitcases he kept under his bed. He took the 1952 girlie calendar down off the wall over the sink and packed it between
layers of his underwear. (I'm surprised he didn't put it down
the front of his pants. I've seen him, when we were out in
public somewhere, take his newspaper and fold it very
neatly and stick it down the front of his trousers and walk
around all afternoon like that.)

He packed his extra combs, first-rate tonsorial equipment
that Phil had given him years ago—long, thin instruments
angled like straight razors, with pointy little tines that dug
into his scalp like tiny claws. He packed his chauffeur's cap.
He packed his Mickey Mouse ears. When he was through,
Mario drove him into Port Authority and put him on a bus
for Ossining, where his equally ancient sister lives. The sister has a garden too. Maybe that was the attraction, who
knows. He must be well into his nineties by now.

She also told me that Mario had been pulled over by the
police the week before, just outside of Hartford. Immediately I had visions of a big drug bust, a burst of automatic-
weapons fire. I saw him sprawled out on the road in a picture
on the back page of the *Daily News*. Riddled with bullets.
His face streaked with zebra stripes of tabloid ink. *Mobster
Killed as Cops Close In.* I don't know why, I just couldn't get
that idea of the Stephanos out of my head.

Of course it was nothing like that. They pulled him over
because he was traveling in a highway commuter lane limited to vehicles with three or more passengers.

The other lanes into town were bumper-to-bumper day
after day, but people could really fly along on the special
ramps and lanes set aside for the car-poolers. The tempta-
tion was too much for him, I guess.

He had three fully dressed mannequins in the backseat of

his Continental, but it didn't fool the cops. They've seen just about every trick in the book, I suppose.

He isn't seeing anybody on a steady basis, and, much to her disappointment, he certainly has no plans for getting married any time soon. Linda says she doubts now if he ever will.

So it is. We bend to our oars, till the current sweeps us out to sea.